ALSO BY M. J. ROSE

Lip Service

Published by Pocket Books

IN FIDELITY

a novel

M. J. ROSE

POCKET BOOKS

New York   London   Toronto   Sydney   Singapore

Jane Hirshfield, "For What Binds Us" from *Of Gravity and Angels*. Copyright © 1988 by Jane Hirshfield, Wesleyan University Press, by permission of the author and University Press of New England.

An *Original* Publication of Pocket Books

POCKET BOOKS, a division of Simon & Schuster, Inc.
1230 Avenue of the Americas, New York, NY 10020

ISBN: 0-7394-1470-4

POCKET and colophon are registered trademarks
of Simon & Schuster, Inc.

Interior design by Kris Tobiassen
Cover design by Brigid Pearson
Front cover photo by Tony Stone Images

Printed in the U.S.A.

For DPS and answered prayers

ACKNOWLEDGMENTS

I could not have written this book without having hope and for that I thank David Scofield for his selflessness, Dr. Marc Lorber, and the entire staff of the Yale/New Haven Kidney Transplant Unit.

Much appreciation goes to Steven Weintraub, who guided me through the mazes of Zen philosophy and psychoanalytic thought, and his daughter Sarah Weintraub for her insights into a seventeen-year-old's romance with Zen.

I am grateful to everyone at Pocket Books, specifically Linda Marrow for continuing to believe and Amy Pierpont for being a true editor in the best sense of the word. And I have nothing but praise for Loretta Barrett, a wonderful agent with whom I am thrilled to share this ride.

Last but not least, thanks to Mara Gleckel and Suzanne Gibbons-Neff—for being there.

FOR WHAT BINDS US

There are names for what binds us:
strong forces, weak forces.
Look around, you can see them:
the skin that forms in a half-empty cup,
nails rusting into the places they join,
joints dovetailed on their own weight.
The way things stay so solidly
wherever they've been set down—
and gravity, scientists say, is weak.

And see how the flesh grows back
across a wound, with a great vehemence,
more strong
than the simple, untested surface before.
There's a name for it on horses,
when it comes back darker and raised: proud flesh,

as all flesh,
is proud of its wounds, wears them
as honors given out after battle,
small triumphs pinned to the chest—

And when two people have loved each other
see how it is like a
scar between their bodies,
stronger, darker, and proud;
how the black cord makes of them a single fabric
that nothing can tear or mend.

—*Jane Hirshfield*

IN FIDELITY

ONE

My daughter stood beyond the fieldstone fence that separated the house from the beach. From the kitchen window, Lilly's slight form was silhouetted against the sunset and the sea. In that wide-open vista she seemed vulnerable and small. Even from a distance, I could see that she was shivering.

Grabbing a jacket for her, I threw one around my own shoulders and walked out, down the sloping lawn that was not yet green because spring had not quite arrived, and out to the edge of the property. It was the last weekend of March and the harsh winds blew against my face. Waves broke wildly against the shore. The sea air smelled briny: seaweed and shells, crabs and mussels.

Climbing down a half-dozen stone steps, I reached Lilly's side and handed her the jacket. "It's cold out here."

When my seventeen-year-old daughter turned to me, her features were distorted by sadness and her eyes, the green-blue of the sea beyond us, were filled with unshed tears.

"Why does being in love have to hurt so much?" she asked.

I wanted to wrap my arms around her and offer sympathy, but I knew the object of her affection was the only one who could comfort her completely.

When you are young, you fall in love with love itself and do not want anything from anyone but your beloved. Later on, it takes great courage and a little bit of stupidity to fall in love and then you need all the help you can get from everyone around you.

But saying anything like that to Lilly would not give her solace. This was her first venture into that madman's paradise of emotion.

Love is a tricky disease to cure. Any therapist who predominately treats women, like I do, knows that. While men can fall hard and feel its sting, women are love's victims in a more profound way. Frankly, I was a bit tired of love. Of its vicissitudes and masks. Of its early bloom and all too easy decay. Of its fickleness and its mysteries. If I could have invented an antidote, I would have been the first one to take it. Having fallen out of love years ago, I did not plan on falling *in* love again. I trusted other things: the solidity of friends, the loyalty of family, each season's beauty, and the ocean's constancy.

I did not encourage or discourage my patients when it came to romance. That was not my job. But in the process of helping them put broken hearts back together, I'd lost my own faith in that elusive emotion that has inspired poets, songwriters, and painters for centuries.

"Come inside, Lilly. I'll make some coffee—no, that green tea you like so much—and we can sit by the fire."

And maybe you'll tell me what's wrong, I thought.

Lilly shrugged and the bulky lumber jacket I had thrown around her shoulders fell off. I bent to pick it up and offered it back to her. Carrying the jacket, she began to walk back to the house, and I followed her, thinking of what I might say to her.

In the kitchen I put on the kettle and shook tea leaves into a fine silver teapot that my grandmother had used as a young bride when tea parties were still popular and well-off women wore white gloves and hats and spent the afternoons, not in the office, but in each other's company. My grandmother had never made green tea in that pot. She had served English breakfast tea with lemon and cream and homemade scones or madeleines. She cared more about her family than herself, went to church each Sunday, prayed every night, and tried to teach her prayers to me, but her rituals never became my own. She knew I said the words only to appease her, and it pained her that I never shared her deep, abiding faith in the goodness of either man or God. But what proof could my grandmother offer that prayers helped—especially after my father was killed?

A long sigh of steam hissed from the logs burning in the five-foot-high fireplace as I entered the living room. Lilly was sitting on the floor. Her back was to me, and in the firelight, garnet highlights shone in her long, dark, and wild hair.

"You're too close to the fireplace. A spark could fly out," I warned her. "Remember Grandma Minnie." There was an oft-repeated family legend that when she was a young girl, my great-grandmother's hair had caught fire because she'd sat too close to the hearth. Although it was certainly a fable, I had often reminded Lilly of it, just as my mother had reminded me and her mother had reminded her.

"I'm not too close," Lilly answered without looking at me.

I put the tray of tea things and a bag of Pepperidge Farm cookies down on the coffee table and poured the tea into my grandmother's fine, Limoges teacups: bone china decorated with a pattern of violets and ivy.

"Do you put lemon or sugar in green tea?" I asked.

Lilly turned and gave me a patronizing smile. "No, Mom. You don't put anything in green tea." Her tone had been more mocking than her words, as if she were saying, Don't you know anything? She was annoyed by my ignorance of a subject so important to her. I was momentarily relieved—anything to replace the forlorn expression of sadness etched on her face.

Handing her a cup and saucer, I tried not to show any solicitude. But she saw past my benign expression.

"Don't look at me like that, Mom. It's okay that I'm upset. It means that I'm alive."

"I don't want a Zen lecture, Lilly. I want to know what's the matter. Why are you upset?"

Reluctantly she started to speak, then stopped. She took a sip of tea and started again. "Why bother? Anything I say about Cooper will be held against him."

Since meeting Cooper Davis, who was immersed in the philosophy and study of Zen Buddhism, Lilly often spouted aphorisms intended to confound me. Interest in religion is healthy, but obsession is not: especially for impressionable teenagers who don't have the intellectual tools to protect themselves from dogma and cultism.

"At least Grandma understands what I'm talking about," Lilly would throw back at me when I objected to her Zen absorption. It didn't help my arguments that my own mother was involved in a myriad of Eastern philosophies and New Age disciplines and had been since my father's death.

My mother was notoriously eccentric and off-center. Although I didn't want her to influence Lilly too much, neither did I want to interfere in their relationship. I wanted Lilly to have that same kinship with her grandmother that I'd had with mine.

"It's my fault your mother is so much better at taking than giving," my grandmother had once said to me. "Being the last child and the only girl, I let everyone spoil her and now she's very selfish, isn't she?"

But she wasn't selfish with Lilly. And watching them together or hearing snatches of their long-distance conversations, I was beginning to like my mother more. As much she had not been there for me when I was an adolescent, she was now there for Lilly.

More steam escaped from the burning logs, and I leaned back, sinking into the chintz-covered couch, gazing around the cluttered room that my grandmother had decorated over sixty years ago. It took some effort, but I did not pressure Lilly to tell me what was wrong; instead I waited patiently, focusing on the china cachepot on the coffee table. My grandmother had always kept lilies of the valley in it this time of year. Forced flowers brought in from the conservatory. Even though the pot was empty, I could recall the fragrance of those fragile bell-shaped flowers. Shutting my eyes for a moment, I saw my grandmother: finely dressed, pearls encircling her neck, a stack of diamond-and-platinum wedding bands glittering on her ring finger.

She wore five thin bands, each different. One was a simple channel-set band made of square-cut diamonds, which had been her wedding band and I had chosen to be my wedding band when Robert and I got married. Each of the other four were to celebrate the birth of my grandmother's children. Some held round diamonds, others baguettes; altogether they stacked one on top of the other as a testament to my grandmother's sentimentality. I had never seen her without them, until finally old age and arthritis forced her to take them off and she had given them all to me. And because they were hers, when Robert and I separated, I chose not to take them off. In my mind, they ceased to be connected to my marriage and became my grandmother's bequest.

In my life, whenever I had been confused or distraught, I had returned to my grandmother in her hundred-year-old house, perched on a tiny peninsula of land jutting out into the Long Island Sound on the Connecticut side, and found instant comfort with her among the familiar furniture and smells—it was coming home.

My grandmother was as solid and constant as her house and I still missed her.

There were others I missed too: my father, who had died when I was nineteen; the man my estranged husband had been before he betrayed me; and my mother, who—though still alive—had always been just beyond the reach of my arms.

"You don't even make an effort to like Cooper," Lilly finally said, bringing me back to the present.

"That's not true, sweetheart. I just worry that he has so much influence over you that you are losing yourself in him."

"That is not at all what's happening. I'm still who I was before I met him; I'm just in love now."

It wouldn't do any good to remind Lilly of the male friends she had forsaken because Cooper was jealous of them, or the extracurricular activities she had abandoned since they'd met.

My knowledge of psychology had never helped when it came to raising my own daughter. Only my grandmother's sage advice had guided me through the minefields of motherhood. But she was gone—dying only weeks after my mother had moved her to San Francisco. I had fought to keep her in her own home, suggesting we hire nurses to help her navigate the maze of senility that was confusing her mind, but my mother and her second husband had moved her out west to be near them.

It had killed the little that was left of my grandmother to be away from her gardens, her beach, and her chintz-covered couches. How could she have been comfortable in a house that was a stark reflection of the Oriental culture my mother had embraced since moving out to California?

Lilly poured herself more tea and rearranged her legs beneath her. She was restless in the one place I never was. When snow covered the ground and dusted the evergreens that sheltered the house from the winter winds coming off the sound, I found solace there. Lighting fires in the great stone fireplace, making spiced cider, and reading mysteries was as satisfying an escape as basking in the summer sun on the small private beach or getting dirty working in the extensive English cottage gardens.

In the winter, the house smelled of pine and burning wood. In the spring the scent of lilacs filled every room until the roses took over in June. It was a house for all seasons. But Lilly, who was a junior in a private high school in New York City, had not been here for months. When Cooper was in the city, she stayed there to be with him, and on the weekends Cooper remained at school, Lilly preferred to be with her father and work with him in his darkroom.

That late March weekend, since it was my birthday, Lilly had acquiesced to come to Connecticut with me.

As a child of separated parents, Lilly's life had been less complicated than most, since her father and I still lived under the same roof, just on different floors. Robert and I owned a brownstone in Greenwich Village on West Ninth Street, and when we split up, he just moved upstairs to his studio, while Lilly and I continued living on the second floor. The office where I practice psychotherapy occupies the first floor.

Even though Robert and I had been apart for five years, neither of us had remarried, so Lilly had not yet felt the full tragedy the dissolution of a union can cause a child. Where he and I slept had less of an effect on her than a divorce would have. At least that was what I hoped.

It had taken years for our separation to cease having an effect on me, but I was over it finally. Cured, healed, and pain free, I had finally called a divorce lawyer to schedule a meeting and begin proceedings.

The grandfather clock chimed the hour, and in the gleam of the fire, I saw a fresh silvery tear mar Lilly's unblemished skin. I longed to take my daughter in my arms and let her cry on my shoulder the way she had when she was younger. As much as I ached for her, I would have welcomed the opportunity to offer her solace. There was not much else she needed me for any longer.

But I would have been the only one comforted by Lilly's tears wetting my neck.

"Lilly, please tell me what's wrong. I'm imagining all kinds of horrible things. Is Cooper in some kind of trouble?" I asked.

She hiccuped a sob, a laugh, and a breath all at once. "But you don't have a problem with him?" she said sarcastically. "Why do you just assume he's in trouble? It's just that he can't come to the city next weekend because he's been assigned some monster project for his design class. That means I won't see him for three weeks." The thought of it caused another sob.

While Cooper tried to come into the city to see Lilly at least every other weekend, it wasn't always possible. The architecture program at Yale was rigorous and demanding. If your average fell below a C you were kicked out, and since Cooper was on scholarship, he was under even more scrutiny.

Lilly complained that I—and Robert, since he backed me up on this—were too strict because we rarely let her go up to Yale for weekends. She had her own schoolwork to do, we had argued. She would be applying for college soon and needed to keep her own grade-average high.

But even more disturbing was knowing that when she went up to visit him, they spent the night together. She was only a junior in high school and the idea of her being sexually active was an anathema to me.

But as much as I worried about her involvement with Cooper, I couldn't bear watching Lilly suffer.

In the shadows of the room, the past hung like cobwebs never brushed away. I watched myself, barely two years older than Lilly, sitting on this same couch, overcome with grief because of my father's sudden death. The emotion was still so strong it reached out and touched me across the span of almost twenty years. Having endured both pain and loss in my life, I foolishly thought I could protect my daughter from those same experiences.

And so, because I hated to see her cry and because I wanted to feel her arms around me for just a moment, I reached out the only way I could.

"Would you like me to drive you up to Yale for the weekend?" I asked.

"You mean I could stay over?"

I nodded, yes.

Of course, I didn't want her to go. I wanted her to be at my birthday dinner along with my brother, his family, my closest friend, and her husband. But I also wanted her to be happy.

Wouldn't her pleasure rebound and give me pleasure, too?

Lilly's eyes, normally round, grew rounder. The green shone brighter despite the tears, and in the depths of the color I saw both my own eyes and my husband's.

My daughter's favorite bedtime story had been how, in the midst of the tragedy of my father's death, I had met Robert, stared into his face, and seen that our eyes were the exact same green-blue color.

"And you recognized yourself in Daddy's eyes?" Lilly would ask.

"Yes."

"And he saw himself in your eyes?"

"Yes, sweetheart."

"And you fell in love with each other and now we all have the same eyes."

Summing up that happy ending, she'd always smiled.

Now she was smiling the same way in anticipation of seeing Cooper.

"Come on, baby, get your stuff packed and let's get on the road."

"Oh, Mom!" All traces of tears were gone and happiness flooded her face. She threw her arms around me and I held her as tightly as I could. As soon as I let go, Lilly jumped up and ran halfway up the stairs. Then, with one hand poised on the polished oak banister, she stopped, and turned around.

"But what about your birthday?" she asked, suddenly remembering.

"It's okay." I waved my hand, dismissing her question. If I was going to let her go, it would be without guilt.

"But being here this weekend was supposed to be my present to you." Her hand began creeping up the railing. She wanted to go, but she knew she should stay.

I shrugged. "It's only dinner, Lilly. I keep telling you, after thirty, birthdays don't matter anymore. It's fine."

That slight assurance was all she needed. She raced up the rest of the stairs and disappeared into her room, and I was left, staring into the fire again.

If Lilly had been receptive, I would have warned her to go slowly and hold some part of herself back. Not to be so completely open to the emotions and excitement she was feeling. Or to the man who was stirring them.

But my child, like both her parents, was not one for half measures.

Instead of worrying, I should have been grateful that Lilly had survived three years of high school without having a serious relationship. Still, I wished it had taken even longer; that she'd had a few more years of innocence, pain-free and lighthearted, before she'd found her first love.

Freud postulated that when you fall in love, you rediscover the love you felt as an infant. If Robert and I had done decent jobs as parents, Lilly would have the stamina and resources to deal with what lay ahead of her. But what lessons had we taught her without knowing it? Had we inadvertently shown her too much of our strife?

It is the actions we don't want our child to see, the nightmares we do not dare speak aloud, the whispered words we do not think they overhear, that impact them the most.

While Lilly was still upstairs packing, the doorbell rang. Passing the window on my way to answer it, I saw the local florist's van parked in the driveway.

Carrying the oblong white box to the kitchen, I put it down on the counter and set aside the card. I didn't need to read it, I knew who the flowers were from.

Each year on my birthday, even after we had separated, Robert had sent me calla lilies. But after I untied the ribbon and laid back the tissue, I was startled to see—not the white lilies—but a dozen long-stem roses. Instantly sickened by the sight and smell of them, I pushed the flowers away from me. The box tipped backwards and the dark red flowers spilled into the white porcelain sink. I was catapulted back in time to the day my father had been shot.

Bullets flew. A bowl of red roses on the countertop had fallen—the glass had shattered, the roses had scattered—one lay at his feet, the color of the petals no different than the color of his blood.

"Mom?" Lilly stood in the doorway. "Are those from Dad?"

"Yes . . . I guess . . . but . . . I'm not sure." I was confused. Robert never would have sent me red roses.

"Isn't there a card?"

Reaching for the small envelope, I opened it and read it. "Yes . . . they're from your father . . ."

Lilly stared into the sink. "They're not lilies this time; isn't that great?" My daughter clutched at every change her father or I exhibited, collecting them as proof that metamorphosis was possible, certain that when we each had changed enough, we might get back together.

Lilly was as good at reading my face as her father was. One look at me was enough for her to know something was very wrong.

"Mom? What is it?"

"It's nothing." I began to pick up the roses, carefully avoiding the thorns.

"I think you're being very ungrateful."

"Oh, Lilly, I'm not being ungrateful." I hadn't wanted to tell her what was wrong and burden her with my memories, but the alternative was worse. "There were red roses in the shop the day your grandfather was killed. Somehow they were knocked over and wound up—" I didn't want to explain any more. "I just don't understand how your father could have sent me roses."

Before I could stop her, Lilly picked up the phone, called Robert, and told him what had happened. Her face relaxed as she listened to him. "I knew it," she said to him, and then handed me the phone. "He wants to talk to you."

"Jordan, I'm sorry about those flowers, but you know I'd never send you red roses, don't you?"

"Well, I didn't think you would have, but the card—" My voice trailed off.

"The florist must have mixed my order up with someone else's. Except I don't know how. I ordered them in person from that florist on Sixth Avenue."

"I should be over this by now. I can't keep breaking down every time I see some reminder of that day."

"You know better than anyone how easy that is to say and how impossible it is to do. You'll never stop loving your father, will you?"

"No, of course not."

"Then how can you expect to stop being horrified by the way he died?" Robert's voice was warm and familiar.

For the first time in years, we were having a conversation that wasn't about Lilly, and yet I couldn't answer him directly. "I'm sorry. Of course it was a mistake." For Lilly's sake, and his, I made an attempt to sound as if I were fine, but I couldn't stop thinking that of all the flowers they could have sent by mistake, why had it been those?

"Any other mix-up would have been all right, but not red roses, especially not on your birthday." So, after all this time, he still could read my mind. "Jordan, listen to me, as soon as we get off the phone, I want you to take the roses and throw them out, okay?"

"That's not necessary, I can—"

"Yes, it is. I want you to take them and put them in the garbage bin outside the house. Will you promise me you'll do that or should I ask Lilly?"

"Yes, I'll do it, Robert." And as soon as I said it, I felt surprisingly better.

How curious that in spite of everything that had happened—his unfaithfulness, my withdrawal, and our separation—some intimacy between us had endured. And how ironic that if not for those red roses, I might not have known it.

The roses had spurred one set of memories; the lilies would have stimulated very different ones.

One night, not long after we had first moved in together, Robert had come home from work, holding out an oblong florist's box, tied with a white satin ribbon. Inside, nestled in tissue, was a slender stalk. A single calla lily. I put it in water, and after dinner, Robert asked me to pose for him with the flower.

Although he'd photographed me several times before, each time I stood in front of his lens, I shed more inhibitions and became increasingly comfortable under his scrutiny. With his cold metal camera, Robert was exploring my secrets and my soul.

"Will you get undressed for me?" he asked. "Just down to your underwear," he reassured.

I was still shy about posing completely nude, but I had let him photograph me in my bra and underpants before; so while Robert set up the lights, I undressed slowly, knowing that even though he was busy arranging the shot, he was aware of every move I made.

The camera had not yet become an intrusion in our life; it was still a revered object revealing the depths and talent of the man I lived with. Robert looked at the world through the viewfinder and saw it in a very special way. And in his photographs, I saw all his passions, but they did not make me afraid. I still believed the promises Robert had made: to be faithful and never leave. Blissfully unaware that all love leads to loss, I never thought he would disappoint me.

My father's death had been the exception, I had thought all those years ago—some loves did last.

With my back to Robert, I took off my blouse and my jeans and then my bra but left on my white lace panties. I sat on the bed, against the pillows, as he adjusted the light meter. He looked up for a moment and his eyes focused on my bare breasts. My nipples hardened. He smiled and went back to setting up the shot.

When Robert had the lights the way he wanted them, he brought me to the window and positioned me the way he wanted me. His fingers felt hot on my skin. He didn't speak. And then he handed me the lily. "It will make you feel less naked," he'd said.

He was right.

I held the lily so that the flower brushed against my skin, the point touching my breast. The stalk lay flat on my belly.

"Yeah, that's good. Lower your head; lift up your eyes. Look at me, Jordan. Do you feel how soft the flower is against your skin? Move it, just a little; let it tickle you."

Wings fluttered in the deepest part of my stomach. I stared at Robert's hands holding the camera, and listened to the clicks of the shutter. Playfully I moved the flower, positioning it so that now the white blossom was between my legs. And then without him asking me to, I took off the lace panties and put the flower back so that it covered me in a modest but provocative way.

He was murmuring encouragement now.

I rubbed the lily against my skin. "It's you, Robert, this flower is you . . ." I whispered.

When I offered the lily out to him, Robert took it and used the thick stem to tease my legs apart. For a long time, he alternated titillating me with the flower and bringing me just to the edge of an orgasm and then backing off to take another shot.

Finally he put the camera down so he could get naked too.

"You're hard," I whispered.

"I've been hard for the last half hour."

"Is it torture to do that, to be hard for that long and not do anything about it?"

"No, it's pure pleasure," he said as he buried his face where the flower had been.

"You smell like lilies. Oh, Jordan," he moaned.

Standing in front of Robert's camera after that, I was brave and brazen. A woman I have never been with another man before or since. I had allowed him to see right into my very soul and held nothing back.

But it's not always best to let a man see you that naked inside and out. To offer up everything including your privacy.

One of the photographs he took on that day was so provocative it set him apart from dozens of other aspiring photographers, landed him his first perfume account, and got him industry notice.

Not only was a career born that night, a child was conceived.

The sound of Lilly's running footsteps and her overnight bag banging against the banister startled me. But what was more jarring was realizing I'd been remembering Robert as my lover.

It had been years since I'd allowed those memories to surface.

"I'm ready, Mom," Lilly called out.

Fifteen minutes later Lilly and I were in my black Jeep driving up I-95 headed toward New Haven. The traffic was light and we were making good time. I almost wished for some delay, so that I could be with her a little longer. It was a thought I'd had too often since the night, two months ago, when she'd woken me up at twelve-thirty to tell me about the boy she'd just met.

"Oh, Mom, he's so wonderful," she had said.

I didn't need to turn on the bedside lamp to see her face. I knew she was smiling and her eyes were shining.

My daughter had crossed the line. On one side was her childhood and on the other was the beginning of her life as a woman. I could hear it in her rapid speech, in her breathlessness, in her need to tell me about her evening and make it real again.

"He's majoring in architecture at Yale and knows all about Japanese gardens and really wants to see my photographs and he's different than anyone else I've ever met."

"I'm so happy for you, Lilly."

"And he looks right too. Exactly how I always imagined he'd look. He's tall, like Daddy, but he has black hair, and he asked me for my phone number. He's invited me to the Cloisters tomorrow. It's like he knows exactly what I'm thinking without me having to say a word. We are so on the same plane . . ."

"Lilly, I'm sure he's terrific, but don't you need time to really get to know him before—"

"Don't do that, Mom. I'm not six years old. I don't believe in fairy tales. I didn't say we're gonna wind up together. I'm just excited, okay?"

"You're right. I'm sorry." I started to reach out to take her hand, but she'd already stood up and was walking towards the door.

Lying back on my pillows, I'd tried to be happy for Lilly and think about the dreams she would have that night, instead of being anxious for her, except I knew there were no guarantees. Sometimes love worked out, but more often it failed.

While Lilly was growing up, I'd avoided reading her the prince-and-princess kind of fairy tales, so of course, every time we went to a bookstore or a video store, all Lilly wanted was *Cinderella* or *Sleeping Beauty*. I found less romanticized tales and more realistic adventures for Lilly, determined to prevent my daughter from being seduced by the happy endings that had warped my thinking and the thinking of generations of women before me.

Men did not kiss women, make them princesses, and take

them to live in towering castles. Most people did not stay in love forever. Endings were brutal.

I hoped Lilly would see men as equals and enjoy them, but not idolize them. I wanted her to be self-reliant and not invest her identity in her relationships.

When she was seven, Lilly finally saw Disney's *Cinderella* at a friend's house. For days it was all she talked about, repeating the story over and over. For weeks she wouldn't answer to her own name, insisting on being called Cinderella. And even though it was a month away, she'd incessantly begged for a Cinderella costume for Halloween.

"It even comes with glass slippers, Mommy," she'd said, and her eyes sparkled imagining such a thing.

I tried to entice her with a Catwoman costume, or an astronaut's outfit, but she wouldn't budge.

One night, over dinner, I lost my patience. "Lilly. Why do you want to be someone who isn't real? Cinderella isn't real, she's just a dream."

"She has to be real," Lilly insisted. "Or else how can she live happily ever after?" She had flailed her arms and kicked her feet on the chair rail. Flinging her plate to the floor, she ran out of the kitchen. Peas rolled in every direction. Ketchup splattered on the tiles. Our dog, Good, scampered to get the scattered pieces of chicken. It took me hours to calm Lily down.

But ten years later, sitting beside my breathless daughter, who was counting the miles to New Haven, I knew all my efforts had been for nothing. Lilly was enraptured by Cooper: he was her dream come true, and nothing I could say would deter her. My interference would only drive her further from me.

Lilly had found something she wanted and that meant she now had something to lose—something that could and probably *would* cause her pain. I wished that, like my grandmother, I were religious, so I could pray that my daughter would survive her first foray into love, that she would not give more than she got, and that no man would ever shatter her heart the way her father had shattered mine.

During the whole ride up to Yale, Lilly talked about Cooper's ideas and why he was going to be a great architect one day. I listened to what she said, not hearing the individual words as much as the tone and the tenor of her chatter. Lilly was infatuated, and no one could compete with the man who was arousing such intense emotions in her.

"I brought some of Dad's shots of me to show Cooper," Lilly said, patting the knapsack that lay on the floor beneath her feet. Peeking out of it was the battered aluminum Nikon that had once belonged to Robert and that Lilly now carried everywhere.

Before I could respond, my cellular phone rang.

"Hello?"

I heard slow, evenly paced, mechanical ticking.

"Hello?" I repeated.

When I didn't hear an answer, I snapped the phone shut. In the last two weeks I'd been getting hang-ups at least once a day. No one ever said anything, but I always heard the same monotonous ticking noise. Pressing my foot on the accelerator, I sped up.

"Does your father know you took those contact sheets out of his studio?" I asked Lilly.

"Dad gave them to me. He's letting me help him choose a shot for a new montage. It's a huge cliff and in the crevices will be my face."

"But that doesn't mean he wants you to show them to Cooper. You know how private your father is about his work. Iago Witherspoon doesn't even see his unfinished work and she owns the gallery where he shows."

"I'm not showing Cooper unfinished photographs. Just a contact sheet. That's different."

I didn't think it was, but kept silent.

Lilly examined the rows of tiny images of herself. "I really like modeling for Dad, but I don't think I'd want to do it for anyone else."

I, too, had enjoyed being one of Robert's models, but it had been almost six years since I had posed for him. At the time, I didn't realize why I had stopped allowing him to photograph me. I'd only known I had not wanted to be part of Robert's landscapes anymore.

But in retrospect, it was obvious: subconsciously I knew something was wrong—I had stopped posing at about the same time Robert had started having affairs.

"Cooper doesn't understand why I'm not bashful in front of Dad."

"What did you tell him?"

She shrugged. "That Dad's always taken pictures of me and it would be weird if he stopped just because I was grown up. It's not like the photographs are sexy or anything."

Even when Lilly entered puberty and became shy around boys, she was never embarrassed in front of the camera.

Although Robert had garnered a reputation for commercial and artistic photography that was on the edge of the erotic, his compositions of our daughter were always in marked contrast to the rest of his work: They were infused only with love. At first he'd melded her soft baby features with rolling hills and cloud-filled skies, and as she grew older, the landscapes changed to reflect her emerging personality.

"Listen, why don't you leave that contact sheet with me," I suggested. "Wait till you can show Cooper the finished collages—he'll understand them better when they're completed."

In response, Lilly pulled her camera out of her knapsack, held it up to her eye, and focused on the road. I heard the click of the shutter closing and the sound of the film advancing. It was the same way Robert avoided subjects he didn't wish to discuss.

Although Lilly's looks mirror mine—with the same dark wavy hair, oval face, small bones but long limbs—her personality is more similar to Robert's. Intuitive and gentle, they also share a love of photography and a dislike of confrontations.

"I'm serious about this, Lilly; it's one thing for you to share what is yours with Cooper, but it's not okay to share something that is your father's. I don't want you to take those photographs with you."

But Lilly had aimed her camera at the changing landscape and was no longer listening. It infuriated me as much when she withdrew with the camera as it had when Robert had done it. I looked at her profile out of the corner of my eye, the high forehead, the full lips, and the stubborn pointed chin.

There was a time, when I was married to Robert, that I began to resent his cameras and devotion to them. No wonder I would have the same reaction to Lilly when she used her camera to distance herself from me.

Having raised this child, and knowing how she would respond, I chose not to pursue the conversation. It was no use. Once she disappeared into "the land of the camera," as I called it, there was no way to reach her.

My cellular phone rang again. Hesitantly, I answered it.

"Hello?"

"Dr. Sloan?"

"Yes?" I didn't recognize the woman's voice on the other end.

"Its Adrienne Blessing."

Adrienne was a new patient I'd been seeing for a month and a half. This was the first time she had called over a weekend.

"I'm still waking up every night at three and can't get back to sleep. I've tried all the techniques we discussed. Nothing works. Can you prescribe something? Anything? I'm nonfunctional here."

"Adrienne, I'm sorry, but you know I can't prescribe drugs. We can talk about you seeing a psychopharmacologist in session, but in the meantime, when you wake up, do something: read, watch a movie, work, just don't lie there."

"I've tried all that."

"I know how frustrating it is. But we can solve this; we just have to work towards understanding the stress that's causing the insomnia."

"Are you sure it's stress related?" she asked.

"From what we've talked about in session, it certainly sounds that way. Falling asleep easily but consistently waking up around three in the morning fits the pattern. Are you still falling asleep easily?"

"Yeah, no problem there. It's just from three on I'm a zombie. Isn't there anything I can take?"

"You can try Tylenol PM or Benadryl allergy pills."

I glanced at Lilly, then back at the road. I would have preferred not to talk to a patient with my daughter in the car.

Suddenly there was a loud horn and the sound of tires screeching. Ahead of me a blue BMW had cut me off. As my right arm shot out to protect Lilly, I looked in the rearview mirror to make sure the driver behind me wasn't coming up too fast. Within seconds, I knew we were okay, but my heart was racing faster than the car.

In maneuvering to avoid an accident, I'd dropped the phone, but Lilly had picked it up and handed it back to me. "I think she's still on, Mom."

"Adrienne, I know how difficult insomnia can be to deal with. Let's focus on this in your next session on Monday, all right?"

"You're never judgmental of your patients, you know that?" Lilly commented after I'd snapped the phone shut.

"I wouldn't be doing my job if I was."

She thought about that for a moment. "Have you ever noticed that Grandma is never judgmental?"

We had reached New Haven. I drove down the exit ramp and stopped too suddenly at a red light. It was my turn not to answer Lilly—I wasn't ready for the lessons my daughter wanted to teach me. Instead, I looked up. In the sky, a first star was visible. Such bright light emanating from something that had died such a long time ago.

The basic precepts of therapy are based on how your past affects your present. Lilly liked to say we should live in the moment. But she spoke out of idealism, out of theory. Her past had no ghosts living in it yet.

A few minutes later I sat in my car in front of Cooper's dorm and watched my daughter walk away.

The luckiest of us learn to use our histories as a ladder to climb to the future. That was what I hoped my daughter would be able to do one day. What I tried to help patients to do—was helping Adrienne Blessing to do. But who was going to help me climb out of my past?

TWO

"How often do you get these calls?" my brother, Simon, asked me.

"A few times a week."

"That often?" Perry, my sister-in-law, looked concerned.

We were having my birthday dinner at the Homestead Inn in Greenwich, Connecticut. Soft lights, white linens, vases of fresh flowers, waiters in starched white shirts and black pants, all contributed to the elegant atmosphere. Piano music drifted into the dining room from the bar.

We were seven at a table that had been originally set for eight. On my right was my niece, Gail, who was nineteen and as petite and blond as her mother. Next to her was my nephew, Harry, a precocious fifteen-year-old.

Chloe Blanchard, my best friend, was on my left and beside her was her husband, John. "And the caller doesn't say anything?" Simon asked.

"No, nothing . . . It's probably just one of my patients."

Perry put down the roll she was contemplating. "I bet you're still taking patients without checking their references. I wish you'd be more careful, Jordan." Perry, who was a professor of twentieth-century English literature, was sometimes unduly influenced by the novels she taught, reading drama into situations where there was none.

"It's sweet of you to worry about me, but none of my patients are dangerous characters. They're all pretty normal as far as neurotics go."

Laughing, she shifted in her chair, and the heart-shaped diamond pin she was wearing gleamed in the light. My father would have told her she shouldn't be wearing it on the right, but on the left. "Where the heart is held," he used to say.

"So you've been getting the calls a few times a week . . . for how long?" Simon asked.

"For the last two weeks or so. I never would have mentioned it except I wanted to know if there's anything I can do to stop them; they're annoying."

But they were more than annoying; they were disturbing me and making me nervous. What was the sound in the background?

My wineglass felt slippery when I picked it up and raised it to my lips.

"And the caller never says anything?" Simon asked.

"No."

"Any ambient noises to help identify where the caller is?" My brother, the district attorney for Stamford, Connecticut, often forgot he wasn't in a courtroom.

"Just a far-off ticking noise."

"From now on, I want you to keep a log of when the calls come in. And use star–sixty-nine to see if we can get the number where the calls are coming in from."

"Do you think this guy could be dangerous?" Chloe's husband asked Simon.

"John, why are you assuming it's a guy? Using the phone to antagonize someone seems more like something a woman would do," Chloe said.

"Do you think whoever it is, is stalking you too?" asked Gail, who was studying psychology at Princeton.

"Goodness, you're all making me sorry I even brought this up."

Ever the family diplomat, Perry tried to change the subject. "Jordan, did Gail mention she's decided to be a forensic psychologist?"

I smiled at Perry and told my niece how impressed I was.

Suddenly an argument broke out between a couple sitting at the table next to us. The man's voice was loud—he'd obviously been drinking—and Chloe, whose first husband had started out as a kind drunk but wound up an abusive alcoholic, cringed.

As a distraction, John quickly engaged her in conversation. "Chloe, didn't you interview a forensic psychologist once?" he asked.

A journalist, Chloe wrote profiles of celebrities and political figures for a well-known magazine based in Manhattan. "No, that was a big coroner out in LA. Now, that's a gruesome job."

"Anything forensic is a little grisly. Jordan, can't you talk Gail out of this?" Perry often wished my brother dealt with IPOs instead of criminals—she didn't want her daughter dealing with them too.

"Obviously, Mom isn't thrilled about my career choice."

"Well, I think it sounds like a terrific job," my nephew said, defending his sister.

Harry idolized Gail, and sometimes watching them, I wished I'd had more than one child. "Aunt Jordan, if someone is harassing you, can't you get a restraining order?"

Simon looked at Henry proudly. "Another lawyer in the making."

"And I'm going to work with criminals too," Henry boasted.

Perry sighed and I gave her a sympathetic glance. When she'd met my brother, he wanted to be a playwright, but after our father was murdered, Simon had gravitated towards the law, eventually becoming a public defender in order to be part of the system that prevented crime and punished perpetrators.

The murder changed both of our career decisions. I had wanted to be a jeweler but instead had turned to psychology so I could understand what motivated criminals. I'd even worked with prisoners and ex-cons for a while, perversely fascinated, until I realized, with my own therapist's help, that my patients were keeping me imprisoned in the past.

It had been years since I'd worked with a convict—in or out of jail.

Two waiters arrived with our appetizers, and while everyone was admiring the artfully arranged plates of food, Chloe leaned towards me. "Jordan, what's the matter? It isn't just the hang-ups, is it?"

She was the kind of friend everyone should be blessed with: perceptive, caring, and smart. "Well, the calls are part of it, but . . . I don't know . . . the whole day's been off. Chloe, do you think letting Lilly stay over at Yale was the right thing to do?"

"She's almost eighteen and she's going to sleep with Cooper whether you want her to or not. Would you rather force her to do it behind your back?"

"But what kind of message am I giving her by condoning it?"

Chloe smiled. "Maybe that you understand how she feels. And that you were once in love too."

"Did my daughter pay you to say that?"

Chloe laughed. "But you've been dealing with this issue for a while, why is it suddenly bothering you now? Jordan, you're trying to throw me off the track with this stuff, aren't you? Whenever you make me dig this hard, it's usually about Robert."

"You're relentless." I took another sip of my wine.

"Well?"

"You know how Robert always sends me flowers for my birthday . . ."

Chloe nodded. "Calla lilies."

"Except this time the florist got his order mixed up with someone else's and they delivered a dozen red roses. I couldn't help it—I got spooked and I wound up telling Lilly more about that than I wanted to."

The waiter took away my soup bowl and Chloe's salad.

"It's bad enough you had to live through that nightmare, but to be reminded of it on your birthday." She shook her head sympathetically and her blond curls bounced.

"I get lulled into thinking the memories are fading, and then something like that happens and it all comes back—just as real and terrifying as it was nineteen years ago."

"It's like that with grief, isn't it? It only hides; it doesn't really ever disappear." Chloe's glance returned to the table beside us, but the drunk had left. She had her nightmares too.

Around us everyone else was eating and talking and having a good time.

"So tell me the rest of it," she said.

"How do you know there's more?"

Chloe smiled. "How long have we been friends?"

"Okay, okay. Lilly called to tell Robert about the mix-up and he asked to talk to me . . ."

"Finally . . ." she said, and took a sip of her water.

I took a sip of my wine. "The closer I get to that appointment with your divorce lawyer, the more I'm reminded of how it was with us before . . . and all of a sudden I'm wondering if I gave Robert enough of a chance to— Damn it! This isn't like me. I'm being pathetic."

"If you were one of your patients, wouldn't you say that it's natural for you to be thinking more about Robert now that you've made up your mind to see a lawyer and finalize the separation? You were so happy with him for so long, Jordan. Just because you cut yourself off and ended the relationship, doesn't mean all your feelings are gone."

"No, but . . ."

"Give yourself a little leeway. You're not made of steel." She poked me with her fingernail.

"Ouch."

"See . . ."

We laughed.

"What would I do without you?" I asked.

"The same thing I'd do without you." She smiled. "But that's one thing we don't have to worry about. Our friendship is much more stable than most marriages."

We were all halfway though our main course when Gail brought up the phone calls again. "Aunt Jordan, can I ask you something about those calls? If it is a patient, why would he just call and hang up?" Gail was tireless when it came to talking psychology.

"Well, if it's who I think it is, he's very jealous. He might be calling me in an attempt to monopolize my time." I speared a shrimp and popped it into my mouth.

John nudged Chloe. "See, Jordan thinks it's a 'he.'"

"So you think that vindicates you from making a sexist comment?" She laughed.

"But, hon," John explained, "you made the sexist comment. I just jumped to a conclusion."

Gail doggedly returned to questioning me. "So he wants all your time?"

"Yes, and since most of the calls come during my sessions, it fits that it's someone who's resentful of my other patients." I tasted the rice that accompanied the shrimp: seasoned with salt and garlic and butter, it was delicious. I couldn't remember the last thing I'd eaten that was as good. I used to cook dinners like that when Robert and I had still been living together.

"Was tonight the first time you got a call when you weren't in session?" Simon asked. I gave him a long look as I tried to figure out why he was making such an issue about something that didn't seem like a big deal to me.

"Yes, it came in on my cell while I was on my way up to Yale with Lilly."

"So, that's why she's not here?" said Gail, who had arrived at the restaurant ten minutes late and had missed my earlier explanation of where Lilly was.

"Well, she was planning on being here. But then she found out Cooper couldn't come into the city for the next two weekends. It was either let her go up to Yale for the weekend or deal with her suffering through dinner."

"I didn't realize you were letting her spend the whole weekend at Yale," my brother said.

Did he seem bothered by the idea or was that just me projecting?

"Lilly is suffering?" my sister-in-law asked.

"Yes, it's something she does now that she's in love."

"Who doesn't suffer when they're in love?" Chloe asked rhetorically.

"It makes for great literature, though . . . all that suffering," Perry observed.

"You know, I'm not sure it's always the best thing that kids grow up," my brother said between bites.

Gail laughed. "No kidding. Sixteen to eighteen were the worst two years of my life." She turned to her father. "And you were an ogre. You just could not let go. If you could have locked me up, you would have."

Simon arched his eyebrows. "Are you accusing me of being overprotective?"

"That's is putting it mildly," Gail declared.

"We can't help it. Even though we don't want to, every parent becomes overprotective at a certain point," John said. He and Chloe had twin boys who had just turned thirteen.

I took a sip of wine. "If there was any way to prevent Lilly from growing up, I'd grab it. The only good that's come of this new stage is that it's given me a new appreciation for what I put Mom and Dad through."

"Adolescence is a war," Perry said. "Parents on one side, kids on the other. We resist letting our kids win even though we know in the end they have to or else they'll never become independent. And if they don't become independent, we've failed as parents."

"That's the problem, isn't it? Independence. Lilly thinks she's ready for it; I don't. So we bicker. Robert's been having better luck with her, but that's because he only talks to her about photography. Actually, I'm sick of being the bad guy. That's why I gave in today and let her go."

"So you're all alone at Grandma's tonight?" Simon asked.

We both still thought of the house as Grandma's even though she had died three years ago. Although she'd left it to both of us, Simon, whose home was nearby, had told me to use it for as long as I wanted. The only thing I couldn't do was sell it.

As I reached for my wine, my watch hit my plate and Simon turned in the direction of the noise. He stared at the black-and-silver chronograph for a moment longer than was necessary and then quickly averted his gaze.

Although I'd been wearing my father's watch for almost twenty years, it still reminded Simon of our father. It is an unassuming watch for a jeweler to have owned and a masculine watch for me to wear, especially with a black velvet dress, but I never took it off. The Swiss-made Croton is on a worn leather band with a black face and silver bars marking each hour. Of the three small silver circles, one is a stopwatch, another a second hand, and the last a timer. The stopwatch had stopped working years ago, but I'd never had it repaired. I couldn't imagine being without the watch even for the week it would take to have it fixed.

Absentmindedly, I spun the outer dial.

Ice plinked against glass as the busboy poured water.

Perry said something to Chloe. John talked to the kids.

Simon got up and came over to my seat. "Jordan, I need to talk to you. Just the two of us." He spoke just above a whisper.

"Is anything wrong. Are you okay?"

"Yes, I'm fine. It's nothing to worry about. Do you want to bring the dog and go for a walk with me in the morning?"

I nodded, curious but not concerned, and we made plans on where and when we would meet.

"Happy Birthday to you. . . ." The waiters had gathered around the table. Simon returned to his seat and joined everyone who was singing. "Happy Birthday, dear Jordan . . ."

The captain placed a small chocolate cake in front of me. Despite myself, I thought of who wasn't at the celebration: Lilly, my mother, my father, and my grandmother—I even thought of Robert—and then wished I hadn't.

At that exact moment, as if she could read my mind, Chloe caught my eye. "Make a wish," she said. "And be careful what you wish for; it just might come true."

I took a breath and blew out the single candle.

"From now on can we dispense with the singing and the candles? I'm getting too old for it." I smiled, chasing away the little bit of melancholy I'd invited to the table.

"My baby sister? Never. And thirty-nine is not old . . . Perry's aunt is eighty-nine and she just started being old."

"Dad, I think Aunt Edie's been old for a while," Henry said.

The waiter handed out slices of the cake and we all indulged. Each velvety bite had a complex combination of tastes: orange, bitter, and sweet. It was so intense that after three forkfuls, I pushed the plate away and noticed Perry had done the same. Of the three adult women at the table, only Chloe, who stayed thin regardless of what she ate, finished every crumb.

"Espresso, please," I said to the waiter who had come over to take orders for coffee or liqueur. And then everyone put their presents on the table and insisted I open them immediately.

Perry and Simon gave me the black cashmere sweater that she and I had seen two weeks before when we'd been shopping in Saks. I had tried it on, rubbing my hands up and down my arms, but hadn't bought it because the price had been obscene.

"This is as decadent as that chocolate cake," I said, and blew kisses across the table at her and my brother.

Next was Chloe and John's gift: a rare first edition of *Memories, Dreams, Reflections,* by Carl Jung. Gingerly, I opened the pristine cover and looked at the title page.

"I can't believe you did this." I squeezed Chloe's hand, kissed her, and then leaned past her and kissed John.

Only Chloe would have remembered that Jung was one of my heroes and would have known how much that book would mean to me.

The next gift was a new pair of gardening shears from Henry. I thanked him and winked at Perry who, I assumed, had made the purchase.

Gail's gift was last. It was a small package and inside under layers of tissue paper was an amber-colored crystal owl.

"What a thoughtful gift, sweetheart. I really love it. Thank you."

My father had started my collection of miniature animal figurines when I was a child. Over the years I'd amassed more than twenty-five, including an alabaster turtle, a lapis bird, a jade frog, and an ivory elephant. When Gail was younger and came to visit me, her favorite activity had been to rearrange the menagerie on its shelves.

I kissed Gail and sat back in my chair. "What a wonderful hoard. Thank you, everyone. Again."

"Wait, there's one more. Mom sent this and asked me to give it to you." Simon pushed a long slim box across the table.

I wasn't surprised. Every year, my mother gave me another piece of jewelry that my father had made for her. I had told her long ago that if she wanted to sell all those pieces, it was fine with me. But she had just brushed my hair off my face and said she'd rather hold on to them for me. Even though I couldn't bear to wear them, I kept them, along with my father's collection of loose stones, in a wall safe in my bedroom closet. Those few dozen suede pouches were all that was left of the jewelry store my parents had owned. Sometimes, late at night, I would take out the cache of jewels to clean them, or just hold them up to the light and linger with the memories they evoked.

Inside the box Simon had handed me was a black pearl bracelet, three strands thick. I sighed and rubbed the pearls on my cheek.

"She doesn't have to do this."

Perry reached over and touched my hand. "It's her way of making sure your father is with you on your birthday."

"My father is with me every day of my life . . ." Tears stung my eyes, but I did not cry.

Instead, I pictured him, in the back of the store, sitting at his jeweler's bench, working painstakingly on the bracelet.

"Look at the color of these, Jordan." My father held out the South Sea pearls. Each one was slightly irregular, but all were well matched. The dark gray iridescent surface reflected cobalt and amethyst and emerald hues.

"Men kill for jewels like this," my father had said.

He had repeated that phrase often about many of the jewels he handled. It was something I had grown up hearing and took for granted. Now I wished I had asked if it had been a premonition. A mantra? Or a message?

THREE

Carefully sipping hot coffee, I walked out of the Dunkin' Donuts shop and back to the car. Good, our cocker spaniel, watched my approach with a hungry look in her eyes. The smell of fresh baked donuts had permeated the parking lot, and while I hadn't bought any for me, I held out a doughnut hole for her, which was gone with one gulp.

The sun was at my back, the car windows were open, the breeze suggested spring, and I wondered how soon I would be able to start working in the garden. I always planted too early, but I was impatient for flowers. I'd learned frost was kind to geraniums, pansies, and ivy. Maybe on the way back, I'd stop at the nursery and spend the afternoon filling my grandmother's stone urns on the steps and walkway with the grape-, magenta-, and plum-colored blooms.

Five minutes later I pulled into the Pinetum's empty parking lot and shut off the car. While I waited for Simon, birdsong would be melody enough.

Donated to the city of Greenwich by its owner, a U.S. Army general, the Pinetum, a forty-acre primeval pine forest, is now a public park and the general's house is a horticultural center. Good sniffed the air, wagging her tail as she recognized the scent of one of the two places in the world she was allowed off her lead.

"Soon, good girl. Soon." Reaching into my jacket pocket, I

pulled out a dog biscuit and gave it to her. Hunkering down on the seat, she attacked the treat. A square yellow sign with black letters at the park's entrance warns that dogs are not allowed, but residents know the rule has never been enforced.

Tires on gravel announced my brother's arrival, and Good's ears perked up. She gobbled the last bit of biscuit before giving him a vociferous greeting. Good barked when she said hello. I had wanted to train her not to, but Lilly had convinced me otherwise. "Only special dogs talk, Mom. If you stop her, you'll be making her just like every other dog."

Simon and I had been walking for five minutes, past the formal gardens and around the back of the pond. I'd told Simon how wonderful my birthday dinner was and how happy I'd been to see Gail. He'd said how sorry he was Lilly hadn't come and then became silent. For a while we just walked and I didn't press him to tell me what was on his mind. Sometimes Simon needed time to organize his thoughts.

"Jordan, Dan Mallory was paroled last month."

A crow cawed as it flew by, and I looked up, searching for it, but the pine trees were so thick where we were I couldn't see the sky.

A cool wind blew away any idea of spring. I buttoned my coat and, hoping to find gloves, stuck my hands in my pockets. "I must have left them in the car."

"Left what in the car?" Simon asked, obviously confused by my non sequitur.

"My gloves."

"Take mine," he offered, holding them out.

"No, I'm fine."

"I don't think so. Not a four-leaf clover's chance of it," he said, quoting one of our grandmother's odd expressions.

We had come to the stream. Some years it was a thin trickle. Others it disappeared entirely. But there had been heavy snows that winter, and the stream gushed and gurgled as it rushed over the rocks.

"I don't understand. He still has three more years to go." The exact day, month, and year of Dan Mallory's release had been incised into my mind since the judge had sentenced him.

Simon crossed the stream and waited for me on the other side. But suddenly I couldn't figure out where to cross. I looked at my brother, helplessly.

"It's narrower here." He pointed to a different spot and held out his hand to me. "C'mon, Jordan. Jump."

Good was waiting on the other side with Simon. Her paws were wet and she was wagging her tail. Taking my brother's hand, I jumped. Good barked, ran ahead, and Simon and I resumed walking.

"I don't understand. How did Mallory get out? Can murderers get out early?"

"Anyone but a lifer can get out early. The parole board is convinced Mallory has been rehabilitated."

"No, Simon, it's impossible."

"I talked to the head of the board myself. Mallory was a model prisoner. Worked hard, stayed out of trouble, and even put himself through school and got a college degree." He paused. "In psychology."

I shivered as I pulled up my collar and tried to hide my face in the warm wool.

For years, I had forbidden myself to dwell on Dan Mallory. Awake, I was successful. But asleep, my subconscious revolted.

In one recurring nightmare I was nineteen again.

Inside the jewelry store, Mallory pointed a 44-caliber gun at my father. From outside the store, I watched through the plate glass. Mallory didn't know I was there. All I had to do was run inside, throw myself against him, dislodge the gun, and give my father a chance to save himself. But I couldn't move. Looking down at my feet, I was horrified to discover I had turned into some kind of precious stone—light green and opaque—and incapable of moving, opening my mouth, or waving my hands. Only my eyes were animated, and I could not save my father with my eyes. Condemned to just watch, I rewitnessed my father's murder, over and over.

When the nightmare scared me awake, I would lie in bed and allow myself to picture Mallory in his prison uniform, sitting on his cot, locked behind iron bars. Wrapping the image around me like a blanket, I'd hold on to it until calmed, until I could let go of the name and the face of the man.

As long as Mallory was in prison, those of us outside were safe, but the minute he stepped beyond the confines of his cell, we would step into ours.

"'Rehabilitated.'" I repeated the word.

"It happens," Simon said.

"Sometimes it happens. But sometimes prisoners are just smart enough to know how to fool the wardens and the psychologists. You and I both have enough experience to know that."

I was shivering and sad. My father would have only been sixty if he had lived. He would have had dinner with us last night, and he would have told Perry to move the diamond pin to her left side.

"The warden insists that Mallory has worked through what happened and takes full responsibility for what he did. He's even become religious."

"Good for him," I said harshly, and saw the dog, hearing her name, stop and turn. "Good girl," I said in a more mellow tone. She ran around me in a wide circle, spotted a squirrel, and took off again.

"I'm telling you because you have every right to know, not because I think you need to worry."

"So I'm not going to get one of your lectures about how I shouldn't walk the dog at night in Washington Square Park—"

"Jordan, stop it and listen to me. I've already talked to Mallory's parole officer on the phone—he's someone I've known for years—and I intend to meet with him later in the week, but based on what Rafferty's already said, I am certain there's no reason for you to be afraid. If you want to be more conscientious about where and when you go out alone, I won't dissuade you—New York can be a very dangerous city and you're not always careful."

"You sound just like your wife," I said, joking. But neither of us laughed.

Like my father, Simon was too protective of me. Had my father lived longer, he and I would have worked out that part of our relationship, but I was still a rebellious nineteen-year-old when he'd died. Typically, my father had been less strict with his son than his daughter, and out of jealousy I stole many of the same freedoms Simon had been given. Trying to prove I was just as capable and equipped as any male, I did foolhardy things and more than once had to be rescued.

I had been fearless then and was not that different now. New York had never frightened me; I wasn't scared to be alone in Grandma's big house; I drove aggressively even in the city and refused to believe that women needed male escorts for safety's sake.

It had been important to me, as a mother, to show Lilly that women could be strong and unafraid. I hadn't wanted her to grow up thinking she was weak and fragile because she was a woman. I treated too many female patients who suffered that delusion.

Perhaps it would have been better to have taught her more concern and caution. But I hadn't wanted her gender to inhibit her.

"Simon?" I stopped walking.

"What?"

"Is Mallory being paroled the reason you were so concerned about the hang-ups I've been getting?"

"Absolutely not. Two different issues," Simon said. "You have to remember, if they thought he was a threat to society, they wouldn't have let him out."

"Simon, he's not a threat to society. Only to me."

"I have more faith in the system than that."

"Oh, please, don't insult me and don't lie to try to make me feel better."

"If I didn't have faith in the law, I wouldn't still be in practice."

I kicked at a rock and it went flying for about five feet before hitting a tree trunk. "I have faith too Simon. In the failure of the system and in the law and in the contracts we all sign. Husbands and wives promise to stay faithful to one another and then cheat. Citizens pledge their allegiance and then spy on their country. And convicts are released only to repeat the same crimes that put them in prison in the first place. Don't forget, I worked with ex-cons for five years."

We'd had this argument before and we would have it again, yet there was some strange comfort in our bickering. For a few minutes, normalcy had returned.

I had spent my early years as a therapist helping people who had committed criminal acts. Hoping to find answers, I had only found more questions. How could a criminal live with himself knowing how much pain and suffering he had caused? How did someone who murdered in cold blood sleep? Marry? Have children? Too many of the criminals I had worked with did not have access to their emotions. Psychopaths, they felt no remorse or guilt. They had done hard time and would again.

Was Mallory a psychopath? Or was he, as my brother wanted to believe, one of the cons who had been rehabilitated?

Simon and I had looped back and wound up at the pond where, as children, we had watched the frogs jump from their sun-baked hiding places.

"Simon, Mallory hates me."

"You're not the one who convicted him."

"But I'm the one who took the stand." I'd stepped in mud; to knock it off I scraped my shoe on a rock. The sound was harsh.

"There was so much evidence they would have convicted him without your statement. Mallory knew that. Everyone in the courtroom knew that."

I was silent.

"What is it?" Simon asked.

"There's more. I never told anyone, but there's another reason Mallory hates me."

"What? That you were dating him and that's part of the reason Dad fired him? C'mon, Jordan. Just because you didn't admit it,

Mom knew, Dad knew, I knew. Did you think you were that good at keeping secrets?"

I tried to remember those few months before the murder, how I'd sneaked around with Mallory, trying to hide the fact that we were dating from my parents, knowing they wouldn't approve: enjoying my rebellion even more than I enjoyed seeing Mallory.

"When Dad caught me with Mallory, I lied. I told him that Mallory had been pursuing me and that I had only seen him a few times because I'd been afraid to turn him down. I never admitted that we'd been seeing each other for months and that I actually *liked* him."

Simon shrugged. "Dad was afraid if he confronted you, you'd go on seeing Mallory just to prove a point."

I shook my head, in retrospect; I had been so immature. "The stupidest part is that when Dad fired Mallory, I was actually relieved. Mallory really was too old for me and wanted much more than I was ready to give . . . not just sexually. He was becoming so possessive of my time that even when I was with my girlfriends, it bothered him."

"So Dad took care of it," Simon said. "He fired him."

"And got killed for it."

Simon stopped walking and turned to face me. "You know that wasn't your fault. Dad would have fired Mallory no matter what you said. Whether you two were seeing each other or not. It wasn't just about you; he wanted him out of the store. He didn't trust him."

"I just wish he'd never hired him," I whispered into the wind.

We parted at the pond: Simon was meeting Perry and the kids at the ten o'clock church service. "Are you sure you don't want to come with us?" he asked.

"It's a little late for me to start praying; Mallory's already been let out of prison."

I veered off the main path and took one of the unmarked trails that led deeper into the woods. After ten minutes of hiking, Good noticed a small group of deer about forty feet away in a clearing and froze. Sensing us, the deer turned and stared but didn't run away. Living in the Pinetum, they had never been hunted or even heard a gunshot. For generations this herd had been allowed to live and breed in the forest, undisturbed. They were fearless.

If confronted with a true threat, these deer would be helpless. Their instincts had been dulled by the decades of tranquillity.

It was a standoff. Finally Good and I headed off in another direction. As my feet sidestepped gnarled tree roots and landed on soft green moss and last year's fallen leaves, I decided to allow myself this one time, alone and in the woods, to focus on the one thing I normally avoided. Its landscape was too rough and rocky to travel any more often.

My father had died and no amount of thinking or dwelling on it would ever change the facts. I had learned that years ago. Better to think about Lilly enjoying her weekend with Cooper or my friends or my patients, who had problems I could do something about. But that morning as I walked further into the forest and the darker it became, the easier it was to slip into the past.

When I was young, I decided I wanted to go to college to study painting and design and become, like my father, and my grandfather before him, a jewelry designer. At sixteen, I started working with my father in the workshop behind the store every summer until August, when my parents closed up for three weeks and our family went to Capri, Italy, where my father's father still lived and ran his jewelry store. But the summer I was nineteen, we never got to Europe.

It was Friday, July 22. My mother was in the front of the store, and my father and I were in the workshop. He was bent over his bench setting a three-carat sapphire ring, and I was cleaning an antique amethyst-and-diamond necklace. The room smelled of coffee, wax, and the apple I had just finished. On the radio, a Frank Sinatra song ended and the news came on. Reaching out, my father turned down the sound.

Over the intercom we heard my mother say good-bye to a customer. A few moments passed and then the front-door chimes pealed again. I wasn't paying attention to the noises coming over the intercom until I noticed my father pick up his head and listen more carefully. I started to ask him what was going on, but he put his finger to his lips, took his small pistol out of the top drawer of the workbench, and stepped on the silent alarm that was connected to the police station.

When my father had installed that alarm, a member of the police force had taken us through a drill. If the store was robbed, none of us was supposed to put up a fight or argue, but rather, as slowly as we could, gather up the jewelry and hand it over to the robber.

"Concentrate on the fact that the police are on their way," my father had told me when we'd practiced. "Let them take whatever they want. We are insured. Nothing is worth risking your life for."

"You know what I want and it's not this gold shit." The robber's voice was tinny and mechanical coming through the intercom's cheap speaker, but I heard every word. I recognized the voice—it was Dan Mallory.

"Here—take these—" my mother was whimpering.

Where were the police? We'd entered another dimension where no time passed. The air did not circulate. The earth had stopped rotating. Was it ten minutes, ten hours, or ten days since my father had stepped on the alarm?

"Stop—" My mother's voice was twisted up as if she were in pain. My father and I rushed to the doorway. With his free hand, my father shoved me back into the workshop, where I fell against a table.

"For God's sake, stay here, Jordan," he hissed, and then stepped out into the store.

My leg throbbing, I crawled to the doorway and stared out.

A frozen tableau. Mary and Joseph and the three wise men around the crèche at Christmas. Tinker Bell flying across the stage with Wendy, Peter, and Michael close behind. JFK, Jr., saluting his father's flag-draped coffin. Movement locked in immovable permanence because of its importance. To the world. To a nation. To children.

This one was mine. Forever. My iconography. The horror against which all other horrors would be measured and come up short. Or so I thought.

My mother was trying not to cry, not to breathe, not to exist, while Mallory held her, hiding behind her, pointing a gun to her temple. Black metal against her cream skin.

My father, his back to me, pointed his gun. "Dan, let her go. Take the jewelry and let her go. Now."

"I don't want the jewelry. I want my job back. I want Jordan back," Mallory shouted.

The only thing louder than his voice was the sound of my heart slamming against my rib cage.

My mother, growing brave with my father in the room, pushed Mallory away. His arm hit a tray of diamond, sapphire, emerald, and ruby rings glittering on the counter. The bowl of deep red roses my mother had delivered to the store every week crashed to the floor. Glass shattered, water spilled, one of the roses fell across Mallory's shoe.

Gunshots from different directions.

One bullet hit the wall behind my father and burst a glass display case. Another bullet—or was it that bullet ricocheting?—hit the mirror behind Mallory, and a rain of my father's reflections fell to the floor. Almost instantly it was followed by another gunshot, but this time it was my father himself who fell. With my eyes, I followed his body as it dropped, the longest drop to the deepest center of the earth. When I looked up again, Mallory was gone and my mother was on the floor beside my father. I ran to his side and put my head on his chest.

My mother was screaming, but there was no way to judge the volume. It was either the loudest or the softest scream I have ever heard. My father was gasping for breath as beneath him the rug slowly changed color from pale gray to the deep dark red of the roses.

I could hear his heart beating. His blood was hot on my cheek, like my own tears. Using my hands I tried to stop the blood. I pressed down. Hard, harder, I heard a bone break. A bone in my hand? I found out later I broke one of my father's ribs trying to stanch his bleeding.

But I could not do it. My hands were not big enough. The hole was too deep. The bullet had gone right through his heart. My father bled out in front of me, under me, while I watched. I smelled fire and roses. Saw the stain growing, reaching towards my mother's feet. She was wearing bone pumps with black toes. Everywhere I looked the carpet was red. (The next time I went into the store, the carpet had been removed. A whole section of parquet stained forever.)

My mother was looking at me. She knew that her husband's life had leeched out of him. I had become her focus.

Taking my face covered with my father's blood in her hands and repeating herself like a scratched record, she screamed: "You've been shot, you've been shot, you've been shot . . ." There was so much of my father's blood on my body it had blinded her, and she ran frantic fingers down my face and my arms and my chest checking to see where I had been injured.

I knew I had not been shot but could not reach that part of my brain where the words were.

In the ambulance, my father on one stretcher, I on the other, the paramedic told my mother it didn't appear that I had been shot. At the hospital they confirmed what she already knew: her husband was dead; her daughter was in shock, but she had not been wounded.

I *have* been wounded, I wanted to explain. But the file in my head where the words were stored was still locked, missing, lost. I had been wounded for the whole of my life. But I did not say anything. In my lap, I clutched my hands, still sticky with traces of my father's blood.

We were in a hallway of the emergency room. I was on a stretcher. An IV needle was stuck in my arm, a bag of something clear dripping into me. I noticed my hands were stained red.

Slowly I lifted my right hand to my face and put my forefinger inside my mouth where it was wet and warm, and I sucked the stickiness off. I tasted something sweet and then salty—the salt from my own skin, the sweet from my father's blood. One finger and then the next and then the next, all licked cleaned but still not clean enough, and my mother said, "Dear God, stop her."

And then a male voice said, "You're going to get a little sleepy now, Jordan. Don't fight it. Close your eyes."

I tried to tell him that I needed to finish cleaning my hands, but I still could not find the words.

The day after the murder, the police came to the hospital and asked me if I could help them find the man who had robbed the store and shot my father. My mother had given them his address from her records, but he was not there anymore. It was the only time during that day that I surfaced from my ocean of grief. I knew more than the details of his face. I knew his name and where he lifted weights and what kind of sandwiches he liked. What he drank. What his kisses tasted like.

But how could I think about him like that? How could I remember that I had liked him and touched him and whispered to him, planning rendezvous without my parents catching on?

I tried to help the police find Mallory, but the one thing I didn't know was his hiding place.

It took two months for them to arrest him. By that time I had gone back to college and my mother had already sold the jewelry store and the apartment, moved in with my grandmother and was planning to move to San Francisco as soon as the trial was over. She was going to run away to the city where she'd gone to college and lived before she'd met my father. It was a place where she still had old friends and no reminders of the tragedy.

"I need to get away from what's happened," she'd tried to explain to me. "You and your brother have school—I have to find something to distract me too."

That semester I changed my major from art to psychology.
There was a lot I needed to understand.

The trial started that November. Mallory's court-appointed
lawyer, in his scuffed shoes and wrinkled gray suit, made a poor
case that his client had been overwrought because he had been
fired by Mr. Sloan the week before and that he had shot out of
fear, not intent to kill.

On the stand, Mallory tried to explain that he'd thought my
father had shot at him first and that the mirrors had confused
him. He had come, not to rob the store, but to coerce my father
into hiring him back. He loved my father, he said. He loved his
job. But Mallory did not do himself any justice. He acted like a
man who was guilty.

I had expected our dating to be part of Mallory's defense, but
his lawyer never brought it up. Had he meant to? Or had he
decided that not even a thwarted romance would justify a cold-
blooded murder. Would a better lawyer have known to use passion
as a motive? Would it have made any difference?

Against my mother's objections, the prosecution put me on the
stand. I would be the most sympathetic witness, they told her.

"Miss Sloan, did you see a man in your parents' jewelry store on
the morning of July twenty-second?"

"Yes."

"And did that man have a gun?"

"Yes."

"And did he shoot your father?"

"Yes."

"Did your father die of that gunshot wound?"

"Yes."

"And did you know that man?"

"Yes."

"How did you know him?"

"He worked for us."

"And what was his name?"

"Dan Mallory."

"And do you see Dan Mallory in the courtroom today?"

I pointed at the spot where I knew Dan Mallory was sitting. I had come in early and the prosecutor had showed me which seat Mallory would be in.

To everyone in the courtroom it must have appeared that I was looking at him, but I wasn't. I had not looked at him once since the trial had begun three days before. Instead I was staring past him and slightly to the left into the face of a spectator.

It wasn't only hatred that prevented me from focusing on his face.

It was also confusion and guilt.

I simply didn't know how to look at the accused and connect him to the man I had known. How could the man who had taken my father's life be the same man who had kissed me? Who had held my hand and talked to me about rubies the color of roses?

The time we had spent together could no longer exist for me: Mallory was no longer my ex-boyfriend; he was only my father's killer.

While the jury deliberated, I tried not to wonder if I was at all to blame for my father's death.

Over and over, I ran through the logic of what had happened. Or the illogic of it. My father had fired Dan Mallory because he didn't trust him: not with the jewels in the store and not with his daughter.

I'd told my father Mallory had been pursuing me.

I'd never told him that I'd dated him willingly.

But would that difference have mattered to my overprotective father?

No. In my heart, I knew, whether I'd actually gone out with Mallory or not, whether I'd liked him or not, my father still would have fired him. He didn't care how I felt about Mallory. All that mattered to my father was how Mallory felt about me.

But if I looked at Mallory on the stand, I might have seen who he had been to me before. I might have understood some of the betrayal he'd felt when he'd been fired.

And I could not dishonor my deceased father with those feelings.

I could only focus on how much I hated Mallory and how I would hate him forever.

After the foreman read the verdict finding Dan Mallory guilty of second-degree murder, I finally looked at him for the first time. And thinking about what he was going to have to give up, I smiled.

FOUR

The big chair in my office was made of leather that had been worn down to a soft finish over the years. It contained me. For fourteen years I had been sitting there and listening to patients talk out their problems and dreams and fears.

Some of them cried, others laughed nervously, but they all talked, except for Adrienne Blessing, who had stopped speaking mid-sentence and had not said anything for over ten minutes.

She had arrived on time bearing a gift—a jar of expensive raspberry jam from the gourmet food store on the corner of Sixth Avenue. After graciously giving it to me, she refused to allow me to thank her, lay down on the couch, and began talking about how easy it was for her to approach men. I had asked her if her father had been an easy man to approach, and she had begun to answer and then had abruptly become silent.

Now she was staring up at the ceiling, examining it as if an important message were encrypted in the paint.

Outside my window I heard a man and a woman arguing on the usually quiet Greenwich Village street. Adrienne didn't seem to notice the commotion. From her body language, I suspected she was struggling with a revelation. A lock of my hair escaped from my chignon, but I didn't tuck it back in. Any movement might have distracted my patient. If I had to sit silently all through that session and the next and the next after that, I could. I'd done it before.

The phone rang on a small ebony table, to the right of my chair. Answering it without taking my eyes off my patient, I felt a sting. Lifting the receiver to my ear, I saw I'd scratched my hand on the amethyst rock my father had given me on my fifteenth birthday. The rock wasn't supposed to be next to the phone but on one of the bookshelves that lined my office walls. Who had moved it? The cleaning lady? One of my patients?

A thin line already dotted with blood proclaimed where the rock's edge had ripped my skin.

"Hello?"

From the couch, Adrienne cast a disgusted glance at me or at the phone. I wasn't sure which.

Lilly's voice sang in my ear.

"I'm in session; can I call you back?"

My daughter knew the shorthand, so she was brief. As I listened to her explain why she wouldn't be home for dinner, I sucked the blood off the scratch on my hand and watched a new line of red appear.

"I'd prefer it if you wouldn't take calls when I'm here," Adrienne said once I'd hung up.

I could have explained that many therapists answer the phone during sessions because if they didn't, they'd never have time to get back to anyone in the short breaks between patients. Instead I thought the interaction between us on this issue might be helpful to me in seeing how she handled certain kinds of situations.

"Why is that?" I asked her.

"Because it interrupts what I'm saying."

She hadn't been speaking when the phone rang, but I didn't comment on that.

"Yes, it does interrupt, and I'm sorry, but don't you take calls at your office?"

"Not when I'm in an important meeting," Adrienne said.

"So how do you feel about my taking that call during our session?" I asked.

"This is ridiculous; I'm not going to waste time talking about your answering the phone. I have more important things to deal with here."

"Maybe how you felt when I answered the phone is important," I suggested.

Adrienne stared at the framed paintings on the wall. Most people thought the two colorful abstracts were the work of a modern artist. No one had ever guessed Lilly had done both paintings in third grade.

There was another protracted period of silence.

"I've told you I've been seeing someone . . ." Adrienne began haltingly.

"Yes." I had hoped she would go back to telling me about her father, but I didn't want to interrupt her now that she was talking again.

"Well, what I haven't mentioned is that he's married." She lifted her head and looked at me with intense curiosity. Her lapis blue eyes bored into me, trying to read my reaction. I knew my face was expressionless—there was nothing she could learn from watching me.

As Lilly and I had discussed in the car on the way to Yale, it wasn't my job to make judgments, regardless of how strongly I felt about a patient's actions. I was there to listen and to lead them to make connections and observations about themselves.

"And how do you feel about that?" I asked.

"I hate that he has another woman in his life. By her very existence she occupies some of his thoughts—and that means she takes up his time. Time he therefore can't spend on me. And to make it worse, there is not only a wife, but a child."

"Could that be why my phone call bothered you so much?" I asked. "I wasn't spending my time on you?"

Adrienne coupled the two thoughts. "Maybe. Or maybe I just think it's rude for you to take calls during my session."

"Okay. Let's get back to the relationship. Have you ever had a relationship with a married man before?"

"A few. Why? Do you think it's wrong to sleep with married men?"

"It's not a question of what I think, Adrienne. All that matters is what you think of it."

"No, I don't think it's wrong. If his wife doesn't make him happy, that's not my fault, is it?"

Rarely in therapy did I allow what a patient was saying to affect me on a personal level, but for one moment I was angry. Not at Adrienne but at all the women like her who didn't think it was wrong to go to bed with someone else's husband. Robert had known at least one of them, and she had helped break up our marriage.

"But it's not a pattern, if that's what you're asking," Adrienne continued. "I'd just rather talk about this new relationship than the ones that are over and done with."

"Okay, what else would you like to tell me about the man you are seeing?"

"He's great in bed, but I knew he would be the minute I saw him. It's not because he's handsome—although he is in an artsy kind of way. It's that he's so comfortable with his own sexuality. Revels in it. He's got this lazy way of moving and a smile that takes forever to complete. All you have to do is look at him and you know he's just as slow and sure in bed."

She waited for me to react and when I didn't, she continued. "Don't you think he sounds attractive?" she asked.

"What matters is that you do."

"But I want to know if you do," Adrienne insisted.

"What I think is really beside the point. We're here to talk about you."

"But I need to know if you understand my reaction to this man."

"Yes, from how you've described him, I can see why you would be interested in him."

"But didn't my description cause a physical response in you? Didn't it stir you?"

"Why does that matter?" I asked.

She let out a long breath. I wasn't trying to frustrate her, but I wouldn't do her any good as a therapist if I shared my personal opinions with her.

Instead of answering my question, she asked another. "What's the first thing you look for in a man?"

If she wouldn't have misinterpreted it, I might have smiled at her persistence.

"Adrienne, why don't you tell me what's the first thing you look for in a man?"

"Boy, you stay right on track, don't you? Okay, we'll do it your way for a while. The first thing I look for is how sexy he is. Sex is my sustenance." She took a satisfied deep breath. "Have you ever been with someone who knew everything about how to please you? Who luxuriated in sex?"

"Have you been with men like him before?" I asked, redirecting the question back to her.

"I specialize in men like him," she purred.

"You mean you find many men like him?"

"I find them or they find me. . . . That's never been the problem," she added.

"Then what is the problem?"

"I want this one to last and they never do," Adrienne said as she crossed one leg over the other and her leather pants rustled. "But suddenly I'm obsessing about it ending, and I think that's the real reason I wake up in the middle of the night and can't go back to sleep. I've never worried so much about a relationship before. Do you do that? Do you worry about your relationship ending?"

I ignored the question she'd asked me and asked her why she had never worried about relationships ending before. But she chose not to elucidate and instead asked me yet another question.

"On the surface, you and I seem very different, don't we?"

"Do you think so?"

"Yes, on the surface we do. Just look at how we're dressed." She glanced from her leather pants to my man-tailored trousers.

Her tight black pants and spiked heels were blatantly sexual. They accentuated her shapely legs and small waist. Her canary sweater was made of expensive cashmere and hugged her breasts suggestively. Her blond, streaked hair fell in waves past her shoulders. When she moved, her Bakelite bracelets clicked together. Adrienne's makeup was plentiful though artful. She could have looked lewd, but instead she seemed vital.

"You're thin enough to wear pants that are more sculpted to your body and that white blouse is buttoned up too high. I like the sweater around your shoulders, but instead of suede loafers you should be wearing higher heels."

"What would happen if I changed the way I dressed?"

"You'd look sexier. I bet your hair is as long as mine, but by wearing it pulled back like that you look severe. And your makeup is too subtle: your eyelashes are long, but you could use stronger eyeliner and a darker lipstick."

"And if I looked sexier, what would happen?" I was curious to see where Adrienne was going with my makeover.

"You'd be even more of a challenge."

"To whom?"

But Adrienne didn't answer my question; she continued looking for ways to compare us. "I'm colors and exaggerations," she said. "You're monochromatic and understated. Where I am obvious, you are obscure. No one knows anything about you from looking at you across a room."

Robert had made a similar observation about me more than once. "You are elusive, Jordan. And that's what is so enchanting about you. It's why I never get tired of photographing you or looking at you," he'd said. But that had turned out to be a lie.

"And what is it about our differences that matters to you?" I asked Adrienne.

"It's just that I bet our differences don't go that deep. I bet that you and I are more alike than not underneath all the window dressing."

"And what does that mean to you?"

"Well, for one thing, if you understand me, it will be that much easier for you to help me."

It wasn't important for me to either confirm or deny her supposition. It was only significant that she was trying to find a way to relate to me.

"Adrienne, let's go back to your obsessing about the end of this new relationship. You said that's unusual for you. Tell me why."

"I usually get bored with the men that I date."

"What about them bores you?"

"I don't know . . ." She thought for a moment. "Men get predictable. I start to be able to guess what we'll talk about, the places we'll go, the way they'll touch me, the positions they'll take when we make love." Her manicured fingers stroked the hollow space where her collarbones met.

"All I've ever wanted was someone to surprise *me* some of the time. Someone who wouldn't rely on me to supply all of the thrills. Someone who's better and stronger and more exciting than I am. And I never have found someone like that." She took a breath, and her chest heaved with the effort. "Until now. This man is smarter, more and more sexually adventurous than anyone I've ever been with before." Adrienne smiled a secret smile to herself. "He likes to hear my fantasies and wants to know about my exploits. My peccadilloes. You know I used to have a hard time having an orgasm but not with him. He knows how to do things to me that I usually have to ask for." She looked at me expectantly again.

She had said so many things I wanted to explore. What fantasies? What peccadilloes? Why was it difficult for her to have orgasms? All this was fertile ground for us to investigate; it was material I needed to hear about.

"Tell me about your relationship with your parents. . . . Did you have to ask them for things?"

"No . . . they completely spoiled me."

"So do you have any idea why it bothers you when you have to ask for something in a relationship?"

"Well, not because I'm shy." She laughed, and I laughed with her.

Adrienne was thirty-two and had never been married. She had moved to New York to go to college and had never left. Her first job had been as a copywriter and now she owned her own agency, a boutique that specialized in iconoclastic, cutting-edge advertising. She was smart, articulate, and successful. No, I couldn't imagine a situation where this woman was shy.

Suddenly she sat up and perched on the edge of the couch. Her face was flushed and she licked her lips before she spoke.

"Can I just tell you about last night?" She didn't wait for me to answer. "I had plans to meet him in a restaurant on the Upper East Side. He'd asked me to wear something long and slit up the side, without underwear.

"When I got to the restaurant, he'd already ordered me a Margarita. While we had drinks, he massaged my leg under the table, and the whole time he talked his hand moved up higher and higher until his fingers were deep inside my cunt and I was wet.

"And then, right there, with all those people eating and drinking around us, he stroked me and played with me until I came. Right there in the bar. Have you ever had an orgasm in the middle of a crowded restaurant?" The memory of the night danced in her eyes. "I knew right then that no matter what happens, I'm already ruined. I'll always want this now. Do you see? Has that ever happened to you? One millimeter of a moment—wham—something happens and then forever your life is different."

"There's a lot about what happened and how you feel that we need to talk about. But we'll have to wait till next time, Adrienne."

Stunned, she pushed her sleeve up her arm and looked at her gold watch. I'd jumped her out of her dream and she wasn't at all happy about it. Standing, she reached for her jacket and her handbag—an expensive Prada bag I had admired with Perry in Saks a few weeks before—and took a step closer to my chair.

"I have to change my appointments for next week," she said. "We're shooting some commercials for a chain of avant-garde clothing stores. All the models are going to be nude."

While I rearranged her appointments, I considered why she'd purposely told me about the commercial. I tried to pay as much attention to what patients said before and after sessions as I did to what they said during them.

Adrienne Blessing occupied my thoughts as I climbed up the stairs and let myself into the apartment. Last night, while I had been home in my robe, watching the news and thinking about the man who had killed my father, this woman was in a restaurant having orgasms with her drink.

Or was she? What was it about the way she had told me her story that made me doubt her? Why had I felt as if I had been listening to someone retelling the plot of a movie they'd seen, instead of describing an incident from life?

I had more challenging patients—a brilliant mathematician who didn't leave his house except to come to therapy, a manic woman who was struggling with a metastasized cancer, and Alex, the jealous young man who might or might not be badgering me with phone calls to make up for the attention his own mother had never shown him—in fact, the majority of my patients were more disturbed and dysfunctional than Adrienne seemed to be, but she was the one who intrigued me the most. Her overt sexuality, the brashness and bravado and the crude language she used, made me wonder about the aspects of her past that she hadn't yet begun to reveal.

In the kitchen, I toasted a bagel, spread margarine on it, and sat down to eat. Suddenly I didn't want anything that basic. I wanted something delicious and tempting. Years ago the refrigerator would have been stocked with Parma ham, fine cheeses, exotic fruits, farm fresh butter, and French chocolate, but that was when Robert and I were still together and before Lilly had become a vegetarian.

My daughter subsisted on nuts, tofu, rice, beans, and vegetables that she steamed herself, while I ate Balance Bars or whatever Lilly left over, ordered out, drank coffee and gallons of water.

And then I remembered the raspberry jam Adrienne had given me. Opening it, I salivated as I dipped the silver butter knife into the jar and then spread the jewel-toned confiture on the bagel.

Savoring the intensity of the jam, I ate slowly. It was unusual for a patient to bring me a gift except at Christmas and since nothing a patient says or does in therapy is irrelevant, I wanted to know what the gift had meant.

I crunched the seeds between my teeth and felt the pulp of the fruit on my tongue. Adrienne wanted me to identify with her, but why was that so important to her?

Finished with the bagel, I stuck a spoon into the jar and ate the jam like ice cream.

Adrienne had all the earmarks of a narcissist: someone who could only relate to the world in terms of how she fit into it and who turned every situation around so that it revolved around her. She had just started group therapy and her group was meeting the following night. Watching her interact with other people would give me even more insight into her pathology.

But how many more clues did I need to make a diagnosis? Hadn't she already insinuated herself into my consciousness without me noticing? Of course I thought about all my patients, but not the way I was thinking about Adrienne Blessing. I flashed on the way she had touched her neck while she was talking to me, as if the very feel of her own skin gave her pleasure.

Like most therapists, I agreed that narcissists were among the most difficult patients to deal with and to help because they were the best at both fooling and manipulating us. Here it was hours later, and I was still thinking about some of the questions she had asked me.

Yes, I had once been with someone who knew everything about how to please me, but not in a long time. And no, I no longer knew what it felt like to have a man luxuriate in pleasuring me. It had been three years—maybe four since I'd bothered to sleep with anyone. I'd lost the drive and the desire to get on that Ferris wheel. After Robert, I'd only dated a few men and none of them more than a few times. No one had gotten inside my head.

Adrienne had asked me one question that stood out from the others—had asked it as if she already knew the answer and maybe she had. Many patients did research on their therapists before they chose them. Perhaps Adrienne had read up on me and knew all about my father's murder and the subsequent trial.

"Has that ever happened to you?" she'd asked. "One millimeter of a moment—wham—something happens and then forever your life is different?"

Yes, my father's murder had been one of those moments. Everything changed for me after that—I'd even met Robert as a result of my father's murder—a single moment that had robbed me not only of a parent but the parent I was closest to. Like Lilly and her father, my father and I shared a passion. Even as a child, I had known I wanted to become a jeweler and work with him. By the time I was seven, my father had made a jeweler's workshop for me at home and had stocked it with glitter, plastic "gemstones," strings of faux pearls, and gold and silver chains—anything that I could use to create jewelry. He examined each piece I made and praised me encouragingly when he saw something that showed promise. When I was ten, he took a necklace I had made out of shells and starfish, cast it in eighteen-karat gold, and gave it to me as a gift.

After my father was killed, I lost all sense of time and place. I don't remember anything of those first few days. I know I was in the hospital, then I was home, and finally I was at the funeral.

Somehow I had showered and gotten dressed. My mother and Simon were beside me in the black stretch limo, but I can't remember any of us talking. We were all too brutalized to be of any help to each other.

There was a service, but I don't recall what was said. Only that the room was crowded and hot. I was sweating and irrationally confused the dripping perspiration with blood. Every few minutes I would wipe my forehead or my neck to make sure my hand did not come away wet and red.

In those days I lived in jeans and clogs and my long hair was always wild and loose. But for the funeral I had pulled my hair back, put on one of my mother's simple dresses, and worn panty hose with pumps.

During the service, while the preacher intoned a homily I did not hear, I worried that my father, floating over the crowd, looking down at the mourners, would not recognize me. The thought plagued me. And halfway through the service I pulled the barrettes out of my hair and let it loose again so my father would know which one of the mourners was his daughter.

Suffering and stricken, and still partially in shock over the atrocity of how my father had died, I was barely present. Flashbacks of the nightmare repeated tirelessly in my mind. For all I knew I had been in the chapel for fifteen minutes or two hours.

There were too many flowers, obscenely alive and fragrant, and I wanted to rid the room of them. It should have been more somber and solemn in the chapel. The noise was too loud; I wanted silence. My father deserved it.

When the service ended, I stood between my mother and Simon and went through the motions of acknowledging the endless line of mourners offering condolences.

Simon had been weeping, I remember that, and he'd gone outside for a moment to try and calm down, so when the Falconers came over, there was only my mother and I, standing side by side, to greet them. Gerald Falconer owned the building my father's jewelry store had been in. Over the years he and his wife had become friendly with my parents. I'd never met their son, but my parents had talked about him—he had done something extraordinary at a young age, but I couldn't remember what it was.

Gerald and his wife, Diane, took my mother's hands. Their son came up to me. For one moment I was aware of something other than my grief. His eyes were the same color as mine. The green of an ocean in the winter. He saw it too. And for a moment neither of us said anything.

Then without any awkwardness, he took my hand.

"I didn't know your father that well, but I know I was enormously lucky to have met him. He was a really wonderful artist. I'm so sorry about what happened."

It was neither particularly eloquent nor wise. Yet what he'd said and the way he had phrased it reached into me and pulled me back from the blood and ambulance sirens and forced me to refocus on my father when he had been the most alive—in his workshop, juxtaposing brilliantly colored gems to create pieces that were whimsical and lovely and wholly individual.

About a month later I was helping my mother pack up what was left in the store before we closed it for good. She was in the workshop on the phone when the doorbell rang. The security guard, who had been hired to stay with us in the store during those last few weeks, looked at me to see if I knew the young man ringing the bell.

I nodded at the guard, who opened the door, and took a step forward.

"My name is Robert Falconer. I don't know if you remember me," he said, nervously shifting the black portfolio under his arm.

I had remembered him immediately because of what he'd said to me at my father's service and because of his eyes.

"I wanted to give you these." He patted the portfolio, put it on the counter, and opened it up.

Apparently my parents had hired Robert to photograph my father's designs so they could include them in a sales brochure.

"I liked working with him. He was a very talented man," Robert said as I flipped through the plastic coated sheets. There were over two dozen shots of my father's work, and looking at them, I thought of Italian still-life paintings.

"My parents chose the right photographer," I told him.

"Thanks."

The last few shots were not of the jewelry but of my father in the workshop, and Robert's portraits immediately brought him back to me: not the pain of losing him, but for the first time since his death, the joy of him.

My tears came as they often did those days. Once the shock of the funeral had worn off and the reality of the days without my father's presence had seeped in, I cried inconsolably.

"Your father and I . . ." Robert hesitated, not sure whether talking about my father was a good or bad thing.

"It's all right to talk about him," I said, realizing that for the first time in a month it was.

"I got to spend a lot of time with your father while I was taking those photographs. He told me all about how a jeweler has to find the personality of each stone and set it to show off its uniqueness. He was a terrific artist."

I looked at the photos again. My father's work really was amazing. Since he had died, I no longer wore jewelry. Its exuberance was embarrassing. I wore only my father's watch, the one he had worn every day, the one I had seen on his wrist ever since I could remember. My brother didn't mind that I had it; my mother had given Simon our father's dress watch—an expensive gold Piaget. All that mattered was that we each had something of his.

My mother closed the store the following week, and I returned to Cornell to start my sophomore year. I loaded up my schedule: not with the art classes I'd been planning on taking before the murder, but with psychology courses. Mysteries more complicated than the play of light and shadow inside a multifaceted gem now obsessed me.

Simon had returned to Princeton for his senior year. We spoke and wrote often, and I wasn't that surprised when he told me he'd decided to apply to law school.

In October, Robert came up to Ithaca to visit for the first time.

I'd had boyfriends before my father died; but no one who'd ever mattered very much or for very long. The last man I'd dated had been Mallory and that had ended in July, just weeks before he took my father's life. Since coming back to school, I hadn't met anyone I was interested in and didn't care to.

But Robert was different. He had known my father and what had happened to him and that made me feel comfortable. He was the only friend I had who didn't ask me to explain my melancholy and with whom I could relax in my sadness.

Robert worked for a stock photo house in New York City and had been given an assignment to shoot a series on the national parks and waterfalls that graced upstate New York. It never occurred to me that he'd asked for that particular job so that he could see me more often. All I knew was that he was frequently in Ithaca that fall and that it was soothing to be with him, to go to the woods together, and to sit silently on a blanket or a rock and watch him work.

At first we talked about the murder. He let me describe it to him over and over and he would just listen. He has an amazing ability, not just to listen, but to hear my silences as well as the words. He always could sense when to give me space and keep a little distance, and when to put his arms around me and hold me as tightly as he could.

One day in early November I brought my sketchbook with me for the first time, and while Robert photographed the falls, I drew. It had been almost four months since my father's murder and the initial pain had become a dull throb. At the end of the afternoon I realized that, for the first time since my father had died, I felt some real peace.

Robert sensed it too.

Once the sun began to set, we walked through the darkening forest, the sounds of the falls growing ever more distant. It was dark by the time we reached the car and it had begun to get cold.

When we arrived back at the apartment I shared with two other girls, no one was home. I made coffee and Robert and I sat at the table and talked about the kind of imagery he wanted to create with his photographs, but we were saying other things to each other with our eyes and a tension was growing between us.

Finally I stood up and walked to my bedroom, knowing that Robert would follow me. I stood by the bureau, but he sat down on the bed, reached out, and pulled me onto his lap.

He traced the outline of my lips with the tip of one finger over and over until my mouth finally opened to him.

"One day I'd like to photograph you. There's nothing obvious about you. Everything is subtle and under the surface. I want to see if I can capture that on film."

"Maybe. Maybe." I was finally experiencing something other than pain—and I didn't want him to stop touching me.

Leaning forward, Robert kissed me. Melting into him, I tasted his mouth and smelled the scent of him—that unique mixture of the patchouli cologne he wears still, leather from the camera strap always around his neck, and mint from the peppermints he liked.

It was me, not Robert, who finally decided when it was time to finally go past those kisses, and reaching out, I unbuttoned his shirt and pushed it off his shoulders.

People always talk about how beautiful the female body is, but a man's body can be beautiful too. There are parts of Robert's body that I could still sculpt without opening my eyes: the cords in his neck, his collarbone, his shoulders, and his long, long thighs. He has a catlike, elegant body, and he moves with a languid ease.

That afternoon I was the one to admire his body the way a man might appreciate a woman's, and Robert luxuriated in my frank examination of him: it pleased and excited him.

Without speaking, we lay down on the bed together and he started to kiss me again. I was still completely dressed: he was just wearing his blue jeans. And then he took off my powder blue blouse. (How do I still remember what I wore all those years ago?) When he kissed my breast, his lips were so hot that I wondered if he would leave an imprint. And he did brand me, but not on my flesh where someone could see it.

We made love for hours that first time, leaving my bedroom only for something to drink, or to eat. We smoked some marijuana and spent the rest of the night listening to a combination of classical and rock music. I watched Robert change the music on my stereo. We listened to records then, and I marveled at the care with which he handled them: only by the edges, not allowing his fingers to touch the surface of the plastic.

At ten the next morning we finally got out of bed. I went to the bathroom to take a shower and Robert joined me and we made love again under the steaming hot water.

I did not ask Robert about his other lovers, but it seemed obvious to me he had had them: he was too comfortable with his sexuality, too sure of how to excite me for it to have been his first time. While I'd had two lovers before Robert, neither of them were more than serious flirtations, and it wasn't until that fall and winter that I learned the details and intricacies of sex. I'm not sure what was more satisfying—what we did to each other with our bodies or the hours afterward, when we would lie in bed and talk about books and paintings and movies and all the things in our lives that had shaped us.

While we sipped rum and smoked cigarettes, I'd tell him my stories and he'd tell me his and we'd swear we could keep the sun from rising too fast.

A year later, in the fall, on a day when the ground was covered with a carpet of fall leaves so vibrant that some of them looked like jewels, I came home and found Robert waiting for me on my porch. Walking towards him, I smiled and ran ahead. I loved this man so much I thought I would die if I ever lost him.

"But it's only Wednesday," I said breathlessly. "I thought you weren't coming up till the weekend?" I put my arms around him and kissed him. "I'm so glad you're here."

Why didn't I notice that he was quieter than usual? Or that his arms had not held me for very long. Or that his kiss had been hurried? Why didn't I notice any of the signs that might have prepared me—even a little—for what was coming so I would not have been as overwhelmed by it?

Once we went inside, I heated up apple cider, poured it into mugs, and handed one to Robert. "Wait," he said, and went to the cabinet where we kept the liquor, pulled out a bottle of brandy, and poured a splash into each mug. Then we went into my bedroom.

Robert sat on the edge of the bed and looked down into the mug. A full minute passed without him saying anything. Finally, in a soft, sad voice I'd never heard before, he began to speak.

"Jordan, I have to stop seeing you." He stopped, took a long drink from the mug, and started again. I did not understand what he meant.

"I know this isn't going to make much sense." He was reading my mind again, but this time I was not comforted by it. "I love you too much, Jordan. You make me too happy and if I don't break up with you now, I never will. I just can't be tied down yet. I need to work on my photographs. To travel. Shit, it's not just that, Jordan. I've never been with anyone but you. I'm too young to spend the rest of my life with one woman. I just can't."

Until that afternoon I'd never guessed I was his first lover.

"For the last year—" My voice broke. I took a breath and tried again. "For the past year, every time I've been upset, you've been the one to make me feel better. But now you're the one who's making me feel bad—and I can't even ask you to hold me."

Reaching out, he took my hand and pulled me beside him on the bed. It was a cruel reenactment of the first time we had been together. "Yes, you can," he whispered as he put his arms around my back and held me so close to his chest I could hear his heart beating.

We sat like that for what seemed like a very long time, and then somehow he was kissing me and I was kissing him back and we were undressing each other, and without either of us saying a word, we began to make love for the last time. I didn't know I could be that violent, but as rough as I was with him, he was that tender with me. I beat on his chest and he stroked my breast. I bit his shoulders and he smoothed my hair. For every pain I inflicted he gave me back pleasure until I finally I began to weep, and then, with his erection still deep inside of me, he rocked me and held me on his lap and licked the tears off my face.

As I came, all I could hear was the same plaintive phrase repeating over and over: this is the last time, the last time, the last time . . .

After Robert left, I stayed in my bed all that night and the next day. And then for five days and nights after that. I barely ate, but I drank that bottle of brandy until it was empty. I listened to all the records Robert and I had listened to together and reread all the love letters he had written me. When I did sleep, I had dreams in which Robert and my father were the same person, and I woke from all of them crying. I hated them both for leaving me, but Robert more because he had left of his own free will.

Towards the end of the week, I got into a bathtub full of hot water and stared at the razor I used to shave my legs and thought about killing myself. Losing my father and Robert was more loss than I could bear.

It was only the idea of all the blood that stopped me: the memory of my father's blood that I could still picture and smell and taste.

Finally one of my roommates got worried enough to call my brother, who came up to Ithaca the next day. Simon was more pragmatic than sympathetic, but it was what I needed. "If you give up like this, Jordan, you are letting Robert win."

"It's not just Robert. . . . It's Daddy. It's losing both of them."

"Okay, if you give up, you are letting Robert win and you are letting Dan Mallory win."

My hatred of Mallory helped me survive Robert's leaving. Instead of feeling sorry for myself and how much I missed Robert, I focused on my anger at Mallory for taking away the one man who never would have left me of his own volition.

On Monday, I went back to classes and immersed myself in work. I couldn't read enough about the mind and its labyrinths. So many people had acted outside of my realm of logic, and those actions had caused me such intense pain—I was not going to stop learning until I knew why.

By the beginning of the next semester, my grade average was a 3.9 and I'd even started dating again.

I was not promiscuous, but neither was I very discriminating. It was the very early eighties during that tiny window of time when birth control pills were easy to get and fatally sexually transmitted diseases weren't. One thing I avoided was emotional commitment. My goal was no more complicated than to prevent loneliness from trapping me in self-pity.

On an afternoon in May, a month before graduation, I came home from class and once again, unexpectedly, found Robert Falconer sitting and waiting for me on my porch steps.

It was early evening, the sun was just setting, and the scent of lilacs was floating on the breeze. Robert's eyes were bloodshot and his hair was disheveled. It had been eighteen months since I'd seen him and he was so thin he looked as if he'd been sick.

I almost turned and ran. I hated him. I never wanted to see him again. I was so very, very glad he was there.

Standing up, Robert pulled me to him. I was too surprised to say anything, and we stood like that, just holding each other, until I drew away—scared of being so close to him again, of how familiar his cologne smelled and how happy I felt to have his arms around me.

"I don't want to be away from you anymore," he said in a shaky voice.

And I believed him. Not because I wanted to, but because at the time he meant it.

Robert described a year of traveling in Europe, getting freelance photography jobs and being unhappy. "I kept thinking, one more week and it won't matter so much. I'll stop thinking about her in one more week," he said. "But the weeks kept coming and I never missed you any less."

Robert spent the next two weekends in Ithaca and then, after my graduation, drove me back to New York. Instead of moving into my grandmother's house in Connecticut, which had been my home base since my mother had moved to California, I moved into Robert's small but charming apartment in Greenwich Village and into his life.

By then, Robert had gotten a job with a well-known fashion photographer and I had been accepted into New York University's master's program and was going to get a master's degree in psychology.

We were never apart after that.

Even eighteen years later, I thought as I got ready for bed, we were still not really apart.

Earlier that evening, I had been trying to get Adrienne Blessing to explore her past in order to help her deal with the present. But somehow it had worked the other way around. I had been the one to travel back in time: to revisit memories and reopen old scars.

FIVE

"I know you're telling me all this because you want me to be careful, but I think you're wrong about this guy, Mom. I spoke to Uncle Simon too. Dan Mallory is a human being who deserves your compassion. Can't you let go of your anger and get past it? How can you just assume he is dangerous because he was dangerous twenty years ago?" Lilly asked as we crossed Fifth Avenue and walked into Washington Square Park.

It was a warm evening and the park was full of joggers, people walking their dogs, and parents with their children. Winter was over and tight buds were showing on the branches of the elm and oak trees.

I tried not to sound exasperated. "Lilly, this man killed your grandfather."

"But that was almost twenty years ago. Isn't it possible that while he was in prison he was rehabilitated? Uncle Simon said he got a college degree and became religious and really turned his life around. Maybe he was able to get in touch with his anger and rage and realize what he'd done was really a reaction to his pain and suffering."

A man walking two Maltese dogs, both white with soot-stained paws, stared at my daughter's chest as he passed. I wanted to give him the benefit of the doubt and believe he'd been reading the message on the T-shirt she was wearing under her leather jacket. Cooper had bought it for her at the Zen center a few weeks before. "Working Hard—Accomplishing Nothing," it said.

Tired of talking about Mallory, I changed the subject. "I don't think people understand what your shirt says."

"That's because in our Western culture, people are too caught up in accomplishments and the idea of achievement. Cooper says they miss all the pleasures and pains of life. All the ten thousand joys and ten thousand sorrows. They just work hard to accumulate more money so they can buy more things that they think will make them happy. They get a momentary thrill and then a few weeks later they're just as unhappy as they were before. So they just work harder to acquire more things."

Good tugged on her leash and pulled me towards the red setter over by the children's playground.

"Maybe they are unhappy because they have unresolved conflicts they need to work out," I suggested.

Lilly shook her head as if disappointed in me. "Mom, psychology isn't the answer to everything."

If I'd thought she would have listened, I would have told her there were no answers. Only experiences. But she had become quick to dismiss whatever I said just on principle.

Returning to the subject I wanted to avoid, Lilly asked: "Why don't you believe what Uncle Simon told you? Didn't he say Mallory had been a model prisoner? Don't you think that after so many years in prison, he might just appreciate his freedom enough to hold on to it?"

Good was sniffing the setter, who was sniffing her back.

"Do you know that we spend more money on the prison system than we do on education?" Lilly continued.

"Sweetie, I think your heart is as big as the whole world and that your idealism is wonderful. But the reason we spend so much money on the prison system is that we have so much crime in this country, and part of the reason for that is because it is so hard to rehabilitate criminals. Over eighty percent of the people in prison are repeat offenders."

"Whenever I don't agree with you about something, you tell me I'm being idealistic. Do you know that you do that? You're trivializing what I'm saying by doing that."

"You're starting to sound more like a therapist every day."

"Some of your lingo may have rubbed off on me, but that doesn't mean I agree with your approach."

This time the sigh escaped from my lips before I could stop it. "I can't wait till you have your own kids and they try to enlighten *you*."

"That's terrible." Lilly's voice was strained; she was walking on the edge of her ire now. I could see the effort she was making not to get mad at me, but I wished she would just let it out. "If you really feel that, you're not living in the present," she continued. "And you'll miss everything. You have to live as if each moment is the only moment."

"The more time you spend around Cooper, the deeper you get into all this. You know, you're losing your sense of humor, Lilly."

Lilly didn't say anything for a moment. Two girls on skates glided by us. One had blue hair. The other had magenta hair and three gold rings in her nose. I supposed I should be grateful that Lilly was rebelling with philosophy, not self-mutilation.

"Cooper thinks it's really curious that you're so uninterested in Eastern religion. I mean, Grandma has spent the last twenty years studying it and you've never even read a book about the subject. He thinks you've avoided it because at the time when you needed your mother the most, she turned to philosophy and religion and you've never forgiven her."

Lilly didn't realize that she wasn't helping Cooper's cause by sharing this information. "I didn't realize Cooper was reading Freud at Yale," I snapped, and then instantly regretted my words. I was losing my self-control with her far too often lately.

Not surprisingly, Lilly lifted her camera up and focused on the playground where a mother was pushing a little blond-haired child on a swing. Click, buzz.

That had become the pattern to our recent conversations. Lilly would say something sarcastic or argumentative, guaranteed to get me to react; then she'd overreact to my response, become frustrated, and would disappear behind the camera.

Lilly advanced the film and took another shot. Click, buzz. The sound had orchestrated more years of my life than I cared to count. How many times had I stood by while Robert aimed his lens at some scene and taken a photograph, changed the exposure, bracketed his shot, and taken the same shot again? How many of our conversations had been interrupted by the staccato opening and closing of the shutter?

I waited in a familiar limbo for Lilly to put the camera down. She thought she was punishing me, but she was the one who couldn't tolerate the isolation for long—even though she'd inflicted it on herself.

"Do you even know what this guy Dan Mallory looks like?" Lilly asked me. She was still holding the camera up to her eye and scanning the park through the lens, but she was speaking to me in a matter-of-fact tone that suggested neither anger nor irritation. "I mean, if I'm supposed to be on the lookout for him—it would help if I had an idea of what he looks like."

I tried to picture Mallory sitting at the defense table, but twenty years had passed and I could no longer see his face anymore. We don't have a choice as to which images we can hold on to and which we can forget. Time blurs the past equally. I couldn't even picture my father's face anymore without a photograph to help me.

"Well, I remember he was intense-looking and muscular. His hair was brown, and he was about five foot ten."

"That's not a great description, Mom. Look around—" She waved her arm. "At least a dozen men we've passed have brown hair and look like they work out."

"When we get home, I'll call Simon and see if we can get a photograph. There were mug shots."

"But those will be ancient. Isn't there a more recent photo?"

"Well, maybe they take pictures of prisoners when they release them; I'll ask." We left the park and crossed back to the other side of Fifth Avenue.

"Lilly, I don't want you to be scared. Just on guard. Just aware."

Lilly laughed—a laugh light enough to float up to the cobalt sky. Just hearing it, I felt better.

"That's all I do, try to be aware. That's the entire purpose of Zen," she said.

I strained to hold on to her laugh and not to react to what she'd said. I had to allow her to find her own balance between Cooper's world and ours. If I didn't, I risked loosing her. The last thing I wanted was to force her to choose between us in order to prove her independence.

At the corner of Sixth Avenue and Ninth Street, I let Good off the leash and she ran ahead of us, bounding up the steps of our brownstone.

"Mom, will you come upstairs with me to Dad's studio?" Lilly asked as we walked into the building.

"I have a patient now, sweetheart."

"Well, when you're done, will you come upstairs, just for a few minutes?"

Lilly, like so many children of separated parents, longed to have us back together and for years invented elaborate ruses to get me to go up to her father's studio with her. Rarely had she been so direct.

"Why?" I asked.

"I want to show you some of my prints."

Of her two obsessions, I preferred photography to Cooper. At least photography only took her away from me for a few hours at a time.

After my last session of the evening, all I wanted to do was take a bath, put on a soft nightshirt, and get into bed with a good mystery. But I'd promised Lilly I'd go upstairs to see her new photographs.

As usual the door was open. Robert rarely locked it, since he wanted Lilly to come and go between floors as she pleased. It created the illusion that we were all still living together.

Before Robert had moved upstairs, he'd always locked the studio door during sessions, and later I discovered, during liaisons. But for the last five years he used a studio on Sixteenth Street for shoots. As for women—well, I didn't think about where he went with them. All that mattered to me was that Robert worked it out so that our daughter wasn't subjected to his sexual dalliances.

When I walked in, Lilly was sitting on the couch looking through contact sheets. Her hair was in her face and her whole body was so intensely focused on what she was doing, it took her a minute to realize I'd come in the room. I walked over to the couch and let my hand slide down her shining hair. She looked up and smiled impishly. For a minute there was no rebellion in her eyes. For a moment I did not ache for her, did not wish to change anything, just savored the feel of her hair on my skin and the simple look of affection on her face. But my mind couldn't refrain from trying to understand it—what was different, why was she like this now and not more often? And then I realized it was because I was upstairs with her in Robert's studio and she had us both together. It was all she had ever wanted and the one thing I could not give her.

"I'll get Dad," she said. "We have a surprise for you."

Off to the right and in the back was the darkroom. Outside that door was a red light. If it was blinking, he was in there developing film.

It was blinking.

Following darkroom protocol, Lilly knocked on the door.

I took a deep breath. Remarkably, Robert and I rarely ran into each other in the building. When I needed to talk to him about Lilly, I called him on the phone. A few times a year—at Christmas, at Thanksgiving, and on our daughter's birthday—we all had dinner together. We were pleasant to each other and the occasions were comfortable for both of us and for Lilly; Robert and I were good at making an effort or a sacrifice for our daughter's sake.

I had learned not to bring up old memories when we were all together. Or at least I thought I had, but that night they were rushing at me like bats trapped in an attic—and I didn't know why.

I sat down on the couch and avoided looking at the darkroom door. To walk into a darkroom unannounced could ruin a print if it was being exposed.

I had walked in only once and had opened the door on the end of our marriage.

It happened almost six years ago, but I could still smell the winter wind and see the snow piling up on the windowsill. Lilly, who was twelve, had a raging fever. I sat by her bed and wiped her forehead with a washcloth soaked in rubbing alcohol and waited for the pediatrician to call me back. I called upstairs to the studio to see if Robert could watch Lilly while I went down and explained to my patient that I'd have to cancel our session. Robert didn't answer the phone, but I knew he was up there.

Suddenly, Lilly thrashed her legs and began to shake. Her neck went limp and her eyes rolled up. The seizure had only lasted a few seconds, but each moment had passed in torturous slow-motion, and when it was over Lilly lay on the bed like a broken doll—legs and arms akimbo.

An insistent buzz announced my patient's arrival. He was waiting out in the cold. I had to at least get downstairs and tell him we'd have to reschedule. But I had to get my daughter to the hospital and to do that I needed Robert to help me.

I covered Lilly in a blanket, told her I would be right back, and ran upstairs. The front door to the studio was unlocked, but the darkroom's red light was blinking. I didn't think—I was panicked. My daughter had a raging fever—she'd had a convulsion—I opened the door.

In the dark red light I saw Robert turn towards me as I walked in.

"Lilly is sick. We have to go to the hospital . . ."

And then I saw several things all at once. Robert wasn't alone in the darkroom, there was a woman on her knees in front of him, and as she stood up, her naked shoulders and breasts were illuminated by the red light. Seeing me, her mouth opened in a wide O, and I noticed her lips were wet. I heard the sound of a zipper closing.

"Where is Lilly?" Robert shouted as he rushed past me. I followed him down the stairs and into our daughter's bedroom.

Robert picked Lilly up in his arms and ran with her down the stairs. While he hailed a cab, I explained the situation to my patient and raced out to the street.

In the taxi, I held Lilly's hand but kept my gaze fixed out the window. Beneath my fingers, my daughter's skin burned.

It was only a few blocks to the hospital, and while I paid the cabdriver, Robert carried Lilly into the emergency room. Within seconds a nurse was taking Lilly's vital signs and a doctor was examining her. He asked me a dozen questions about what had happened. Several he asked me over again.

Finally, but not quickly enough, the doctor told us that other than the high fever, it didn't look like anything was wrong. "It's more common to see this reaction to fevers in younger children, however, so to be safe I'm going to give her something to bring her fever down and keep her under observation for a few hours, if not for the rest of the night."

Lilly lay sleeping on the gurney. Sweat had made the hair near her face curl. I took her hand, enclosed it in mine, and sat down by her side. Robert and I had not said a word to each other since we'd left the house. There would be time to talk once Lilly was past this crisis.

An hour later the doctor came back to tell us the fever had broken. "I think you can both relax now. Why don't you go get some coffee?"

"But what if she wakes up? I want to be here," I said.

"I guarantee you, this kid is going to be sleeping for the next four or five hours nonstop. A cup of coffee or a drink across the street only takes a half hour. It would do you both good."

"No," I said, holding back tears.

"We shouldn't leave," Robert said to the doctor. "I don't want her to wake up in a strange place without either of us here."

For the next few hours we sat there silently, staring at our child, watching the thin white blanket rise and fall with every breath. Thankfully the fever had stayed down and she continued to sleep peacefully.

After the fourth hour, the doctor returned. "Lilly's bloodwork came back and everything looks fine. Why don't we just watch her for another hour? If her temperature remains normal, I'm going to let you take Lilly home. I really don't think there's anything more serious than a flu to worry about."

Except for our marriage.

"Jordan, can we talk about what happened in the studio?" Robert asked when the doctor had left the room.

"No."

His hands moved, as if he were about to reach for mine, and then fell back in his lap. So well-proportioned and expressive were his hands, they might have been carved by Bernini or Michelangelo. It hurt my eyes to look at them and wonder, for the first time, where they had been and whom they had touched.

"We have to talk, Jordan. I need to talk to you."

I didn't want to listen to his voice; it repulsed me.

"Not here and not now." I was adamant.

I watched Lilly, still concentrating on my daughter, but now that she was better, I couldn't continue to push aside the reality of what I'd seen in the darkroom. Eventually I was going to have to deal with what Robert had done and what it meant. Was I going to lose him? Had I lost him already? Did I even care? I hated him more now than I had when he'd left me so many years ago. I'd survived without him then. I could again. I'd lost my father; I knew how to handle loss. I'd be fine— No, I would not be fine.

"Jordan, please," Robert pleaded.

"Be quiet: the last thing I want is for Lilly to wake up and hear any of this."

Robert got up and walked to the door. "Just come out in the hallway for one minute so I can talk to you."

"I'm not leaving her."

"Just stand here in the doorway, just for a second. You can still see the bed."

Too worn out to argue, I got up and followed him into the hall, but I stood facing Lilly in case she woke up.

"Jordan, please don't assume it's more than it was. I need to explain what happened. It was nothing. I love you."

"First, don't you dare tell me you love me. And don't try to explain away what happened—I'm not a therapist who can listen dispassionately to what you need to say. I'm your wife." And then I laughed—a short broken sound. "As if being your wife means anything to you."

"You mean everything to me—Christ—that sounds so hollow. Jordan, you are part of me. What we have—"

"No. Be quiet. I can't listen to you anymore. I only want to listen to Lilly breathing. That's all I want to hear."

As I walked back to my daughter's hospital bed, I started to cry.

Robert followed me, stood behind me, and wrapped me in his arms. I smelled his warm skin: woods, leather, and mint. Just for a moment, I thought, just for a little while, let me rest in his arms and accept the comfort he's offering. Just for a little while let it be all right to forget about what happened. Our daughter was in the hospital and I needed her father.

Robert held me in his arms, and in his throaty, low-pitched whisper he promised me everything was going to be all right. Temporarily overwhelmed and, perhaps, I think, temporarily insane, I began to deny what I had seen. Somehow he would make sense of what had happened in his darkroom so that I could forgive him and we could go on. He would have to—he was Lilly's father, he was my husband.

We had written our own vows.

"For richer, for poorer, in sickness and in health . . . in love and in fidelity . . ." he had intoned in front of the preacher and our parents and friends. I heard his deep voice say the words, and then in response, lighter and less resonant, my own voice repeated each one.

Lilly was released at midnight, and Robert carried her out of the hospital in his arms, her head resting on his chest. I ached to hold her, but he had her and she was fine.

When we put her in her bed, we both stayed in her darkened room watching over her sleeping form for a while longer.

Finally, reassured, we both went into our bedroom. Without talking, Robert undressed in front of me while I sat sullen and exhausted on my side of the bed, not knowing what I was supposed to do. He dropped each layer of his clothes on the floor until he was naked. I walked away, to undress in the bathroom. I'd never done that before, not even when I was pregnant, but I didn't want Robert to look at me now. I was suddenly lonely and ashamed. I didn't want to be naked in front of my husband for fear he would be able to look past the flesh and see the rent in my heart—a tear I had allowed him to create by making him more important to me than I had been to him.

My own fidelity made a mockery of Robert's infidelity. I had been open to him. In lust, in pleasure, in comfort, yes, but I could not be open to him in pain that he had caused.

I had already suffered enough by loving and then losing. First my father, then Robert in college, and now Robert again. Hadn't I learned my lesson?

Getting into bed, I stayed as close to the edge and as far away from Robert as I could. So he had gotten used to me. I pulled the covers tighter around me. My breasts were no longer tempting. My hips and thighs not enough of an invitation.

Trying to calm myself, I summoned up everything I had learned as a therapist about the difference between love and lust, and men's promiscuity. But all the theory in the world couldn't pacify me or erase Robert's betrayal. I was no longer his to have or to hold.

If that had been his only transgression, our marriage might have survived. But what he confessed to me a few days later took away my options.

I could have dealt with a patient's promiscuity, but not my own husband's.

Although I suggested he get professional help, Robert resisted. Meanwhile, I tried to give him time and to trust him, but he had broken something in me. And once I realized that I was watching him and checking for signs of other affairs, I asked him for a separation.

Five years later, I was thinking about how, in addition to other things, I'd lost so much of my pride behind that locked darkroom door, and just then it opened and Robert came out.

He smiled at Lilly and then looked over at me. "Hey, Jordan," he said.

Usually when I was with Robert, I looked around him and past him and beyond him and paid only polite attention. But that night, his voice had its old effect on me. I was feeling it, not just hearing it. Damn, I thought. I hadn't been prepared, I'd been thinking about the past; I'd let my guard down.

At forty-two, he was almost as lean and long as he had been in his twenties. His golden skin was only slightly weathered. His hair fell across his forehead the same way it always had. I ignored the urge to reach up and brush it out of his way. Robert leaned against the door with that same casual stance that had always made him look as if he weren't afraid of anyone—as if he could do anything. Since I had stopped living with him, it had become an effrontery. How could he continue to look so capable when there were obviously many things he could not do?

"Hello," I said, and turned to Lilly. "What is it you wanted me to see, sweetheart? What's the surprise?"

"Dad, help me set up the shots; it will only take a minute, Mom."

I moved to the window and looked into the blue-black night studded with the city's one hundred thousand lights. For years the only light that had mattered to me was in Robert's eyes when he looked at me.

"Mom?"

A half-dozen photographs were lined up on the easel-like shelf where Robert usually displayed his works in progress.

But he worked only in black and white.

These oversaturated color prints were Lilly's.

In the first shot, shafts of pale sunlight illuminated a cluster of deeply green pine trees. A fiery red bird perched on the highest branch of the tree closest to the frame and on the ground, glowing like a flame, lay a single red feather.

"Oh, it's beautiful, Lilly," I told my daughter. "It's like one perfect line of poetry. Complete, evocative, memorable."

Lilly didn't wait for me to finish looking at the rest of the shots to tell me the news.

"Dad talked to Iago tonight, and she's decided to show all these in that small exhibition hall off the gallery during Dad's next exhibition." Lilly's voice raced ahead. "You know, that place where she puts new artists?"

"My God, your own show? That's wonderful, Lilly."

"And guess how much Iago's going to charge?" But she didn't wait for me to guess. "Three hundred dollars each. Isn't that amazingly incredible? She really thinks someone might buy my photographs."

I was so caught up in Lilly's excitement I was even smiling at Robert, silently thanking him for arranging all this. "Well, I'd like to be the first person to buy one," I said.

"*M-o-m.*" She had stretched the word into several pained syllables. "You don't count. It has to be a stranger who doesn't have to buy them because her daughter took them but who wants to buy them because she sees something in them. Because she sees the place I found."

I can see that place, I wanted to tell her. But she wouldn't believe me, not yet.

SIX

"I saw Dan Mallory's parole officer this morning," my brother said.

It was three o'clock on Thursday afternoon, and we were sitting at a window table in a café only a few blocks away from the brownstone. Rain ran in rivulets down the glass, car lights splashed over us, horns honked. New York City seems to have trouble with rain. Good drivers who can navigate oncoming buses and out-of-control bikers lose all confidence when the streets are glossed with water. A little girl in a yellow slicker, holding a red umbrella, stopped and pushed her face up to the glass and looked inside. Her breath made fog on the window. She drew a house in the condensation and then moved on.

Simon had asked me to meet him so he could tell me about his conversation with Jim Rafferty.

But as soon as he did, I was going to tell Simon about the letters Dan Mallory had sent me from prison. I'd kept them secret long enough—they were relevant now: those eighteen-year-old letters were proof that Mallory was dangerous.

The first innocent white envelope had arrived among an ordinary pile of bills and magazines. Except there wasn't a return address in the left corner. Or on the envelope's back flap. Slitting it open, I extracted a single sheet of paper and looked down at the signature.

The letter landed on the kitchen counter, and the words blurred into dark intelligible scratches. I folded my arms across my round belly as if I might protect my unborn baby from this intrusion into our lives.

I wanted to burn the letter in the sink, or rip at it with a kitchen knife.

When I finally picked it up, my hands shook so violently the paper reverberated like distant thunder. Before I'd finished the second paragraph, a sudden attack of morning sickness or revulsion at Mallory's words, or a combination of both, had sent me running to the bathroom.

"So did you find out where Mallory's living?" I asked.

Simon centered his coffee cup in front of him, scraping the china on the marble. He returned the sugar bowl to the middle of the table, placed his spoon on his saucer, and refolded his napkin. Once order had been restored, he answered me.

"Yes. Mallory's here, in New York City."

"Oh, shit!" Cappuccino sloshed out of my cup. My hand was trembling. "Where, exactly?"

"I can't find that out." Simon pushed his coffee away.

"Why not? You're a DA; you know everyone. Rafferty is an old friend of yours, isn't he? You have to be able to find out exactly where Mallory is."

Simon shook this head. "It doesn't matter who I know. It's illegal for the parole board to give out that information. But listen to me, Jordan; Rafferty is certain Mallory isn't a threat. They never would have released him if he was."

"We've already talked about this. We both know anyone is capable of deception."

He was watching my hands, watching me twist my grandmother's diamond-and-platinum bands around and around on my finger. The metal edges pressed into my flesh as I continued spinning the bands.

Simon frowned.

"What's wrong?" I asked him.

"I don't want you to be this worried."

"Wouldn't you be if the man you sent to prison had been released and was living somewhere in your city?"

"Jordan, you didn't send him to prison. His crime did. The judge did. Rafferty assured me that Mallory doesn't blame you for anything that's happened to him. He's not only reformed, he's repented."

"I know, you told me he's become religious. You told Lilly too. Thanks, by the way: now she's telling me that I have to have compassion. She also said you told her people change. Simon, don't you realize how idealistic she is? If she's not at least a little suspicious of people, how can she protect herself? I want her to be afraid of Mallory. He could come looking for her. He could come looking for me. How does anyone really know what his plans are?"

"His plans are to get a job and stay out of trouble. You have to believe me."

When we were teenagers, Simon was so good at pretending everyone had assumed that he was going to become an actor. Every night he used to come down to dinner as a different character from one of the plays he was always reading. One night it would be Lear, another Julius Caesar, and another Willy Loman.

As a trial lawyer, he'd honed that skill and used it to his advantage in the courtroom, but among friends and family it was frustrating. You never knew whether or not he was telling you what he really thought.

"You really aren't worried?" I asked doubtfully.

"Rafferty is a smart man. I've never known him to read an ex-con wrong."

"Okay, but tell me, what if this is the one time Rafferty is wrong?" I asked.

"Jordan . . ."

"You know something, Simon, Lilly asked me to describe Mallory to her and I couldn't. Oh, I have a vague image of him as a twenty-two-year-old, but I don't know what he looks like now. Do you realize how vulnerable that makes me? I don't even know if

I'd recognize him if he walked into my office and asked for an appointment—"

The ringing of Simon's cell phone sounded shrill in the quiet café. While he listened to whoever was on the other end of the phone, I sipped the lukewarm cappuccino and tried to think of anything other than Mallory.

Outside the trees branches were swaying in the downpour. Raindrops settled on the swelling buds, dripped off the still unfurled leaves. I glanced at my father's watch. I still had forty minutes before my next appointment. Forty minutes to dwell on Dan Mallory and wonder where he was and whether or not he was thinking about getting revenge.

Simon, who had my mother's temperament, was now shouting into the phone.

Getting up, I walked over to the counter, where a dozen different kinds of pastry were showcased behind glass. The tarts were perfectly formed, the strawberries and raspberries fresh and plump, the apples golden and glazed with sugar, the edges of the pastry buttery brown. I should ask the clerk for three of the raspberry tarts; Robert loved them and— Robert? Where had that thought come from? Robert didn't have dinner with Lilly and me. I hadn't bought food with him in mind for over five years.

"Can I help you?" the waitress asked. I asked for two of the tarts in one box and another in a separate box for Simon and watched her gingerly remove the jeweled pastries out of the case and slip them into boxes that she tied with red-and-white string.

When I was a child, on the way to visit my grandmother, we'd stop in town at the local bakery and buy a box of cookies. I would watch the woman in the store pull exactly the right amount of string off the cylinder, wondering how she knew precisely how much she'd need. Her fingers moved in double time, securing the box and making the knot. I tried to memorize the way she tied it, but she moved too quickly.

It was my job to hold the box and keep it straight so the contents wouldn't slide around and crumble. Taking this responsibility seriously, I handled the white cardboard package as carefully as if it were full of butterfly wings.

"Don't open that box," my mother warned. "I'll know if you do. You're clever at taking things apart, but not as good at putting them back together."

Inhaling the intoxicating mixture of butter, chocolate, coconut, and raspberry, I'd stare at that red-and-white string and its intricate knot. Did I dare untie it? Maybe this time, finally, I'd get it retied correctly.

Simon was still talking loudly when I returned to the table.

"How many times do I have to repeat it? For God's sake, Marjorie." It was the same judgmental tone my mother used when we were growing up. She never just shrugged her shoulders and moved on as she did now. Dirty fingernails, a missing button, a broken toy, anything could set her off.

He listened for a minute and then said: "I have to go, I have another call."

Deftly he punched one of the keys and said hello, listened for a moment, and then hung up quickly.

"I have to get back to Stamford; the jury is asking for a readback." He threw a twenty-dollar bill on the table. "That should cover the coffee and whatever you didn't get me that's in those boxes."

"No—I did get you one. Here." I handed him one of the boxes. "But, Simon, I didn't tell you—"

"Can't it wait?—I really have to get back." He was already standing, anxious to go. "Call me tonight and tell me, okay?"

"Yes, go, it's nothing that can't wait until tonight." I hadn't told him about those letters for eighteen years, a few more hours wouldn't matter.

He bent down to give me a quick peck on the cheek, and then he was gone.

The waitress came over, and I ordered another cappuccino. Decaffeinated, this time. Finding out that Mallory was in New York was a more potent stimulant than a whole pot of espresso would have been.

While I waited for the waitress to return, I tried to figure out what was making me more anxious—that Mallory was out of jail and living somewhere in New York or the fact that I was helpless to do anything about it.

"You will be a good therapist, one day," Mona Westover had told me years ago. "But only if you let go of wanting control. You have to stop trying to solve your patients' problems and help them to solve the problem themselves."

In order to become a therapist, you have to undergo therapy yourself. And no one could have a better therapist than Mona Westover. I still occasionally went back to see her, either to work out my own issues or to get a professional opinion regarding one of my patients. Maybe Mona could help me deal with Mallory's return.

Mallory being in New York unnerved me even more than I had admitted to Simon. I wasn't only scared for me; I was scared for Lilly, who was so trusting, who wanted so badly to believe that people could change and that life did sometimes have storybook endings.

I had seen her face the other night up in Robert's studio. Lilly still had faith that one day Robert and I would be together again.

Living in limbo was no longer fair to her. It was time for Robert and me to formalize our separation and move on. When Lilly had been younger, it made sense to keep her environment intact and give her access to both her parents. But at seventeen she was old enough to understand Robert and I had to move on.

I almost laughed out loud.

The mind was capable of great deception and trickery, wasn't it? What better diversion from Mallory's release—which I had no control over—than to think about terminating my marriage—which I did have control over.

But as clever as the smoke screen had been, it had proved only a minor distraction. Not even my divorce could stop me from thinking about Mallory for long.

Simon thought he had been reassuring, but he hadn't been in the jewelry store that day. He hadn't had our father's blood on him or seen Mallory's face or sat in the courtroom and testified against him.

"I didn't mean to shoot Mr. Sloan," Mallory had said on the stand. "I was confused. I just wanted him to give me my job back."

He looked right at me, but I refused to return his gaze and looked away.

"I respected your father. I loved him," he cried.

Liar, I thought.

Mallory had been fired two weeks before he came back with a gun.

According to Simon, he'd been back in New York for ten days. How long would he wait this time?

I finished what was left of my cappuccino, picked up the pastry box, and walked the three blocks back to my office.

Simon did not believe that Dan Mallory thought I had betrayed him. But I knew. I had the letters he'd written me from prison.

SEVEN

I was back in my office, staring out the window, looking at the people and the cars, wondering if Mallory could be one of those people or if he could be in one of those cars, when my next patient arrived.

"Hi, Steve." I looked at him as I let him in, but he didn't meet my gaze. It was only Steven O'Keefe's second visit and he wasn't yet comfortable with the idea of therapy.

"So, how did your week go?" I asked once we were seated.

"Okay, I guess. Is that what I should talk about? What I did last week?" he asked.

"When you come here, you can talk about anything that's on your mind."

It took him a few minutes to collect his thoughts. Steven was a pleasant-looking, balding, forty-five-year-old. He had told me that he had two children who were in high school and that he was divorced, worked in a brokerage house, and his boss had a violent temper. That afternoon he was still as nervous as he had been the week before. He kept his eyes downcast, and he clasped his hands tightly in his lap as if he were hiding something in them.

What if Steven O'Keefe had lied to me about who he was? What if he were really Dan Mallory pretending to be a patient to get access to me—would I recognize him? Surely, something about him would be familiar—some facial expression, some mannerism.

But what if Mallory had undergone a profound change in prison? What if he had been ill or had aged prematurely behind bars? Just from the time of the murder to the time of the trial he had changed so drastically I had barely known him when they'd brought him into the courtroom. He'd lost weight, his long hair had been shaved, and instead of standing up straight, he'd been hunched over.

But it was preposterous to think he'd changed so much that if he were sitting in front of me, I wouldn't know it.

Leaning forward, I made eye contact with my patient. "Just tell me whatever you're thinking, Steven. Sometimes when you don't plan what you are going to say, it's even more helpful for the therapeutic process."

He relaxed a little and began to tell me about an argument he'd had with his boss.

Forty-five minutes later, just moments after Steven left, my phone rang. I hesitated, as I did now whenever the phone rang— was there going to be anyone on the end of this call? Or was I just going to hear that persistent ticking noise again?

"Dr. Sloan?" The man spoke with a strong Brooklyn accent.

"Yes . . ."

"This is Jim Rafferty, Dan Mallory's parole officer—"

Once the session with Steven had gotten started, I'd stopped thinking about Mallory, and the sudden mention of his name made me shiver.

"Mr. Rafferty, why are you calling *me?*"

"Because your brother asked me to. He suggested it would be helpful for me to tell you what I told him about Dan."

I sighed.

"Dr. Sloan, Dan is reformed. Believe me, he's worked through his anger. He's doing well at work—"

"*Where* does he work?" I asked.

Outside the rain had stopped. It was almost six o'clock, and soon my next patient would arrive.

"I can't tell you that."

"Why not?"

"Because as hard as this is for you, it's just as hard for Dan. You probably don't want to hear this, but he has rights too. He's paid his debt to society. He's been in prison for almost all of his adult life."

"You're making *him* sound like the victim. He's not. He killed my father in cold blood. He's dangerous—"

Rafferty interrupted me. "I appreciate how you feel. But Dan is no longer dangerous."

"I know inmates can have a tough time after so many years of confinement. Freedom can be its own prison. How is he coping now that he's out?" I asked.

"He's coping fine. He never liked being behind those bars."

But I'd liked knowing that's where he was. Lying on a hot beach in the summer, watching Lilly playing in the sand, I'd think about how much hotter the sun must be reflecting off the concrete prison courtyard.

Dining out with Robert, celebrating an anniversary or a birthday, I'd take a bite of some delicious meal and enjoy it even more knowing that the food on Mallory's plate was barely edible.

Over the years, the sensations I enjoyed the most were the ones I knew Mallory was being denied. I'd thought the only way to triumph over what had happened to me and my father and my mother was to eat, smell, listen, watch, kiss, swim, run, roam streets, and travel . . . to do every single thing that was denied Dan Mallory.

"Dr. Sloan, I know how hard this situation can be, and I thought maybe you'd like to talk to someone at Victim's Rights."

I laughed. I had actually been thinking about telling Rafferty about the letters, but he was so obviously Mallory's advocate, it would be a wasted effort. I'd wait just a little longer and tell Simon about the letters first.

"Mr. Rafferty, I appreciate your offer, but that's not the kind of help I need. What I do need is a recent photograph of Mallory. I haven't seen him for almost twenty years and I don't know what he looks like anymore. If he were to walk into my office or corner my daughter and me in the park, I wouldn't even know it was him. Can you at least do that for me?"

"I don't have a photograph of him. And even if I did, I couldn't give it to you. Please don't take this the wrong way, but just because you are a therapist doesn't mean you can cope with this situation without some help. That's why I thought you might want to talk to the Victim's Rights—"

The buzzer rang. "I'm sorry, Mr. Rafferty, I have a patient downstairs. And honestly, short of you telling me where Mallory is and what he looks like so I can protect myself and my daughter, there's nothing you can tell me that will make me feel any better."

"Dr. Sloan, take my word for it, Dan Mallory is not going to contact you or your daughter. He is not living in the past."

But there was the distinct suggestion in Mr. Rafferty's tone of voice that I was.

Once again, Adrienne Blessing had come to my office bearing a gift—this time it was a wooden box of plump, green figs. When I tried to thank her, she waved her hand and said it wasn't necessary.

"You're very generous." Bringing me presents was an interesting dynamic, one I wanted to explore.

"That's what men tell me in bed too." She laughed. "But what so few people understand is how selfish giving can be."

"Tell me more about that."

"When I do something unselfish and unexpected for a man, he's that much more in my debt. I make myself indispensable."

I nodded and waited to see what else she was going to say.

"And I'll do anything a man wants me to do. Anything to get further under his skin." While she spoke, Adrienne drew a lock of her hair across her cheek. "It's hardly an effort on my part—I love everything about men—the whole perfect maleness of them. Have you ever had a female lover, Dr. Sloan?"

"Adrienne, let's talk about why you keep asking me personal questions when you know I'm not going to answer them."

"I'd just feel better if I knew you could relate to what I was saying," she said impatiently.

"Except that's not how the process works. I'm not here to relate to what you are saying but to listen and understand so I can help you. Why don't you just talk, Adrienne; don't worry about me."

Without parting her lips, she lifted the corners of her mouth slightly. When some people smiled, they invited you in; when Adrienne smiled, she teased from a distance.

"I prefer male lovers because I like to be penetrated, to take a man inside me, to surround his cock with my flesh and wetness. It makes me excited to know that I'm making him excited. But when there haven't been enough good men around, I've had female lovers. What I don't like is that you can't prove anything with a woman."

"What do you mean 'prove anything'?"

She shrugged. "I don't accomplish anything when I sleep with a woman."

"Do you see sex as some kind of an achievement?"

So it was Adrienne's insecurities, not her passions, that were powering her.

"I don't know if I can be faithful to one person," she said, making what seemed like an odd leap in logic.

"Why is that?"

"Because it's always been more important to get someone, not to keep them. But I don't want to fool around anymore. I'm ready to be with just one man, but I can't do it without you. I need your help. And fast. Before I blow this one." Adrienne smiled at her own pun.

"What is it about being with one man that bothers you?"

"I get bored." As Adrienne went on to describe how she felt when the thrill of a new relationship lost its edge, how the highs became harder to reach and how the sameness dulled her senses, she stroked the leather couch with her fingertips.

"What about your emotional investments in these relationships, Adrienne?"

"What emotional investments?" Her laugh, unlike her smile, was intimate: meant to pull the listener in.

"Are you saying that you don't fall in love with any of the men you sleep with? You don't get attached?"

"No, I never have gotten really attached. I've never met one person who mattered to me as much as the passion itself matters. Until now. It's possible that I might be ready to form an emotional attachment now. Dr. Sloan, have you ever gotten drunk on fucking?"

"Adrienne, have you ever gotten drunk on fucking?" She needed to hear and feel the impact of her own words.

"So you think I'm showing off by using words like that," she said.

"I don't know, are you showing off?"

"No . . . that's how I talk about sex. No purple prose. No hearts and flowers. When I look at a man I've just met, I imagine him fucking me. I wonder what his sperm will taste like. Whether his cock will be thick or long? Does he seem like the type who only takes or a guy who gives back? My whole body comes alive when I meet a new man. If I get wet just talking to him, then I'll take him to bed. If I can look at a guy's hands and imagine them on my breasts . . ." Adrienne cupped her breasts. ". . . on my thighs . . ." Her right hand caressed her leg under her skirt. ". . . I know we'll be hot together." She was no longer aware of being in my office: her eyes were half-closed, and her head was tilted back: she was in the ecstasy of her own fantasy.

"Adrienne, you told me you'd been in therapy once before, is that right?"

She opened her eyes and there was a flicker of resentment in them; she was obviously angry that I'd interrupted her.

"Oh, yeah, she was just terrific . . ." Her sarcasm was thick and her laugh was nasty.

"Dr. Helga Grand told me I was a sex addict. Came right out and diagnosed me in the third session. Oh, please, what an obvious conclusion. I'd read the books too. But I don't fit the profile. My sex life doesn't interfere with my work. I don't drink to excess and I don't do drugs. If I'm without a partner, I don't get panicked or depressed; I just masturbate a lot more. I don't obsess about sex to the point that I alienate friends or family.

"Some people love to eat chocolate or read juicy novels or go to the movies—I like to go to bed with sexy men and stay there for a long time. I love the smell of the sheets after we've come, the feel of my skin when it's rubbed raw. I adore walking to work the next morning and being aware of my cunt—all sore and stretched. But none of those things make me a sex addict, do they?"

She waited for my answer, without guile and in earnest, with a narcissist's self-satisfied smile playing on her lips.

"Can you just imagine how much men enjoy me?" she asked before I'd even begun to answer her last question, and then she continued talking. "I just like sex, and I don't have and never have had one shred of guilt over anything I've ever done. Once I slept with three men in twenty-four hours. It was glorious. Heady. Intoxicating."

"Let's talk about guilt, Adrienne. You say you don't have any guilt over any sexual encounters. Do you have guilt about other things?"

In the last fifteen minutes of the session, she described three incidences in her life where she had felt guilt, proving she felt it in the appropriate situations and could identify it properly.

After she left, I stayed in my office for a few minutes assessing her session. Adrienne was right; she didn't exhibit the typical symptoms of a sex addict. Even if she had, her previous therapist should never have diagnosed her so bluntly. Like every patient, Adrienne needed to be led towards conclusions about herself in her own time.

Bringing the box of figs with me, I left the office and went upstairs. It was seven o'clock and I was hungry, but I was also drained. It had taken an enormous amount of energy to stay ahead of Adrienne. I poured myself some vodka, threw in a handful of ice cubes, and sat down at the kitchen table. I had taken a few sips of the drink and was about to bite into a fig when the phone rang. I looked at the panel of lights. It was the office line.

"Hello?"

There was no answer.

Tick . . . tick . . . tick . . .

"Hello? Who's there? *Please*, who are you?"

The only response was the hollow mechanical sound. I hung up and punched in star–sixty-nine.

"The number you are trying cannot be reached by this method," the mechanical voice droned.

Damn it! Who kept calling?

Was it Mallory?

No longer hungry, I sat there sipping my drink; the ice cubes melted before my panic subsided.

Maybe I was overreacting. Maybe that parole officer—Rafferty—was right and Mallory had been rehabilitated. But how much could a man change? Could the man who had written those letters really no longer be a threat to me?

The figs abandoned, the drink drained, I left the kitchen and went to the closet in my bedroom. Behind the clothes was the wall safe. Twisting the dial to the right, to the left, and then to the right again, I listened for the last tumbler to click into place. I pulled the door open and felt inside, past the suede pouches of my father's jewelry to the small stack of letters at the very back of the safe.

They had arrived while I was pregnant with Lilly. One a week for four weeks and then no more. Why had he sent them? Why had he stopped? I never knew.

At first, I had kept the letters a secret from everyone but Chloe and my therapist because they embarrassed me. I'd thought I deserved those letters as punishment for the part I'd played in my father's death.

But Mona helped me deal with my misplaced guilt and see that my rebellion against my father had not caused his death: a very disturbed man had.

Once I understood my reaction to the letters, it seemed unimportant to tell anyone else about them.

If I'd ever received another, I'm sure I would have gone to the police with it. But no more ever arrived.

Handling them now as if they were toxic, I put them on my

desk. Each was addressed to me in the same precise cursive hand. All were postmarked Ossining, New York, and all dated in January 1982.

J—

Do you have any idea how addicted you can become to an idea, an object, an act, a person? Have you ever thought about how a mind can lock onto someone and become a slave to them the same way you can become hooked on nicotine or alcohol? I have been mainlining you these past few years. I take my obsession to bed with me and wake up with it, and it sits beside me at every meal, nudging me. It never leaves me for long, nor can I bear to stay away from it for long. Maybe for a few hours at a time I can concentrate on something else, but in the joint, time inches by. There are never enough distractions, so you spend too much time ruminating on why you are here and who put you here or what you did to yourself to get here, and for me—you are part of the answer to those questions.

I read in a newspaper article at the time of my sentencing that you started studying psychology, and I have been studying it along with you. While you read books about Freud and Jung, I read books about Freud and Jung. I study the ego, the id, and the superego, study dreams and fetishes and criminality and depression and repression and denial and psychosis. While you read to learn, and maybe control, I read to discover my own soul. And one of the things I have learned is my psychology is not healthy. If you were going to draw a picture of my mind, it would be a banged up metal box with its latches busted. It's tied shut with a wire—but that wire's twisted and frayed and corroded with rust.

But the top of the box is encrusted with jewels.

Gems are mysterious, multifaceted; catching the light from one angle, they gleam; held another way, they go dark. There is seduction to the glitter of the color, drama to the cost. And because of their value and allure, people yearn to possess them.

You are one of those expensive gemstones. Not a sapphire—its depth is hidden in the darkness. An emerald is too opaque; a pearl has the opalescence of your skin, but a pearl is rounded and you are sleek and straight—angles without that softness that some women have. Almost a diamond, but a diamond is too cool, too reserved.

You are a ruby—a square-cut, four-carat ruby set in platinum.

When I close my eyes, behind my lids, that color is there. Rich and thick, the color of rose petals, the color of beating, pumping blood: of passion.

I am your secret and you are mine. We are connected in a place that has no present: only a past and maybe a future.

I still dream about making earrings, pins, and necklaces in your father's shop. But mostly I dream I am setting a ruby. Four carats in a platinum ring. And from what I know about how the mind works and about the subconscious and dreams, I can tell you it isn't healthy that I have this dream so often. There is not one good goddamned thing about it.

I let go of a long breath and put down the letter. Like the first time I had read it my hands were shaking and the back of my neck was damp with sweat. Eighteen years ago when I'd taken that letter to Mona, the man who'd written it was locked up in prison.

Now he was out.

EIGHT

It was seven-thirty by the time I finished reading all of Mallory's letters and realized it was time for dinner. Lilly was still upstairs working in the darkroom. Rather than call, I decided to go up. I didn't mind running into Robert. The letters had unnerved me and left me anxious; I needed some company.

But Lilly was alone in the darkroom.

"You're just in time; I was about to lock the door. . . . I have to develop these prints. Do you want to stay?" she asked.

"Aren't you hungry, baby?"

"This won't take much longer, Mom. Can't dinner wait? I really want to get this done."

Sitting on a stool, watching her work, I was able to stop thinking about the past and take pleasure in Lilly's competence and skill. Standing over her shoulder, in the glow of the red light, I watched with her as images appeared in the developer bath.

She was working on the roll of film she'd taken in Washington Square Park, and while I recognized the scenes, because I'd been there with her, the photographs presented the park in a way I hadn't seen it before. The specifics she'd chosen impressed me. Lilly had Robert's eye for picking the most interesting faces, for freezing the most dramatic moment, and for seeing the balance and symmetry within a busy landscape.

It was a wonderful thing that she had discovered her talent early. I thought of the pleasures she'd have being able to express herself artistically. No matter what had happened to Robert, his artistry had gotten him through and past each trouble spot. For once the camera seemed an enviable escape; it would be a relief sometimes to disappear from things that disturbed me the way both my daughter and her father could.

A new picture was emerging, and as I watched it deepen and darken and come to life, I noticed a figure I'd seen in the previous shot. Both pictures had been taken from a different location in the park, but the same man was in each of them.

All I could see of him was a New York Yankee baseball cap, the top rim of his sunglasses, and his right shoulder. Although his features were blocked by the man in front of him, his stance indicated he was facing the camera.

I went back to the first shot, which was now drying, and looked at it again.

"Lilly?"

"Yes?"

"When you were taking these pictures, did you notice this man?" I pointed to the figure.

"I can barely see who you're pointing to."

"This man wearing the baseball cap."

Lilly looked away from the photograph and turned to me. "No. I didn't. I can't even tell that's a guy."

"Isn't it strange that he's in both shots?"

"Not really; a lot of people walk through the park the way we do. He must have just been following the same path we were."

But what if it wasn't the path he was following? What if this man was wearing a baseball cap and sunglasses and cowering behind other people to make certain he wasn't noticed or recognized?

As Lilly continued to develop the rest of the roll, I examined each shot, but the man only appeared once more. Again he was obscured, but his hat was unmistakable.

If only I could have seen his face.

I kept trying to imagine what Dan Mallory would look like almost twenty years older. Would he be heavier? Thinner? Would he have lost his hair? Would he be gray? How had time and all those years in prison changed him?

Soon the darkroom was hung with dripping prints and Lilly was done. She turned on the lights, and together we looked from one to the next.

"Mom, you're right. I can pick out that hat in four of the shots. You think he's Dan Mallory, don't you?" Lilly asked.

"I don't know. I wish I could see his face."

"I can't believe I'm doing this, but if I prove to you that it isn't him, maybe you'll stop worrying about this so much."

Lilly shut off the lights and pulled out her negatives. Placing a strip of film under the enlarger she adjusted the lens and blew up the area that included the man. After exposing the film, she proceeded to slip the paper into the developer bath.

I didn't realize how tightly I was clasping my hands until I unclenched them

"Damn," I said. Even in the enlargement, there was nothing to see but the baseball cap and the rim of the sunglasses. There were just too many people around him, obscuring his face. "How tall do you think he is based on the man next to him?"

"Mom." Lilly's tone was disapproving. "You are being so paranoid, I can't believe it."

"I'm being cautious."

"No, you are being paranoid. They wouldn't have let him out of prison if he were going to follow you. The shrinks tested him. That's what Uncle Simon said. He's changed, Mom. He's past all that. He's sorry and he's suffered."

I didn't want to stand in the darkroom arguing with her. I wanted to go downstairs and make dinner and turn on an old movie and try to convince myself that everyone else was right and that this man was not Mallory and that I had nothing to worry about.

As impossible a goal as that seemed.

And for a while, talking to Lilly in the kitchen while the pasta boiled and the sauce simmered, I did manage to put the image of the man and the idea of my father's killer out of my mind.

NINE

As I waited in the reception area of the law office of Gold, Wein, and Bullard, flipping though a women's magazine, I scanned the articles: "Married and Happy—Ten Tried-and-True Tricks." "When an Extramarital Affair Is Just What the Doctor Ordered." "Sex and Marriage—How to Keep the Honeymoon Alive."

Annoyed, I dropped the magazine back on the coffee table. Those articles were like doing open-heart surgery with a nail file. No woman can save her marriage by reading one thousand words in April's issue of *Self* magazine. A decent marriage—not even a good marriage, but an okay one—takes more hard work, patience, and compassion than most people can find in one lifetime.

"Dr. Sloan?"

The woman was in her fifties with brilliant white hair and dark eyes. A pair of glasses hung on a pearl chain around her neck.

"I'm Laurie Gold." She smiled and extended her hand. She wore several silver bracelets that jingled almost merrily as she pumped my hand.

"We didn't talk much over the phone. Why don't you tell me a little about why you want to get divorced?" she asked once we were settled in her office and she'd put a mug of fragrant coffee on the table in front of me.

"That's a question I would have expected of a therapist, not a lawyer," I said.

She laughed. "Well, a divorce lawyer in many instances is forced to double as a therapist. I've discovered that the more I know about the whys of the divorce and the marital history, the easier it is to negotiate the settlement and terms."

"Well, I think this one will be pretty straightforward, Mrs. Gold."

"That sounds refreshing. Let's get started, then." She uncapped a pen and wrote the date on the legal pad in front of her. "Now, how long have you and your husband been together?" she asked.

"We've been married for eighteen years, but for the last five— almost six—we've been separated. It's an unusual living arrangement, though; Robert lives on the third floor of our brownstone, and our teenage daughter and I live on the second floor."

Her eyebrows arched. "Why is that?"

"Robert and I didn't want what we were going through to affect our daughter any more than absolutely necessary."

"How has she handled it?" Laurie asked.

"She still thinks our separation is temporary and that eventually we'll get back together. When we are all in the same room, I see her looking for signs that Robert and I are still connected to each other. I was hoping she'd finally come to terms with the situation and give up. But she hasn't stopped giving us anniversary presents."

"I take it you haven't had any serious relationships with other men in the last five years?" Laurie asked.

"No . . . I wasn't interested . . ." I used my hands to finish the sentence.

"Because?"

"The one good thing about a having a failed marriage is that it makes you finally understand how alone you are. How alone we all are. In the last five years I've had to concentrate on who I am and what I want for me, not just who I was as Robert's wife and Lilly's mother. It's taken me a while to get there."

Laurie nodded as if she'd heard this sentiment before, and I was sure she had. "But you are there now?" she asked.

"Yes, I think so. I'm pleased with my life."

"Has your husband had any serious relationships?"

"I'm sure he sees women, but no one that he has made a point of introducing to our daughter."

Laurie chewed on the tip of her pen. "If you don't mind, would you tell me why you and your husband separated."

Laurie was watching my hands. I stopped twisting the stack of wedding bands on my finger, took a large sip of the coffee, then put the mug down.

"If you don't want to—" she said.

"No," I interrupted her. "It's all right. Robert is a photographer. One night I walked in on him with one of his models. I might have been able to deal with that one incident, but there were others. And I couldn't stand watching and waiting for yet another. You see, we'd been—well, *I'd* been very happy with him. I'd never doubted the strength of our relationship. I just loved him. Maybe I made him too important in my life or took him for granted . . . maybe I put too much pressure on him . . . I don't know." I looked away from Laurie's sympathetic face and out the window at an ugly brick building. It had started to drizzle.

"Robert's very wise; he's always understood me better than anyone I've ever known. What I thought, what I felt, always seemed to matter to him; we used to talk out everything . . . I'm sorry. None of that matters. I'm rambling. Robert thought that because we were so close, he could tell me the truth about his affairs and that I would be able to help him. He said all the typical things— about how he didn't want to lose me and how they had just been there and it was so easy.

"I'm a therapist—I knew the signs—he wasn't describing one mistake, he was describing a real problem. But I was the last one who could help him. He needed to see an objective therapist. Except he refused. So we separated."

"Why wouldn't he go to a therapist?" Laurie asked.

"He said he wanted to work it out with *me*, not with a stranger. Except I couldn't help him—I was too involved. About six months after he'd moved out, he did finally go see someone. That was almost five years ago."

"You keep mentioning five years; is that somehow significant?" Laurie asked.

"Well, therapeutically, five years is the average amount of time it takes to work out a serious issue. So by now Robert should be at a point where he can have a nurturing relationship and a new life."

"And so should you," Laurie said.

"Yes, but I was just explaining about Robert."

"Right." She wrote something down on the yellow pad and looked up at me again. "So now that he seems to have it all under control, you're ready to divorce him."

"Yes."

"You don't think it's slightly odd timing, Jordan?"

"What do you mean?"

Laurie put the tip of her lacquered pen back in her mouth as if she were trying to stop herself from saying anything.

My cellular phone rang. Apprehensively, I reached into my bag to get it, hoping that someone other than my phantom caller would be on the other end. "Excuse me," I said to Laurie, and answered it.

Even as I said hello, I knew no one was there—I could already hear that now familiar but no less disturbing mechanical ticking.

"Are you all right?" Laurie asked after I snapped the phone shut.

"Yes. No . . . I'm not sure." I waved my hand as if I could wipe away the problem.

"So are you and Robert legally separated?" Laurie asked.

"No, we never filed any papers."

"Tell me a little about your finances." Her pen was poised to take notes.

"My husband is a talented artist and a successful photographer, and I have a good practice. Plus I've inherited a small amount of money from my father. I don't want anything from Robert except that he pay half of Lilly's college education."

"And what about the brownstone?" she asked.

"We have a small mortgage that Robert pays. The last time we talked about it, a few years ago, Robert said he'd continue to pay the mortgage and wanted me to stay there for as long as I wanted. It's Lilly's home. The only home she's ever known."

Laurie made some more notes and then looked up. "I know you said you haven't had a serious relationship in the past—but you're not involved with anyone now, are you? I just want to make sure."

"No, I'm not, but why is it so important?"

"It can affect how we handle the divorce. If there were any other men in your life, I would recommend certain precautions. Do you have the name of the attorney your husband will be retaining for this procedure?"

"No, I don't—I—we haven't actually discussed this."

"When were you planning to tell him?" She laughed, and I laughed along with her. I knew only too well what usually went on in divorces and how different this one must sound.

"Well, I wanted to talk to you first and find out what the simplest way would be to handle this; just file papers and get it done?"

"That has a lot to do with the attorney your husband hires, but I can recommend someone who won't turn something that is obviously amicable into an ugly fight. And then the whole procedure will be fairly cut and dry—legally at least."

"Robert wouldn't let this turn into a fight. He's not that kind of man. He'd never go to war with me over money or things."

"You'd be surprised. Not many divorces start out ugly. It's the fighting over assets and alimony and child care that turns them into battles."

Laurie explained what kind of fees she required and gave me a list of financial information she'd need. "And I'll call you with a recommendation of a lawyer for Robert," she said.

Suddenly, I felt tears spring into my eyes. "I'm sorry . . . I can't imagine why I'm getting emotional now . . ."

"Jordan, it's normal to feel sad. You're dissolving a marriage."

"No, I did that years ago." Other than when my father died, I rarely cried and was embarrassed at the sudden rush of emotion. Even when I was a child, I just wasn't one of those little girls who cried all the time. Lilly cried, though. Too often, I thought. It was her sensitivity to the world and its suffering. Even beauty could make her weep.

"You might think you ended your marriage years ago, but nothing is as final as a divorce. I'm sure you've seen this happen to your patients, but when it happens to you, all the professional expertise in the world doesn't help. If you choose to go through with the divorce, you might want to—"

"If I *choose* to go through with it?" I interrupted her. Squaring my shoulders and brushing the hair out of my face, I took a drink of tepid coffee. "Why would you question whether I'm going to go through with this?"

"I'm not sure—just a sense I'm getting."

Her statement made me feel as if I had not explained myself correctly.

"It's what I want. I'm just not looking forward to telling my daughter or dealing with her disappointment. No matter how old a child is, a divorce is devastating."

Laurie nodded sympathetically. "And it can be just as traumatic for a child if she thinks her parents sacrificed their happiness for her."

"No matter how I handle this, Lilly is going to suffer." I looked away from Laurie and out the window again.

"Jordan, as a psychologist, you know that no matter how good a parent you are, you're going to cause your child pain in some way or other during your lifetime. It's no easier to be a perfect mother than it is to be a perfect person. You can only be the best mother you can be, and I'm sure you've been a damn good one."

I laughed. "Sounds like you're a pretty good therapist yourself."

"It's all been on-the-job training. Divorces are obviously highly emotional legal actions."

"It must be very difficult and disheartening to do what you do every day. Do you ever get depressed?" I asked her.

"I shouldn't admit it to a new client, but yes, sometimes."

"How do you keep doing it?"

"I like to think that I'm helping give people second chances at being happy."

Her words struck me as odd. With all the hundreds of divorces she handled, she still believed in the possibility of happy endings. "So you're an optimist." I laughed.

"Aren't you?"

"I'm not sure . . ."

Laurie's secretary stuck her head in the door and said her next appointment had arrived.

I leaned down and picked my bag off the floor, preparing to go.

"She's a little early, Jordan; there's just one thing left."

Laurie explained the difference between getting a legal separation, then waiting two years for an automatic divorce, and the faster alternative of suing for a divorce in court, and then she asked me which route I wanted to take.

"I don't know if I should wait. I've already waited years."

"Take a few more days and let me know what you decide," she suggested.

I stood up, we shook hands, and I walked to the door.

"Jordan." She stopped me just as I was about to leave.

"Yes?"

"I know you say you've wanted this for a long time, but from the look on your face when you talked about Robert and some of the things you said about the two of you, it seems to me you and your husband might still have the foundations in place for a good marriage."

I laughed. "Compared to other marriages you see?"

Laurie laughed too. "It just sounds like you have a lot of love and respect for each other. Marriages built on less than that succeed."

I didn't know what to say.

She smiled. "It was an observation, that's all."

It took a great amount of effort for me to hail a cab when I emerged from Laurie Gold's office building. I was suddenly exhausted, and in the back of the taxi I shut my eyes. As the driver navigated the city streets, I didn't think about Robert or Lilly but about the marriages I had helped to save in my practice.

There were so many couples who'd had such great expectations for their union but had been so terribly disappointed for one reason or another.

Should I have worked harder to save my marriage? Had I been too tough on Robert? Had promiscuity been his reaction to a failing of mine? Had I been working too hard at being a therapist and a mother to give him what he'd needed?

But I was sick of those questions. I'd asked them every time Lilly said good night to her father and walked down the stairs to our apartment making it seem as if she were crossing continents.

The taxi had pulled to a stop. I paid the driver, got out, and went into the market on the corner to get some food for dinner.

No, leaving Robert had been the right thing to do. Whatever pain I'd caused Lilly would be offset by what I had showed her— that women were not weak, that we did not need a man more than our own self-respect.

At home I found Lilly's meditation sign hanging from her doorknob. I greeted the dog, poured myself a glass of wine, and sat down in the living room. Listening to a Pavorotti CD, I laid my head back and tried to disappear into the music.

"That's too loud."

Lilly was standing in the doorway with a scowl on her face. Her skin was pale, her eyes looked bloodshot. Had she been crying? She was wearing black jeans and a black turtleneck; the same outfit she'd been wearing for days. Or was it weeks?

"Isn't this a backward conversation? You're the teenager. Aren't I supposed to be telling you that your music is too loud?" I smiled, but she didn't smile back.

"Someone called for you," she said.

"Yes?"

"Stephanie—she said she was from Laurie Gold's office and wanted to give you the name of the divorce lawyer she was recommending. Mom, are you getting divorced?"

This wasn't how I'd wanted her to find out. "I've been thinking that maybe it's time," I said.

"Have you told Dad?" Lilly asked.

"No."

For a few moments she was silent. I knew the look on her face; she was straining against the onslaught of emotion she was feeling.

"Cry, scream, rant, anything, but please, Lilly, don't keep it inside. Tell me how angry you are at me; it's okay."

"I'm not angry." Her voice was almost inaudible.

No, she wasn't angry; she was disconsolate. So strong was my desire to go to her and comfort her that my arms involuntary lifted by my sides.

"So are you going to tell Dad?"

"Yes, soon."

"You do that," she said, then turned and walked out of the room.

I listened to her door shut firmly behind her and felt defeated.

It wasn't right that Lilly had to bear the burden of keeping something like this from her father.

In my bedroom, behind my own closed door, I hesitated for a few seconds but then dialed Robert's number.

"Hello?"

When I heard his voice, I realized I'd hoped he wouldn't be home.

"Hi."

"Lilly okay?" he asked right away.

I wasn't surprised. I never called him except to talk about Lilly. "Yes, she's all right, she's fine."

"Are you okay?"

For a moment I didn't know what to say. No, I wasn't. I was frightened and worried and concerned, and it would have been such a relief to tell him about everything that was bothering me. But the couple we had once been—so capable of comforting and caring for each other—hadn't survived our breakup.

"Jordan?"

"Yes, I'm fine, Robert." I had a sudden visceral reaction to forming his name with my lips—a sexual response that surprised me with its intensity. I could see him then, his hair falling over his eyes, his hand holding the phone, the pulse point on his neck where I had liked to put my mouth and breathe in the scent of his skin.

"Do you want to come up for a while and talk about whatever it is?" he asked.

"Why do you think there's something wrong?"

"Because I can hear you taking short breaths and you only do that when you're upset."

Tears welled up in my eyes for the second time that day. What was wrong with me?

"I'm fine."

"Jordan, are you crying?"

What clues was he hearing? "No—why? Do I breathe differently when I'm crying too?" I said, attempting to sound light-hearted.

"Yes—and when you're trying not to cry, your voice gets higher and tighter, as if holding in your emotions is taking an enormous effort."

"I can't tell that much about anyone from listening to them on the phone."

"I bet you can—I bet you can tell that I'm smiling, can't you?"

He was right. I had known he was smiling. I could tell from the sound of his voice, and I could picture the laugh lines that would be more pronounced around his eyes, that certain lift in the corners of his mouth.

Something inside of me started to ache.

"Jordan, if you'd let me, I could listen, I could help," he said.

And I knew then that he wasn't smiling anymore, but that something in him was hurting too. I could tell from how slowly he'd said my name.

"You know what, you have helped. But I'm tired, Robert; I should go to sleep."

"If you need to call again—don't worry about waking me up, all right, sweetheart?"

I was certain he hadn't meant to use an endearment, but that it had just slipped out. Did he realize he'd said it? Did he know how the word had come across the phone wire and wrapped itself around me? How for the briefest second I could smell his skin and feel his arms? Did he know all that from the sudden intake of my breath and the silence that was all I had offered in response?

"Talking to you, I remember things I've been trying to forget," he said.

"It's the same for me," I whispered.

And when he said good night, I knew he was smiling once more.

TEN

The next night, my Tuesday eight o'clock group therapy session was rife with tension. The two newest members were making the other eight uncomfortable. In different ways both Steven O'Keefe and Adrienne Blessing were sending out signals that they didn't want to be there. Steve looked down at the floor and would not make eye contact with anyone. Adrienne sat with her arms crossed defiantly over her chest. She'd also moved her chair back slightly so she was not quite part of the circle.

"She isn't my type and I don't have anything in common with her," said Tony, a twenty-two-year-old man who'd been in the group for two years. "But my parents expect me to marry her."

"You can't marry someone to please your parents," said Sonya, an unmarried middle-aged teacher from Brooklyn who still lived with her mother. She sighed. "You can lose yourself if you try to please other people and not think of yourself."

"Are you at least attracted to her?" asked Harry, another long-time group member.

"No. No, I'm not."

For the first time in half an hour, Adrienne spoke. "Don't you think the woman you marry should arouse you? Don't you want someone desirable? Someone you want to touch, who wants you to touch her?"

As she spoke, Adrienne's right hand stroked her suede jacket. Tony, and every other man in the room, was riveted by the motion.

"Of course I want to marry a woman who I'm attracted to. But my father say's that doesn't matter, that a man never stays attracted to any one woman for very long."

"Sure men get tired of fucking their wives, but at least most of them start their marriages off wanting to," Adrienne answered.

"Do you have to talk like that, Adrienne?" Sonya admonished. "It disturbs me."

"Maybe you just don't like me talking about sex because you're not getting any."

"How do you know whether or not I'm involved with anyone?"

"Well, are you?" Adrienne asked.

"No."

"Then you must miss having sex and that's why you're so touchy," Adrienne quipped.

"Sex isn't that big a deal to me," Sonya shot back.

She had been so shy and easily intimidated when she'd started therapy, standing up to Adrienne was a great leap for her.

"C'mon, that's not possible." Adrienne was looking right at me. "Sex matters to everyone. If you don't think it does, you're just hiding something from yourself, aren't you?"

"Talk to the group, Adrienne. Not to me."

She frowned and with a little less energy reposed the question to the group members.

But in my mind, I did answer her. Of course it's possible. Sex doesn't have the same value or importance to everyone. Or even to oneself at different stages in one's life.

When Robert and I had first split up, I missed him in my life and in my bed. But I hadn't allowed myself to think about what I no longer had. At first it was an effort, but in time it became easier. Although I'd gone on a few dozen dates with some fairly interesting men, I had no desire to sleep with any of them just because I was frustrated and missed my husband.

"Isn't there anything else to talk about but sex?" asked Ursula, a married private-school teacher. She turned to Adrienne. "You're making me uncomfortable too. You're so provocative. Do you realize you've already flirted with every man in this room?"

"Ursula," I said, "can you rephrase that and tell Adrienne how she is making you feel by talking about sex?"

"Okay, I feel uncomfortable when you talk like that. You exude sex. It's unseemly. I even feel like you are flirting with me sometimes, and with Dr. Sloan and with Sonya."

Adrienne laughed sarcastically.

"Adrienne, can you respond to Ursula with words?" I requested.

"That's just who I am," was all she offered.

"I think we've abandoned Tony and his problem," Harry said. At sixty-two, he was the oldest member of the group and the self-proclaimed mediator. He never failed to watch out for lost threads and abandoned feelings, and his kindness extended to everyone in the group except himself.

"Tony, I think you should just tell your father that you won't marry this girl just to make him happy," Sonya said.

"If it's so easy to stand up to parental authority, how come you can't tell your mother you want to move out?"

Harry intercepted before I could. "Tony, how do you think that comment made Sonya feel?"

"He doesn't care how I feel."

Tony was contrite. "Yes, I do. I'm sorry. I'm just all freaked out about this thing."

"Why can't you talk to your parents about this, Tony?" Ursula asked sympathetically.

"No matter what I say, my father tells me I'm too young to know what I'm talking about. And my mother—she just backs him up."

"Can't you talk to your mother when your dad isn't around and ask her to explain it to him?" asked Ursula.

Tony laughed sardonically. "My mother? She married my father because her father wanted her to. She'd never see it my way."

"Is your father happy with your mother?" Adrienne asked.

Tony basked in Adrienne's attention. "Is he happy with her? He doesn't think of my mother in those terms. She is his wife and the mother of his sons. He has girlfriends to make him happy."

"So does half the male population of New York City," Adrienne joked.

"That's not true. All men are not animals." Sonya crossed her arms over her ample chest. "Are they?" she asked me.

"Ask the group," I suggested.

"Well, quite a few of the men I've dated have been married." Adrienne had become animated and was eagerly participating now that she was dominating the conversation. It was the reaction a therapist would expect from a narcissist.

"If I was married to someone like you," Tony said bravely to Adrienne, "I wouldn't want to be with any other women."

Harry laughed. "No man sets out wanting to find a woman other than his wife, but sometimes life drives him to it. It happens because he needs to find an escape from his problems and disappear for just a little while. Even if it's only for a few minutes." His voice dropped on the last few words and when he finished there was silence in the room.

"The only thing men do faithfully is cheat on their wives," Adrienne added.

"You're disgusting," said Ursula in a tight, angry voice. "How can you date married men? Don't you ever think about their wives? Don't you owe it to the women in these relationships to stay away from their men?"

"Ursula, it's not helpful to attack anyone. Why don't you tell Adrienne how her comment made you feel?"

In private sessions Ursula had revealed her husband was cheating on her, but she had not yet told the group about the affair that was devastating her marriage.

Adrienne didn't wait for Ursula to explain. Instead she responded, her voice stoked with indignation, "I do not owe anyone anything. I have to take what I want. That's usually the only way to get it."

Something flickered in Steven's eyes, and I asked him what he thought about Adrienne's comment. When he spoke, his voice was so soft I had to lean forward to hear him.

"Aren't you worried that you are doing something immoral? That God is going to punish you?" he asked Adrienne.

Adrienne smiled at him. "God? Oh, no! Don't tell me you

think abortion is wrong too." Her voice was tinged with con-tempt.

Sonya, who so far had not missed an opportunity to correct Adrienne, jumped in. "I don't think you understand what we are doing here; we're supposed to interact and respond and support each other. Making fun of other people's religious beliefs doesn't help anyone."

"Chill. Chill. I wasn't making fun of what Steven said. Just reacting, sweetie."

"You know all you've brought here tonight is cynicism and filth," said Ursula. Her pert nose was wrinkled as if she smelled something foul. "And I for one resent it. Why don't you at least try to offer something constructive? And for all your talk about sex this and sex that, you haven't revealed a single real feeling."

I had known that Adrienne would stir up the group when I invited her to join us. The whole point was to get people to inter-act with those around them the way they would outside the group. It not only gave me a chance to see how my patients functioned in the world, but also gave them insight into how they affected other people.

"I'm sorry if you don't like it, but those are my real feelings. I love to fuck."

"What hurts so bad in you that you do that—that you shut us out no matter what we say? You are so beautiful, but when you talk like that you look ugly." Ursula had finally said something to Adrienne that reached her. I held my breath.

"Once you let someone help you, you owe them. That makes it hard to just walk away when you want to," Adrienne answered.

"I don't believe you really feel that. Why don't you tell us why you can't participate in here? Why can't you reach out and ask for help? We all ask each other for help. Why can't you?" Ursula asked.

"Accept help and you start to count on it. When it's not there, you're disappointed. Screw that."

"Who did that to you?" Sonya asked.

"Who didn't?" Adrienne quipped.

"Come on, be specific. Who did that to you? Sonya asked you a question, honey. Who did that to you?" Ursula repeated. She was talking to Adrienne as if she were a child. "And don't just come back with a flip answer. Who disappointed you so much that you hurt all the time?"

Adrienne stared at Ursula without revealing a single emotion.

Now Tony leaned forward in his chair. "It's hard, isn't it? But we've all been there. We all had a difficult time opening up to each other at first."

Adrienne seemed to retreat, pushing herself as far back in her chair as she could. But the metal chair was not very giving. Suddenly, she lifted her purse off the floor, flipped her hair over her shoulder, stood up, and walked out of the room without saying another word.

For the rest of the session my patients discussed their reactions to Adrienne's exit. And then, barely five minutes after everyone had left, my office door buzzer rang. "Who is it?" I asked.

"Adrienne Blessing, can I come in?" the disembodied voice asked.

I met her in the hall.

"I wanted to talk to you about what happened in there. I waited in the restaurant across the street until I saw everyone leave," she explained.

"We can talk about it the next time group meets. If I let you come back in now that everyone's left, it's only going to augment your feelings that you aren't part of the group."

"But I don't care about being part of them."

"Yes, I understand that. But that's not between you and me, that's between you and the group."

"I want to come in for just a few minutes." She was annoyed with me. "I waited all this time."

Obviously she didn't like being turned away.

"I'm sorry. But please try to understand; it wouldn't be fair to you or to everyone else in the group." I watched her, looking for any emotion—be it anger, frustration, acceptance—but there was nothing. Curtly, she said good night and turned and walked away.

Back in my office, I looked out of the window at the restaurant across the street. I'd often seen people sitting in the cocktail area having drinks, but I'd always thought my curtains blocked their view.

Leaving on the lights, I left the building and walked across the street. It was nine o'clock and the bar area was thinning out, so I didn't have to wait for a window table.

As soon as I sat down, a waiter took my order, and when he left I stared across the street at the brownstone where I lived and worked.

Through the drapes, which during the day prevented anyone on the street from seeing in, I could clearly make out a circle of chairs, a standing lamp, and a flowerpot on the windowsill.

The waiter returned with a bowl of nuts and my vodka and tonic. As I took a long sip of the drink, I watched a man slow down as he reached my building. It was Robert. Carrying a portfolio and bag of take-out food, he walked up the four stone steps to the front door and then using his keys let himself inside. Mellow light, warm and inviting, illuminated our front hall. I could make out the chocolate-colored carpeted steps, the creamy walls, and a stained-glass lamp.

The scene was so conventional: a man coming home after a long day at work to an inviting home, a loving wife, and a typical teenage daughter. There was no way to guess it was a broken home, that the husband and wife were separated or that the teenager was anything but typical, distancing herself from my physical world and sinking further and further into a metaphysical one.

I took another sip of my drink and continued staring out the window. In the pale light of the streetlamps, someone else had stopped close to my building. Partially concealed by a broad oak, I couldn't tell if it was a man or a woman, but I could see by the person's stance he—or she—was looking in the window to my office.

I immediately thought of Mallory.

Opening my cell phone, I punched in Robert's number without spending the time to weigh the rationality of the call. If I'd gone outside, I might have scared the stranger away, but if Robert looked down from an upstairs window, he might see the person's face and—

"Hello?"

"It's me," I said.

This time he didn't ask me if I was calling about Lilly. "What's up?"

"Could you look out the window? There's someone standing in front of the building, and—" My words came out in one long rush.

"I'm walking over to the window now . . ."

"Shit. Whoever it is, is leaving," I muttered.

The tree branches swayed in the breeze as the shadowy figure turned and walked away in the opposite direction from the house.

"Is that the person you wanted me to look at? The guy walking away?" Robert asked.

"Yeah."

"What's this about? A rejected swain?"

"Was it a man? I couldn't tell. Did you see his face at all?" I asked.

"No. Jordan, where are you? How did you know someone was outside? What's wrong?"

"I'm across the street. And I'm just being paranoid. I'm just spooked about Mallory being out of prison."

"What are you talking about?"

"Didn't Lilly tell you? I asked her to. Dan Mallory was released from prison a few weeks ago. Robert, they let him out early."

I heard him let out a deep breath. "Is that what's been going on? Christ, I'm sorry, Jordan. Are you all right?"

"Not really." I laughed and drained my drink. "Did you ever check with the florist about that mix-up with the roses?"

"No, I forgot to . . . Why, do you think that Mallory had something to do with you getting those roses?"

"I don't really know what I think." I was annoyed at how frightened I sounded.

"Are you alone there, Jordan?"

"Yes . . ."

"I'm coming over. I'll listen to you worry for a while and buy you a drink."

I hesitated. Our conversation from the night before was still fresh in my mind. If talking to him over the phone had stirred up so many feelings, what was going to happen if we were alone together?

"No, that's okay. I'm all right, really," I lied. "I don't need to talk about Mallory."

"Fine, then we won't talk about him; we'll discuss our difficult teenage daughter and her all-too-interested boyfriend and what we are going to do about them."

Or we could talk about finalizing the end of our marriage, I thought. Like I'd meant to the night before. But was I up to that?

"I don't know, Robert. I should get home, I have some work—"

"Jordan, order me a glass of port, okay?"

"No—" I started to say, but he had hung up.

Yes, Laurie Gold was right, there were people whose marriages were based on less than what Robert and I had. Couples who couldn't talk to each other. Spouses who didn't listen the way Robert did. He understood the machinations of my mind, but he was also the man who had made promises and broken them—which according to my misguided patient, was what all men did.

Perhaps it was a good thing that Robert was meeting me. Perhaps in person it would be easier to tell him about the divorce than it had been over the phone. Of course, it would be easier here, away from the house, in a neutral place.

I motioned to the waiter and ordered Robert's port and another vodka and tonic for me.

"Hey."

On Robert's face was a look of concern and empathy and just a little hint of something softer I didn't want to acknowledge.

Smiling that ironic half smile of his, he pulled out a chair and lowered his tall frame into it just as the waiter returned with the drinks.

"I know you said you don't need to talk about Mallory, but I think I should have all the info. By the way, why do you think Lilly forgot to tell me?"

"Sometimes I think we're losing Lilly," I said, not really answering his question.

He smiled again. "No, we're not. Well, we are, but not the way you think. Not in a way that should upset you. She's just growing up and trying to find out who she is. Part of that is rejecting some of who we are. Don't you remember being her age and rebelling?"

"No. I wasn't like Lilly." I tried to picture myself. At seventeen, eighteen. At nineteen all I could see was a frozen image—of my hands on my father's chest. Of my father fighting to stay alive. Of trying to stop the blood. I shook my head, trying to make the red-tinged images disappear.

Robert looked down at the table, at my hand. His smile reappeared. "You're doing it."

I didn't have to look to know what he was talking about; I was twisting the platinum and diamond bands. "So many wedding bands, Jordan. Most women think one is enough," he used to tease me when he caught me playing with them.

Robert reached across the table with his large, so very capable hands and stopped my fidgeting. "You're trying real hard not to be, but you're scared to death of Mallory, aren't you? It's okay, Jordan, talk about it. You don't have to deal with everything by yourself."

I didn't answer him right away because I was distracted by the sensation of his skin on mine, by the shiver his touch induced. He let his hands rest on top of mine for much longer than was necessary, and although I noticed, I didn't move my hands away.

⌐

"So you've finally taken down the firewall," Robert said as we got ready to leave an hour later.

"What?"

"You've been keeping me at arm's length for so long. But last night and tonight—it's different. You're different. Do you realize how long it's been since we've been together without our daughter chaperoning us?"

"It's the atmosphere here, the drinks . . ." I shrugged.

"If that's what you want to believe," Robert said, looking right into my face and into my eyes.

"We should go," I said.

He nodded. Something instantly tightened in his face; there was a flicker of anger and then he shook it off. For a moment neither or us said anything, and then Robert leaned forward and kissed me.

What surprised me was not that he had done it, but how much I'd wanted him to.

The pressure of his lips, the worn leather of his collar against my neck, the smell of the port, the stubble on his face, all overwhelmed me.

When we pulled apart, he spoke before I had a chance to. "Don't say anything, Jordan, please. Don't analyze what just happened, not yet. Can you do that?"

I nodded in agreement, knowing that even if I'd wanted to, I wouldn't have known what to say.

We walked across the street, the silence still charged with the kiss we'd exchanged. Robert opened the front door, and I proceeded him upstairs. At the door to the second-floor apartment, I stopped. He reached out and touched my cheek with his fingers in a parting gesture.

"Thank you," he said, and started climbing the next flight of stairs without waiting for me to say anything.

Inside, Lilly was in the living room, sprawled out on the sofa, the phone in her hand, talking. Her shoes were off, the lights were low, and on the stereo was a CD of Gregorian chants. She looked up at me, waved, and went on talking.

I went into the kitchen to get myself something to eat and realized I had never told Robert about going to see Laurie Gold. For the second night in a row, I'd never mentioned the subject of divorce.

ELEVEN

By eleven o'clock I was in bed, eating grapes and trying to find something on television that would distract me from the feel of Robert's hand on my skin. Rolling a single grape around on my tongue, I burst the skin with my teeth, felt the juice run out, and bit down on the wet flesh. It was wet and dry, sweet and sour, at the same time.

Robert's skin on my skin had been as new and shocking a sensation as if we'd never touched before. I thought I had accepted living without physical contact or the heady thrill of a man looking at me because he wanted me, but all it had taken to bring it back and make me remember what I had forgotten were Robert's fingers on my hand.

I took another grape, held it between two fingers, and peeled it with my teeth. Four pieces of skin and then the fruit was naked. The flesh had a similar consistency to the flesh on the inside of my mouth.

One night, years ago, I had taken Robert in my mouth while he was still sleeping and let him grow inside me while he dreamt. He woke up surprised to find me under the covers with my lips around him. Barely conscious, he put his hands on my head, laced his fingers through my hair, and held me there. It was his hands, so gentle and so insistent, that I recalled.

The truth that I had not told myself for the last five years was that I missed his body as much as I missed everything else about him. But his body had betrayed me.

I quickly bit down on another new grape, chewed, and swallowed. I didn't savor the next few but ate them quickly, devouring one after another, losing the specialness of each but getting an intensified, satiated feeling. I hadn't eaten dinner, and the grapes were like drinking and eating at the same time. Soon all that was left was a twig with its bare branches.

My windows were open, and it was cool outside. I shut the light off and pulled the down comforter up to my neck. Good was lying on the foot of my bed, snoring slightly, and the rest of the house was quiet. A low murmur emanated from the living room: Lilly was probably still talking to Cooper.

I closed my eyes. My hand crept down and came to rest on my stomach. I slipped my fingers in between the buttons on my nightshirt and touched my skin, trying to imagine these were not my fingers but Robert's, but I couldn't summon up the extra element of electricity his touch would have delivered.

Slipping down further, my hand found what it was looking for, what my body had been waiting for, without me knowing it, for the last few hours.

I stroked my inner thighs with both hands, and then one hand traveled further, making the journey from the inside of my thigh to the inside of me.

Like the juice of the grape, I was wet.

That night very long ago, he had forced himself to pull out of my mouth.

Too soon, too soon. It's my turn to taste you now.

His hair softly tickled the inside of my thighs and he pressed his face up against me.

Suddenly, it wasn't my hand between my legs, but Robert's mouth, and the faster and harder I rubbed, the more I disappeared into the illusion that he was doing this to me.

He had spent a long time that night torturing me with his tongue and his teeth and lulling me into a place where nothing existed but my hunger for his mouth.

You look so beautiful, he'd said.

It's what you're doing that makes me look like this.

My breathing had changed. I was the rhythms and the motions of my body and of his mouth.

Tell me what it feels like, Jordan.

Like I am awake and asleep at the same time.

More.

Like I am lost.

But I'm finding you.

Yes.

We changed positions again and he kissed my mouth.

Can you taste yourself? he asked.

Yes.

Lick yourself off my lips.

His body was stretched out on top of me; the length of his erection was pressed up against my stomach.

Show me how big you are, I whispered.

He pulled himself up and proudly showed himself. His eyelids were heavy, his lips were wet, and his skin was flushed

Will you make yourself come? Can I see you do that? I asked.

Yes.

His engorged penis disappeared into his fist and then emerged again, and I could not take my eyes off it. Robert watched me watching him.

Do you like how it looks? he asked.

Oh, yes.

It's yours because you're the one who makes it like this.

His words penetrated me and excited me as much as his body could have.

It's your cock, Jordan; it doesn't belong to me anymore. Do you like having your own cock?

I want it inside me. Now. Please. Now.

He slipped inside me from behind. With one finger he gave my clitoris a tiny beating while he pressed his other hand flat against my stomach and pulled me close to him.

With your hand there can you feel yourself pounding inside of me? I asked.

Yes.

My legs were bent at the knees and my feet were in the air; my thighs pressed together, opened, and pressed together again.

Faster, Robert, faster.

He changed his rhythm.

Like that? Is that how you want it?

Yes. Don't stop, Robert.

No, not until you tell me to.

Never.

Faster and faster, my hand did its own dance while I writhed to a remembered music until a blast of intensity crested upwards and pelted me with insane bliss.

It was over when I became aware of my heart beating, my breath straining, and of the warmth spreading upwards in an over-flow to my stomach and breasts and neck.

Rolling over, I lay my cheek against the cool cotton sheets. Hungry again, I sat up, turned on the light, and reached for the bowl of grapes. I'd forgotten I'd finished them all.

The lights were off in the living room, and now from behind Lilly's closed door, I could hear her laughing. She was probably still on the phone with Cooper. Suddenly, I felt nothing but happiness that she had met Cooper and that he could elicit that enchanting laugh from her.

In the kitchen, I opened the refrigerator, took out a loaf of bread, and the jar of jam Adrienne Blessing had given me.

Many patients talked about how long it's been since they've had sex. Some count days, weeks, or years. I didn't know how long it had been; I'd never kept track. I hadn't cared.

Therapists spend hours working with patients to break down their defense systems and get to the truth of their lives. But patients are in therapy because their lives are not working. Some-thing is interfering with their functioning. Whether they are depressed, angry, lonely, addicted, or shy—they go to a therapist because they want to improve their life and if not enjoy it more, then at least function better in their day-to-day existence.

But nothing had been interfering with my life. I was enjoying it and functioning well in it. I didn't need to have my defense mechanisms torn down to discover hidden truths.

I didn't.

Sitting in my kitchen, eating bread smeared with raspberry jam, I didn't want to think about my practice or any of my patients, but Adrienne Blessing was as present as if she were sitting at that table with me. In a quick succession of insights, I realized something so obvious that I actually stopped chewing. How could I have been so oblivious?

Adrienne closed off her feelings and treated sex as if it were a contact sport because to acknowledge that she needed anything more would require her to also acknowledge and experience disappointment and pain.

Identifying with your patients is detrimental to the healing process. A therapist has to remain an objective listener. But because I was in the same kind of denial as Adrienne was, I'd missed understanding her main motivation. Adrienne had shut down and closed off her feelings rather than deal with how badly she'd been hurt.

She had wound up with half a life.

She was a competent, capable woman. Seemingly in control and satisfied. But she was alone. It wasn't sex she craved; she was starved for someone to love and to be loved by.

And so was I.

TWELVE

Simon took a tentative sip of the steaming coffee. "So what did the florist say?"

"That he got a call a few hours after Robert left the store—from a man he assumed was Robert—who changed the order for calla lilies to red roses."

"It is possible that the florist just screwed up and was covering his ass."

We were sitting in my office on Wednesday afternoon a few hours after Robert had called me to tell about his visit to the florist earlier that morning.

"Of course it's possible."

"But you think Dan Mallory called the florist, don't you?" Simon asked.

"Yes, I think it is possible."

"How would he have even known about the flowers in the first place?"

"Maybe he's following us. Robert and me. Maybe he followed Robert into the store and overheard him place the order and then called back later and changed it."

"Do you want this coffee I brought you?" Simon asked. "It's getting cold."

I reached out and took the proffered cup.

"Jordan, I think Mallory is so relieved to be out of prison that the last thing he'd do would be to come anywhere near you."

I took a sip of the coffee. "Do you remember that you told me to try and get the number my hang-up calls were coming from."

"Yes."

"Not a single one has been made from a phone that accepts the star–sixty-nine function."

"But that doesn't point to Mallory any more than it points to one of your patients. No matter who is making those calls, they wouldn't want you to be able to track them."

"Then why did you tell me to do it?"

"In case someone was stupid enough to slip up."

I sighed and looked at the manila folder on the table. "Simon, there's something else. I wanted to tell you the other day, but you had to get back to court. Mallory sent me letters from prison."

"Letters? Shit, Jordan!" Simon slammed his hand on the coffee table. "Why didn't you tell me sooner?" he shouted. "Why didn't you tell the police?"

"I couldn't tell anyone back then. It would have meant explaining so many things I still felt guilty and embarrassed about. But what Mallory says in these letters makes it sound like—"

Simon held up his hand to stop me. "Wait a minute. What do you mean 'back then'? When exactly did you get these letters?"

"One a week, for four weeks in January of 1982."

"But that's eighteen years ago." He shook his head. "Jordan, what's in eighteen-year-old letters isn't going to pull any weight with the parole board. Mallory was what—twenty-four when he wrote them? He's forty-two now and he's been through all those years of rehabilitation. He's not the same man."

"*Maybe* he's not the same man."

"Jordan, didn't you talk to Jim Rafferty? Didn't you hear what he said? Mallory has been through every psychological test that exists. If he were still dangerous, he would still be in prison."

"Don't patronize me. You don't know how Mallory thinks; I do."

"No, you know how Mallory *thought*. Not how he thinks. Only the parole board, Mallory's shrink, and Rafferty know how he thinks."

"Will you just listen to some of this stuff?" I asked.

"Will it make you feel better?"

I didn't answer. Instead, I picked up the manila folder, opened it, and began to read.

When I close my eyes, I never just see darkness—you are always behind my eyes. Occasionally when I think of you, I connect to a feeling of love—of wanting to care for you. Other times I can only feel anger because of where you have brought me.

I look at the watch my mother brought me. Oh, yes, I have a watch, even though it's not allowed, because there are ways to break the laws in here.

You bribe a guard, he looks the other way—it's so easy. Most guys smuggle in cigarettes or drugs. But I wanted this watch. It only cost twenty-five dollars, but it looks like one of the watches your father sold for a thousand dollars more. This one is just like the watch he always wore. That was his watch you were wearing at my trial, wasn't it?

Now that I have a watch, I play games with the time. It's one hour since I have thought about you. It's twelve minutes since I have thought of you.

They say you can't make it in the joint if you hold on to wanting, to wishing, to needing. If you hold on—they say—you go crazy. You've just got to eat and shit and jerk off and work and sleep and exercise and then do the same thing all over again. You've just got to exist from one day to the next and not look forward or back. The most dangerous thing is to think about how long you have to wait to get out because if you actually start counting or calculating . . . my God, the numbers would drive you insane. Imagine knowing something will happen in seven thousand and three hundred days? Or worse yet in one hundred seventy-five thousand and two hundred hours?

How do you even contemplate something so incalculable?

But that's how long it will be before I can see your face again.

I put down the sheet of paper and took a sip of my coffee.

"Goddamned bastard!" Simon's eyes had narrowed, and his hands were clenched into fists in his lap.

I picked up the next letter.

There's a lot of time to watch TV in here, and sometimes I catch an old black-and-white starring Audrey Hepburn. I stare at the screen with my eyes bugging because of how much you two look alike. Long neck, big wide eyes, dark hair, and skinny.

But in my head I don't see you in those TV blacks and whites—in my head you are still that deep red ruby. The one gem I had to have. That I screwed up my life for. Sometimes when I think about you, I want to strangle you. But then I take my cock in my hand and it's your image that makes me come.

I have to decide if I want to punish you or fuck you. If I want your love or your apology. Maybe I just want it all.

"You hurt in me like a scar that still hasn't healed. But when we are together again, the pain will go away because we will be able to share it.

I deal with my pain by naming it over and over or by trying to push it away or bury it, but nothing works. Only when I am able to taste your skin, your sweat, and your tears—when we can swallow each other's pain—will we be able to release each other from it. And then you will want me the way that you should and we will be together.

I was still shivering after I read the last sentence.

Simon stood up and walked to the window. He took a deep breath and let it out, and when he spoke, his voice filled the whole room with its volume. "How dare he write those letters to you? How dare he after what he did to Dad!" My brother spun around to face me. "Why didn't you come to me when you got those letters?"

My fingers trembled as I put the last letter back in the folder, and my voice quivered when I answered him. "I told Mona about them and we dealt with them in therapy. And I showed them to Chloe. But if I'd let you or Robert read them, I would have had to relive my relationship with Mallory. And I just couldn't to do that back then."

"But you must have been frightened to death when you got them." Simon sat down again.

I shrugged. "Yes, but I wasn't as frightened as I am now. Back then Mallory was safely locked up in a prison cell. Now, he's out there on the street." I glanced out the window and then looked back at the folder of letters.

Leaning forward, I pushed the folder across the table towards my brother. He picked it up and held it without opening it for a minute, as if he were weighing it, and then he rested it on top of his briefcase.

"Jordan, I'm going to show these to Rafferty. But I want you to understand—they *are* eighteen years old. And eighteen years is a long time to get help, to become religious, to feel remorse, and to be rehabilitated. To change. No parole board in the world would have released Mallory if he was still the same man who wrote those letters."

Getting up, Simon came over to where I was sitting and squatted down so that we were face-to-face. "I promise you, I'm taking this seriously. But I've done my homework on this one, Jordan. Every single person who was involved in releasing Mallory is certain he is no longer a threat to you—or to anyone. Can you trust me on this and not worry?"

"It's not you I can't trust; it's the man who murdered our father."

THIRTEEN

"I need a friend," Chloe said.

It was Friday night and we were standing on the ticket-holder's line at a movie theater in SoHo. The film we were waiting to see had won so many film festival awards the line stretched down the block. Chloe had chosen it because she was writing a profile of the director for her magazine.

"Why? What's wrong?" I asked her.

Reaching into her bag, Chloe pulled out her cigarettes, shook one from the pack, lit it, inhaled, and then blew out the smoke. A man in front of us turned, gave her a dirty look, and moved off to the side.

"I feel like an idiot or a sixteen-year-old or something. I met someone, Jordan." She took another deep drag of her cigarette.

"You met someone? You mean you met a man."

She looked up at the movie marquee. "The guy who wrote and directed this picture."

He'd gotten so much press for this film even I knew his name. "Max Brecht? The guy you're interviewing?"

She threw down the half-smoked cigarette and stomped it out. "It's just so stupid. . . . I didn't tell you about it at first because I kept thinking I was imagining it or that I'd get over it, but . . ."

"We can figure that out later; first tell me what happened."

"A few weeks ago I E-mailed him to set up an interview. He was out in LA and suggested that I start the process by E-mail and then we'd meet up when he got back to the city."

"Oh, no . . . I know what's coming: two writers and two laptops."

"The man writes notes that are better than most novels. Before I knew it we'd written a few dozen letters back and forth. From the very beginning it was different. How can I explain it? He is so damn disarming, not just answering my questions, but making really astute observations about me. I started getting up in the middle of the night to see if he'd written me back and was amazingly disappointed if he hadn't. It's more than just two writers flirting with words. Anyway, it never occurred to me that he was feeling it too."

Finally, the line began to inch ahead. A young girl in front of us asked us to hold her place while she went and looked for her friend.

"But he's just as interested as you are?" I asked.

She nodded her head yes.

"Have you met him yet?"

"No. I've seen photographs of him, though. He's not handsome—it's nothing like that. But, Christ, he's just so brilliant. Yesterday, I talked to him on the phone for over three hours. He has an accent like one of those Americans who were lucky enough to have been educated in England."

"Was he?"

"Yes. His father was one of the screenwriters blacklisted in the forties. So he moved his family to London and that's where Max went to school—this is ridiculous; you don't need to hear his bio. Just give me the lecture."

The line suddenly stopped its slow crawl and we were standing still again.

"What lecture?"

"You know, the lecture that one friend gives to another friend that talks her down from the infatuation high, makes her realize that even good marriages get boring, but that boredom is no excuse to have an affair, that I should not meet him tomorrow but finish up the interview on the phone and just walk away."

"If I tell you all those things, will you listen to me and just walk away?"

Chloe looked at me but didn't answer.

"I don't like giving lectures anyway," I said.

We were facing the theater's plate-glass windows where the movie posters were displayed, and in the reflection, I could see that a man was a few feet behind us, just standing by a car in the street, staring at us. Something about his stillness or his stance made me spin around. But in the time it took me to turn, he had disappeared. Had he looked like the same man I'd seen in front of the brownstone on Tuesday night? Like the man in the crowd in Lilly's photographs?

"What's the matter? Is it Mallory again?" Chloe asked. She knew how worried I was now that he had been released, and she'd been relieved when I told her I'd finally given my brother Mallory's letters.

"I'm so spooked that I keep thinking I'm seeing him—but we're talking about you now, and your problem, which unlike mine, is real."

The line started to move once again.

"Jordan, I want to tell you to stop worrying about Mallory and relax, but I'm afraid if I do that you'll think I'm not taking you seriously."

"I know you better than that. You can just tell me what you think."

"Okay. I think you should believe what Simon and Rafferty have told you but you still need to be careful."

Finally reaching the theater entrance, we handed our tickets to the attendant and were pushed inside by the crowd behind us.

Chloe and I had gone to enough movies together over the years to have a routine. She rushed ahead to get seats while I got on the line at the concession stand. When my turn came, I ordered one large unbuttered popcorn for us to share, a small Coke for her, and a diet Coke for me.

I found her a few minutes later halfway down in the center section. After settling in, I asked Chloe what was bothering her the most about Max Brecht.

"I guess I'm disappointed. I thought I was safe, that this couldn't happen to me. I mean I haven't even noticed a man since

I met John. I thought if you loved your husband, if he still excited you, if you were happy with your career and not facing some kind of life crisis, that you were immune to getting crushes on other men and wanting to jump into bed with them."

"Marriage is a commitment to a relationship; it isn't a vaccination against noticing other people. We put so much pressure on our marriages it's almost impossible to live up to our expectations."

She smiled. "So what do I do?"

"Well, what do you want to do?"

"I want you to tell me that I'm not allowed to even be seriously thinking about any of this. That it's a normal, healthy thing to fantasize, but that taking it to the next level would be not only wrong but dangerous."

"You know it's normal. It's even healthy. Of course it's exciting to meet new people and want to get to know them better. Do you realize if it were a woman you'd met instead of a man, we wouldn't even be having this conversation?"

"Because I'd only be having lunch with her, not thinking about sleeping with her."

We both laughed.

"Okay, I'll tell you what I'd do," I said.

"What?"

"Reverse the situation. What if John met someone and was attracted to her the way you're attracted to Max? What if he said he still loved you but he was a little bored and wanted to have a fling? How would you feel?"

"I'd want to kill him, I'd be insanely jealous, and I'd start worrying about our marriage."

"Do you think Brecht is a threat to your marriage?"

"Not in the slightest. This has nothing to do with John. He's my husband; I want to be with him forever and grow old with him, but . . ."

"Max makes you feel alive and excited?"

"Yes. Exactly. And I like it. It's exhilarating. And I don't want to stop feeling it. Not just quite yet." She reached over and took a handful of popcorn. "What if I go ahead with this? How will I be able to ever look at John again? I don't want to cheat on my husband, Jordan."

"I don't think most people want to cheat. It happens because we're fragile and needy and it's really hard to keep saying no to something that feels so unbelievably good. By making sex so damn precious and inviolate, reserving it for just one person, we've put unbearable pressure on ourselves. We're not saints and yet we demand this great sacrifice from each other."

"I'm not sure you're helping me very much here." She laughed.

"I'm sorry. It's just that I keep seeing this over and over with people who come to therapy. Sometimes, I think it's really strange how couples get so jealous of their lovers sleeping with other people, but don't care how much they talk to other people. I mean animals can have sex . . . but only human beings can share what's in their heads. Why don't we make talking sacred? Sorry, I think you just got your lecture."

"But it sure wasn't the one I expected to hear from you."

And it hadn't been the one I'd expected to give. Why hadn't I been able to grasp any of that before?

The theater was filling up and we had to endure two more people squeezing by us on their way to getting the last two seats at the end of the row.

"Jordan, I do have to meet him and do the interview, right? I mean, it's work."

The lights started to dim.

"Right."

"I can't possibly write a profile about him without sitting down and meeting him face-to-face. Right?"

"Right."

"Jordan, am I just rationalizing?"

But I never got a chance to answer her because the coming attractions began and the woman in the row behind us asked us to be quiet for the second time.

After the movie was over, we shared a taxi uptown. Just before Chloe dropped me off, she turned to me with an odd expression on her face, put her hand on my arm, and said: "You should think about what you said to me tonight about my infatuation. You made a lot of sense, Jordan. Some of it might just help you finally forgive Robert's infidelity."

I walked up the front stairs of the brownstone. Maybe I didn't need to forgive him anymore, but perhaps it might finally be time to try to understand him. I put my key in the lock and went inside.

FOURTEEN

On Sunday morning, I got up early to do chores. A few hours later, arms laden with freshly laundered clothes, I knocked on Lilly's door. She opened it for me and I laid the fresh-smelling shirts and jeans on her bed. My daughter had just gotten up and her long hair was a disheveled mess. She was wearing a man's shirt—which must have belonged to either Cooper or Robert.

Since she was a child, she had appropriated her father's shirts and sweaters and wore them like lucky charms. I'd noticed a few new ones since she'd been dating Cooper and assumed she had carried over the practice to the new man in her life.

Opening her closet door, Lilly began to put away the laundry. I was surprised to see so many naked hangers and empty spaces on the shoe racks. At least half of her wardrobe was missing.

"Lilly, where are all your clothes? Your shoes?" I asked as I scanned the inside of the closet.

"I gave a lot of them away. Everything extra. I only kept what I really needed," she said proudly.

"Who did you give them to?"

"To a thrift shop the Zen center operates. I don't want to get stuck in materialism. All those clothes disguise the real issues." She finished putting away the jeans and started on the shirts.

My daughter had always been generous with her things. As a child she'd been eager to share her toys, offering them to her friends when they came over to play—my mother was like that too.

During one visit to San Francisco we drove over the Golden Gate Bridge and my mother paid the toll for the car behind us.

"Watch what happens when they realize what we've done," she told Lilly. My little girl had leaned out the window and watched the two businessmen arrive at the tollbooth. We could see their initial confusion; then they looked to see if they knew who we were and when they realized they didn't know us and saw Lilly leaning out, waving and smiling at them, they erupted in smiles and waved back. Since then, even now, whenever we go through a tollbooth, she insists we pay for the car behind us.

But this wasn't a two-dollar toll. These were her clothes. I wanted to take her by the arms and shake her. Or yell. I wanted to disconnect her telephone and ground her. Instead I sat down on the bed and calmly asked her if perhaps she could have discussed it with me first, since I was the one who'd purchased all those clothes.

"You gave them to me. And I gave them away. We don't really own anything, Mom, not even our bodies. We only rent them for a while. I hardly ever wore all those extra pants and skirts, and there are tons of people who need them. Mom, it was a good thing I did."

Her expression was so earnest, so sincere.

I had a choice—try to get her to see my point of view or accept her actions and try to deal with the situation a different way. Above all, I didn't want to start another battle with her. Our days were fraught with too much tension as it was.

"Well, don't expect me to replenish anything in the near future." I stood to go. And then I noticed that there were other things in the room that were missing. There were gaps in her bookshelves, and the guitar Robert had bought her a few years ago when she wanted to learn how to play no longer stood in the corner on its stand.

"Did you at least keep your camera equipment?" I asked.

Lilly shot me a withering look. "Oh, Mom, of course I did."

"And you didn't sell any of the jewelry I've given you that your grandfather made?"

"Of course not. Why are you being so impossible? I had too many things. Too many other people have nothing. The state of the poverty in this country is deplorable—"

"Don't lecture me, Lilly. I'm not asking you to become a free-market capitalist. But there's a line, and you've crossed it and I know that you know it. If you didn't, you would have mentioned that you were giving away most of your worldly possessions and wouldn't have waited for me to discover it like this. What's next? Are you going to take food from the kitchen and offer it to the homeless on the street?"

"You're getting upset . . ." Lilly was biting the inside of her cheek. It was what she did whenever she was trying to control her emotions. Or mine.

"You're damn right I'm upset. You just gave away thousands of dollars of things that your father and I bought you. Lilly, what's happening to you? The more involved you get with Cooper the less you seem like a member of this family, and—"

"This family? We don't have a family. You're destroying it."

"Lilly, your father and I failed in our marriage, but that doesn't mean we are not a family and you know that."

"Prove it," she challenged. "Have lunch with Dad and me today."

"You're manipulating me."

"I knew you were going to say that. I knew you wouldn't come." She was pouting. Her lips were pursed, and I could clearly see the three-year-old she'd been.

I walked out of her bedroom without saying another word and went into the kitchen to make myself coffee. In the quiet I could hear Lilly playing a CD of those annoying chants.

Over the last few years I had heard about Eastern religions and practices from my mother who, at forty-five, had begun studying at a Buddhist center outside of San Francisco. There she met Horace Templar, a Jewish businessman who, at thirty-five, had stopped manufacturing athletic wear and had opened up a New Age catalog company.

Horace was as different from my father as a man could be. Five years younger than my mother, he was as wiry as my father was muscled, as cerebral as my father was emotional, unencumbered by things whereas my father was fascinated by them, and spiritual in ways my father had never been. The only trait they both shared was an ability to love. Especially to love my mother.

Once she found philosophy and met Horace, my mother had been able to put my father's murder behind her. I loved Horace for helping her to do that.

My mother had met a man and married him only three years after my father died. I had been separated from my husband for five years and hadn't met a single man who had warranted more than a few dates.

But then, my mother had had real closure and I still was confronted with my husband day after day and Lilly's constant attempts to throw us together, like this lunch she was trying to back me into.

Now that Lilly had gotten involved with Cooper and Zen, she and my mother were closer than ever. But what was fine for my mother—who was an adult—wasn't necessarily as good for Lilly, who was still so idealistic and impressionable.

But could I really complain when other kids were experimenting with drugs, alcohol, and piercing their noses?

"Is there any coffee left?" Lilly asked when she walked into the kitchen a while after our argument. Her face was scrubbed and her hair was shining; she looked as calm as if nothing had happened between us.

"I can make you some. Caffeine or decaf?"

She thought about the coffee. "Never mind, I think I'll make green tea."

Her ritual began with washing out her glazed teapot, then carefully measuring out the loose tea, boiling water, and pouring it into the pot. It was a ceremony she performed every day, but on this Sunday she reminded me more of a monk in a temple than a teenager in the kitchen.

"So, are you coming to lunch?" she asked.

If I went to lunch, she'd be happy, I thought. For an hour or two the tension would be gone and I could enjoy her, laugh with her, talk to her without any animosity. All because her father would be there.

"Okay, I'll go."

"Will you come upstairs with me before we go?"

Lilly gave me a wide smile that was almost as good as an embrace.

"To the studio? Why?"

"We're choosing the photographs for Dad's exhibition catalog. He said he'd love it if you would come and look."

Lilly waited, with anticipation. I knew what she wanted; she had wanted it every day for the last five years.

"I don't think so, sweetheart. I've got a bunch of patients' notes to go through."

Lunch would be bad enough. Lilly would sit there like a cat, watching each move we made, judging, weighing, and interpreting our body language, our glances, and our every word. Her overwhelming desire that her father and I get back together would be as palpable as the sound of the silverware hitting the china.

"Mother, *please*." It was an annoying expression she'd heard me say to my mother when I wanted something from her that she wasn't giving me. As our children grow up, they play back our worst flaws and illuminate our insecurities, and make us cringe.

"I have to get some work done. You go upstairs and call me when you and your father are ready to go out."

"That's not why you won't come, and you know it. You're scared, aren't you? You have unresolved issues with Dad that you refuse to face."

"That's quite a trick—using my own psychological jargon as a weapon against me."

"Well . . ." Lilly was smirking.

"It's Sunday morning. I'm having coffee. Can't we make this a peaceful interlude instead of another argument?"

"I'm not arguing. I'm asking you to open your eyes and your mind and live in the present. In this very moment. Not look back or forward, just deal with now. What is wrong with coming upstairs and looking at Dad's photographs? Don't you know what kind of karma you are creating by being so negative?"

"Don't you know what kind of karma you are creating by being so insistent?" I asked, but with a smile.

My daughter smiled back at me. She was too smart to keep hounding me. And so a few minutes of silence ensued.

For a moment, I actually believed she'd decided to back off, and then . . .

"Iago wants to promote the fact that these shots are of me to get the exhibit more press, and now Dad's not even sure he should have the show at all."

Lilly had finally gotten to me. I frowned and drank what was left of my cold coffee. "Your father would never exploit you to sell more photographs."

"Of course he wouldn't . . . but that's why he wants you to see the shots. He wants your opinion of them."

And so when Lilly went upstairs fifteen minutes later, I went with her.

Robert was wearing his usual uniform of black jeans and a long-sleeve white shirt. His hair was still damp from a shower, and I could smell his scent the minute I walked into the studio. Leather, patchouli, and peppermint.

He got up from the table where he was reading the paper and gave his daughter a kiss. Over her head he looked at me. I often had a hard time reading Robert's face: as a photographer he'd learned to keep his expression impassive so he wouldn't influence his subjects. But that Sunday, I had no trouble discerning his pleasure at seeing me. I was disarmed and slightly flustered by my own rush of emotions.

"So Iago wants to promote the fact that your model is your daughter?"

"Good morning, Jordan. Nice to see you. Would you like a cup of coffee?"

He was being sarcastic, but he was smiling. I said hello and accepted the coffee, which was stronger and more potent than the brew I had made for myself. Robert drank his coffee black and considered anything else an affront. I went to his refrigerator and helped myself to a long pour of milk.

"Sit down; I'll bring the shots out," he suggested.

I sat on the couch and Lilly sat down next to me.

"I know that you think I manipulated you to get you here," she said in her most beguiling voice.

"Are you apologizing?" I asked.

"No." She laughed, and I could see in her face the same joy I'd seen when she first tasted ice cream, when she'd picked out Good from the litter. For a moment I didn't see the other face, the accusatory, sad face I'd been seeing since her father had moved upstairs.

Lilly had told me this couch opened up to a bed, but if you didn't know that, there was no indication that Robert lived in the studio. In fact, the only visible sign of his personal life was a framed photograph next to the telephone. Taken ten years earlier, it was of Lilly and me on a beach at sunset. The pale amethyst sky behind us reflected on the water and the sand beneath our feet.

In the steel file cabinets were hundreds of other shots of our daughter but only this one magical shot of both of us was on constant display. If he'd kept all the photographs that he'd taken of me over the years, they were probably in there too. But had he kept so much tangible evidence of our time together? I would have kept them . . . Destroying them would have been like denying what was between us. What *had been* between us, I corrected myself.

After I'd discovered Robert with the model in the darkroom, I never let him photograph me again. I was so angry I'd wanted to take all those shots of me and burn them. I didn't want him to have even that much of me anymore.

I'd held on to that anger for a long time. Forgiveness, I told my patients, is accepting what has happened and ceasing to want revenge for it.

In theory it works, but revenge is hard to give up. I had lain in bed at night during those weeks before our separation, watching my husband while he slept and imagining ways to hurt him. I would take Lilly and move somewhere where he would never find us. Deprive him of his daughter forever. Or I would divorce him in the messiest way imaginable and tell the court he had become a sex addict so that they wouldn't grant him joint custody.

Instead, I had done nothing. I hadn't been able to risk what that revenge might do to Lilly.

"Okay, all done," Robert said.

Over two dozen photographs lined the walls, sitting on the wooden shelf that ran the length of the studio.

All the montages were composed of images Robert had taken when he and Lilly had been in Japan the summer before.

I looked from the first shot to the last: Lilly's face superimposed on the surface of a sandpile spiral in a Japanese garden; her elongated body half hidden and half revealed in rice paddies; her face, neck, and shoulders rippling on the surface of the water in a pond of koi.

The photographs revealed more than a unique vision. Robert had reached a new level of sensitivity and grace. Were the photographs sensual? Yes, but not in a lewd or lascivious way. There was no question his was the work of an artist.

This was what Robert had always given me, I thought. A view of the world I could never have seen with my own eyes.

Just as I had been proud to be the daughter of a man who painted with jewels, I had been proud to be the wife of a man who could take disparate images and merge and meld them into poetic meditations. No matter what our relationship, I would always respond to his visions. An artist's ability excited me: emotionally, intellectually, and in Robert's case, sexually.

But wanting him and having him were two different things. Of all the things I wanted, it was a life without any more grief. And I could not trust Robert to protect me from himself.

"You're not going to ask me what I think?" I asked Robert.

"I can see what you think from your face. Thank you," he said humbly.

I nodded. "These are guaranteed to get you more attention than you've ever had," I said.

"And more controversy?" he asked.

Robert had been taking photographs of our daughter since she was born—each one not only showed Lilly superimposed against an enchanting landscape but also revealed the terrain of a father's love.

Nevertheless when this new exhibit opened and the public found out these were photographs of his daughter, Robert would be under a new kind of scrutiny. He had a reputation for creating erotic images, but there really was nothing overtly sexual in the actual photos of Lilly, except that my daughter's legs were long and her skin was silken and her shoulders were suggestive on their own. Lilly's body was sensual and Robert's photographs showed that.

"Mom, do you think these are about sex?" Lilly asked.

"No. Of course not."

"So you'll come to the opening with us?" Lilly delivered what I now understood was the ultimate reason for this meeting.

"We need you with us. And we want you with us," Robert said in that way he had of stating something simply, with sincerity.

I need you and *I* want you, was the subtext in his eyes.

"Mom, if you're at the show, no one will think that there is anything suggestive about Dad's photographs."

"No, sweetheart. Some people will always see what they want to see, no matter what's really there."

"Like Cooper." She sighed.

"What did Cooper say?" I asked.

"I told him I was wearing a bodysuit, but he keeps saying I look naked. That everyone will *think* I'm naked. He's really upset."

"Cooper's seen these?" Now it was Robert's turn to be angry.

I'd warned Lilly not to show Cooper the photographs.

"I only showed him one contact sheet, but he got all weird. He wouldn't even talk about it for a while. And then finally he asked me a bunch of questions about how I felt when you were taking the shots and stuff like that. But after I explained it to him, he was all right about it."

"Lilly—when did you show him the photographs?"

"A couple of weeks ago when I went up to Yale."

"Goddamn it, I told you, no one sees the shots until we are finished with them and they are hanging in Iago's gallery."

Lilly's bottom lip quivered and her eyes filled with tears. It was bad enough that Robert and I fought with each other, she couldn't bear to create any more dissonance.

"I had the contact sheets with me because you and I were working on them and they were in my backpack and I was just so excited about them . . ."

Robert didn't let her finish the thought. "I don't ever want you to do that again. Jesus, Lilly, you can't show the pieces of these prints out of context. It's like asking someone to look at the foundation of a house and understand it."

"Do you think that's why Cooper freaked over them?" Lilly asked me. "Because what he saw was a work in progress?"

"Yes, I think so, sweetheart. But when he comes to the exhibition and he sees the finished montage, he'll understand," I assured her.

"So do you understand why you can only show someone the finished photographs, Lilly? Because once the shots are put together, there's no question about their intent, and—" Robert wasn't finished making his point about respecting the privacy of the work in progress.

"I'm hungry," Lilly interrupted. "Can we go eat?"

Unable to stay mad at his daughter for long, Robert grabbed his wallet and stuffed it in his jeans. "Are you coming with us, Jordan?"

"Yes, she is," Lilly answered for me, just in case I had been thinking about changing my mind.

This can't do any harm, I thought as I walked down the steps with them.

Except it could. It could keep me connected to them as a unit and keep me from moving on just as I was on the verge of finally breaking free.

At the restaurant, I looked from Robert to Lilly and realized they were, for better or worse, my family.

"It's the thin red cord . . ." Lilly was saying.

"What's the thin red cord? I'm sorry, I was thinking about something else," I said to Lilly.

"In Buddhist teachings there is a red cord that connects people to each other. It's a visualization of the concept of soul mates," she explained.

For a moment I was confused. It seemed as if Lilly were answering my unasked question, telling me why I still felt connected to Robert.

"Cooper gave it to me." She pulled back the cuff of her shirt and showed us the thin cord of blood-colored silk encircling her wrist.

She had been talking about her connection to Cooper, of course, not of mine to her father.

"Lilly, you are only seventeen . . ." Robert mused as he sipped a Bloody Mary.

"So?" she asked.

Robert stirred the tomato juice with a celery stalk. "And Cooper is nineteen—"

"Weren't you nineteen once?" Lilly interrupted.

Robert stole a glance at me; it was so intimate and revealing that I blushed remembering what I had been like at nineteen. What *we* had been like.

"Yes, I was nineteen once, and that's why I think it would be better if you played the field a little more, didn't get so entangled with one person. You do things with such intensity, and I'm afraid that Cooper—that no boy at nineteen is really ready for such a big commitment," Robert said.

She shrugged. "Cooper and I belong together, like you and Mom do."

"Lilly—" Even to me my voice sounded sad. "I know you wish it was different between your father and me, but it's not and you have to stop saying things like that every time we're together."

"No, she doesn't, Jordan . . ." Robert said my name almost too softly. I was embarrassed, but Lilly smiled. I turned to him, but he didn't say anything else. Not knowing what else to do, I picked up my fork, and took a mouthful of salad and began to eat.

We talked about Lilly's debut at Robert's show, her work at school, the new ad campaign Robert was shooting, and we talked about Cooper.

I was trying to be my daughter's parent and watch her face when she talked about her boyfriend: a seventeen-year-old has not yet learned that she has to hide her lust behind her eyes. Being with Lilly and Cooper together was even more uncomfortable; despite my presence they made no effort to refrain from constantly touching each other.

Although I remembered what it was like to be in heat, watching my daughter in the throes of it was different. I fled the room when she was with Cooper. I hid behind an open book when we were all in the living room together, and yet I couldn't stop myself from stealing looks at their intertwined hands and legs and how they had to lean against each other on the couch.

Over the years, I'd had numerous conversations with my daughter about safe sex, birth control, and the value of waiting until she was older before she slept with a man. But I knew all the conversations in the world wouldn't stop a seventeen-year-old if she was determined to have sex with her boyfriend.

I did, however, make a rule that when Cooper came over, he could only be in Lilly's room if the door was open. Cleverly, she had devised a way to obey my rule yet still get some privacy. She'd open her closet door all the way and close her bedroom door halfway so that my view inside her room was blocked. When I caught her doing it, I'd threatened to not let Cooper come back if she did it again, but part of me was thankful for the slightly closed door; I didn't want Lilly to disobey me, but neither did I want to accidentally walk by and see Cooper's hand on my daughter's breast or her lips on his mouth.

Robert and I had a phone conversation about the rules when the relationship between Lilly and Cooper became serious. We'd agreed that when Cooper came into New York to spend the weekend with Lilly, he would sleep upstairs in the studio, in the dark-room on a futon. We both hoped that Lilly wasn't having sex with Cooper and certainly didn't want to do anything to encourage it, but we also knew we were powerless to control them when we weren't around, and despite all our efforts, there were times when Robert went out and I was downstairs with patients.

Once I had come home at the end of the day to find them eating ravenously in the kitchen. My daughter's hair was damp, Cooper wasn't wearing a shirt, and they were both yawning.

I left the kitchen distressed; there was also something familiar about the scene but at the time I didn't know what it was.

Now, sitting across the lunch table from Robert, I remembered the afternoon his mother had walked in on the two of us. We had been so full of sex and naïve about knowing how to hide it that we chased her out of her own kitchen. Just as my own daughter and Cooper had done to me.

FIFTEEN

NYU students filled up Washington Square Park, playing Frisbee and in-line skating, while parents walked hand in hand with toddlers or pushed baby carriages. It was the kind of day that makes New York worth all the trouble.

We'd finished lunch and Lilly and I were walking down to SoHo to look for a Mother's Day present for my mother.

"I think we should get her a singing bowl." Anticipating my question, Lilly continued. "They ring it at the end of a Zen sitting, Mom."

I'd heard that slight exasperated edge to her voice but chose to ignore it.

"And I assume you know where we can get a singing bowl in SoHo?"

"There are three stores that sell Tibetan arts and antiques all within a block of each other off of Houston Street. They all have different ones."

"I was thinking, Lilly, maybe in August when I'm on vacation, I'll take some time and read one or two of the dozens of Zen books you have out at the house," I said. "Is there one you think I should start with?"

For my effort I got a surprised and pleased smile: I felt as if I'd been blessed.

"Why don't you go out to San Francisco and do a retreat with Grandma?" Lilly asked.

"Spas are too serene for me; imagine how I'd do at a retreat."

"But you would become aware. You'd wake up. You'd see what harm you're doing to your life and learn how to open up—"

"Lilly, can you just recommend a book?"

I was happy when she laughed instead of pouted. "Let me look through them. Some are easier to start with than others."

"That would be great." I smiled, delighted that we'd avoided yet another debate.

After crossing Houston Street, we turned right and walked up to Thompson and arrived at the first of the three Tibetan stores. I knew Lilly was going to inspect each store, making sure that the bowls in the first were as good as the bowls in the second and that the third didn't have something better. I prepared myself for the challenge of watching how my daughter went about choosing the perfect gift.

The days of allowing her to test each flavor of ice cream in Baskin-Robbins had led to this. I had nourished this trait and now was fated to endure it. Whether it was buying shoes or a new coat, Lilly insisted on going to several stores to make sure that there wasn't something better priced or more attractive just around the corner. If only she were as discerning about the men she chose.

Standing at the counter, my daughter carefully struck a small brass bowl with a wooden mallet, releasing a celestial sound. An angelic and otherworldly chord resonated, and in it I heard the sun rising.

In the case beneath the bowls were an array of beaded bracelets. "These are lovely," I said. "What are they?" I asked.

"Wrist malas," she answered. "People use them in meditation to help them stay centered, the way some people use mantras and others use breathing."

Eventually Lilly and I explored the next store and then the next but finally returned to the first store. While Lilly was buying the singing bowl, I went to look at the case of malas.

One was made of coral beads; another was made of ivory and carved bone with silver beads mixed in.

Lilly's birthday was in the middle of May. Perhaps I would take some of the stones I had at home in the safe and have a mala made for her. While Lilly was still occupied at the cash register, I asked the woman behind the counter if the beads needed to be of a certain material to be authentic. She said no, that they could be made of anything. "They don't have to be blessed or anything?" I asked.

"Nope. Just beads on a string. They are all very different. This one is over five hundred years old," she said, pulling out a coral strand. "Would you like to see it?"

"No, but thank you," I said, and hurried to the front of the store before Lilly came back to see what I was doing.

Afterwards we stopped for coffee at a café and then went on to Dean and Deluca, a gourmet grocery store on Broadway. Walking down the aisles, we looked at the fruits and vegetables artistically arranged in baskets and on shelves.

"Do you want some peaches?" I asked.

"One," she answered.

I took four.

"Will we eat all four? Why don't you just get two?" she asked.

"Because I like peaches."

Lilly's eyes never stopped moving as she assessed the array of colors and shapes. She wasn't seeing food anymore. Like her father, she saw the world and everything in it as a potential photograph.

My cellular phone rang, and I reached inside my bag and opened it.

"Hello?"

There was no answer except for that damned ticking sound.

"Who are you? Why don't you just tell me who you are and we can talk about this . . ."

Lilly was watching me, her eyes curious but not alarmed.

There was still no answer. I tried one last time. "Please tell me who you are." But when there was no response, I shut the phone and threw it back into my bag.

"Mom, why would someone keep hanging up?"

"I wish I knew. I think it might be a patient who's upset about something. I hope it's a patient."

"Why do you 'hope it's a patient'?"

"Because if it isn't, I'm going to start thinking it's Dan Mallory."

"You're still not giving him a chance, are you? Why can't you just believe that he's changed—"

I listened to her with half my attention while I continued to shop, choosing two fat red tomatoes, a head of bibb lettuce, a plump eggplant. At the pasta counter I bought some fresh pumpkin ravioli. At the cheese counter, a wedge of aged, golden Parmesan. My mouth was watering with the smells and anticipated tastes of the dinner I was putting together.

When we got to the cash register and Lilly saw the total, she was appalled.

"It's crazy to spend that kind of money on food. It's too extravagant," she said.

"We can afford it."

"That's not the point. It's about greed. About being aware of what things cost. You know, there's a Zen story about a very rich man who died and someone asked what he'd left. And someone else said—Everything. You can't keep it. You have to share it. It's not really ours."

I shot her a warning look.

The day had worked some magic—she smiled. "Okay, Mom, no lecture."

I yearned for the days we had fought over whether or not she could have a pair of two-hundred-dollar shoes that she wanted because her best friend had just gotten them. I had refused to buy shoes at that price for a teenager who was still growing, and Lilly had been furious with me. If only she wanted those shoes now, I would buy her two pairs.

That night after dinner, I went to the closet in my bedroom and opened the safe where I kept the treasures that my mother had given me when she sold the store, the pieces my father had made himself as well as the collection of raw stones and beads that he had been saving for years.

I cherished this hoard of jewels, even though I no longer thought I'd ever make jewelry again.

My dreams of working by my father's side had died along with my father, but I still imagined that one day I'd find a way to bring my father's designs to life.

Once or twice a year, when missing him was too hard to bear, I would take the precious and unique stones out of the darkness and revel in their tones and hues. The collection had been appraised and valued at over one hundred fifty thousand dollars, but I knew I'd never sell it. I got too much comfort knowing that whenever I needed to, I could look into the depths of those brilliant sapphires, rubies, and emeralds and for a moment, at least, feel close to my father again.

But that night, almost twenty years after my father had died, it was hard for me to touch the gems that he had handpicked and pored over without choking back tears.

Searching through the suede pouches, I finally found what I was looking for—a handful of smooth cabochon emeralds with a deep mystical glow to them.

Laying a chamois cloth on the top of my desk, I shook out the beads and inspected them as I had seen my father do dozens of times. These stones were all that was left of a very elaborate and extremely expensive necklace my father had bought long ago in India.

I didn't know what he had planned to do with them, but I was going to use them to make a birthday gift for his granddaughter.

I laid the beads out, counting as I went along, and found there were enough to make a wrist mala. But I needed something to hang from the end. Back in the vault, in another suede pouch, I found some of the tiny jade animals I didn't keep in the cabinet, including a frog, which Lilly had once told me was a Buddhist symbol.

"A frog just sits," she once had explained. "Just sits and is aware. The same way someone who practices Zen sits in meditation and becomes aware."

"Is that how you become enlightened?" I'd asked her.

"Oh, Mom, if you want to be enlightened," Lilly had answered, "just love."

I loved Lilly.

I would string the beads together and hang the frog from the end. I wouldn't dare tell my overly generous daughter what the stones were worth—if she knew, she might sell them to raise money to save Tibet or feed the homeless.

One day, I'd tell her. But for now, I'd just let her know that they had belonged to my father and that would ensure their safety. Lilly knew how precious my father's possessions were to me.

In a box of my father's supplies, I found dark green silk thread and began to string the beads. I tied a knot between each, as my father had taught me, but I was rusty. The silk was difficult to manipulate, and despite my initial efforts looking amateurish, I did not give up.

When had I last strung beads or pearls? The last summer that my father had been alive?

As I worked, I thought about my father. Not about how much I missed him, but about his artistry and his skill, and for the first time I realized that even though I had not become a jeweler like him, in a way I had followed in his footsteps.

My father had looked into stones and searched their internal landscapes for occlusions and flaws. I did the same with people and helped them to find the veins and fissures that caused difficulty and pain.

Lilly's mala sat on the chamois, gleaming in the soft glow of the lamp. I took it into my hands and, using it like a rosary, moved from one bead to the next. Rolling each irregular oval in my fingers, I wondered what my daughter thought about when she meditated. Did she see her own flaws and fissures? Or mine?

I wasn't completely sure I'd strung the mala correctly, but for now I wrapped it in soft tissue and put it inside a suede pouch that had the name of my father and mother's store embossed on it in tiny gold letters. With the tip of my finger I rubbed the words.

For a moment, I was back in the store breathing in the scent of the vanilla candles my mother burned and the pine oil my father used to sharpen his instruments. But then the air was full of the sick sweet smell of blood and the harsh smell of gunfire and flesh burns and then the sweat of the ambulance driver who picked me up and laid me on a stretcher and, mixed in with all the other smells, the incongruous scent of Joy perfume, which had been in my mother's bag and must have somehow broken in the melee.

My mother never wore her favorite scent again. And now almost twenty years later, just the slightest trace of that perfume made me gag and forced me to breathe through my mouth so that I wouldn't have to inhale the memories of the day my father died.

Putting down the suede pouch, I walked over to the window. I wanted the smells of the city street to fill the room and chase away the ghostly scents I was recalling. It took me several minutes to return from the past and refocus on the present scene of the street below me. Finally I saw that in the shadows, across the street, a man was staring up at my window.

I stepped back involuntarily but continued to look out, wondering if it was the same man I'd seen the other night from the restaurant; I just couldn't tell. Was it Dan Mallory? It was easy to think of him, just having had the jewels out. No, I was overreacting. It was a passerby stopping for a moment to admire the graceful sweep of our stone steps or notice the wisteria vine that was growing up the side of the building.

But I couldn't be sure. It might be Mallory. Watching me. Waiting for me. Trying to gauge when I went out or came in.

Picking up the phone, I called my brother, but he wasn't home. You're being paranoid, I told myself as the figure walked away and disappeared into the shadows. I looked at the clock. It was almost midnight. How long had it taken me to string the beads? How long had I been standing at the window?

I was willing to admit, at least to myself in the quiet darkness of that night, that I wished Robert were there with me, in the bed, waiting for me, listening and soothing me, and giving me his hand to hold while I fell sleep.

Except he was not there because I couldn't trust him and I couldn't trust myself with him. Wishing it were different wouldn't do me any good. One day, I might find someone to be with, but if that never happened, it would be all right—I had learned to live without a man and to be thankful for my friends and my family.

I lay down on my bed against the cool sheets and closed my eyes. But rather than being thankful for what I did have, I could only think about the warmth and comfort I was missing.

I wondered if Robert was home. Was he in his bed in his stark white studio staring up through the skylight at the night sky? Or was he out sharing some woman's bed, touching her body and bringing her pleasure?

It was none of my business. Although he was Lilly's father, he was no longer my mate. So why was it happening more and more that my thoughts—no matter how hard I pushed them away—they kept returning to Robert?

"Mom?" It was Lilly at my door. "Are you awake?"

"Yes, sweetheart."

She opened the door. Illuminated by the light in the hallway, she looked like a ghost in her white nightgown and with her wild wavy hair.

"I just wanted to thank you for going to lunch with Dad and me and for taking me shopping."

"You're welcome, Lilly."

"You know, sometimes Dad stares at you." She walked in and sat down on the edge of the bed.

"What do you mean?"

"Well, I guess I didn't understand it before—the way he looks at you, I mean—but I've seen the same look on Cooper's face when he looks at me."

"Oh, Lilly, it was so sweet of you to come in to thank me. Let's just enjoy the moment. Let's leave your father out of this conversation."

The air changed, her energy surged, her body language shifted. I had disappointed her and not followed her lead. She got up, turned, and walked away.

"Good night, Lilly," I called after her.

If she answered me, her voice was as soft as her footsteps in the carpeted hallway and I didn't hear her.

SIXTEEN

That Monday evening, when Adrienne Blessing arrived, she looked me over and raised her eyebrows. "You look awfully austere tonight. You're still wearing your hair in that chignon?" she said as she handed me a small shopping bag. Her chocolate brown velvet skirt cut her mid-thigh, the deep V of her sweater showed ample cleavage, and her suede boots stopped at the knee. Even from across the room, I knew how soft and supple they would be and how expensive.

As she settled herself on the couch, I took a sip of my iced tea and smelled a hint of peppermint. Immediately I was reminded of Robert and just as quickly forced my mind off him and onto my patient.

"Aren't you going to look at what I brought you?" Adrienne asked.

Opening the shopping bag, I glanced inside.

"Thank you for the strawberries; they look delicious."

She waved her hand, dismissing my thanks, lay down, closed her eyes, and without preamble leapt into a description of her weekend.

"We barely left the bed. You know, I've slept with hundreds of men, but I've never met anyone who fucks like this . . . like he loves me . . . but I don't know if I can trust that," she said.

"Do you realize you always come back to whether or not you can trust your own emotions? Why do you think that is?"

"Because I've never been faithful to any man for more than a few months. Not even the ones I thought I loved."

"Why?" I asked.

"I told you it gets boring. The sex becomes expected."

"How do you feel about being unfaithful?" I drank more of my tea.

"It never bothered me. In fact, sometimes, it's a thrill. I remember once I was out in LA on a shoot. Staying in the Beverly Hills Hotel. I'm such a hotel slut; I love the oversize beds, the anonymity of the room, the room service—just one big sexual playpen. Anyway, my lover had flown out as a surprise for the weekend, and I was glad to see him. Eric was good in bed, not amazing, but I could count on him. His cock was too big, though . . . not that it hurt . . . but it took him a long time to come and it actually got tedious after a while. I know everyone raves about size, but . . ."

Outside I heard a bicycle bell shrilly interrupt the quiet of the street, adding a jarring note to Adrienne's monologue.

"How does this connect to trust?" I wanted to get her back on track.

"The next day I had a meeting with the production company: the director, assorted personnel, and Mitchell, the cameraman. I had worked with him and slept with him on our last shoot. He was a wild man with a notorious reputation. He looked like a gypsy with his curly black hair, dark skin, and the small gold hoop earring he wore in one ear. You could tell just by looking at him that he loved women. You know the type?"

She was baiting me again. "Go on," I said.

"Mitchell was—is—a terrible flirt, and he kept making eye contact with me through the whole meeting, and afterwards he made sure he was in a convenient spot to stop me as I left. He said something about taking a drive with him, and I went. It didn't matter that someone who had flown out to be with me was waiting for me back at the hotel. I wanted to go with Mitchell. For the adventure. For the thrill.

"The next thing I knew I was with Mitchell in his car and his hand was on my leg and he was stroking my skin and we were driving on the Pacific Coast Highway with the sun beating down on us. He drove with one hand and played with me with the other. After a while of driving me crazy, he told me to pull off my underpants . . . I must have been wearing a skirt . . . and I did, and he took them and threw them out the car window and started to finger me. I remember how he glanced at the other drivers on the road to see who had noticed the flying panties.

"Mitchell sure knew what to do with his fingers . . . I must have had two or three orgasms in that car. And he just gave them to me . . . like presents.

"It wasn't too far to the house he rented on the beach, and when we got there he opened champagne and took out some cocaine and we got into bed and I went to work on him. He had the body of a swimmer and was tan and muscled. He had all the moves right. Not just the macho stuff. He knew how to nuzzle and whisper and kiss too.

"He took a slug of champagne at one point and put his lips against me and washed me with the wine . . . licking me clean when he was done.

"And the guy at the hotel? I just left him there. Didn't call, just forgot. I stayed with Mitchell for the rest of the day and the night. We stayed naked—just fucked and ate and swam and slept."

I wondered if she knew how her face looked; suffused with the memory of the lovemaking, her muscles were relaxed and there was a smug slant to her lips. Her breaths were coming more quickly; she was getting excited.

"Adrienne, how do you feel right now?"

"Am I making you jealous?" she asked.

"Adrienne, I asked how *you* felt."

"Can you imagine competing with a woman like me for a man? Any man?"

I rephrased the question I wanted her to answer. "What happens to you when you relive nights like that one with Mitchell?"

"I get horny. I want to leave here and get into bed with a man and get lost in all his smells and tastes."

"But what about sharing these private moments? How does that make you feel?" I asked.

"What does that have to do with anything?"

I didn't want to make her self-conscious, but I needed to under-stand why she talked about her sexual exploits to the exclusion of everything else. I guessed she was hiding something, and I wanted to know what that was. I needed to know in order to get to the next stage of therapy with her.

I changed the direction of my questions.

"Let's get back to the issue you are afraid of . . . if you give up all these men and concentrate on just one, what would happen?"

Adrienne took a while to respond and then only said: "I don't know . . ."

"First thing that comes to your mind?" I prompted.

"When I was a kid we had a cat and it was getting old, so my mother went out and brought home a new kitten. And when the older cat died, it was okay, because we had the kitten there to dis-tract us." Adrienne opened her eyes and tilted her head and looked at me for the first time since she had lain down on the couch. "Weird. Where did that come from?"

"A deep place. Let's talk about how that felt. To lose one cat, to have the other kitten. Was that a good thing?"

"Having the other kitten made it easier to not stay stuck in feeling sad for the one who had died. If I always have a man or two waiting in the wings, then I can leave when it's time and not have any kind of emptiness in between."

"But what would happen if you waited until it was past the time to leave? What would happen if you stayed?"

"First boredom so big and so vast that I'd lose myself in it. Then, I'd be alone." She crossed her arms over her chest.

"And if you are alone? What then? What will happen to you if you are by yourself?" I asked in a soft voice, trying to keep her cen-tered on her feelings.

"If I'm alone . . . I don't know, Dr. Sloan."

"If there's no excitement, no experimentation, if there is same-ness and empty spaces and silence, what will happen?"

"I'd have to think . . ." Her voice had dropped to a lower regis-ter. For the first time in therapy I saw her slip into a place where she was not editing what she was saying. "I'd have to think about how alone I was and then I would disappear," she whispered.

Good, we'd gotten someplace.

"Disappear? What do you mean?" I asked her.

"You don't exist unless someone else can see you. Did you ever look in the mirror long enough that your face turns into a stranger's face? In the dark, you can turn any stranger's face into a lover's face. I'm never worried about disappearing when I'm wrapped up in a man's arms, pinned to the bed by his legs. I am certain that I will never disappear again. But in the morning, in the light, I want to go prowling again. To look for the backup cock, to get it ready, to have it waiting."

"Have you ever disappeared? When were you ever invisible?" I asked.

Adrienne laughed. "It's ridiculous; I'm so in-your-face I could never be invisible." She had snapped out of the moment. "This isn't why I'm here, to talk about this sophomoric shit."

"Feel it, Adrienne; don't think it. Where were you, how old were you, it didn't matter what you looked like or what you wore or what you said . . . when was the last time you disappeared?"

She didn't move. Said nothing. I heard a woman calling out to someone on the street. I waited. Adrienne's breath came faster. Outside a car door slammed.

And then Adrienne broke. A wounded animal sound—halfway between a whimper and a cry escaped from her lipsticked mouth. Her face didn't crumple; her nose didn't get red. She was crying from inside her chest; it didn't get further than her throat. Dry, hard sobs. She was lovely even as she wept.

"My father . . . when he drank . . . when he came home from work and sat down with my mother and drank . . . then he couldn't see any of us, and he yelled and screamed, and you couldn't reason with him because he wasn't rational anymore, he was drunk."

"Okay, that's okay. That's good. Now we know."

"I disappeared," she said in a childlike voice.

"Yes, you did. Do you think that might be part of the reason you always want another man in the wings, so that when the one you are with disappoints you, you can flee?"

"This isn't why I came here . . ." She had opened her eyes again and was staring at the ceiling. She seemed stunned.

"No? Why did you come here?"

"To talk to you about my lover."

"I still want to hear about your father when he drank. About how it felt to have him leave you for a bottle of what was it—scotch, gin?"

Her armor was back on. "It happened a long time ago. It was bad. Now it's over."

"Yes, it's very bad when your father leaves you. It's awful, especially when he leaves you voluntarily. It's even worse than if your father dies when you are a child—if he died, that would have been out of his control, you couldn't really blame him. But your father knew he was drinking and he knew that was hurting you and he did it anyway."

"Yes. It all comes down to the fucking pain we feel, doesn't it? No matter what we do we just can't escape it."

"No, Adrienne, we can't escape it. And when we try to, it just winds up controlling our lives. We have to accept that there is the pain and that there is also pleasure, and try to find a balance between the two."

She hesitated for a moment. "You know, my father didn't know he was hurting us," Adrienne said defensively.

"Yes, and that makes it even harder for a child to understand." My voice was soothing. However your father leaves—if it is because he drinks or because someone kills him—ultimately all that matters is that he is gone.

"I'm going to get married," Adrienne blurted out. "And you are going to help me."

"How?" I asked.

"You are going to help me get rid of the obstacles in my way."

"And then what will happen?" I asked.

"I will be this man's wife. I want that. I act like I don't. But I do."

"What is 'that'?" I asked.

"I want to know the comfort of being a couple. Of climbing towards a future together. Even if it is an illusion, I want to be able to count on someone—just a little bit."

Adrienne had surprised me with the sudden warmth in her voice. I had known it was in there. It was in everyone. We are all like those Russian dolls, our secret selves hidden inside our secret selves. And we are all so good at keeping the most vulnerable ones hidden from view.

"I don't want to be restless anymore. I've had it with being the predator." Adrienne sighed. "Surviving on your own is hard work. Being lonely is exhausting. I'm tired of living alone in the world no matter who I'm with and missing someone who isn't there for me anymore and maybe never was."

Of all the patients I'd ever had—this one who resembled me the least, who spoke in a way that set my nerves on edge, who fucked her way through life, and who if I met outside of my office, I would not befriend—she was the one I had connected to the most.

A patient like Adrienne can be dangerous for a therapist. If I began to identify with her, it would get in the way of my treating her.

"It's time," I said, closing my notebook to signal the end of our session.

"You have no fucking idea how right you are," she responded.

I stayed in the office for a while doing some paperwork. Since Lilly was at a friend's house working on a school project, there was no reason to rush upstairs. When I finally stood in the hallway locking my office for the night, I heard a key in the front door. Checking my watch, I knew it was too early to be Lilly; it must be Robert. If I started walking up the stairs right away, I wouldn't have to see him, but if I stayed, if I lingered, then . . .

He smiled as soon as he saw me. "Hey there . . ."

Even the simplest words can be invested with meaning if they are part of your history. My response to Robert's familiar greeting was visceral: here was my husband arriving home at the end of the day. Bypassing logic or reason, I reacted emotionally and took a step forward to kiss him hello.

And then I stopped myself.

Robert leaned against the door in his lazy way. He had noticed what I'd started to do and then not done, and now he was waiting for me to say something.

For so many years I had avoided looking at him, but in that moment I took in the full measure of what I had walked away from.

"Do you want a cup of coffee or a glass of wine?" I asked.

"Something up with Lilly?"

Of course he would still assume I wanted to talk to him about Lilly. Despite the few times we'd been alone in the last two weeks, she was still what connected us.

"No, she's at Wendy's. She's fine. I just thought . . . Never mind . . ." Suddenly embarrassed, I took a step towards the staircase.

Robert stepped forward, reached out, and held me back. Even through my sweater, I felt his fingers hot on my skin.

"Yes. A glass of wine. I'd love one," he said.

He followed me upstairs and stood in the doorway a moment. Robert didn't live here anymore. He didn't come here to see his daughter; she climbed twenty steps to see him. It had been a long time since Robert had been inside the apartment where he and I had lived together for twelve years. Yet, he sat on the couch, not like a guest, but like he was home. And I fumbled with a bottle of wine and the corkscrew. Finally, taking it from me, he uncorked it and filled two glasses. We sat for a few minutes in silence.

"Any news about Mallory?" he asked.

I shook my head no. There was an awkward pause, and without any editing, I told him what I was thinking. "You know, I don't know you anymore really, except as Lilly's father. Isn't that strange? You have a whole life that is separate from mine, and I don't know anything about it."

"No, Jordan. You still know me; you always have."

I shrugged. "I'm not so sure."

"Well, even if you don't know me, I know myself pretty damn thoroughly." He laughed sardonically. "I've spent the last five years learning about why I've done everything I've ever done."

I nodded. "Five years, yes, that's the magic number all the therapists use. That's how long a cure takes. Has your therapist told you that?"

And then I realized I never should have asked him that. "I'm sorry, it's none of my business."

"Of course it is. And, yes, he has told me that. And I'm the one who should apologize. For what I did, back then, to us. It's no excuse, but my fooling around was a stupid response to being jealous. You'd become so self-sufficient, so successful—your patients were all in love with you—it all sounds like so much bullshit now, but I was just trying to find the woman who you'd been. I know it's no excuse, but I missed the nineteen-year-old whose whole life centered around me and—"

"I don't want to go back there—" I couldn't open up those old wounds again and watch them bleed. "Robert, I've been to see a divorce lawyer."

His body jerked back as if I had struck him, but I continued talking, not willing to acknowledge the discomfort I was causing him. "Maybe it's time we did this for Lilly's sake. And for ours. We both need to have fuller lives and show our daughter that we can make other lasting connections. Prove to her that love isn't some terrible hurtful thing."

"Is that what you think we've shown her, Jordan?"

"Isn't it?" I asked.

"Look at her. She's in love—with the wrong guy, as far as I'm concerned, but then again, that's what fathers always think—she's happy. Obviously she's not afraid to get involved with a man."

"But she's not just dating Cooper; she's disappearing into this Zen thing with him. Do you know that last week she gave away half her possessions to a charity? She and I argue constantly . . ." I said. "I'm afraid I can't reach her anymore."

"Jordan, don't you remember what it was like with you and your mother when you were Lilly's age?"

"But my mother was different; she didn't understand anything about me."

Robert didn't say anything; he gave me a minute to realize what I'd said. When I started to laugh, he joined in.

"Don't worry so much about Lilly. You've done a wonderful job as a mother, Jordan." Robert lifted his wineglass in a silent toast. I watched his Adam's apple move and stared at the golden skin where his shirt was open at the collar.

"But Lilly's too trusting. She's going to get hurt because of it and feel all kinds of pain," I said.

"You can't save the world, Jordan."

"She's not the world; she's my daughter."

"You still can't solve her problems for her. You can only show her the way and be there for her if she gets lost. Like you were for me."

"But I wasn't—I left you." I didn't understand what he was trying to say.

"I deserved nothing, yet you were still gentle with me," Robert said.

Moving closer he put his hand on mine.

I leaned forward and kissed him lightly; a gesture of gratefulness because he had always known how to listen to me.

And then, not lightly at all, Robert kissed me back.

Until that moment I had not admitted how very much I'd been wanting him since we'd kissed in the restaurant the week before.

He held my face between his hands and traced the outline of my lips with his tongue. I wanted to lose myself in this, not think about what had happened before or what was going to happen after. Just this—to live on the edge of his lips. And suddenly I thought of Lilly's lecture about being aware, and I knew this was what she meant. This one moment was the only thing that was real and that mattered. We could have been undressed and naked and in bed and he could be inside me and we would not have been able to get any closer.

"Jordan . . ."

He said my name as if he were reminding himself of something important.

I looked at him, not sure of how to respond.

"No, you don't have to say anything now. You talk too much anyway," Robert said with that smile that let me know he was half joking and half serious. "We can talk about it all later. Just sit here and be still and be glad for things that endure despite time and logic."

He put my head against his chest, and I rested there, listening to his heart beating and his breath going in and out of his body, and I tried to quiet my ever-questioning mind.

We kissed again for a long time, and somewhere during that kiss, I moved my hand inside Robert's shirt and touched his bare skin. A sigh escaped from between his lips.

My fingers made circles on his chest, and he kissed me again. I knew that he was allowing me to set the pace.

Unbuttoning my own blouse, I put his hand on my breast. His fingers immediately curled to hold me, and I felt his erection against my leg.

Like two teenagers, we touched each other for a long time, as if that preliminary touching was all we were allowed. And it was enough. Lovemaking with someone who could see inside your soul was more than pleasurable: it was joyful and life affirming. The emotions and sensations and connections it generates can be transporting.

"Lilly should be home any minute," I finally said. "We should stop."

Robert smiled. "Quite a role reversal we have here, my dear. The parents worried about getting caught by the teenager."

I laughed.

Robert kissed me on the forehead and got up to go. "If you want to, call me later."

"Call you . . ." More words that were loaded with memories. When I'd been in college and he was in New York, we used to make love on the phone when there was no other way for us to be together. "Do you mean the way we used to?"

"I mean call me any way you want, Jordan. Take your time, sweetheart," he said, and then let himself out.

I remained on the couch, looking at the two empty glasses and the rings of condensation that had pooled on the glass coffee table. And when I heard the downstairs door open and close and Lilly's footsteps on the stairway, I got up quickly, put the glasses and the wine bottle in the kitchen, and hurried into my bedroom.

I had needed to know Lilly was home and safe, but I didn't want her to look into my face because I was afraid of what my all-too-wise daughter might read there.

For the first time in a very long time, I got into my bed naked and felt the sheets against my thighs, my stomach, my breasts. I touched my skin and it was hot. And then without thinking about it or weighing it or deciding whether or not it was a good idea or a bad idea or a risk, I picked up the phone and dialed Robert's phone number.

"Hello."

"Hi," I whispered.

"I was hoping you'd call." His voice resonated in my chest like a musical chord.

I held my breath.

"And I'm glad you called." Robert could be so generous with his words.

"Are you?" I asked, feeling suddenly shy.

"Yes."

"Why?"

"I've been missing you for years; I didn't want to miss you tonight," he answered.

I held my breath again, as if by not breathing I would be able to hold his words inside my body and believe every one of them.

"Robert . . . I'm not sure of anything . . . I mean all this time I've been so certain that we—"

"Jordan?"

"Yes . . ."

"Don't think about it now. Don't question it. Just tell me how you feel."

I laughed. "You sound like me."

"I know."

"Robert?"

"I'm here, sweetheart."

My voice caught in my throat. "Are you in bed?" I asked.

"Yes."

"Are you undressed?"

"Not yet. Do you want me to get undressed, Jordan?" He was smiling; I could hear it in his voice.

I felt brazen. "Yes. I want to take you in my hand. I love holding you and stroking you and having you grow hard because of the way I'm touching you." I was shocked at my own words.

"Yes, you can do that, with just one finger, you can do that."

"I'm touching myself," I told him.

"Yes? Tell me."

"I'm rubbing myself. I'm all wet and slippery and imagining that they're not my fingers but yours," I said.

"Those are my fingers. I'm stroking you very lightly, just the way you like it, and I can feel the waves of heat coming from between your legs. God, you are hot, aren't you?"

"Yes. . . . I want you to kiss me while you are touching me. Kiss me like you did tonight."

"Do you want me inside of you?" he asked.

"Yes . . . now, please. But I want you to go in slowly, very slowly."

"I keep my hand on you and keep massaging you . . . so that you don't know which feels better, my penis inside of you or my fingers . . ."

The orgasm wasn't a slow build, but an eruption of molten lava exploding inside of me. The phone lay nestled in the crook of my neck. I moaned just loud enough so that Robert could hear me. Still in the throws of my orgasm, I heard his moan follow: harder and louder than mine.

We both were breathing erratically when his voice brought me back to wakefulness: "What?"

"I said that was wonderful. You were falling asleep, weren't you?" He laughed.

"Yes, Robert." I liked saying his name. "I was falling asleep, and yes, Robert, it was wonderful."

"I'll talk to you tomorrow. Good night, Jordan."

SEVENTEEN

The next morning I lingered in bed, half awake but still dreaming about the night before and expecting that any minute I'd start feeling guilty or, even worse, foolish about what I'd done. But it wasn't until I was sitting in the kitchen with a cup of coffee that I acknowledged what I was feeling—fear. Could I risk trusting Robert to be mindful of my heart?

But maybe he's changed, Lilly would have told me if she'd known what I was thinking. One thing was certain, I wouldn't pursue a relationship with Robert in order to please Lilly. I would have sacrificed my life for my daughter, but I would not endure another betrayal for her.

I sat thinking about what I had said and done on the phone with Robert and a half hour passed in what seemed like minutes.

At ten-forty-five, with three hours until my next patient, I took a taxi uptown to Forty-seventh Street and Sixth Avenue so I could show Lilly's mala to the woman who had strung pearls for my father and make sure I had done it right.

Herta opened the door and looked at me through her bifocals for a few seconds until she figured out who I was. *"Mein Gott!* Look at you. All grown up you look just like your mother!" She threw her heavy arms around me and clasped me to her chest.

After she had introduced me to the three other stringers who shared the space, I showed Herta the mala, explaining that I wanted to be certain I'd strung it correctly.

"You're rusty," she said in her thick accent. "Ach! Look how tight you did this. And on the frog . . . What kind of knots are these?"

Herta pulled out some green silk, and while I watched, she restrung the mala in less then ten minutes.

I liked that my father's stringer was stringing my daughter's prayer beads. It kept alive even more of a connection between the past and the future. I kissed Herta good-bye and tried to give her money, but she shooed me out the door.

Downstairs, I walked through the booths looking at the cases glittering with every conceivable kind of jewelry. My father used to come to buy his diamonds from one of these merchants. I remembered the wizened Hasidic Jew who spoke English with a thick Yiddish accent, not unlike Herta's. His black suit was always wrinkled; he smelled slightly sour and was very old.

"But he has the diamond eye," my father explained when I complained about how odd the man was.

Before I was old enough to understand the expression, I took it literally and would stare at the diamond merchant intently whenever my father brought me along on a buying excursion.

Finally, one afternoon, the old man asked me why I was staring at him.

"I want to know which of your eyes is the diamond one?" I'd asked.

Years later, it was that Hasid who recommended Dan Mallory to my father: "Mr. Sloan, the boy has a diamond eye!"

The ghost of my father walked with me down one aisle and up the next, and before I could stop them, tears blurred my vision.

The walls behind the booths were mirrored, and as I walked towards the exit, I noticed a man in a baseball cap who seemed to be following me. Walking more slowly, I looked down, pretending to inspect the cases that glittered in the harsh overhead light, but when I raised my eyes one second later, he had disappeared.

I shivered. Was this the same person who had been standing outside of my brownstone? And if it was, who could it be but Dan Mallory? Who else would be following me except him?

Nothing that I could remember about Mallory could help me now. He had been lean but muscular with long hair when he worked for my father, then thin with a crew cut at the trial. My last memories of Mallory sitting in the courtroom did not even correspond to the man I'd been dating behind my father's back—so how could I possibly recognize him now? What was his nose like? What shape was his face? The lines ran together; the colors were smudged. Our brains do not hold faces well over the years. How often did I look at snapshots of my father to bring him back into focus and see him clearly again?

Stop it, I said to myself, as I held on to a glass counter and waited for my heart to stop banging against my ribs.

"Can I help you?" asked the proprietor of the booth where I had stopped.

"No, I'm just looking," I said.

And I was, but not for anything in his case: I was looking for the man in the shadows and the man in the mirror.

Out on the street I pulled out my phone and called Lilly's school.

"She missed a dentist's appointment," I ad-libbed. "And I wanted to check that she just forgot and make sure nothing is wrong."

"I just saw her in the lunchroom. Do you want to talk to her, Dr. Sloan?"

"No, that's fine. I'll talk to her when she gets home. Thank you."

I walked another half a block, but I still wasn't any calmer. I needed to talk to someone who wouldn't think I was crazy to be so worried, and so I called Chloe.

After listening to me and reassuring me, she suggested I meet her at a Japanese restaurant a few blocks away. "We can have lunch. And some sake. I think we could both use it," she said.

Suddenly, I remembered that she'd met with the film director the day before.

"You had your interview . . . Was it that bad?"

"No, it was that good. I'll tell you when I see you."

On the way to the restaurant, I used the phone once more to call my machine. There was one message, but when I played it back, instead of someone speaking, I heard a recording of a popular song I'd listened to in my college days. "You've got me thinking of you . . . always . . . every day every night . . . and when I'm thinking of you . . . always . . ."

Five minutes later, Chloe and I were sitting in a corner of a Japanese restaurant, drinking sake and waiting for our sushi. I had just played my phone message for her.

"I think Mallory left that song on my machine."

"I know you do. But I think that after spending all those years in prison, he'd be so relieved to get out and get on with his life that he'd want to go forwards, not backwards."

"But sometimes you have to go backwards *before* you can go forwards."

"Let me just play devil's advocate here. Isn't there anyone else who knew you back then who would know you liked that song?"

"Chloe, why would someone call me out of the blue and—" But I had thought of someone who knew that song. And Chloe had thought of him at almost the same time as I did.

"Could it have been Robert?" she asked.

And despite everything else that happened that day, and how old I was, and how silly it made me feel, I blushed.

Our food came and while we ate, I gave Chloe an abbreviated version of what had transpired between Robert and me the night before.

"If John had ever been unfaithful, could you ever trust him again?" I finally asked her.

"Have you heard something I should know about?" she joked.

"Of course not."

Chloe stared down at a piece of fresh salmon on its bed of rice. "I think it would depend on whether it was a fling or a real love affair." She speared the piece of fish. "God knows, this is not the time for me to be judgmental about anyone else's extramarital affairs."

"Tell me what happened yesterday." I was glad to listen to her story rather than spend any more time on mine.

"Max Brecht is not and could never be a harmless flirtation. He is too smart, too intuitive, and much too sexy." She stopped talking and looked down at her food again.

"And so you are going to—"

Chloe drank what was left of her sake and then laughed. "Never see him again or meet him tomorrow for drinks. I know what I should do . . . but I'm having trouble reconciling it with what I'm dying to do. He is just so damn tempting. But then I think about John, and I get very nervous." She smiled at me. "Tell me to stay away from him, Jordan."

"Will you listen?"

"I'll try."

We both laughed.

"Tell me something to scare me out of seeing him again."

"Okay. Most female patients don't leave when they find out their husbands are cheating on them. They make excuses, blame themselves, and turn the other cheek. But when men find out that their wives are cheating . . . they usually do leave."

"We're wimps. We have such lousy self-esteem we blame ourselves and worry that if we left, we'd never find anyone else."

"I left," I said softly.

"Yes, but you were different. You knew you could support yourself," she said. "And you were still young. There was no reason for you to settle for a situation that you found deplorable."

I toyed with a slice of tuna that had fallen off its rice pillow. Would staying with Robert and trying to work out our problems really have been settling?

"Do you think I did the right thing?" I asked.

Chloe looked at me and then at the way I was playing with the chopsticks and not eating.

"You did what you thought was right."

"But do you think it was right?" I asked.

"I can't presume to know. But from what you told me at the time, it sounded like you did the right thing. And I have enormous respect for how you did it—no fights, no ugly scenes. You didn't take Lilly away from Robert and you didn't change her environment."

"When I met with Laurie Gold, she said something to me that keeps resonating in my head. I was telling her how I thought it was time for me to go through with the divorce because I was setting a bad example for Lilly, living like a nun, not making an effort to meet anyone else—"

"Jordan, if you want to tell that to Laurie Gold, fine. But if you want to talk to me about whether or not you are going to get divorced, if we are going to have this conversation, let's have it honestly. Don't hide behind Lilly. You don't have a relationship with a man and haven't had one for five years, because you can't find anyone who measures up."

"But my father wasn't that perfect and my parents didn't have an ideal marriage."

Chloe burst out laughing and pushed away her plate. There was a piece of salmon roe sushi left, the orange eggs glistening in the overhead lights.

"Are you going to eat that?" I asked, chopsticks poised for her answer.

"No," she said, and my sticks swooped down to claim it. Safely in my mouth, I bit down onto the liquid-filled eggs and tasted salt and the sea.

"It isn't your father no one matches up to, you nitwit; it's Robert."

"But Robert cheated on me. He was unfaithful. How tough is that to measure up to?"

"Jordan, how can you sit in your office and make sense of other people's lives but understand so little about your own?"

A waitress gently placed two cups of green tea down in front of us. I watched the steam waft into the air and then dissipate.

"Do you want that tea?" she asked.

"No. I know you're dying for a cigarette. Let's go."

While we stood outside and Chloe lit her cigarette, I noticed there were tiny pink blossoms on the trees in front of the restaurant. Early spring was the best time of the year in the city; winter's chill was gone and flowering trees broke up the monotony of the buildings.

"So, are you going to see Max again?"

"I won't see him as long as you promise you will see Robert again."

"You nut, you mean you won't if I will?"

It was a relief to be laughing.

In the taxi on the way back downtown, I took Lilly's birthday gift out of my bag and touched the cool emerald beads and wondered what she would do with them. Where would her meditation take her? The ringing of my cellular phone interrupted my thoughts. Apprehensively, I answered it.

"Hello?" There was no answer, only that infernal ticking. "Who the hell is this?" I asked, even though the last thing I expected was an answer.

"I'm a ghost." The voice was mechanically altered and therefore unrecognizable. It froze my blood. "You look right through me all the time, Jordan. But I'm watching over you and your daughter and keeping you from harm. I'm everywhere. Outside of restaurants, in doorways, behind the trees, and in all the old haunts."

And then, before I could breathe, before I could say a word, the line was disconnected.

When I got home, I raced up the stairs, quickly locked the door behind me, and called my brother. "Did you get the number he was calling from?" This time Simon didn't try to reassure me.

"No, it was blocked," I said.

"Let me call Rafferty. If there's a problem, he's in a position to do something."

I had five minutes until my next session started.

I checked that Lilly was home and found her on the phone with Cooper, and then returned downstairs to let in my next patient.

Just as I shut the door behind me, Simon called back.

He hadn't had to call Mallory's parole officer; Jim Rafferty had called him.

"Jordan, Dan Mallory has disappeared. No one knows where he's gone."

EIGHTEEN

The rest of the week passed slowly as thoughts of Dan Mallory slipped in and filled up every empty slot I had between patients, and by Friday I was distracted and exhausted.

When I finally finished for the day and went upstairs, I was surprised to find Lilly packing a duffel bag. Seeing the confusion on my face, she reminded me of the trip she'd planned with Wendy and another friend weeks before.

"I'm going to a retreat; did you forget, Mom?"

All the clothes she was going to take with her for the weekend were folded and laid out on her bed. Two T-shirts, an extra pair of jeans. Some shampoo, toothpaste, and her purple toothbrush. A bar of oatmeal soap, her rock crystal deodorant, underpants, a tube of mascara, and a tube of lipstick.

"Is that all you're taking?" I asked. There was something so forlorn about the meager pile.

"It's a meditation weekend, not a party."

"I know, but it still doesn't look like you're taking enough."

"That's only because you are comparing it to what you take when you go away. I don't need four pairs of shoes for a retreat in the mountains," she said, and put the pile of T-shirts into the bag.

"Lilly, I don't take that many shoes."

"No? When we went to California at Christmas, you took six pairs."

"Okay, so I have a problem with shoes. I need to have the right shoes for each outfit."

"I know. I'm not criticizing you; it's just that no one wears shoes when they meditate." Lilly went over to a drawer and pulled out some socks, then turned and smiled at me.

"See, if I hadn't said anything, you wouldn't have had any socks."

Lilly laughed and went into the bathroom and came out with her hairbrush, mousse, and conditioner. Inwardly I was relieved. At least she was still obsessed with her hair. My daughter had pared her life down to such an extreme I was happy for whatever excesses she still had.

Finally, she opened her camera bag and began to check its contents.

"You're taking your camera?" I asked, and then answered before she had a chance to. "Then, when have you not taken your camera? I'm sure you'll take it with you when you walk down the aisle and into the birthing room when you have your first child."

"Dad did," she said.

"I know, sweetie, but he wasn't the one giving birth."

"Mom, can I take your phone?" Lilly asked.

"Aren't there phones at the retreat?"

"Yeah, but they're only for emergencies. I won't be able to call Cooper from those phones."

"Maybe you should follow the rules. Perhaps there is a good reason for you not to use the phone."

"You're suggesting I take the retreat *more* seriously?" She looked at me askance. "Oh, I get it; it's about Cooper." Lilly sat down on the edge of the bed and smoothed out the bedspread in a circular movement. "Mom, what is it about Cooper? Why don't you like him?"

While she waited for my answer, she picked up her sweater and started to stroke it as if it were a pet. It was a gray cashmere sweater that I had bought for Robert in Italy years ago. At ten, Lilly had appropriated the sweater and made it her security blanket. Sometimes it was stuffed in her backpack. Other times it was tied around her waist or her neck. But it was always nearby.

My seventeen-year-old daughter shouldn't still need her security blanket. But many children of broken homes had lingering insecurities and separation anxieties. I hoped one day she would forgive us the damage we'd caused her when we'd failed to keep our marriage intact.

"Oh, hon, we've gone over this before. It isn't that I don't like him . . ." I hesitated. It was important how I answered her. I didn't want to have another fight with her just as she was about to leave for the weekend. "You're just so young to be so serious about one boy."

"I'm not the type to date a lot of different guys."

"I know, but this way you are making Cooper so important in your life that if it doesn't work out, you're going to be devastated. I don't want you to get hurt like that."

"What makes you think he's going to hurt me? Maybe I'll be the one to hurt him. I think this is really about the fact that *you* made Dad too important in your life and that *you* don't trust people—you especially don't trust *yourself*."

I laughed. "Goodness, Lilly, you've gotten really good at taking on the role of my therapist. Here I was talking about you, and suddenly we're analyzing me."

"I'm just pointing out the truth, Mom. Just because you have chosen to think the worst of people and doubt everyone doesn't mean I have to adopt your negative attitude."

But I had proof that people—especially men—shouldn't be trusted; she didn't. I had been burned; she was still unscarred.

"All I'm suggesting is that you occasionally see other boys too. I don't want you to be suspicious of people. That's not what I'm saying. It's simply not wise to fall in love so fast and become exclusive right away. You are so open to him; you don't hold anything back. I wish you'd protect yourself a little."

"No, that's what you do—you protect yourself too much, and I think you are just as wrong for doing it as you think I am for not doing it."

I sighed. It didn't matter what I said, Lilly was as certain of her opinion as I was of mine.

She shrugged. "You'll see, Mom. One day you'll see."

"Nothing would make me happier than if you were right and I was wrong."

"Then change. Cooper says you attract negativity by thinking negatively."

I held my tongue. It's a stage, I said to myself. She will outgrow this fascination with Cooper and Zen philosophy. She will lose some of her fervor and let go, and we will not always be adversaries facing each other across a wide divide.

"I'll go get you my phone," I said. "Except, I'm still getting those strange calls, and I don't want you to have to deal with them."

"We can set up a signal." It was a game to her, but then she hadn't heard that awful mechanical voice or the ominous message. "You can call, let it ring once, then hang up and call right back. I'll tell Cooper too."

In my bedroom, I grabbed my bag, pulled out the phone, and walked back to Lilly's room. It wasn't the best solution, but at least using a signal, Lilly wouldn't be subjected to the disturbing calls.

Lilly left an hour later for her weekend retreat, and while it was still light out, I decided to go jogging and take the dog with me. Since Dan Mallory had disappeared, I'd given up walking the dog after dark and instead let her out in the enclosed courtyard at the back of the brownstone. But there was at least an hour until the sun started to set and I needed to get some exercise.

Out on the street I stretched my legs on the stoop and noticed that the lights were off upstairs in Robert's studio. He'd gone away for the weekend on a shoot in Southampton, Long Island. He'd asked me to go, but I'd said no. A weekend was more time than I'd spent with him in over five years; I was frightened we were moving too fast.

When I got home, the phone was ringing.

"Any news on Mallory?" Robert asked.

Since I had told him about the song on my machine and the mechanical voice, he'd been checking in with me a few times a day.

"No, nothing yet."

"They'll find him, Jordan."

"I know," I said with a bit more confidence than I felt.

"I called before, but you were out."

"I was just out walking the dog. Lilly left for the weekend," I said.

"I know. I talked to her before she left."

I sat down on the couch, picked up one of the velvet cushions, and hugged it to my chest. "So, what's new?" I asked.

"You, baby."

We had fallen back into all our old familiar shorthand, those odd, nonsensical phrases couples adopt that connect them to each other. When we were dating and then later living together, whenever Robert had called me, I'd always asked him what was new and he'd always answered with that phrase, *You, baby.*

It had been so long since I'd heard that particular expression, and suddenly I wondered how many other women had heard it in the last few years.

"Do not think about the other men your wife knew before you met her," I had once told a patient. "Each time your mind starts to go there, take three deep breaths and come back to the present. You can't do anything about the past, and by focusing on it, you are losing your chance for any happiness in the here and now."

Either I should take my own advice or I shouldn't talk to Robert—not if this was what it was going to do to me.

". . . everything went great today and I finished up early, but I've still got this wonderful cottage for the whole weekend, so I was wondering if you might reconsider my offer and drive out. We could go to the beach in the morning, go out to dinner, relax."

"Well, I . . ." I hesitated.

"I'm sorry; do you have other plans, Jordan? I don't want this to be awkward for you. Lilly told me you weren't doing anything."

So Lilly had been playing matchmaker again.

"I knew I never should have dressed that child up as cupid for Halloween when she was eight. She's never gotten over it."

Laughing, Robert said: "I don't know . . . I think she's pretty good at it. So what do you think, Jordan? Come on, I'd love to spend the weekend with you."

I looked around the empty room and saw the weekend stretching out before me. I knew if I stayed here I would only obsess about Dan Mallory.

"Can I bring the dog?"

At eleven that night I pulled into the parking lot of the Southampton Inn. I could smell the salt in the air and hear the waves crashing on the beach. Robert had said there was a main building but that he was in one of the cottages on the beach.

Robert must have been waiting for me, because he came out to the car while I was taking out my overnight bag. It was the same size as my daughter's duffel bag, but while hers was half empty, mine was overstuffed. I could have packed less if I had had more time to think about what I'd need, but I had been too nervous to keep my mind on clothes.

I am going to be spending the night with Robert—the thought made me shiver. But if I was thrilled, I was also apprehensive. I couldn't afford to make the same mistake again; it would destroy the relationship I'd had with Robert over the last few years, and I didn't want to do that to Lilly.

After dropping my bag at the cottage, Robert and I took the dog for a walk on the beach. Barefoot, wearing an oversize white cashmere sweater and jeans, I luxuriated in the feel of the sand between my toes and the mist on my face. Good raced up ahead sniffing the ocean smells, and as we strolled by the sea, Robert described the job he'd just finished shooting for a new perfume called Waves.

"The whole idea was to create a classic but still provocative message."

"Well, at least they chose the right photographer."

"Why, thank you. But it's been nothing but torture from the beginning. The creative director is close to a genius but damn difficult to work with."

Good raced back and dropped an errant tennis ball at our feet. I rubbed her head, praised her, threw it, and she took off again.

"What was the problem?" I asked.

"She wanted me to work with an old 1940s art film, which unfortunately was shot on nitrate film and practically falling apart. I've had to learn all about how to handle it. I now know more about nitrate film than I ever wanted to."

"What are you doing with the old footage?"

"Taking stills from it and superimposing them over the footage I've shot out here on the beach. A nude in black-and-white and the waves in color—all kind of unreal and arresting."

"It sounds wonderful. . . . When can I see it?"

I was listening and at the same time thinking of how quickly we'd slipped back to who we had once been together, and I was surprised at how much I liked being in that place again.

Or was it the same?

It was the future I was attracted to, not the past. I'd already lived that. I'd been mangled and hurt by this man and in the process had known an anger as great as any love I'd ever felt. It had been my companion in bed and kept me company when Lilly was with Robert.

Like the pain of childbirth, I could still remember how it had overwhelmed me, but I couldn't summon the exact feeling, and like anything else you have gotten used to, in a strange way, I missed it. Without that anger to protect me, I was vulnerable again.

But wasn't that growth? To let go of the old feelings and discover what remained once the anger was gone. To find out what might develop in its place.

Robert pulled me down, and we sat side by side looking out at the ocean.

The sand was warm for early May, and it felt soft on the soles of my feet. The moon was bright in the sky, and without any light pollution, the stars burned brilliantly. Although those stars had died hundreds of thousands of years ago, we could still see them shine. How could I question emotions and connections that lasted a mere five years?

"What are we doing?" I asked Robert as we watched Good playing with a crab shell she'd found.

"Riding the wave. Seeing how long we can stay standing before it knocks us down."

"Is that smart?"

"I don't know. It just feels like what we have to do."

"Why?"

"I don't know. But I'm afraid if we try to define it, we'll disturb its course," he said.

"You sound like Lilly."

"Our daughter knows some stuff we haven't even guessed at."

I laughed. "But you won't tell her that, will you?"

"Not for a very, very long time."

When we got back to the cottage, Robert opened a bottle of wine and poured us both a glass. I sat down on the couch and looked out at the beach, imagining I could see the afterimage of the two of us walking there just moments before.

I took a sip of the cold white wine, and then Robert sat down next to me and intertwined his fingers in mine. It was more sensation than I could tolerate. All he'd done was put his hand on mine and I'd felt my insides liquefy.

I shut my eyes.

For a few minutes we sat there, still and quiet except for the sound of the ocean. When Robert leaned over and kissed me, it was a long sure kiss that had no urgency to it.

After the kiss ended, Robert led me into the bedroom and over to the bed. I sat on its edge while he disappeared into the bathroom; when he came out, he was holding a hairbrush. Sitting beside me, he began to brush my hair just as he had when we had first been together. I forced myself not to remember the past, but to enjoy the smell of salt air and the feeling of the bristles gliding through my hair.

I heard Lilly telling me that when we cease to think and let ourselves become our sensations, time seems to stop. What has come before or what will come after no longer matters.

Robert took his time, not rushing a single stroke—he was simply brushing my hair and in that moment, it seemed to be enough for him.

At some point—it might have been minutes or hours later—he put down the brush and undressed me. When he had taken off all my clothes and I was naked, he stood back and looked at me.

"I hope you'll let me photograph you again, Jordan. Your body is wonderful."

"Don't stare at me—" I turned away self-consciously.

Sitting down beside me, he ran the flat of his hands down my shoulders and arms. I started to shiver.

"One day, you will let me take pictures of you again . . . one day when you're not scared anymore."

"I'm not scared. I just don't want you to—"

He kissed me silent, and we lay together on the bed, my bare skin against his clothed body. It felt both indecent and exciting to be naked while he was still dressed.

Robert started kissing my shoulders, light sweet kisses that landed on my skin like sparks, while his hand traveled further down my back, around to my stomach, and then in between my legs. For a moment I thought to ask him why he was still dressed, and then it didn't matter because the sound of the ocean and the smell in the air and the tastes in my mouth all disappeared and there was only Robert's breath on my skin and the concentric circles he was making with his fingers and I came in a great shuddering rush.

When I opened my eyes, he was smiling.

"I wanted to give you that. Not take anything. Not yet. Just give you something," he said.

Tears filled my eyes for all the things we had done to each other and the things we had not been able to do.

"No, not now, Jordan. Please don't be sad now."

He left the room and brought in the unfinished bottle of wine, and we lay in the dark without talking.

I watched him as he took off his shirt and then his pants, revealing the body I remembered: the long legs covered in blond hair, broad shoulders, and flat stomach. When I looked at Robert naked, I wanted to be an artist again, to take his camera and shoot roll after roll of film of him, to sculpt him and paint him.

Once he came back to bed and lay down beside me, I leaned over him and like a cat, I licked his body, starting behind his ear, taking my time down his neck to his shoulders. The longer it took me, the better it would be. Waiting did not matter. We'd been waiting for five years.

I felt myself get wet between my legs, and by the time I'd reached his erection, I was more than ready for him. I teased him—licking him, biting the soft skin of his inner thigh, doing everything to him except for taking him in my mouth.

Nudging him, I turned him over and began the whole journey back up his legs, his buttocks, following the line of his spine and his shoulders up to his neck.

Moaning my name, he finally grabbed me and deliberately lowered me onto him until his erection just touched me. And then he held me there, suspended in air, forcing both of us to wait while the wanting grew more insistent.

Slowly, I lowered myself onto him, only taking in an inch of him at a time and then stopping, holding back for yet another moment, and then taking one more inch.

The orgasm rocked me with its intensity. Robert's arms were around my back, his head was buried in my neck, my breasts were crushed against his chest, and he was so high up inside of me that when he came, it felt as if his orgasm had reached my heart.

Everything broke apart then, shattered, shimmered, and exploded, and I lost all sense of myself and of him. Tears spilled out of my eyes and sobs broke loose from deep in my throat; the tears were the only way that I could respond—both emotionally and physically. In the exhaustion that followed there were no words, no thoughts, just a desperate gasping for air—I needed to hear his breath and mine and know for certain that we had survived.

I wanted to say something to express my gratitude and surprise and fear and relief and happiness. Instead, I fell asleep in my almost–ex-husband's arms.

NINETEEN

I woke up in the middle of the night and lay quietly in the bed listening to the ocean and Robert's breathing, both following the same rhythm.

There would be other nights to wonder about what I had done and whether it had been the right or the wrong thing to do.

"You awake?" Robert asked.

"Yes."

"That was nice." I could hear the smile in his voice.

"Nice? Well, that's one word for it."

"Jordan, I have something I want to say to you, and I don't want you to interrupt me, just let me get this out, okay?"

"Okay," I answered with a laugh. He knew me almost too well.

"I've learned a lot in the last five years. What my weaknesses are and my strengths. I know that I was unfaithful to you. But I was also faithful to you in the way that matters the most. I've never loved anyone else, Jordan. I didn't *make* love to anyone else. I had sex the way people who are grasping for something but don't know what it is have sex. The way drunks and drug addicts take another drink or another snort, for the thrill, for the momentary oblivion."

I had no trouble listening to patients talk about being obsessed with sex, but listening to Robert was almost impossible.

"I'm not asking you to forgive me. Christ, I know it's way too late for that. But what about giving me another chance? We belong together. What does Lilly call it? That thin red thread? We are connected like that. Not just because of Lilly. We were connected way before we had a baby.

"I'm not asking you to take me back all of a sudden and be my wife again. I'm just asking that you don't shut the door on this but spend some time with me and see what happens."

There was one beat of silence.

"Are you done?" I asked.

"You just interrupted," he said, laughing. "I knew you couldn't do it; you just couldn't wait to start talking."

I laughed too.

"I was almost finished." He took a long breath and then continued. "Jordan, I don't want a divorce."

There was another beat of silence, and this time I stayed quiet.

"Now I'm done," Robert said.

"I don't know what to say." My eyes had adjusted to the darkness, and I could see the surprise on his face.

"That's impossible," he said, laughing.

"Don't make fun of me. I'm just overwhelmed."

Reaching out, he brushed the hair off my face, leaned over, and kissed me very tenderly on the lips.

"Robert, I didn't expect this. I need to sit with it for a while. Can you just hold me?"

And in the darkness, he did.

It can be a difficult thing for someone to understand that you want to be together and yet also need to be alone with your thoughts. But Robert and I had never misunderstood that need in each other. It had always been easier for me to be quiet when I was with Robert than when I was by myself. No one else put me at ease and quieted my mind the way he could.

My daughter has said that the major lesson of Zen is that "it changes" and we have to learn to love the change. But if we are extremely lucky and the stars are positioned in the heavens the right way, and the Fates are not angry with us and God is in a good mood, some things change for the better.

We fell asleep, holding each other, and woke four hours later to a bright sun and the sound of waves hitting the beach. Robert opened the windows and let in the breeze and then came back to bed and we made love again. Our dance was slower this time and sweeter, and for me, sadder, because in the daylight I knew that we were older and had lost five years together. After all this time that we had been separated, after we had struggled to go on with our lives and Lilly had pined for what she had lost, we were still these two people who could be so good together.

Once we had dressed in jeans and sweaters, we drove to town for breakfast.

After we'd each had a second cup of coffee, we took a doggie bag back to the car for Good, gave her a breakfast of bacon and eggs, and then the three of us took a walk.

Southampton is a small town with a big-city sensibility. The store owners and restaurateurs cater to the rich weekenders who have summer homes nearby and shop with the same abandon and vengeance as they do in Manhattan. We had stopped in front of a bookstore and were looking in the window when a biography of the Dalai Lama caught my eye. "I forgot to call Lilly. She doesn't know where to reach me if there's an emergency. I don't know what to tell her."

"Do you want me to call?"

"No, I'm fine."

He handed me his cell phone. "I'm just going down the block to buy a newspaper. I'll be right back."

I sat down on a bench under a tree and called my own cell number. It rang once. I hung up, waited a beat, and hit redial. Lilly answered tentatively.

"Hello?" she said.

"Hi, sweetheart, how are you?" I asked.

"I'm okay."

"Have you gotten any of those hang-ups on this phone?" I was hoping she hadn't.

"No, you're the first person who called. What's up?"

What was I going to say? I wasn't ready to tell her about Robert and me—it was too soon. I didn't know what it meant yet, and the last thing I wanted to do was raise her hopes and then let her down.

In the background on her end, I could hear street noises: cars and buses. "Where are you? It sounds a little hectic for a Zen monastery in the woods."

She didn't answer. I heard a horn blast. "Lilly, where the hell are you?"

I knew my daughter did not believe in lying. It was not one of the eight or nine paths to rightful being—she'd explained it to me once, but I couldn't quite remember the phrase. I guessed that in the silence she was struggling with a lie.

"You're not at Mount Temper, are you?" I asked.

"I was."

"And where are you now?"

More silence. "Lilly, I asked you a question."

She still didn't answer. She didn't want to tell either the truth or the lie.

"Lilly, what happened?" I tried to keep my tone understanding.

"I went to the Zen thing, but it was awful. So Wendy and Pam and I left. We're at Yale."

I sighed. "Did you plan this all along?"

"No."

I believed her. And yet she had done something she knew I wouldn't have approved of. The impact of spending the night with Robert and the weeklong stress of worrying about Dan Mallory suddenly hit me—I didn't have the energy or the desire to fight with her.

"What time are you coming home?" I asked.

"We're going to take the four o'clock train, tomorrow."

"All right, we'll talk about it then."

"No, Mom, I'm not going to let you leave me with *a talk* hanging over my head for the next day and a half. If you want to talk about it, let's do it now." Lilly always acted tougher when she was around Cooper.

"Okay. We'll do it now."

"I'm not doing anything so terrible," she began. "Not taking drugs, not drinking. I'm just in love and spending time with the person that I love. Maybe you're jealous. Maybe if you had a man in your life, you wouldn't begrudge me having one in mine."

I was furious that she would speak to me like that, and at the same time I couldn't help but wonder if she was right.

As if she could read my mind she said: "You know, I'm not a kid anymore. And you can't expect me to keep all my opinions to myself. You don't."

"Lilly, this isn't about anything but the fact that you left Mount Temper and are up at Yale with Cooper."

"And with Wendy and Pam." She tried to diffuse the issue.

"Having friends with you doesn't change the fact that you are at Yale."

"Don't you understand that no matter how hard you try you are not going to stop me from seeing Cooper?"

"I'm not stupid enough to think I can stop you. But you have to have some respect for the fact that until you are eighteen—"

"Which is next week."

Of course I knew her birthday was the following week, but it seemed impossible that she was already going to be eighteen. For years I'd always told her that when she was eighteen she could do what she wanted, but until then she'd have to abide by what Robert and I thought was right.

"Maybe you should have told me I could do what I wanted when I was twenty-one," she said.

I laughed at her comeback.

"Or thirty-two."

Then Lilly laughed—that musical laugh that always sounded like bells.

"Okay, Lilly. We won't talk about it when you get home. We're done talking about it. We'll figure out some way to compromise about all of this."

"Thanks, Mom." She sounded surprised at the way the conversation was ending.

"Just be careful, okay?"

"Okay. I love you."

"Love you too, sweetheart."

I smiled, feeling the breeze on my face, and looked down the block. Robert was walking towards me, and Good was pulling on her lead.

"Did you tell her to call you up here if she needs you?" Robert asked after I filled him in on the conversation.

"Damn, I forgot. Let me just call her back."

"Don't. She has my cell phone number. If she needs one of us and you're not home, she'll call me."

Robert and I had reached the corner. "Come this way," he said, leading me past the library into a hidden garden surrounded by pine trees.

"How do you feel about Cooper?" I asked Robert.

"I don't know. Does any father like his daughter's first real boyfriend?"

"No, not usually."

"Know why? Because we remember only too well what it was like to be those boyfriends." He laughed. "Remember me when I was twenty?"

I laughed along with him but then sobered immediately. I had only been thinking of Robert's love and his lust . . . but then I remembered his leaving. I would do anything to protect Lilly from the pain I'd felt when Robert had left me. I couldn't tolerate the thought of my daughter lying in a bathtub, staring at a razor, and contemplating suicide.

"Jordan?"

I looked at him.

"Where did you go?"

"Nowhere particularly good." And hearing her name, my dog jumped up and licked my hand.

"Lilly is going to be fine. She's your daughter. She's not going to fall for the wrong guy."

I looked wryly at Robert. I had . . . hadn't I?

That night, Robert told me he had been invited to a party being given by George Lawson, the owner of the fragrance company manufacturing Waves, and he asked me if I'd mind stopping by before we went out to dinner.

Lawson's house was only a short drive from where we were staying, and on the way, Robert began to describe the people he expected to be there. He'd only just finished telling me about Lawson's wife, who ran the company with him, when we arrived.

At the end of winding driveway that twisted past stately oak trees, Robert pulled up in front of a white Victorian summerhouse complete with a wraparound porch where a band played.

"There are going to be some characters here from the creative side who I wanted to warn you about," he said as we walked up to the front door. "But you'll just have to see for yourself."

Inside at least a hundred guests stood around in clusters talking and drinking and nibbling on the hors d'oeuvres that waiters passed.

After getting cocktails, we went in search of Robert's host and found Lawson on the deck facing the ocean. I was startled but not displeased when Robert introduced me as his wife.

Carrying plates of finger food, we made our way back out onto the porch, where a dozen small tables had been set up. We sat down with some people Robert knew, and we were all chatting amiably when I looked over towards the French doors to the living room and noticed her. She was holding a glass of wine in one hand and a cigarette in the other.

Adrienne Blessing was wearing a brightly colored Pucci dress that was cut high on her tanned thighs, and I remember thinking it was too early for her to have a tan or to be wearing that dress. An acid green sweater was tied around her shoulders, but did nothing to hide her cleavage. I must have been staring because Robert followed my glance.

Adrienne's eyes rested on Robert. Then she waved to him.
When Robert raised his arm to wave back, I almost reached out to
stop him.

What was I doing? Adrienne and Robert knew each other, but
how?

As Adrienne began to walk towards the table, it was obvious
she hadn't noticed me yet and didn't until she was only a few feet
away. I'm sure it was imperceptible to anyone else, but I noticed
her lose a step and saw her eyes narrow. Recovering quickly, she
continued walking towards us.

It is always uncomfortable when a therapist and a patient confront each other in a social situation, but it wasn't always possible
to avoid it. I would leave it up to Adrienne to acknowledge me
and would understand perfectly if she preferred to keep the fact
that she was in therapy a private matter.

Adrienne put her drink on the table and sat down as Robert
began the introductions.

"Adrienne Blessing, this is my wife, Jordan Sloan."

Adrienne smiled at me. "It's nice to meet you, Jordan."

I have been a therapist for too long to believe in coincidences.
I'm not sure if it's fate or the collective unconscious, as Jung called
it. But I knew it was not a coincidence that this woman was
acquainted with Robert. I just didn't know how well she knew
him.

A breeze blew in off the ocean and I was suddenly chilly.
Pulling my sweater tighter around my shoulders, I noticed that the
cool air didn't seem to be affecting Adrienne despite her bare
arms.

Robert explained that Adrienne was the creative director and
president of the advertising agency that had hired him to shoot
the print ads and TV commercials for our host's new perfume.

"In fact, Adrienne is responsible for naming Waves," he said.

The conversation flowed easily. Adrienne was loquacious, full
of her own power: the center of the conversation. And she paid
attention to everyone at the table but me.

What *was* the connection . . . What did it mean that she was both Robert's client and my patient? If Robert still saw clients at his studio, she might have been there and simply noticed my office downstairs. But Robert's clients had been going to his studio on Sixteenth Street since we'd separated.

I'd wait until he and I were alone to ask him if he'd ever mentioned that I was a therapist to Adrienne. It wouldn't have been the first time that someone who knew Robert had come to see me professionally, but I usually referred them to other therapists.

If I'd known Adrienne was a client of Robert's, it would have been a conflict of interest to treat her. A patient needed to be free to discuss anything with her therapist and not feel inhibited if she needed to talk confidentially about her business dealings.

But business dealings weren't what Adrienne had been discussing in therapy, and while I watched her interact at the party, I wasn't surprised by how much more comfortable with business associates she was than with the members of her Tuesday night group therapy session. There she had to deal with her feelings; here she was the president and creative director of an ad agency and could discuss her work.

"I found the old footage from a collector of erotica." Adrienne was explaining how she had come by the vintage film. "The woman has that kind of innocent sexiness of a young Monroe."

"Who's the actress?" Hank Mellors, the other man at our table, asked.

"We never discovered who she was, but I think it's better that she's a mystery; if she were someone well known, every viewer would already have an opinion of her, but this way she's whoever you want her to be—slut or angel. It's more provocative, don't you agree?" She had turned to Robert and was waiting for his response.

To me, it seemed as if he purposely sipped his drink in order to avoid answering her. I wondered why.

"How old is the film?" Hank asked, his eyes riveted to the swelling of Adrienne's breasts.

"It's from the early forties," she said.

"Is it that nitrate film?" Hank said.

"Didn't I read something about that kind of film in an issue of the *Smithsonian*. Can't it explode?" Hank's wife, Debbie, asked.

"Yes, but I've had it checked out, and it hasn't degraded much. I have to be careful with it, of course, but it's safe in the darkroom; the big threat to nitrate film is intense heat," Robert explained.

I drank more wine and watched Adrienne turn her charms on everyone at the table one by one. Oh, she was enjoying having an audience. She leaned towards whomever she was speaking to, touched their hands, and looked right into their eyes, as if they were more important and interesting than anyone she'd ever met.

"I didn't know they made X-rated movies back then," Hank said, trying to win back Adrienne's attention.

"Every century has produced great erotica," she answered. "But you'll never guess who owns the largest collection. The Vatican. They've confiscated so much erotic art over the years, they wound up with more of it than anyone else. Can't you just picture all those bishops and priests stealing into the storage rooms and vaults to jerk off over the same lewd images they preach against." She laughed and the two men joined her. Debbie was clearly embarrassed.

As soon as Adrienne noticed Debbie's discomfort, she turned to her.

"The woman's skin in the film is luminous. You should see it. You have skin like that, you know?"

But Debbie didn't relax; if anything Adrienne's attention had made her even more uncomfortable.

Accustomed to the way Adrienne discussed sex and flirted with everyone—men and women alike, I wasn't surprised at the turn the conversation had taken, but I didn't want to bear witness to Adrienne in action. It would only make it harder for me to be objective with her in therapy. That was, if I kept her on as a patient: we'd have to discuss that in her next session.

I caught Robert's eye and looked at the French doors. He nod-ded, stood up, and we said our good-byes.

As much as I wanted to ask him about Adrienne once we were alone in the car, professional ethics stopped me. No matter how curious I was, I couldn't break a confidence.

"Are you still hungry enough for dinner?" Robert asked as he pulled out of the driveway.

"No, I ate too many appetizers."

"Me too. Let's go to Sag Harbor for coffee and brandy," he suggested.

"That sounds perfect."

"By the way, thanks for dealing with that scene," Robert said as he drove onto Route 27. "Ordinarily I wouldn't show up at a client's party. But I like Lawson. And I like working on his account. I just wish Adrienne Blessing hadn't been there."

"Why?" I asked.

"She's given me a hard time on this job."

"I can imagine; she seems very intense."

"That's putting it mildly."

Ahead of us the long stretch of road was dark and twisting, and Robert concentrated on his driving.

By the time we'd parked the car on the main street of Sag Harbor, I still hadn't figured out how to broach the subject of Adrienne being my patient without breaking a confidence.

We walked into The American Hotel, a quaint three-story inn located in the center of town. "In the summer it's impossible to get a table. People wait on line for hours," Robert explained as we sat down.

I knew that since we'd separated, Robert had been spending a large part of his summers out here. He rented a cottage in East Hampton and often brought Lilly with him. "Why aren't you staying at your house this weekend?" I asked.

"The rental doesn't start till Memorial Day weekend. Maybe this summer you'll come out here with Lilly and me."

"Robert, we need to talk about Lilly. It wasn't an accident that I didn't tell her I was with you when I spoke to her this morning."

"Why didn't you tell her?"

"She wants us to get back together so badly I can't bear to think of the campaign she'll mount when she knows—I'm just not ready to deal with that."

Robert leaned closer to me and inhaled. "You always smell so much better than anyone else."

Than any other woman—I thought.

"I have worked with a lot of women, Jordan," Robert said, once again reading my thoughts. "And I have a mother and two sisters and a daughter and she has friends. More than half the world is made up of women. So every time I refer to women, don't automatically think the worst, okay?"

"I wasn't thinking the worst." I tried to sound convincing.

"I wouldn't blame you if you did. But, Jordan, I'm not going to make the same mistakes again. Do you think you can believe that?"

I had no desire to argue with Robert. I never did. It wasn't that I was afraid of arguing, but being right never seemed that important.

"But I'm not sure it's a good idea to hide our relationship from our daughter. What if she finds out on her own? We'd hurt her worse if she thought we had lied to her," Robert said.

I took a sip of my drink. "I don't want to get her hopes up."

"How can you be so sure that's what she'll do?"

"Because Lilly still wants all those fairy tales I wouldn't read her to be a little bit true."

"But maybe they are a little bit true."

Robert's words were sweet and satisfying to hear, and I wished I could *believe* them because I had grown up on those same fairy tales I tried to protect Lilly from—only to watch them come crashing down around me, first when my father had been murdered, and then when I found out about my husband's infidelity.

"Robert, I don't want to sneak around either, but I can't disappoint Lilly again."

"You won't."

"You can't be sure of that, not yet."

"From my end I can be sure. Jordan, haven't you ever wondered why I continued living upstairs in the studio? Why I didn't go out and get a nicer apartment where I could have a bedroom and a living room? Didn't you ever wonder why I never introduced anyone I was seeing to Lilly?"

"I assumed you did all that for Lilly's sake."

"Maybe at first. But after a while I realized that I was staying because I didn't want to leave you. I didn't want to live in another building. I didn't want to be more than a staircase away from you. Yes, I dated. I was lonely. But I never met anyone who mattered to me the way you do, Jordan. I don't want to be married to anyone else but you."

"It sure is the weekend for speeches," I said flippantly. From the look on his face, I realized I'd insulted him. "I'm sorry, Robert, but it's not easy for me to hear all that sincerity from you."

"Why?"

"I don't know."

"That's not an answer."

Why did the very things I'd wanted most to hear make me so uncomfortable? Robert waited patiently, listening to my silence.

"Maybe it's not Lilly that you are trying to protect," he finally said. "Maybe it's yourself."

He had heard the words I hadn't said. Robert was intuitive in a way that I wasn't. I looked for clues, for insights. I had an excellent memory and was good at puzzles. But Robert had a different gift. He could look inside people and know what they were feeling even when they didn't know themselves.

Reaching inside his jacket pocket, Robert pulled out a jewelry box and put it on the table between us. I recognized the name on the case; it was one of Southampton's finest stores.

"This is for your birthday. I know you don't ever wear jewelry other than your grandmother's rings, and I know it's because of your father's death. But I hope you to can make an exception and wear this."

"But my birthday was last month," I said.

"Well, I wasn't with you a month ago and I'm with you now."

"What is it?" I asked him, looking at the box.

"Jordan!" He laughed. "The box is right in front of you. Open it."

"First tell me why you bought it for me, and then I'll decide if I'm going to open it."

I'd had too much wine at the party and had finished an entire snifter of cognac; I didn't trust my reactions. I wanted some warning here, some signposts. I couldn't afford to misinterpret what was going on between us.

"This is like a scene out of one of those silly 'first-date movies' I make fun of. The ones we used to make fun of together," I said, still looking down at the jeweler's box.

"Except this isn't a movie. There's no fake sunset backdrop and no orchestra playing, just a radio and smoke from some guy's cigar. And nothing is easy and I don't expect it to be. But there's no one I want to tackle life's challenges with more than you."

I sat there, just holding the leather box.

"Aren't you going to open it?" he asked.

"No. A lot of what you said tonight needs examining. I know I have to find out who I'm trying to protect, but I also know that if I'm not ready to tell Lilly about us—and I'm not—then I'm not ready to open this box. I can only do that when I'm ready to wear what's inside in front of our daughter."

And wondering if that day would ever come, I slid the box back across the table towards Robert.

TWENTY

If I had escaped worrying about Dan Mallory for a little while over the weekend, all concerns rushed back at me on Monday afternoon when Simon called to tell me that Mallory had now missed two meetings with his parole officer.

I looked out of the window from my office. A weekend gardener had planted pansies at the bases of the trees all up and down the block. New York has a million gardens, some of them only window boxes or a two-by-two-foot square on the sidewalk. But I wasn't inspecting the scenery; I was looking for a shadow of a man.

"Jordan, how would you feel about hiring someone to watch your house?"

"A private detective? Won't the police watch the house?"

"No. Technically you aren't in danger. There's no proof that it was Mallory who called you—"

"Who else do you think could have made that call, Simon?"

"It doesn't matter what you and I think. Rafferty needs concrete proof. You have to understand that from his point of view, until last week Mallory had been the model ex-con. He showed up early for his parole meetings, wasn't having any major adjustment problems, and he was well liked on his job. From all reports he wasn't drinking or doing drugs. Rafferty thinks it's just as likely that Mallory might have been in an accident, or have gotten sick."

I took a sip of my coffee and I held the warm cup in my hands as if it offered some kind of comfort.

"What about the man who was following me?"

"The man who you *think* was following you. Jordan, I'm not doubting you; I'm just telling you how Rafferty sees it."

"What if I had pictures of Mallory following me?"

"Do you?"

"I don't know." I told Simon about the photographs Lilly had taken in the park and about the man who had shown up in so many of them. "You can't see his face clearly, but maybe the police can do something with the film. Or maybe Rafferty might recognize him. Would that be enough to convince him?"

"Yes. Let me call him and get back to you."

I had just put the receiver down when it rang again.

"We have a date today, don't we?" Chloe asked.

"Oh, I forgot."

"If you forgot our shoe search, something must be wrong. Is it Mallory?"

I filled her in on my conversation with Simon while I made myself more coffee.

"All the more reason for you to meet me. Get your mind off of that monster. Besides, I need advice," Chloe said.

"Max Brecht advice?"

"Oh, damn it, Jordan. Why is it so damned seductive to be wooed?"

"I don't know. But it is, isn't it?"

"Okay, now I hear something else in your voice. Is it Robert?"

"We were talking about you. If I meet you, it's to work on the Max Brecht issue. Not Mallory, not Robert."

"Since when have we been able to stick to one subject?"

After my eleven o'clock patient, I left to meet Chloe on Madison Avenue and Sixty-fifth Street at the Walter Steiger store. We had a shoe route. Over the years, we refined it, though occasionally we would alter it when we heard about a new store or a big sale.

As I walked out of the brownstone, I checked up and down the block. Everything looked normal. But there were so many places someone could hide. So many ways to be invisible. I noticed a Federal Express man walking towards me—that uniform could be a disguise, I thought. A man in a baseball cap was delivering groceries to the brownstone next to mine. Was he too young to be Mallory?

Maybe it would be a good idea to have someone watch the house for a while.

Twenty minutes later I got out of a taxi in front of the store. In the window I saw a pair of black mules. Pointy toes, backless, elegant stacked heels. I wanted them as soon as I saw them and was trying them on when Chloe walked in.

"Kind of sexy for the office . . ." She giggled.

The dark-haired saleswoman, whom we both knew from years of frequenting the store, laughed with us.

"But they are kind of great for weekends. Black wide-legged pants, white silk T-shirt, black mules," I said as I inspected my foot in the mirror.

"Sexier than your usual fare, even for the weekends," Chloe said, and examined my face. "What happened with Robert?"

I smiled at her "Chloe, we're not talking about me today. We're concentrating on you."

"Jordan, let's just do five minutes on you. Believe me, I won't let you go on about it for too long. Then it's my turn."

While Chloe tried on the same mules, I briefly told her about the weekend with Robert. "But don't ask me what I'm going to do. I don't know."

"Okay, I won't ask. But I know what you *should* do. Get over your pride. You love him. Accept it. Now, do these look as good on me as they did on you?"

Over the years we had bought dozens of pairs of the exact same shoes. We were sole mates, Chloe once had joked. But the reality was that Chloe and I were not similar. That was why we could be friends. We didn't look alike; we didn't like the same men. She was athletic, outgoing, and spontaneous. And she was a harmless flirt who, for the first time since marrying John, had gotten in over her head.

We both bought the black mules and strolled down Madison towards our next serious stop, on Sixtieth Street.

"Jordan, do you think it sounds like I'm falling in love with him?" Chloe asked after describing her last meeting with Max.

"No, I think you are falling in love with falling in love."

"I interviewed a therapist once who said it's not always the worst thing to have an affair. Margo Lynch . . . did you ever hear of her?"

"Yes . . . she's not in practice anymore."

"What happened?"

"A couple of husbands and wives sued her for breaking up their marriages."

"Are you serious?"

"Yes."

We stopped at a streetlight.

"I remember she said having an affair can make someone realize that their spouse isn't so bad," Chloe said.

"There are easier ways to find that out. Just turn on a TV talk show. No, the only positive thing I've really ever heard come out of an affair is the realization that even illicit thrills eventually become routine."

"That's not what I wanted to hear right now." She laughed, lit a cigarette, and took a breath.

"As hard as I can try to be objective, Chloe, infidelity is a bit of a loaded issue for me."

"I know, I know. Is it selfish of me to talk to you about this?"

"Of course not."

We had reached our next stop. In all of New York, the fourth floor of Barneys had our favorite assemblage of shoes. It was dangerous to be in there in the mood we were both in.

Chloe tried on powder blue ballet slippers with a tiny heel. I had on strappy sandals.

"Why isn't it enough to just know Max is interested?" she asked. "Why can't I stop there?" She got up and walked to the mirror and did a twirl in the blue shoes. "I hate the rules, Jordan. I wish I could be a man. Why can't we just sleep with someone else every once in a while and get it out of our systems? Just do it without threatening what we have, without feeling guilty?"

Involuntarily I winced. For a second she didn't understand my reaction to what she'd said, and then she quickly apologized.

"That's okay. It really is. Just don't think that a man does it without repercussions. Some men lose things that matter to them a lot. Some men actually have feelings."

"There you go again. Trying to convince me that the two sexes aren't that different," Chloe said, and then slipped out of the ballet slippers to try on leopard suede pumps, but the heel was so high she wobbled as she walked. Abandoning those, she tried on yet another pair.

"Of course the sexes are different. But men and woman do have certain things in common. Men crave love and security too. It's just that they don't often show it, and we show it too much."

"I still wish I was a man," she said as she examined her feet in the new shoes.

"Why? You have a career and kids, and you earn as much, if not more, than your husband does. You pay half the bills, and you don't rely on him for anything. But you make it sound as if you are totally dependent."

"And you are just the opposite," she said. "You make it sound as if you don't need a living soul, but you do."

Chloe bought the ballet slippers, and we decided to take a break and get something to eat downstairs at Fred's, the store's restaurant. After the waitress took our order, Chloe returned to her problem.

"Anyway, I really am in trouble this time," Chloe said. "Max is just too interesting. Do you think I should be seeing someone?" she asked.

"Chloe, don't ask me to tell you to stop seeing Max."

"No, you idiot, I was asking you if I should see a therapist?"

"Of course. I think everyone should see a therapist. There is a terrific woman who—"

"Forget it. If you can't be my therapist—and I know you can't—I don't want to see anyone else. I'll just keep dragging you out under the pretext of shopping and get shrinked in the process."

We both laughed.

After spending the afternoon looking at shoes, I couldn't help noticing Adrienne Blessing's shoes when she showed up for her session later that day. They were the leopard pumps that Chloe had been unable to walk in, but Adrienne seemed to have no such problem.

"I picked these up for you," Adrienne said as she handed me a bag from Balducci's. Inside were three large peaches.

"I'm not having a good day," she said as she stretched out on the couch. "I had a fight with one of the art directors that works for me," she said.

"We certainly can discuss that, but first we need to talk about the fact that you are working with my husband."

"Why?"

"Because if I had known that you worked with him—worse yet, hired him—I probably would not have accepted you as a patient," I told her.

"Then I'm glad I didn't tell you."

"So you did know?"

"Of course I knew."

I wasn't quite sure what to make of what she was saying. Why would she have purposefully not told me she knew Robert? "Well, now that I know about it, we should discuss whether or not I can continue to treat you. I can recommend another fine therapist who—"

"No. I want to be in therapy with you—precisely because you are married to Robert."

Something in her tone alarmed me. None of this was making sense. "And why is that?"

"I'm not ready to talk about that." She crossed her feet at the ankles.

"I'd like you to talk about it anyway," I suggested.

"I'm sure you would. But I'm not ready to talk about it yet." Adrienne recrossed her ankles. Then she crossed her arms over her chest. She was as closed off as she had been when she first came into therapy.

I waited. Five minutes went by. Adrienne lay quietly on the couch without speaking for the next ten minutes. She was so still that I wondered if she had fallen asleep. I could hear the sounds on the street outside. A truck stopping. A horn blasting. A dog barking. Music—Mozart, I thought—drifting out of a window somewhere. A phone rang upstairs. A plane flew overhead. I could even hear my watch ticking. My eyes stopped on the amethyst rock on the bookshelf, and I thought about my father and Dan Mallory. Change focus, I thought.

"Adrienne, sooner or later you are going to have to communicate with me."

"Or?" she asked.

"Adrienne, what are you feeling right now?" I asked.

"Rage."

"Good, tell me about it."

"It is overwhelming, gargantuan. I want to be violent." Her voice was tremulous; I could hear the suppressed emotion. "To do something to hurt someone. To make sure I get what I want. To destroy what I want so I can stop wanting it. To get revenge for having been betrayed."

"Who has betrayed you?"

"You have. The man I'm seeing has," she said.

"And how has he betrayed you?"

She laughed a tight laugh, and my antennae went up. There was an edge of hysteria to the sound.

"Aren't you interested in why you've betrayed me?" she asked.

"I just assumed it's because I suggested you see another therapist."

"Oh, is that what you think?" Adrienne smiled, but it was a nasty smile.

"I'd like you to see another doctor next week. Not instead of me. But in addition to me. I'd like him to evaluate you for medication."

"Medication? Yeah, I need medication. I need a big cock. That's the only medication I need."

"Will you go see Dr. Tyler?" I asked.

"Is that what I have to do to stay in therapy with you?" she asked.

"Yes."

"Then I'll go see him," Adrienne responded docilely.

"Adrienne, why is it so important that you stay in therapy with me?"

She leaned on her elbow and faced me. Her eyes bored through me, trying to communicate without words. "This is a standoff, isn't it?" she asked.

"Is that what you want—a standoff?"

"No, not at all, Dr. Sloan." She flung my name at me as if she could insult me with it. "No, I want to win."

"And my job is to help you win. You just have to give me a chance to do that," I answered.

Her smile broadened and Adrienne's face was suddenly suffused with light. "Oh, you will. You will. You will help me win."

TWENTY-ONE

I would have spent more time rethinking the session with Adrienne, but Simon and Jim Rafferty were waiting in the anteroom for me. I showed them into my office, where Rafferty took a seat on the couch and Simon pulled up one of the chairs I used for group.

"Dr. Sloan, first I want to assure you that I don't believe you are in any danger," Rafferty began.

"Well, you certainly sound certain. How can you be so sure?" I asked.

"I've been talking to Dan twice a week for six weeks. He hated prison. It robbed him of everything that mattered to him. Dan's greatest regret is that he never became a jeweler, and all he wants is to find a way to get back into the profession. I just don't think he'd risk his future to see you."

"So what do you think has happened to him?" Simon asked.

"I think that he's sick and in a hospital somewhere."

"Are you searching the hospitals?" Simon asked.

"Yes. Not just in Manhattan but in all five boroughs."

Simon was staring at my hands, and I looked down. I was twisting the wedding rings around and around my finger. I stopped.

"If Dan is AWOL, he's the first ex-con who has fooled me in ten years. I would bet my job on the fact that he is not the one calling or following you," Rafferty said.

Our jobs were similar and we both knew the warning signs to

look for in sessions. Adrienne had given me at least three or four that evening. I might not understand them yet, but I had noticed them. But what if Rafferty had missed the signals that Mallory had given him?

Opening his briefcase, Rafferty pulled out a manila folder. "As certain as I am, I'm not foolish," Rafferty said as he held out a police drawing. "Have you seen this man?"

I stared at the drawing, trying to connect the sketch to my memory of Mallory, but it was too generic. No matter how long I looked, I couldn't see either the young man I remembered as Dan Mallory or the elusive figure I'd glimpsed in the jewelry district, or across the street in the shadows, or in Lilly's photographs.

"He doesn't look like what I remember of Mallory from years ago. And he doesn't look like anyone I've seen since."

Rafferty glanced at the police sketch and then back at me. "It's not a particularly good likeness, and I'm ashamed to say that's my fault. Even though I had half a dozen meetings with Dan, I had a hard time describing him. When he first got out of prison, he was clean-shaven, but then he started growing a beard. Sometimes he wore sunglasses; other times he wore a baseball cap. He was readapting, trying out different looks, trying to find himself again."

"The man in Lilly's photographs . . . and on Forty-seventh Street . . . he was wearing a baseball cap." I was trying to ignore the sweat that suddenly drenched my body.

"Can I see the photos?" Rafferty asked, and then stood up quickly. "Are they here?"

"Yes, my daughter has them upstairs. I'll be right back."

Lilly was in her room doing homework on her computer.

"Honey, Dan Mallory didn't show up at the parole office or at work again today. His parole officer is here and he'd like to see those photographs you took."

"Just because he hasn't shown up doesn't mean—"

"Not now, Lilly. *Please*. Just get the photographs and come downstairs with me." The tone in my voice must have convinced her. She pulled the photos from a stack on her desk and followed me downstairs and into my office.

Rafferty inspected the shots Lilly had taken and the one blowup she'd made. He shook his head. "I don't think there's enough here to work with. But I'd still like to see what the lab can do."

"But what about those sunglasses and that baseball cap? Do they look like the ones Mallory wore? Could that be him?"

Rafferty looked up. "It could be, Dr. Sloan. It could also be a dozen other guys I know too. But, yes, it could be Dan."

It was no surprise to me that Rafferty thought the man in the photographs might be the man who had killed my father.

"Shit," Simon said.

Lilly looked from her uncle to me. I went to her and put my arm around her.

"We'll put a detective on your house for a couple of days. At least until we find Dan or he shows up with a damn good explanation for where he's been," Rafferty said as he ran his fingers through his hair.

Simon nodded. "I feel better—and worse now that you're taking this seriously." He turned from Rafferty to Lilly and me. "You'll be safer now with someone watching the house."

Rafferty spent some time talking to Lilly about the precautions he wanted her to take. For a moment I was remembering the day the police had come to my parents' store after a string of violent robberies in the neighborhood to tell us about the precautions we should take if a thief ever confronted us. And how pointless all those precautions had been in the end.

I concentrated on Rafferty's voice as he told Lilly that she should not under any circumstances leave the house alone at night.

"Do you understand?" he asked her.

"Yes, but why have you given up on him? Don't you still think he might have changed? Even if it is him in my photographs— why couldn't it just be a coincidence that he was in the park the same day we were?" she asked.

"Of course it's possible. But it's still better to be careful. The truth is that Dan Mallory did kill your grandfather and your mother was the main witness for the prosecution. It was her testimony that helped send him to prison for nineteen years."

Something in Rafferty's tone reached her. Her eyes narrowed, and under my hands her body stiffened.

"If he is following us . . . what do you think he wants?" Lilly asked.

"I'm not sure. All I know is that if he isn't sick or dead, then he's broken his parole, which means all bets are off. He once liked your mom very much, and I really don't think he'd do anything to hurt her or to hurt you. He might just want to see her to apologize. But if he fooled me . . . if he fooled the whole parole board, we can't take any chances."

When Rafferty left, Simon and Lilly and I went upstairs. I made a vodka and tonic for my brother and one for me, and then turned to Lilly. "Sweetheart, come sit down."

Lilly was standing behind a chair, holding on to it as if it were all that was keeping her upright. When she didn't move, I went over to her and put my arms around her. Immediately her arms went around my back. I half expected her to start to cry, but she didn't. Instead, she took a deep breath and then disentangled herself from my embrace. "I'm fine," she said. But she wasn't convincing.

"Jordan, why don't you give Lilly a drink. It wouldn't hurt her," my brother suggested.

"I'd like a glass of wine," she said in a voice that alerted me this would not be the first time she'd had a drink. It was not the right time to confront her with my suspicions that she was drinking behind my back. I'd deal with that later. Right now, she needed something to relax her, and so I relaxed the rules.

"Here." I handed her a crystal goblet. "Sit down, sweetheart. Don't be frightened; we can handle this."

"Frightened?" Lilly arched her eyebrows. "Mom, I'm not frightened. I'm furious. Jim Rafferty spends so much time around negative people that all that bad energy is oozing out of his pores. Didn't you hear him? He doesn't know if Mallory is sick or dead? He doesn't care about him at all. He has no compassion for him.

It's terrible. He only cares about his own job and that he might have made a mistake."

Simon looked at me over the rim of his glass. He wasn't as familiar with Lilly's new slant on things as I was. "Rafferty has compassion, Lilly. For you, your mother, and for Mallory—"

Lilly interrupted him. "I can tell when Mom has been with a disturbed patient because it's all over her. Like bad perfume. And it takes her hours to get rid of the stink."

Lilly's observation was right. Like stale tobacco, some patients' negative energy clung to me.

"Rafferty's not just picking up on other people's energy. His soul is corroded."

"Call me callous, but I don't care about Rafferty's soul right now, Lilly," my brother said. "I just care about you and your mother being safe. Your mother said she's noticed someone outside the house twice. Have you seen anyone?"

Lilly didn't say anything.

I knew what her silence meant.

"Oh, Lilly, was it the same man from the park? For God's sake, please tell us." I realized I was shouting, but I couldn't control myself.

"Not a person, just a shadow. I was taking pictures out the window the other night and saw someone across the street. It was an interesting effect—the way the shadow had more presence than the person."

"Did you take a picture of this person?" Simon asked.

Again Lilly didn't answer.

"Oh, Lilly, why didn't you tell us when Rafferty was here?" I asked.

"Because you can see even less of this man than the man in the park."

"Lilly, can I see the photograph?" Simon asked in a much calmer voice than I would have used.

Simon and I waited while Lilly went upstairs. I made him another drink, and he came into the kitchen to keep me company while I put some chicken breasts into the oven to heat up for dinner.

About ten minutes later, Lilly returned, holding out a contact sheet and a photographer's loop. First I peered at the sheet and then gave Simon a look. Just as Lilly had said, the scene was completely in shadow.

"Who but Mallory would be so furtive?"

"Can I have the negatives, Lilly? Maybe the police lab can lighten them, blow them up—"

"I can do that, Uncle Simon."

After Lilly went back upstairs to the darkroom, I turned the oven off so the chicken wouldn't dry out and Simon called Perry to tell her he would be home even later than he'd expected and that he'd fill her in then.

Robert had just come home and was with Lilly when she came back downstairs. We all examined the photos, but the figure in the shadows was totally obscured by limbs from the trees, and we couldn't make out any of his features.

Lilly actually seemed relieved.

Robert walked over to the window, glanced up and down the street, and then turned back to us.

"I don't want either of you going out alone."

"Rafferty already read us the riot act, Dad. Boy, this guy gets out of one prison and we go into another one."

I remembered thinking just that when Simon had first told me about Mallory's release the morning after my birthday dinner.

"Until the police find Mallory, either your mother or I will walk with you to school and one of us will pick you up." Robert's tone left no room for argument. If anyone could get through to Lilly, it would be her father. But so far he wasn't having any more luck than either Simon or I had.

"Like I'm eight or nine. Oh, great." She pouted.

"Lilly, he shot your grandfather. He was in prison for nineteen years. He's a criminal," I said.

"But that doesn't mean he is going to do something bad again. It doesn't. People change. Don't they, Dad?" Lilly asked, turning away from me and imploring her father to take her side.

It was at that moment that Lilly's opinions about Dan Mallory finally became clear. This was more than Lilly wanting to believe that Dan Mallory was rehabilitated; this was about Robert changing so that we could get back together and be a family again.

And Robert knew it. He looked from his daughter, to me, and then back to Lilly.

"Yes, people do. People can change. Sometimes for the better. But sometimes for the worse."

"But you are just assuming that in this case Mallory has changed for the worse. That's not fair. Is that how you'd want to be treated—"

"Lilly!" It was a single word, but it was as harsh and sharp as Robert's voice ever got, and it stopped our daughter. "We just need to be careful. We are not putting Mallory back in prison. Not damning him. Just taking precautions. So stop it, all right? Don't make us the enemy in this. You don't have to disagree with everything that your mother and I think and feel just to prove a point, okay?"

Lilly looked down at the floor and remained silent. Robert's short speech had embarrassed her.

At about nine o'clock Simon left and Lilly asked Robert if she could go back upstairs and work with him in the darkroom for a while. Once they were gone, I got into bed and opened a book. I was still on the same page five minutes later when my phone rang.

"Hello?" I said.

Silence.

"Damn it, say something. Who is this?" I shouted in frustration.

"Did you ever eat one of those hard candies with a drop of honey inside?" a mechanical voice asked. "You suck and suck waiting for the shell to dissolve so you can get to the soft honey center. That's what your voice is like. Melting honey. And I can't wait till it's whispering in my ear, stroking my skin, confessing to me and apologizing."

I heard a click.

Immediately I punched the star key and the six and the nine buttons, but a recorded voice told me the number I was trying to reach could not be accessed this way.

I called Simon on his cell phone and told him what had happened. He said that he'd call the police and try to get a tap on my phone to trace my calls.

After hanging up, I turned on the television and scanned the channels, looking for some distraction.

People change, Lilly had said.

Do they? Not typically. More often they learn to tolerate their feelings so they won't have to hide from them or act on them. Addicts do not stop wanting their fix, but they can learn to live through a tough situation without running to a bottle or a medicine cabinet. Introverts do not become extroverts, but they can learn why their insecurities cripple them; instead of focusing on past fears, they can learn to be more outgoing.

How much had Robert changed? How much had I?

The phone rang again, and I let the machine answer it. When I heard Chloe's voice, I picked up the receiver.

"Hi." My voice even sounded strained to me.

"Are you all right, Jordan?"

I told her about Rafferty's visit, including Lilly's reaction, and the last phone call I'd gotten. After commiserating with me and trying to shore me up, Chloe hesitated when I asked her what was new.

"It can wait till tomorrow," she said. "You have enough on your plate for now."

"No, you don't sound like it can wait. Is it about Max?"

"No, it's not. It's about Robert. Are you sure you want to deal with something else right now?"

"Yes, tell me."

"I heard something at the magazine this afternoon I thought you should know about," she said. "The culture editor told me that some right-wing, religious group is planning a protest at Robert's show when it opens next month. They're calling him a child pornographer and claiming that the nudes of Lilly—"

"For God's sake, she isn't nude."

"Well, our editor is planning to crucify the nuts. She says she knows Robert's work and there is no way he's capable of pornography. But I'm sure that doesn't help much."

"Oh, Chloe, I don't want anyone writing about Lilly—good or bad—right now. With Mallory missing this makes us so vulnerable. Who knows, he could be masquerading as one of those right-wing nuts and come to the opening and—"

"I know. But the show's not opening for six weeks, right? They'll find Mallory way before then."

When I got off the phone, I walked upstairs to Robert's studio but then hesitated at the door—my hair wasn't brushed . . . I was wearing an old robe. I smiled at my sudden vanity. How much I'd changed in a few short weeks.

How much Lilly would have liked knowing that, I thought as I walked into the studio where she and Robert were arranging his photographs, trying to organize the flow of the upcoming show.

I told them both what Chloe had said.

"But they haven't even seen any of the photographs. No one has but us," Lilly said. "How dare they call Dad names!" She loved him so much and was so sure of him; I only hoped she'd never be disappointed. It seemed unlikely. Robert was far more responsible as a father than he'd been as a husband.

"Mom . . ." Lilly gestured to the photographs. "How can anyone see these and call them pornographic?"

Moving from one image to the next, I drank them in. My husband's work, my daughter's body—her spirit and his sensitivity.

"I think I'm going to call off the show," Robert said.

"No!"

"Lilly, please. You are much more important than any show," he said.

"But I don't care what anyone says," she insisted.

"But I do," Robert said.

I smiled at him and put my arm around my daughter's shoulders.

"Lilly, your father is right. Now, let's get going; it's late. There's school tomorrow. And it's your birthday."

"Dad . . . will you just think about it for a while before you call off the show. Please?"

"Yes, I'll think about it."

We took a step to the door, and then Lilly stopped, turned, and ran back to her father to kiss him good night. "Oh, don't forget, Cooper is coming in tomorrow for my birthday dinner. He's getting in around three."

"How long is he staying?" Robert asked.

"For the night, if that's okay with you. It's the end of the semester and he's got too much work to do to stay longer. He has finals next week."

Over Lilly's head, Robert looked at me with a glance that said he was glad Cooper's visit was going to be a brief one.

Half an hour later, Lilly was in her room and I was back in my bed when the phone rang again. Once more I let the machine answer it but picked up when I heard Robert's hello.

"I feel like Lilly is my parent instead of my daughter and I have to sneak around behind her back to see you." He was being funny, but I knew it was bothering him.

"I'm actually enjoying it; not many people get to have an illicit affair with their own husband." I laughed and then stopped, realizing what I'd said.

Robert, who had always been able to hear the meaning behind my words, heard the sudden shift in my voice.

"I'm sorry I ever hurt you, Jordan."

"Regardless, that was a stupid thing for me to say."

"Forget it. Listen, is Lilly asleep?"

"She should be."

"Do you want to come upstairs for a while? Just for a while. I think we could both use some company," Robert said.

As tired and worried as I was, I didn't hesitate. I wanted the respite that he was offering.

Each step I climbed to Robert's studio made me feel lighter and less anxious. He must have been listening for my footsteps, because he opened the door before I knocked. Opera music was playing, and he had uncorked a bottle of red wine and was waiting for me, glass in hand.

I took a sip of the wine and put the glass down. Robert smoothed my hair off my forehead and kissed me. After we'd sat down on the couch, he kissed me again.

"Last night, I wanted to creep down in the middle of the night and get into your bed."

I hesitated—opening up to him still took courage. "I was thinking about you too."

"I'm the only one allowed to think," he joked. "Once you get started thinking, you overthink. And that's not what you need right now."

Robert pulled me down beside him on the couch. We lay beside each other, kissing, our hands entwined and the full length of our bodies pressed together. This was how it had been when we were younger—in his parents' house on their couch, in the park on the grass, at the beach. We had never tired of touching. Back then I had been sure we would never get enough of each other. But Robert had gotten enough of me . . .

I tried to concentrate on the feel of his hands on my breasts, but I couldn't help wondering when I would finally be able to let go of the images of him with other women.

Sensing that he'd lost me for a moment, Robert got down on his knees next to the couch. "Just lie there, Jordan. Just quiet your mind and relax."

He held my legs apart and kissed the inside of my thighs, succeeding in chasing away every thought and replacing it with sensation. For a while the only thing that mattered was his tongue and the way he was moving it in tiny flickering motions. I pushed myself against him, fiercely, hungrily; all I wanted was to get to the place he was taking me.

"I don't care how hard you are or how much you want to come, you can't stop . . ." I gasped. "You owe me, Robert. You owe me hundreds of orgasms."

"Will you tell me how you want each one of them?" he asked as he caught his breath and laughed at the same time.

"Yes."

"I'll give you each one exactly the way you want it. It doesn't matter how long you make me wait as long as I can smell you and taste you and as long as at the end you will let me come."

"Maybe I will. Maybe I won't. Maybe for weeks, for months, you will just give them to me . . ." I teased.

He was using his hand now, rubbing me back and forth in a slow, languorous gesture. "That's fine. Until you decide it's my turn, I'll just do what you want."

"I'll just keep making you hard . . . but every once in a while I'll do this . . ." I repositioned myself and sucked on the tip of his erection for a few seconds, just long enough for him to begin to get lost in the sensation, and then I stopped. "But I'll only do it for a moment. Just long enough to make you crazy. To make you want me so much you'll do anything I tell you to. But never long enough to make you come."

Once more Robert's head was in between my legs. His tongue was moving in small circles and his breath was hot against my skin, and then for a moment he stopped and pulled back. I pushed forward to find his mouth again.

After a few moments I took him in my mouth and held him there, moving back and forth on him, letting him think I was going to keep going, and then I pulled back and listened as he moaned.

"Do you like this? Controlling me? Teasing me but not quite giving me what I want?"

"Oh, yes." I laughed again.

But it was becoming more and more difficult for me to concentrate on the punishment I was supposed to be inflicting. Pressure was building inside me and I no longer wanted to play the game. Suddenly, I pulled away, climbed on top of him and lowered myself slowly onto his erection.

"This is one crazy punishment, Jordan."

"I know . . ." I was laughing again and rocking back and forth, feeling Robert grow even harder inside of me.

He raised his arms, encircling my head in his hands, and pulled my face down to kiss me. There were a thousand unsaid words in that gentle, passionate kiss, and while I didn't hear one of them, I felt them all.

Then—as if sent from a long distance—a thought interrupted the pleasure: I'd had the courage to leave Robert when he'd been unfaithful, but did I have the courage to take him back?

He must have sensed the interruption, because he increased the pressure of his lips and thrust far deeper into me than he had before, and then we both slipped into the vortex of our climax.

TWENTY-TWO

The following day was Lilly's birthday, and she'd asked for a small dinner party in the studio with just her father and me and Cooper.

"Wouldn't you rather have a big party with all of your friends and our family at a restaurant or at least downstairs in the dining room?" I'd asked.

"It's just another day, Mom. No different than yesterday or tomorrow. And this is how I'd like to spend it. Every day should be a celebration," she'd said. "Let's just get pizza from John's. No balloons, no fuss."

But there were no distractions either, not from thoughts of Dan Mallory, or from what Robert and I were becoming to each other, or from the fact that my daughter was so involved with Cooper that she hadn't taken her eyes off him all night. The only time Cooper had not looked at her was when his eyes returned to the photographs of Lilly that Robert had left up on the walls: images of Lilly intertwined with trees and superimposed on mountains and hidden in canyons.

Cooper was sitting on the couch as close to Lilly as he could be without sitting on top of her. Robert and I were cleaning up before dessert, and Lilly had just finished telling us about Cooper's summer job with a landscape designer.

"So, Cooper, tell us a little about these gardens you'll be designing," Robert said.

"My boss has been hired to build a Zen garden for a client in Westchester. It's better than anything I could have imagined."

"Sounds challenging," Robert said enthusiastically.

"And it fits in perfectly with what I'm studying. The dean of the architecture school even said he's going to give me credit for the summer's work."

"Cooper's already sent his boss three designs that have been incorporated into the final plan," Lilly elaborated proudly.

"Where does the plant material come from? Will your boss have to travel to Japan?" Robert asked.

"No, we'll be able to get most of what we need here."

"And there's going to be a wisteria pergola. Wisteria grows in Japan too, did you know that, Mom?"

"I've always loved wisteria. We don't just have it here," I explained to Cooper. "It grows all over the porch at my grand-mother's house too."

"I know, but it's really overgrown. If you cut it way back, it would flower much more," Cooper suggested. "You know you have some really fine specimen trees out there, Dr. Sloan, but the umbrella spruce, the weeping pine, and the ginkgos all need drastic pruning."

"When did you see the trees in Connecticut?" I asked, since I couldn't remember him ever coming out to the house.

"That weekend I went to the retreat. First we went to Yale and then down to the house," Lilly said, slightly nervous.

"When? For the day?" I asked.

"Well . . . no. We left Yale on Saturday afternoon. There wasn't enough room for all of us to stay at Cooper's."

"You stayed in your grandmother's house alone without dis-cussing it with either your mother or me?" Robert asked.

"Wendy and Pam came with us. We all stayed there. What's the big deal?"

It wasn't that she'd taken Wendy or Pam to the house, but that she'd stayed there overnight with Cooper.

Robert took a deep breath. I saw his jaw working. I knew he was deciding, as I was, if he wanted to confront Lilly on this flagrant disobedience now, on the night of her birthday, or let it drop.

Cooper's eyes darkened in preparation to defend Lilly.

I stood up. "I think it's time for coffee and presents. Robert, would you help me?"

Robert followed me into his small kitchen, but he stood on the threshold, watching what was going on in the studio.

"They are in a full clench, kissing. Her eyes have been glued to him all night. They've never left each other's side," Robert said to me in a low voice.

"Robert, let it go." I started to put the candles on Lilly's cake.

"I can't. She ignores all our rules and regulations. Jordan, she's sleeping with him."

I tried to stifle my laughter. "Of course she's sleeping with him. What did you think? That you were going to keep her a little girl forever?"

"But she's—"

"You know, no man has an easy time with this—"

"Don't talk to me like this is a therapy session, Jordan. Isn't it bothering *you*?"

"That she's sleeping with him? Yes, of course. I'm worried sick about AIDS and pregnancy. But I also know there's no way to stop her. Could my mother have stopped me?"

"You were *nineteen*."

"Sweetheart, come on, be realistic; would you be less bothered by this if Lilly were one year older?"

"No, of course not. But it's all happening so fast and she's not just dating him she's obsessed with him."

"I know. Believe me, I wish she wasn't in so deep—it makes her so vulnerable. I'm afraid she might get hurt."

Robert looked at me for a moment, reading beyond my words. And then he took me in his arms and held me. "Of everything I've done, I can't forgive myself for making you suffer."

"I'm not worried about Lilly because of what happened between us; I'm just plain old worried." I forced a laugh. "Come on, let's enjoy Lilly's birthday and not be the kind of parents we'd hate if we were kids."

I lit the candles, Robert picked up the cake, and we walked back out to the studio.

"Happy Birthday to you . . ."

"No, no, please don't sing," Lilly said as Robert put the cake down in front of her. But we kept on singing while Lilly picked up her camera and took pictures of us—shying away from the attention.

When we'd finished singing, Lilly lowered the camera. Then, suddenly like a little girl, she closed her eyes and made a silent wish.

I cut the cake while she unwrapped her first present. It was from Robert—a new Leica camera with a case full of lenses. Lilly got up and put her arms around him. "Oh, Daddy, it's awesome. Thank you."

After she'd spent a while examining the camera and its accessories, loading it, and shooting a few pictures of Cooper and her father and me, she was ready for her next gift.

Cooper retrieved a big box from the hallway and put it down on the coffee table in front of Lilly.

For a few seconds, she was happy just staring at the package.

"You might like it better if you looked inside," Cooper said.

The unwrapping took a few minutes, but Lilly finally pulled off the last layer of tissue to reveal a bonsai tree: an eighteen-inch pine that grew on a large rock. On the moss that covered the rock sat a china figurine of two old people on a bench. The miniature worked perfectly to skew one's perceptions. If you saw the people in scale, the tree towered above them, sheltering them in the forest.

"I wanted to give you something that would last as long as we will," Cooper said, and kissed her full on the lips. For a moment I felt my heart soften towards him. What he'd said was so sweet and loving; it almost seemed all right that they were together.

Finally, I handed Lilly my gift. After ripping off the wrapping, she examined the suede pouch, reading the gold letters that spelled out the name of my father's jewelry store. Lilly gave me a curious glance, hesitated, and then pulled out the beads and inspected them.

"It's a mala," I said.

"I know . . ."

"The stones are from your grandfather's collection," I said proudly. "They were once part of an Indian princess's necklace, and they're very old."

"But, Mom, don't you know that I don't use a mala?" She was surprised at my ignorance. "In the kind of Zen I practice, when you sit, you meditate on your breath. Not on a mantra or a mala. This just proves how little you know about what I do." Lilly dropped the mala back in the pouch and put the present down on the table.

"Lilly, how can you be so rude? Your mother went to a lot of trouble to have that gift made for you. I think you owe her an apology." Robert's voice was stern.

"Come on, Dad. This is all so hypocritical. Mom can't stand me being involved with Zen, and you know it."

"Oh, Lilly, it's not that I don't approve. It has never been that. It's just the zeal . . . the single-mindedness. Let's not do this now— it's your birthday—let's just have some cake and enjoy the night." I looked down at the cake, away from my daughter's face, and stuck my fork into the thick chocolate icing.

The phone rang interrupting the tension, and Robert answered it.

"Hello? Oh, hi Mom, she's right here; hold on." He held out the phone to Lilly. "It's your grandmother calling to wish you a happy birthday."

Lilly took the portable phone into the darkroom and talked to her grandmother for about ten minutes while Robert and Cooper and I talked about the bonsai tree he'd given her.

When she came back, she handed the phone to me.

I went into the kitchen for some privacy and immediately told my mother what had happened with the mala. "I swear I could kill you for encouraging her with all this stuff. Between you and Cooper, she's in way over her head and it's really ripping us apart."

"Be patient, sweetie. She's overly involved right now, but it's just a stage, I promise. Even if I told Lilly that what she was doing was wrong, she wouldn't hear me. She has to learn it for herself. Lilly is doing something we call strong sitting—being too zealous, myopic. I promise when she comes out of it, you'll have your daughter back."

"If I want her by then," I said sarcastically. "I made the mala out of Dad's emeralds from that Indian necklace, remember?"

"Jordan, did you tell Lilly how valuable those stones are?"

"Of course not. She'd only get even more upset that I was being materialistic. I thought she'd see how beautiful it was whether she knew it was expensive or not."

"That's something your father would say." My mother's voice had lowered, and there was a hint of sadness in her words.

Why does love and its loss have to cause so much pain? I wondered. It was similar to the question Lilly had asked me almost two months ago out at the house in Connecticut the weekend of my birthday. But they were questions I would never have answers to.

Even after so many years and a new marriage and a new life, my mother missed my father.

It is one thing to lose someone you love to someone else. But when someone you love is killed, they are gone, not just from you, but from the world. And your wound never completely heals. When a word is said, or a smell wafts by on the air, or on your grandchild's birthday . . . you feel fresh pain.

"Don't be sad about your father, Jordan. He's always with us. In everything we do. He is part of our universe. Yours, mine, Lilly's."

For some reason my mother's Eastern reference did not disturb me the way Lilly's did but rather, miraculously, brought me some peace.

When I hung up the phone and joined everyone around the cake, Lilly was excitedly talking to Robert about her grandmother's birthday gift.

"And we're going to be able to take a retreat with a Zen master who is visiting from Kyoto."

"What's all this?" I asked.

"Oh, Mom, it's terrific. Grandma's giving us two weeks at the Zen center in August—"

I looked up. "'Us'?"

A shadow crossed my daughter's face.

Cooper smiled. "I'm going with Lilly to San Francisco."

"When did all this get decided?" I asked.

"Just now, when I talked to Grandma. She's sending plane tickets for me and Cooper—the tickets and the retreat, for both of us—that was her present."

Why hadn't my mother discussed this with me first?

"Robert—do you think—?"

Lilly interrupted me. "This doesn't have anything to do with Daddy. Or you. This is a present from Grandma to me. She invited Cooper, and it doesn't matter what you and Daddy want."

"I'm sorry, Lilly, but it does—" I started to say when she interrupted me.

"I can't believe this!" she said, and then she was on her feet, her fists clenched tightly by her sides. "I just turned eighteen and I am old enough to do what I want. It's my life—not yours. You two don't own me. You never did. *I* don't even own me. You can't protect me and you can't stop me; you can only make it so I wind up having to lie to you and do things behind your back."

"While you are living under my roof—" Robert started to say.

Lilly started to laugh. "I can't believe you are using that line on me. All my friends' fathers use that line, and I've always bragged that you never do. That you understood. But you don't! You've forgotten what it's like to want to be with someone and be in love."

"Lilly, sit down," Robert said softly.

"We have to talk about this. You have to hear what we are saying—" I added.

"No, I don't. I'm not paying you to talk to me. I'm not one of your patients. I don't want your advice. I didn't ask for it."

She ran out of the studio, slamming the door behind her.

Cooper turned to us. "I'll go get her," he said in an ice-cold voice. After he left, I slipped the mala into my pocket, where it rested against my hip; a pressure reminding me of the disaster the night had turned into.

While Robert and I cleaned up, we tried to talk about what we should do, but all too quickly I heard the downstairs buzzer ring. I looked at my watch. Damn, it was ten of eight. I had to go; my regular Tuesday night group was arriving. If Lilly had not been so insistent on treating the evening as if it were just another night, I might have canceled that night's session. But I hadn't.

I went down to my office and let in Harry, the first patient to have arrived. I checked to see that the detective was across the street watching and then left the door unlocked, as I always did for the first ten minutes of the group. My policy was that everyone waited in the anteroom until eight-ten; then I'd lock the door again and start the session. I didn't like starting early because the latecomers too often felt uncomfortable walking in after the group was in session.

With ten minutes left, I returned to our apartment to see if Lilly and Cooper were there, but they weren't. Well, at least she wasn't out alone, I thought. I needed to calm down and stop thinking about the scene that had just been played out upstairs.

In my bedroom, I put Lilly's mala into the safe and then returned downstairs to my patients.

Adrienne was late and walked in just as I was shutting the door. By the time we started, I'd slotted away most of the sadness and anger and was ready to work. Sometimes I wondered what was wrong with me that I could disassemble and block my own emotions so efficiently.

It was a difficult session. Steven was being typically quiet, and it annoyed several members of the group. I worried that they were picking up on what was left of my unsettled feelings and tried to relax and let go of what had happened with Lilly.

Adrienne was, as usual, taunting everyone with her caustic comments and challenging me every chance she got.

"Why are you looking at Dr. Sloan that way?" Sonya finally asked her.

"What way?"

"You know," Tony said. "You're acting like you have something you want to say, but you don't want to say it."

"It's none of your business," Adrienne shot back at him.

Everyone's back went up at this.

"That statement makes me feel as if you don't care about me," Tony said.

Several other members of the group echoed his thoughts.

"Well, to be completely truthful, I *don't* care about any of you. Why should I? I don't know any of you. I didn't pick you as friends or colleagues. I'm only here because Jordan wants me here. And I've decided it suits my purpose to humor her." Adrienne was seriously overreacting.

But why? I wondered.

"Her name is Dr. Sloan," Harry said.

"Her name is Jordan. That's what her husband calls her," Adrienne retorted.

"How do you know what her husband calls her?" Sonya asked.

Adrienne stood up. "I know her husband. I know him really well, but Jordan doesn't know *how* well I know him." Everyone looked from her to me. Adrienne continued talking. "What your poor, pathetic *Dr. Sloan* doesn't want to believe is that all men are pricks. At their core, at their deepest center, they are all just pricks. They think with their pricks, they fuck with them, and they fuck women up with them. She just doesn't want to believe how little they care about anyone. Not even our oh so smart Dr. Sloan understands that."

She spewed the words out like venom. I heard what she had said and understood its implications, but I couldn't think about that now; I had to gain control of the situation.

"Everyone relax. Adrienne is obviously upset. Please, Adrienne, sit down."

She stared at me like I was the one spouting gibberish, and then she started laughing. It was a slow, languid laugh. Sexy, seductive, and off-balance.

Sonya, tears in her eyes, got up and went over to Adrienne. "I can feel how upset you are, but don't you dare attack Dr. Sloan."

Adrienne pushed Sonya away.

"It's all right; please, Sonya, please sit down." Before I could say anything else Steven started talking to Adrienne in a soft, gentle voice. "You are really angry, aren't you? Someone took away something you wanted very badly, didn't they?"

She nodded at him. Just a quick movement of her head. But it was enough. Adrienne had focused on the present moment. The wild look left her eyes.

It was ten-fifteen and the session was over, but I needed to keep everyone a little longer to talk about what had just happened.

"I think we should all—" I stopped, interrupted by a loud and pitiful wail coming from upstairs.

What was going on? It sounded like Lilly. Had she come home? Was she with Cooper? Was she hurt?

As I raced up one flight of stairs and then the next, the cries grew louder and more horrible. It *was* Lilly's voice, but her words were unintelligible.

It wasn't until I was just outside the door to Robert's studio that I finally made out the two syllables my daughter was shrieking over and over again.

"Dad-dy, Dad-dy, Dad-dy . . ."

TWENTY-THREE

The studio door stood wide open, and Lilly's cries came from the direction of the darkroom. I found her on the floor, leaning over her father's inert body. A red photographic light, the only light that would not damage light-sensitive film, dimly lit the room.

"Is he breathing?" I asked.

She looked up but didn't seem to understand what I was asking. She continued repeating the same two syllables over and over as if they could rouse him with their repetition. "Dad-dy . . ."

I grabbed the phone and dialed 911, my words rushing out of my mouth so fast the operator had to ask me to slow down. My eyes never left my daughter hunched over her father's prone body. I was seeing them as separate and removed from me. My daughter and my husband were frozen in a grotesque pose. And superimposed on them was a twenty-year-old image of myself hunched over my own father's body.

The two images fused. The red light of the present and the blood I had seen in the past merged. "He's been shot," I said into the phone.

Lilly looked up at me. "He's not moving," she said.

"He's not moving," I repeated to the woman on the other end of the phone.

"We have your address and are sending an ambulance. Is his heart beating?" she asked.

"Lilly, can you hear his heart?" I asked.

Lilly, her head against his chest, listened for a moment that did not seem to end. I could hear my own heart loud as thunder in my ears.

"Yes. Yes. Daddy, Daddy, please, wake up."

In the strange red glow of the darkroom, everything seemed out of context and surreal. Robert's fingers were splayed against the floor. My daughter's long dark hair spread out on his white shirt. Photographs of nude bodies hung from glinting steel. The room was shaking. No, I was shaking; the room was still. As still as the body on the floor.

"Is he breathing? Tell her to put her hand under his nose . . ." the operator asked.

"Lilly, put your hand under his nose, can you feel his breath?"

"No—"

"She can't; why are you wasting time talking to me? Why aren't you sending someone?" I screamed into the phone.

"The ambulance is already on its way, Mrs. Falconer. They're only about a minute from you now. I'm talking to them over the radio as they get closer, giving them the information you're giving me so they can arrive prepared. Can you go downstairs and let them in? They should be there in about thirty seconds. Can you do that? Or is there someone else who can go downstairs?"

"Let them in?" I needed to make sure that I understood her. "Yes, I can let them in."

I put the phone down without hanging it up, and half ran, half fell down the steps until I finally reached the front door, where several of my patients were still congregated, watching the ambulance approach.

The detective who had been watching the house ran up to me. "What's going on?"

"My husband—he's hurt—upstairs," I said.

He pushed past me. My patients stepped aside as I rushed out into the street to flag down the ambulance.

In the midst of all the craziness, I noticed that Harry was holding Sonya and that Tony was smoking a cigarette. The emergency vehicle careened down the block and pulled to a stop in front of our brownstone. Three medics carrying equipment raced towards the steps, and I pointed them upstairs. A police car screeched to a halt behind the ambulance, and the policeman followed the medics inside.

"How many flights?" one of the medics asked.

"Three," I answered.

There was some conversation among them, and one of them ran back out to the ambulance.

By the time I got upstairs again, one medic was positioning an oxygen mask on Robert's face while another jabbed his arm with an IV needle.

"Any allergies?" one of the medics asked me.

"No . . . What's wrong with him?" I asked.

"Is he on any medication?"

"Not that I know of . . . What's wrong with my husband?" I shouted.

"It's going to be okay; we're going to find out," the medic said, and then he leaned over and listened to Robert's chest with a stethoscope.

"I can't get a pulse," another medic announced.

Lilly, who was standing by the sink, started to sway, but I got to her side before she lost her balance. I desperately wanted to cover her eyes and her ears so that she wouldn't see or hear any of this and would never be able to replay it again in her head. From witnessing my father's death, I knew too well how this scene would haunt her for the rest of her life. But I also knew I couldn't have protected her from it any more than my mother could have protected me.

"Do not let him die. Whatever is the matter with him, do not let him die," I heard myself say to the medics. "It's his daughter's birthday. He cannot die on her birthday. It's my daughter's birthday," I repeated. But no one was paying attention to anything I was saying.

"The dispatcher said he was shot—where's the point of entry?" one of the medics asked.

I didn't know.

Finally Lilly turned away and buried her face in my neck, and I felt her tears, hot and wet, on my skin. I held her as tightly as I could in my arms. It was impossible that this was happening.

"There's no gunshot," the medic said.

"Let's get him to the hospital, then," another medic responded.

As the paramedics clustered around Robert, I lost all sight of him except the one hand that was stretched out behind his head. They strapped Robert to a portable gurney and lifted him up, two of them carrying him down the steps, while the third gathered up some of the medical equipment they'd brought upstairs.

Lilly and I followed them down to the street. "We want to go in the ambulance with him," I told them.

Good was barking, jumping up on us. Even the dog knew something was wrong. "Put her inside, sweetie," I said to Lilly, who, moving like a zombie, grabbed the dog by the collar and pulled her inside. A few seconds later she came out, shutting the door behind her.

"There's no room in the back of the ambulance, Mrs. Falconer," one of the medics explained. "The police officer will take you and your daughter to the hospital."

"No—I—" I started to say we had to go with him but realized I would only be distracting them and Robert needed all of their attention.

The detective said he would take us, and opened the back door. "Do you have your keys? A bag?" he asked me.

"No—I don't—"

"Why don't you go back and get them? It's going to take the medics that long to get your husband settled into the ambulance anyway," the detective told me.

I ran back into the apartment. As soon as I stepped inside, Good rushed me and I had to push her away while I grabbed my bag. Lilly had followed me and turned on the radio—which is what we always did when we left the dog home alone.

Good whimpered, and of all the things that had happened, that was what triggered my tears.

Lilly and I went back downstairs and were in the back of the detective's car within seconds of the ambulance's taking off. The hospital was only a few blocks away, and we were there in less than five minutes.

Lilly and I got out of the car and waited while the paramedics lifted the gurney out of the ambulance, and then we followed right behind them as they rolled Robert into the ER.

Once inside, a group of doctors and nurses immediately surrounded him, and all we could see was the IV pole above their heads.

How odd, I thought, they have made the emergency room look like the set of a TV show. And then I realized how ridiculous I was being; it was the other way around. My mind wasn't working right.

There was no sense of time, only of dread. Concentrating on Lilly's face, I reached out with a tissue from my bag and tried to wipe away her constant flow of tears.

Around us, other emergency cases were brought in, people with gaping wounds and broken limbs. Somewhere an infant cried incessantly and a man shouted in Spanish.

The doctors took Robert into a partitioned cubicle and pulled the curtain shut.

"What are they doing to him? Why can't we be in the room with him?" Lilly asked me.

I had to make an effort to open my mouth and speak. "As soon as they know what's wrong, they will come out and talk to us, sweetheart. It's more important that they figure out what's wrong."

About an hour later a young doctor did come out to give us an update.

"Your husband is in a coma, Mrs. Falconer. I'm not sure why, yet. But I do have some questions. Can you tell me if he was on any medication?"

Dozens of questions and very few satisfying answers later, Lilly asked the doctor if she could see her father.

"We're transferring him to intensive care in a few minutes. It's on the second floor. Why don't you meet him up there? He's hooked up to a lot of life support but don't be frightened. We're doing everything we can to help him."

"Do you have any idea what's wrong? What's going to happen to him?" I asked.

He looked into my eyes. "I don't know, Mrs. Falconer. Not yet."

Lilly and I took the elevator up to the intensive care unit, where it was much quieter and much colder than it had been in the emergency room. We were both shivering as the nurse showed us into a small partitioned-off room where Robert lay on the bed. Lilly took a step back, frightened despite the doctor's warning. I took her hand, trying to be strong for her, but I was frightened too. There were tubes coming out of his nose and IVs going into each arm, and he was hooked up to at least three large monitors, which flanked the bed.

His skin was devoid of color, and the only proof that he was alive came from the blinking and bleeping machines he was connected to.

The nurse, who was standing behind us, finally spoke. "You can stay as long as you want. But we're going to be checking him every fifteen minutes, so sometimes we'll have to ask you to wait in the lounge down the hall."

"Can he hear us?" Lilly asked the nurse in a hoarse voice.

"We don't know for certain. But we think it helps if you talk to him. You can even hold his hand. I think he'll know you're here."

Suddenly one of the machines started to sound an alarm. "What is that? What does that mean? Mom?" Lilly turned to me, panicking.

The nurse hit a button on the offending machine. "That's nothing. Not every noise means something's wrong. You have to remember that, okay? And every machine in here is connected to a computer at the nurses' station. So even if one of us is not in the room, we are constantly aware of what's going on."

"Do you think it would be all right for us to have a few minutes alone with him now?"

"Sure, that would be fine. I'll be back."

I held on to the edge of the bed for support while Lilly walked up to Robert's side and took his hand.

"Daddy, I know you can hear me. Squeeze my hand if you can hear me, that's all, just squeeze my hand."

But nothing happened, and after a few minutes Lilly dropped his hand and turned to me, weeping anew.

I took her out into the hall and into the waiting room, where I held her and rocked her and let her cry.

I wasn't crying, yet, and I wouldn't. I had to stay in control for Lilly. All I could think about while my daughter sobbed in my arms was why loving someone always came to grief and if it was worth it in the end.

Abruptly, Lilly stopped crying and began to talk. "It was awful. I went up to the studio, but no one was there. I was going to leave when I smelled something weird and started to look around, and then I found Dad on the floor in the darkroom. He looked so helpless. I've never seen him like that. Even when he's asleep, he looks so strong. I called out to him, but he didn't answer, and I tried to shake him, and then I poured water on him. Did I hurt him by doing that? I don't even know why I did it. I just poured water on him. Did I make it worse?"

I knew Lilly would have to talk this out, repeat the facts of the evening over and over until she began to accept them.

"No, you did the right thing." I was trying to figure out what she meant by the smell. "Where did you go, sweetheart, when you left the studio?"

"I went to Wendy's house."

I nodded. Her friend's house was only two blocks away. "I thought you'd gone downstairs and that Cooper had gone down to get you and the two of you had gone out together."

"No. I don't know where Cooper is—I thought he stayed home."

"All I know for sure is that he went looking for you after you ran out of the studio. Does he have a key, in case we don't get home? Or can you call him, sweetheart, and tell him to go back to school? I don't think he should be in the house all alone. Not with Mallory still missing."

"He has a set of keys. I gave them to him this afternoon. He wanted to go pick up my present and didn't want me to go with him. But I can call him. He has a cell phone."

I handed her my phone, and she called and got his voice mail and told him that her father had had an accident and that he should go back to Yale because she and I were going to be at the hospital all night.

"I wish he'd answered," she said after she hung up. "I would have liked to talk to him."

"I know, darling," I said, and pulled her closer so she could lean against me, and I could lean against her.

TWENTY-FOUR

There was no day or night in intensive care: the lights were bright all the time; nursing shifts changed without announcement; doctors came to look, listen, prod, and poke Robert and then left, often without giving us any news.

There were no real walls separating the patients of the ICU, and so I was aware of everything going on beyond the partitions bordering Robert's.

The antiseptic smells soothed me, but the human smells that emanated from the cubicle next door, where an old Russian woman lay dying, made me sick. Her sons were with her, praying over her tiny body, and their keening frightened Lilly.

Finally at about two o'clock in the morning, Lilly fell asleep in the waiting room. I went back and forth from there to Robert's cubicle and spent the night watching them both sleep.

The mechanical sounds of Robert's machines made me drowsy until one of them would blast an alarm and a nurse would come in to check on him. And each time I held my breath until she told me that he was all right, that he was still alive.

I desperately wanted to know what had happened to Robert and what was going to happen to him, to find out if he was ever going to wake up or if he was going to die. But no one knew anything yet.

Staring at the unconscious form on the bed, I wondered what Robert was thinking—if he was even thinking. Do you dream when you are in a coma? No one could tell me. Willing him to wake up so that I could look into his eyes, I said his name over and over as if it were some kind of prayer. I needed to look into his eyes, even if it was only once more.

Why wouldn't he wake up? What had happened? Why didn't anyone come and tell me what was wrong? Why wasn't it the next day or the day before, why wasn't it any other time at all except for that time and that place?

At about seven in the morning, Lilly came in, bleary-eyed and groggy. When she saw that nothing had changed, her tears began again. I sent her home to shower and eat something and walk the dog and to bring me back some clean clothes. At nine o'clock my brother arrived with a detective named Frank Tadlock. They took me down to the cafeteria and over coffee told me what they had figured out so far.

I stirred sugar into my coffee with a wooden stick. Only when Simon put his hand out to stop me did I realize I'd been stirring it obsessively.

"There was a contained fire in a garbage can in your husband's darkroom last night. We don't yet know what was burned, but we do know that the heat caused a can of nitrate film to explode and that the inhalation of the fumes from that explosion induced your husband's coma."

"We have to tell the doctors—" I started to get up, but Simon stopped me.

"We've already spoken to Mr. Falconer's doctors," the detective said. "Unfortunately the information was not that helpful. This isn't like a snake bite where there's an antidote."

"We just have to wait and pray that Robert will come out of this very soon," Simon said.

"How long do they think it will take?" I asked.

Simon shrugged. "All the doctor said was the longer Robert remains in the coma the more dangerous it is. We have to stay positive and believe he'll wake up. And be there for Lilly and . . . try to find Mallory."

"Do you think Mallory had something to do with this?" I asked. Suddenly, it was all confused in my head. "Do you even know about Dan Mallory?" I asked the detective.

"Yes, I've been filled in on the whole story and have spoken to Jim Rafferty at length," Tadlock said.

"Do you think Mallory tried to kill Robert to get back at me?"

"That depends on how and when that can of film got into your husband's darkroom," Tadlock said. "Do you know?"

"Yes, he's had if for several weeks; it's part of a job he's working on."

"And did your husband know how dangerous that film was?"

"Yes. Yes, he knew."

"In that case, I doubt the fire had anything to do with Dan Mallory. How would he have known about the film?" Tadlock asked.

"I can't imagine he could have."

"But you knew about it?"

I nodded yes.

"Who else knew about it? Who else has access to the darkroom?"

"Only my husband and my daughter use the darkroom. And Lilly left the studio before I did. I was the last one to leave. Except for Robert. He was still there when I left." I watched Tadlock uncap a pen and scribble something in his spiral-bound notebook. Then he flipped backwards to a previous page full of notes.

"But I'm confused. Why are you asking me these questions? Don't you think it was an accident?"

"An accident is possible but unlikely. It's more probable that someone set that fire deliberately." He recapped his pen and laid it down on top of the notebook.

"Why is that?"

"Your husband wouldn't have burned anything in his own darkroom knowing how dangerous that film was. You are certain he knew how dangerous it was, aren't you?"

"Yes, absolutely. He was just discussing it with some people at a party last weekend." Last weekend . . . it seemed so long ago. "Can I go back to Robert's room now? Are you done?" I stood up.

"Mrs. Falconer, I know this is a terrible time for you, but I need just a few more minutes. The undercover policeman watching your brownstone last night reported that a dozen people came and went between the hours of eight and nine-thirty. Can you tell me who they were?"

"People? What people?" I couldn't think. Around us the cafeteria was filling up. The clattering of plates and silverware and the smell of coffee and eggs distracted me. You could tell the visitors from the hospital staff by the emotion on people's faces. The staff laughed and joked and ate quickly. The visitors stared off into space.

"Oh, you mean my patients," I realized finally. "I had a group therapy session last night at eight o'clock. But there are only ten patients in the group."

I had to think about it for a few seconds before I figured out who the other two people were. "Ten patients plus my daughter and her boyfriend."

"Could I have a list of your patients' names and their phone numbers. We need to talk to them and find out what, if anything, they noticed."

"I don't think I can— Oh, no!" I said.

"What is it?' Simon asked.

"I had three patients this morning. I completely forgot about them. Someone is probably standing there right now ringing the bell, waiting to get in. I have to call—"

"Before you go, can I have those names and phone numbers?" Tadlock asked.

"No, I can't do that."

"It's important that we talk to them. One of your patients might have seen something," Tadlock insisted.

"Would it be all right if I called them first and let them know you will be calling? Make sure they feel comfortable with me giving out their phone numbers."

Detective Tadlock nodded. "How much time do you need before I send someone over to get the names and numbers from you?"

"A few hours. I have . . . I think I have everyone's work number in my book. I can call Lilly and ask her to bring my book with her when she comes back."

"Or I can take you home for a while, Jordan. You can take a shower. Change," Simon offered.

"No, I'm not leaving Robert."

I felt safe at the hospital. The doctors in their green pants and shirts and the efficient nurses all in white comforted me. At home there would only be the silence and the phone and the waiting.

"Are you sure that it wasn't an accident?" I asked Tadlock again.

"Pretty sure. One last thing, we need to arrange to take your fingerprints and your daughter's and anyone else's who might have been in the darkroom with your husband."

"I told you, Robert never let anyone else into the darkroom but Lilly." And then I remembered that Cooper had slept there, but that hardly seemed important enough to mention.

"Okay. But if you think of anyone, let me know." He capped his pen and then remembered something. "Your brother told me that quite a few people are upset about your husband's upcoming show. Has he gotten any threats?"

I didn't know. Suddenly I wondered how many other things I didn't know about Robert's life.

After Detective Tadlock left, Simon came upstairs with me and sat in Robert's room and watched him sleep. When Lilly came back with my bag and my address book, Simon left to go to his office but promised to return at the end of the day.

I left Lilly with Robert and went out to the waiting room to call my patients and let them know that the police would be phoning and that their sessions were canceled.

Their reactions were varied, and I no longer remember who said what. But no one from Tuesday night's group objected to speaking to the police. The only people I didn't reach were Adrienne Blessing and Tony Riggio, and I hoped I would remember to call them again before the police reached them. I didn't want to leave messages on their machines. But if I had no other choice, I would.

Our first full day in the hospital passed slowly. Lilly and I were both exhausted by the inactivity and Robert's unchanging condition. Chloe came during lunch to keep us company and to hold my hand. She brought sandwiches, which she tried to get us to eat, but neither Lilly nor I had any appetite. Nor did Chloe after she'd seen Robert lying unconscious on the bed.

Bravely, she tried to look at him, but I could tell how frightened she was.

"You don't have to pretend; it's all right. We know how bad he looks, how serious it is."

Chloe shook her head. "The last thing you need is to try and make me feel comfortable. I came here to help you."

"The only way anyone can help us is to make Robert well," I said.

At around two in the afternoon, a policeman from the detective's office came by to get my patients' phone numbers and our fingerprints. At three Lilly went back home to walk the dog.

When Lilly returned, she sat in the corner of the room, closed her eyes, and began to meditate. Sitting still and breathing deeply, she retreated deep into herself, and I suddenly felt as if I was the only conscious one in the room. Where was my daughter? The child who needed to hold my hand, who cried and came running to me when she was scared or hurt? Where was Robert with his ironic smile and calming presence?

After about twenty minutes, Lilly opened her eyes—and there was some light in them again. She went over to Robert's bed and took his hand. "It's all right, Daddy, you can sleep. I know you're tired and need rest, but tomorrow you will wake up." Her voice cracked. I reached out for her hand, and for a moment she let me hold it. Her hand was as large as mine was. When had she become an adult?

Sitting in the chair beside Robert's bed, I fell asleep for a while. In my dream a man who stood in shadows grew larger and larger, taking up more of the air in the room, making it harder and harder for me to breathe—the next thing I knew someone was shaking me.

"You're having a nightmare, Mom. Wake up. Wake up."

I opened my eyes. First I saw Robert, still and quiet. Then I turned to Lilly. "I used to wake you up from nightmares. Now it's your turn, huh?" I tried to joke.

"Dad is going to wake up too," Lilly said with confidence.

I hadn't noticed until then, but she had her camera with her, hanging around her neck. I watched with surprise as she lifted it up to her eye and began photographing Robert.

"What are you doing?" My voice was harsher than I'd intended.

"I want him to hear the sound. It's a good sound to him. It's a life-affirming sound. It might help. And I have to take these pictures. He'll want to see them."

"I don't think you should take pictures of him, Lilly."

"It's what is going on now. He'll want to know. I'm going to develop them tonight so I can show them to him tomorrow when he wakes up."

"But, Lilly, Lilly, don't you understand how sick your father is?"

"No, you're the one who doesn't understand. This is not your father who didn't get better. This is my father, and he's going to be fine. Where is your faith? What's wrong with you? You have to believe in him getting better. You have to."

Underneath I knew she was angry, but she was exerting enormous self-control, remaining calm and staying centered.

"Lilly, it's all right to get angry," I said.

"I'm not angry."

"You must be angry, sweetie. And scared and confused. Your father is lying here in a coma. He may not live—"

She put her hands up over her ears and shut her eyes, like a child. I could see her at six, at seven, taking this stance when she didn't like something I was saying to her.

Then she sat back down in the corner and resumed her meditation pose and left me again.

"Lilly, don't—"

Without opening her eyes, and in a voice so soft I had to lean forward to hear her, she whispered: "I need to breathe now. I have to breathe. Please, Mother. Let . . . me . . . do . . . my . . . breathing."

Perry came a little while later, and we all took turns talking to Robert and breaking up the monotony with trips downstairs to the cafeteria for tea or coffee or something from the vending machines. Once, I went outside and walked up and down the block in front of the hospital. In my head I was talking to my father . . . *Don't let anything happen to Robert. Not now that I've finally found him again. Please. Haven't we all been through enough? I don't want to spend any more of my life missing people. I miss you enough. Please.*

Perry went home when Simon arrived with more sandwiches, and he sat with us by Robert's bed, watching for some sign of change. After several hours, he tried to convince us to go home and get some sleep, but we both refused.

"I don't care what you want. Neither of you are going to be any good to anyone if you stay here another night," he insisted.

I looked at Robert in the bed. He had been in a coma for twenty-four hours. That was already a long time. Every hour he stayed in that state made his chances of recovery worse. Why wouldn't he wake up?

Simon took me by the arm and tried to move me. "Come home, Jordan. Lilly needs you to take her home."

My brother was right. I walked over to the bed and touched Robert's forehead with my fingertips. I whispered good night to him and then followed Simon out of the room. Lilly stayed behind for a few seconds to say her good night.

In the hallway, I paced, worried about leaving. The doctors hadn't given us any real hope—there was simply nothing they could do for Robert but keep him on life support and wait. "Should I leave, Simon? What if he doesn't t make it through the night? What if we are home and they need us here?"

"Jordan, if there is any change, the hospital will call you. You only live five blocks away," Simon reassured me.

I started to cry as soon as we stepped inside our brownstone.

"I'm staying here with both of you tonight," Simon said. "And by the way, neither of you are going upstairs to the studio. First of all, the police haven't finished up there yet, and second of all, you don't need to do that to yourselves."

My brother poured brandy for both my daughter and me, and the three of us settled down in the living room. Lilly got tired first and started to fall asleep on the couch. I woke her up and helped her to her room. Without getting undressed, she walked to the bed, rubbed her eyes, lay down, and almost immediately fell asleep.

When I came back to the living room, I saw that Simon was hanging up the phone. He looked grim.

"Is it Robert? Did something happen?" I asked.

"No. Nothing new from the hospital. But I just spoke to Detective Tadlock. The police just got finished talking to one of your patients—Adrienne Blessing?"

"Yes, I assumed they talked to all my patients by now. She and Tony were the only ones who I couldn't get to personally; I left them both messages."

"Jordan, she told the police that she was having an affair with Robert. That he was planning to leave you to marry her."

My laughter sounded hysterical even in my own ears, but I couldn't stop it. No food, no sleep, and then the single shot of brandy had done me in.

"Jordan?"

"An affair? With Robert? No. She's one of my patients. She hired him to shoot a commercial for her agency—"

Yet even as I tried to deny it, I knew it could be true. Adrienne had made so many allusions to the affair during Tuesday night's group therapy session and in our last private sessions. She had told me she was in therapy with *me* specifically because I could help her get what she wanted. She'd said— What *had* she said?—I had to get my notes. I needed to know exactly what she'd said.

"Oh, Simon, I don't know. Maybe she had dated him once or twice, but Robert told me he wasn't seeing anyone—"

My brother was looking at me strangely.

"There is something else, isn't there?" I asked. "What is it?"

"Adrienne told the police you had the motive and the means to try and kill Robert. She claims he told her you wanted him back and that when he explained that he was with Adrienne, you went crazy and threatened him. She has given the police the names of two witnesses who were there with you when Robert described that he was working with that nitrate film and how dangerous it was—"

"Simon, am I a suspect?"

"Not yet. But you are now under suspicion."

I knew my brother well enough to know he still hadn't told me everything. "What else?" I asked. "What else could there possibly be?"

"She's gone to the newspapers with the whole sordid story."

"This is crazy." I was twisting the rings on my finger. Around and around, faster and faster.

"Jordan, listen to me, the police are still investigating. They aren't ready to charge you yet."

Tears did not come. Nor shouts or cries or even whispers of words. Nothing mattered. Nothing was logical. Nothing made sense.

"We have to talk about hiring you a lawyer," Simon said.

"Simon, was Robert lying to me? I don't understand. Not this time. He told me he wanted to—" But how I felt didn't matter. "I don't want Lilly to find out about all this. Not now. Not while Robert is in a coma."

"Lilly will be fine. I'll sit down with her and explain that it is only an allegation and that the woman who made it is not psychologically sound."

"Lilly shouldn't have to deal with all this. Not now, Simon. Not now."

He took my hands. "Jordan, listen to me. Lilly is a strong kid. She'll understand. You have to have some faith in her. She loves you and Robert. She's not going to believe some nut who—"

"I know Adrienne Blessing. She's credible, Simon. I know her. I know how she looks and speaks and how smart and successful she is. People are going to believe her."

"No they aren't. It's all going to be okay."

"But my fingerprints are all over that studio. I was the last one to see Robert alive—I even told Tadlock that I was alone with him."

I was shouting because I was frightened. The image of Lilly looking down at her father in that hospital bed haunted me. How could Lilly deal with losing both her mother and her father at the same time?

Starting at the beginning, I made Simon repeat everything Adrienne had told the police. Somehow my own patient had manipulated me. But why? Nine other people could testify Adrienne had said she was sleeping with my husband. Two people who'd sat at our table at George Lawson's party could testify that I knew that can of film was in Robert's studio and how dangerous it was.

But I could prove I was the one who'd gone to the divorce lawyer, not Robert. Robert had told me he wanted us to be together again, not to get divorced.

"Wait, Simon. Maybe Adrienne did it. Maybe she *did* know Robert and maybe he broke off with her when he and I started to see each other again and maybe she set that fire to get revenge. People do have psychotic breaks. They do desperate things. Maybe she's a dangerous woman. *She* was in our building that night. *She* was late to get to group. The front door was unlocked for almost fifteen minutes. Maybe while I was downstairs with the rest of the group, she went upstairs . . ." As upset as I was, I knew, from the expression on my brother's face, that I had given him something to work with.

"All right, Jordan. We'll figure it out. But now you need to get some rest." Simon took me by the arm and led me to my bedroom. He did not tell me I was hysterical; he did not patronize me; he did not use words to calm me. Instead he took off my shoes, my sweater, and ran a bath for me. He left me in the bathroom and told me to get undressed and get into the tub, and that in the meantime he would call Tadlock and tell him everything I'd just explained.

I did what he said. I took off my clothes, settled into the warm water, and let its heat soak into my skin. On the other side of the bathroom door, I heard my brother's voice repeating my story to Tadlock.

~

When I came out of the bathroom in my robe, Simon helped me get into bed and then sat by my side.

"Do you think you can fall asleep?" he asked.

"Not yet. Will you talk to me for a while?"

"Do you remember when we were kids, how I would call out to you from my room and ask you to come in and help me do something. You'd be all happy and excited, thinking I wanted to play with you, but when you came in, I'd ask you to change the television channel? And you would do it because you always thought that, maybe this time, if you did what I asked, I would let you stay in my room and watch TV with me. Or how I would convince you to go into the kitchen and make me a sandwich. And you would. For years you did everything I wanted. Until you finally figured it out and you went into the kitchen and made me that last sandwich, the one where you mixed the tuna fish with the Tabasco sauce, steak sauce, and dishwashing liquid, do you remember? After I ate it, after I threw up, I got so mad at you that I dumped all your Barbie dolls and their clothes down the incinerator. And then we sat there and waited to see if I was going to start blowing bubbles like that episode of the *Little Rascals* where Alfalfa blows bubbles out of his mouth because he's eaten the soap. Do you remember when Mom found us, and demanded we tell her what was wrong, and both of us kept quiet?"

I could hear his voice; it was even and steady and slowly relaxed me.

"Remember how Mom and Dad always said that I was your older brother and I had to protect you? And I would argue with them and tell them I didn't want to protect you. That you could protect yourself and I didn't want to have to worry about you all the time?"

Simon's voice had the same soothing effect on me as the bath-water had. I wanted all of this to be over and done with and to be with Robert and Lilly and Simon and Perry and their kids in my grandmother's house, where we would all be safe. I'd even let Cooper come, I was thinking. I'd go easy on Lilly and wouldn't give her a hard time.

I had never bargained with God, I wasn't even sure if I knew who God was, but I was ready to offer prayers and promises if it would help Robert and give Lilly her father back.

I woke up at five in the morning and called the hospital before I got out of bed but was told that there was no change in Robert's condition.

When I walked into the kitchen an hour later, Simon was sitting at the kitchen table sipping coffee. I poured myself a cup, sat down, and looked at the pile of newspapers on the table. He must have gone out to the deli on the corner because I didn't have a subscription to the *Daily News* or the *New York Post*. But there they were.

On page three of the *News*, the headline read: "Photographer victim of attempted murder." The reporter had interviewed Adrienne Blessing, owner of the Alternative Agency, who had been questioned by the police about her lover, Robert Falconer, who was hospitalized due to an accident that had involved nitrate film. "Dr. Jordan Sloan, Robert Falconer's ex-wife, the successful psychotherapist, had been trying to resuscitate the marriage . . ."

I didn't even bother with the *Post*.

Other brothers might have kept the articles away from their sisters. But Simon was smart enough to know that the best thing, the very best thing he could do for me was to get me angry. To give me a challenge.

Yes, Robert was in the hospital, but while I waited for him to wake up, I was going to fight back.

TWENTY-FIVE

Lilly and I spent another day at Robert's bedside, but there was no improvement. The tubes dripped their chemicals and nourishment into his body while other people lived their lives. My friends came and went. More nurses changed shifts. More doctors arrived, poked, and prodded and left. But Robert still remained in a coma.

At eight that night I convinced Lilly to go home with her friend Wendy and spend the night at her house and, except for the nurse, I was alone with Robert and his machines.

There is a stillness in a hospital after the visitors have left that is as strong a presence as noise might be. The droning voices of overhead television sets are the loudest thing you hear. The nurses move around quietly on their crepe-soled shoes, checking on vital signs and drawing blood for tests. And occasionally there is the mechanical beeping of a machine reacting to a loss of pulse or breath or life itself.

The man I married eighteen years ago lay in a deeper sleep than he had ever known, while I held his hand and whispered to him.

Earlier that afternoon the day nurse had promised that he could hear me, but the night nurse stood at the foot of the bed and, in a very solicitous tone, told me that he probably couldn't.

"Did I ask you? I didn't ask you. I don't want you to tell me," I said, and the anger in my voice caused her to back away from the bed and from me and take refuge near the door. I did not care what she said or what she thought. I wanted to believe Robert could hear me, needed to believe it. He had always heard me, no matter what lay between us. It was my job to hear other people, but only Robert took it upon himself to hear me.

So I continued talking to Robert, regardless of whether he could hear me or not. As much for my own sanity as for his well-being.

"Talking is a cure," I said to him, even though I was not at all sure of it anymore. And I should have been sure of it. I made my living talking and listening to my patients talk.

Robert had now been in this hospital for two days, and every time another hour passed, I wondered if this would be the hour when he finally woke up or . . . I couldn't finish the thought.

"Lilly brought her camera here again today," I told Robert. "Is it macabre that she wants to take pictures of you like this? Or is it just the way you and she process pain? Through the lens?"

If Robert could have spoken, he would have told me not to worry and to let Lilly be.

It was a favorite expression of his. "Let Lilly be." He used to say it to the whole room when our daughter was in her nightmare stage and afraid to go to bed. "Let Lilly be!" He'd shout into the closet and under the bed. None of my therapeutic jargon helped her, only his words. Before he'd leave her for the night, he'd lean over her bed with his golden hair falling into her face and he'd tickle her until her laughter chased away whatever demons had been visiting her. Then Robert would laugh along with her and his eyes would crinkle in the corners.

But on Thursday evening his eyes were closed and his hair was greasy. Tomorrow I would ask the nurse to help me wash it. And shave him. He was so proud of his looks and his hard lean body—he'd have been horrified if he could have seen himself.

"They think . . ." I said to my husband, needing him to hear me, "there was some kind of foul play."

I stared at his face for some flicker of acknowledgment. For a twitch of his eyelid or a parting of his full lips.

His arm lay on top of the blankets. It was well-toned and muscular but motionless. I put my hand inside his and curled his fingers around mine, pretending for the moment that he had taken my hand.

"You are so handsome," I said.

He always smiled when I told him that. And I always told him. No matter how much I loved him or hated him, and I have done both.

But that night he did not smile. There was no reaction—he just continued to lie motionless in that bed. Robert had not moved for forty-eight hours. There were times when I wanted to make his mouth move and form words for him because I couldn't stand to watch so vibrant and vital a man be so still and slack.

These machines are keeping him alive, I was thinking. If not for these machines . . . If there were a blackout—

I looked up at the nurse. "What would happen if the city had a blackout? What would happen to his machines?"

"We have a generator, Mrs. Falconer; it's okay."

The relief was so great and I was so worn out by worry, I started to cry.

Staring at Robert through the blur of tears, I suddenly noticed a bowl of fruit on his bedside table. When had it arrived? Who had brought it? I stared at the grapes, the peaches, and the figs—just like the fruit Adrienne had brought me so often.

Had she been here when I was out? Had she sent the fruit? I asked the nurse if she'd seen who had brought the basket into the room, but she had no idea.

I knew, though; it had to have been Adrienne Blessing.

"Who was she to you, Robert? Robert? Answer me," I shouted.

But the stone-still man in the bed remained silent. Greater than my anger was my fear. And greater than both was my sadness for our daughter, who was as much in love with her father as I was. Even though he might still have been cheating on me.

"Mrs. Sloan?"

I looked away from Robert and towards the door. A man was standing there, holding a well-worn notebook.

"Mrs. Sloan, I'm Detective Gershon," he said, nodding at me. "I'm sorry about the hour, but I need to ask you some questions." And as he entered the room, he pulled the cuff of his shirt down over his watch, as if further apologizing for the time.

TWENTY-SIX

What was going on? Hadn't Simon said the police weren't ready to question me? So what was this detective doing at the hospital?

"I'm sure there is some kind of mistake." I was staring at one of the monitors that showed Robert's oxygen rate. After two days and three nights of being riveted to the screens, I knew exactly how to read his vital signs.

"No, there's no mistake. I need to talk to you, Mrs. Sloan."

I turned back to the man in the doorway and wondered why Detective Tadlock had sent someone else instead of coming himself. But it wasn't the detectives that mattered. It was the doctors I cared about and waited for, hungry for any morsel of information they could give me about Robert's condition.

"I need you to come to the station house with me," the detective said.

"No, I'm sorry. My brother worked all this out. I can't leave my husband now."

"Mrs. Sloan, please don't make this difficult for me. This is a criminal investigation. You don't really have a choice."

I stared at Robert. Why wouldn't he just wake up and tell them what they needed to know?

"Mrs. Sloan?" the detective repeated my name.

Oh, Robert, get up, please. But he didn't move.

I bent over and kissed Robert's cold, gray cheek, grabbed my bag, and followed the detective out of the door and into the hall.

I looked at my watch. It was almost ten o'clock.

"I have to go home first and walk my dog. Can I at least meet you at the station house later?"

"Listen, would you rather if I took you home and talked to you there?"

"Yes, please." It was a small thing, but I felt grateful. "I only live a few blocks away. I usually walk. Is that okay? I need some air."

The detective asked polite questions about Robert's condition as we walked the five short blocks home. As soon as I opened the front door, the dog started barking upstairs. I ushered the detective into my office and told him I'd be right back. "I don't want to alarm my daughter. I'll just let her know what's going on and be right back."

"Sure, I have kids too. It's fine. I'll wait here. Do you have an ashtray?" He was looking around the room, examining the shelves, staring at the drawings on the wall.

I pointed to the ashtray I kept on the bottom bookshelf for patients who needed it. As he reached for it, I noticed his watch. It was almost identical to mine, to the watch that my father had worn every day.

"I have to go tell Lilly I'm here," I said, and left the detective to his cigarette.

Upstairs, Good jumped on me, wanting to be petted. She was so lucky that she didn't know what was going on. Her eyes were wide in anticipation. She was waiting for her treat—habit told her she usually got one when I arrived home.

And then I noticed that the apartment was dark. Why had Lilly shut off all the lights? As I walked toward her room I had a moment of panic followed by one of relief when I realized that Lilly wasn't home. I had forgotten that she had gone to Wendy's.

Detective Gershon was waiting outside my office door, watching me come down the steps.

"In all the confusion, I forgot, my daughter isn't here."

"Not here?" He seemed perturbed.

Why did it matter to him where Lilly was?

"Don't you know where your daughter is?" he asked.

From inside my bag, my cellular phone rang, and I ran to answer it.

Gershon was saying something, but I wasn't paying attention. I'd given the nurse at the hospital my number and she'd promised to call if there were any changes.

"Mrs. Falconer, this is Dr. Heller."

"Did he wake up?" I asked. "Oh, no, is anything wrong?"

"Not a thing. Quite the opposite. Your husband moved his hands several times. It's very significant, and we wanted you to know right away. I also think it might be a good idea if you were here to talk to him. He's still sleeping, but we think he might—"

"Yes. Yes," I interrupted him. "Thank you. I'll be right there."

I snapped the phone shut, grabbed my bag, and ran out of my office.

"Where are you going?" Gershon demanded as he followed me out the front door.

"I have to get to the hospital, my husband's waking up," I said as I raced down the front steps and onto the street. "I'm sorry, but I just can't answer your questions now." I glanced back one last time and saw him still standing on the steps, holding on to the handrail. He didn't look pleased.

I rushed into Robert's room in ICU and found the night nurse sitting in the chair where I usually sat. She smiled at me. "He's showing quite a bit of physical response. Why don't you talk to him, try to get him to wake up."

I sat by the bed and took Robert's hand in mine. His fingers didn't move. What if the doctor had been wrong? What if Robert had moved involuntarily and it was all a mistake? There was no response when I pressed my fingers into his. Robert's hand was as slack as it had been for the past two days.

I waited. I talked to him. I did what Simon had done with me; I told Robert stories from our life. I told him what I could remember about each of our trips to Europe. I described in detail all of his photographs and told him which ones I liked the best.

Going all the way back into the past, I told him what I'd done in the year that he had left me. I listed the name of every man I'd gone out with to try to get over him. I told him stories about Lilly, reminding him of all the firsts we'd witnessed together. I talked about how he'd been the only one I could talk to about my father after the murder, and how he'd given me a future to look forward to, to believe in. I talked about our wedding at my grandmother's house, our honeymoon in California. I even told him how awful I'd felt when I found him in the darkroom with that model.

I'd never spoken aloud about it, but I did that night. I told the man I had been married to how he had ripped apart my heart and how the pieces had never quite fit back together again. Anything to rouse him.

But nothing made him move. Not all that night. Not early the next morning. Yet I kept talking, going over and over our lives together in excruciating detail. I was trying everything I could think of to stir him.

At seven, the nurses changed shifts, and the morning nurse told me she'd take over so I could go downstairs and get some coffee, but I was reluctant to leave the room.

"Come on, get out of here. Take a walk around the block. We'll be fine," she said, and patted me on the hand.

Fifteen minutes later I was back in Robert's room, talking to him again.

"I'm going to get his meds, Mrs. Falconer," the nurse said. "I'll be right back."

"Did you hear her call me Mrs. Falconer, Robert? They all do. And I haven't corrected a single one of them. Everyone takes for granted that it is my name too. That's one of the reasons it's so hard for a woman to be married and stay independent." There was no response. "Men don't understand what it's like, but you understood better than most. You never needed to own me, and it was all right with you that I kept my name . . . wasn't it? You understood that I wanted to keep 'Sloan' to keep something of my father alive. But it's strange—I'm so used to being 'Dr. Sloan' and all of a sudden everyone is calling me Mrs. Falconer. You know what, Robert—I love it whenever a doctor or a nurse or even one of the detectives calls me Mrs. Falconer; I—"

Suddenly I thought of something.

"Except for that detective who was here last night. He called me *Mrs*. Sloan. Isn't that odd? People who know me professionally call me Dr. Sloan, and sometimes people who know me through you or Lilly call me Mrs. Falconer. But that detective last night called me Mrs. Sloan. I don't even understand why he was here. Simon said the police weren't ready to talk to me. But this detective insisted. He was nice enough to offer to question me at home, but then the hospital called and I never found out what he wanted to know."

I stared down into my husband's placid face . . . was he listening? Could he hear me?

The nurse came back and began changing the IV bags that hung above the bed.

"Something else that didn't make sense was how upset he was when I told him Lilly wasn't home." Shivers ran down my arms. "Robert? Do you think . . . Why do you think he called me Mrs. Sloan? No one ever calls me that . . . It was my mother's name—"

"Lillll . . . Lillll . . ." Robert was trying to speak. He was awake. He was listening.

I held my breath, afraid to believe that he really was waking up. I didn't want to be imagining this. I looked over at the nurse; she smiled at me.

"Yes, Lilly, our daughter; she's fine."

His eyes were still shut, but his face was alive with the effort of trying to wake up and form the words.

"Where's . . . Lilly . . . now?" Robert said in a slow, intelligible whisper, clear enough for me to understand it.

"At Wendy's. I'll call her. Oh, sweetheart, she's going to be so glad—" I choked on my words and put my head down and kissed Robert's fingers. They moved under my lips, and I picked my head up.

"Mall . . ." Robert struggled with the word.

"Now, don't strain yourself, Mr. Falconer. You take your time," the nurse was saying as she took his vital signs and fussed over him.

He opened his eyes, not all the way, but enough to look at me. "Mallory . . ."

"Everything is all right now. You're awake. You are going to be fine." I was holding his hand and he was gripping my fingers with urgency.

"Mallory . . . is Detective . . ."

I didn't understand what he was trying to tell me.

"Mrs. Falconer, he shouldn't be getting upset now," the nurse admonished me.

I started to move out of her way so she could check his pulse, but Robert reached out and grabbed my hand so hard I flinched.

"What is it, Robert?"

"Mallory is . . . the detective," he said.

A dozen separate pieces of the puzzle suddenly fit into one complete picture, and I knew what Robert was trying to tell me, what he had figured out even before I had.

"Oh, God, yes, Robert, you might be right. I have to call Lilly. I have to call her and tell her not to go home. Not to go anywhere."

By then it was after nine in the morning, and no one answered the phone at Wendy's house. Frantically, I dialed our home number. When I heard the machine answer, I hung up.

"Did you find Lilly?" Robert's voice was still straining, but each word was clearer.

"No. I'm going to go home. She's probably on her way there, or here. If she gets here, tell her to call me on my cell phone." I was talking to both Robert and the nurse. I wanted to hold him, to cry over him, to rejoice now that I knew he was going to be all right, but first I had to find Lilly. Mallory might be out there somewhere looking for her.

"Get the police, Jordan." Robert's whisper was insistent.

"Yes, of course; don't worry."

As I hurried down the hall and into the elevator I knew Robert was right and that I needed to take a policeman back to the house with me.

There was a squad car outside the hospital, and I quickly explained to the policeman what was going on. "Get in," he said, and called Detective Tadlock as he drove to the brownstone.

Once we arrived, the policeman double-parked the car and accompanied me up the steps.

I fumbled with the keys and flung open the door, calling out my daughter's name.

"Lilly?" I rushed up the stairs.

Lilly stepped out of the door to our apartment and into the hall. "Mom . . ."

"Yes, sweetie. Are you all right?"

"Yes—" Lilly noticed the policeman, and her eyes widened in fear. "What's wrong?"

"I just needed to make sure you were all right. I'll explain in a second."

I turned to the uniformed officer. "Thank you for coming. I wasn't sure and I didn't want to take any chances."

"No problem, ma'am. I'll circle the block a few times to make sure everything stays calm. Detective Tadlock should be here in about fifteen minutes."

"I appreciate that," I said.

As he walked out the front door, I walked up the last few steps towards our apartment.

"Lilly, your father is awake. He's talking. We have to call the hospital and tell your father you're okay, and then I have to call your uncle and leave a message about Mallory. Lilly, I know what he looks like now; I know what to tell the detective—"

"Dad is awake. Oh, God, oh, God . . ." She started to cry in great huge gulping sobs. I put my arms around her and held on to her. And then over her shoulder I saw him.

"You did a very good job of not giving me away, Lilly. You were an excellent little actress."

It was the man who had told me he was Detective Gershon, who I now could see, if I strained and squinted and added pounds and subtracted hair, was Dan Mallory. The man who killed my father was standing in my home and holding a gun on my daughter and me.

TWENTY-SEVEN

Mallory smiled at me.

There was no longer any question who he was, but I understood why I hadn't recognized him when he had first come to the hospital room. We see what we are looking for. It had been so many years since I had seen Mallory, years during which I had forced myself not to imagine his face but block it from my mind.

Now he stood before me in my own kitchen, leaning against the sink, staring at me as hard as I was staring at him. Lilly and I stood by my side in the doorway.

"Sit down, both of you." He used the gun to point to the kitchen table. From the way she flinched, I knew he'd been tormenting her with that gun since he'd gotten there.

"Are you all right, sweetheart? Has he hurt you?"

She shook her head no.

"Hurt her? How could I?" Mallory smiled at me again.

I ached for her. I had wanted her to be more realistic, but I hadn't wanted her to learn her lessons like this.

"The gun is to protect me, not to hurt either of you. Come here, Lilly," he said.

But Lilly didn't move; her eyes were still glued to the gun.

"I'm not here to hurt you. I already told you, I love you, Lilly, the same way I loved your mother. You are an even finer ruby than she was."

In confusion, Lilly looked at me, trying to understand what

Mallory was talking about. Sweat was dripping down my back, and my blood was pounding in my ears as I fought to stay in control and not get lost in the fear that gripped me. I smiled at Lilly. "It will be all right, sweetheart. Let's all sit down at the table. Come."

Like a child who needs to be led, Lilly followed me to the small round table and we sat down on either side of Mallory.

Detective Tadlock would be here soon, I thought. Yes, the policeman had told me Tadlock was on his way. I knew that, and so Mallory knew that too. He must have heard the policeman on the steps. All I had to do to protect Lilly was to keep this confrontation relaxed and keep Mallory calm until the police came. And they would come. Because they had to. Because Robert had come out of his coma, because we loved our daughter, because enough had happened to us.

"Jordan, do you know how much your daughter looks like you used to? She's the girl I remember. I'm sorry about that, I really am. I wanted you to stay the same way, wanted your hair to be as long and your skin to be as smooth. I wanted it all to be the same as it was." His voice was laced with both a madman's hysteria and a criminal's contempt.

Lilly's eyes were wide with fright. I had to think of some way to get her out of here or to get him to leave, but I couldn't think straight—I was too scared. Forcing my mind to concentrate on my training, I tried to remember what I knew about dealing with disturbed patients.

"Dan, it's dangerous for you to be here; why don't you leave before you get into even more trouble than you are already in?"

"Leave? Now that I'm finally here? Are you crazy? I've been planning this for weeks, watching you from the park, from across the street, following you—and do you know what the hardest thing was?"

He didn't wait for an answer. "Trying to get used to who you've become, to stop looking for your younger face—until I saw Lilly— her face is the one I remember.

"For almost two decades I had been feeding off that image and I'd never thought about how age would change you. In my mind you stayed a nineteen-year-old with shining hair down to your waist, purple eye shadow, wearing blue jeans and clogs, and smoking cigarettes.

"I might not have recognized you at all if I wasn't looking for you, but I would have recognized this daughter of yours in an instant, whether it had been on the street in Paris or a subway in Tokyo."

We were in the room where I had made hundreds of meals for my family, a safe room, full of mementos of Lilly's childhood. The refrigerator's surface was covered with snapshots of summer vacations and school plays. On the windowsill was a ceramic pot that Lilly had made in an art class.

Mallory had invaded our home and was poisoning the air. He was putting my daughter in danger, and I didn't know how to save her.

"I really think you should leave." I knew my only chance was to stay focused and appear calm and be logical, but I was shaking. Could Mallory see my body trembling?

"I once read that there is a ninety-nine percent chance that in every breath we take there is an atom of Julius Caesar's dying breath. Do you know how many times I have thought about that for the last twenty years? It meant that we were exchanging breath: some of your breath in me, some of my breath in you. We were fucking each other just by breathing."

His eyes were shining maniacally. I had to get Lilly out of here. "Dan, will you let Lilly take the dog out for a walk. Just for a few minutes; she'll come right back." I turned to my daughter and tried to shout to her with my eyes—please, while I am talking to him, get up, Lilly, and go.

Mallory seemed to think about it for a minute. "No, I don't want her to leave, Jordan. I want Lilly here. Maybe even more than I want you here." He turned to Lilly and leaned closer to her. "I want you to listen to what your mother has to tell you. She has a confession to make. Don't you, Jordan?"

"I'm not sure what you mean."

"Do you know what it's like to be betrayed by someone you love with all of your heart?" Mallory asked me.

"Yes."

I could remember so much about Mallory now that he sat close to me. All the days I had known him when I was a teenager played out in my mind. Images I'd blocked came flooding back. Mallory had been clever, sexy, and talented. He had been rougher than the private-school boys I knew, and that had scared me a little, but in retrospect I knew this was what had made him so appealing to me.

"Do you think that kind of betrayal is something you can ever forget?" he asked.

I knew that it wasn't.

"No, you don't forget it," I said.

"Why don't you tell your daughter how you betrayed me?"

"I didn't . . ." I argued, and then realized it was time for the truth. "I didn't mean to," I said.

"But you did betray me, didn't you? You laughed with me and sat next to me in the movies and held my hand and let me smell your hair—I still remember you used shampoo that had coconut oil in it—your hair smelled like tropical islands and warm summer sun. And you let me kiss you and you kissed me back. With those lips. The same lips Lilly has. Full, moist, red—even without lipstick. How can your lips be so red? You know, in prison, in the dark, I would imagine your lips were on my pillow and I would kiss them in my sleep."

Lilly's entire body was shaking.

"You were some little cocktease, weren't you, Jordan? You let me touch you and you touched me back . . . but only up to a point. . . . And you are just like that, aren't you, Lilly?" He turned and looked at her, and she shrank back in her chair. "I've seen you with your boyfriend in the park. I've seen you kiss him and touch his hair.

"Are you going to let your boyfriend play with you until you have him where you want him and then are you going to run away too?

Like your Mom did?" He looked from Lilly to me. "You just couldn't stand up to your father, could you, Jordan? You had to lie and say that I was pursuing you, when you were the one who had come after me. When you were the one who had made me want you so badly that I couldn't sleep at night without imagining you. You lied to your father because you were afraid of him and didn't want him to punish you for being such a bad girl. For playing with the help."

"Dan," I was speaking softly. "I did like you. Of course I did. I had nothing to do with my father firing you."

"Lilly, what do you think now that you know your mother was a cocktease back then? Maybe I should make you tease it now in front of your daughter?" he said to me. "Or maybe I should make your daughter tease it now in front of you. How about it, Lilly?"

I had to force Mallory to look away from Lilly, to stop fixating on her.

"Dan, do you remember my father? How strict he was? He knew you were attracted to me, and he didn't like it. He wasn't ready for me to grow up. He wanted to keep me a child forever, so he fired you. I didn't have anything to do with it."

"But you didn't try to stop him, and you made it worse by not standing up for me," he hissed.

"Dan, none of that matters now. I'm sorry if I hurt you. I didn't mean to. Why don't you go now before anything happens? The police have been watching the house. They are looking for you. Why don't you go before they come back. Haven't you spent enough time behind bars?"

"But you lied about how you felt about me," he repeated.

"You're right Dan. I didn't tell my father how I felt."

"*But you lied!*" he shouted.

"Yes, I lied."

Mallory laughed, and it was an awful, tortured sound. "Your father loved me. I was his apprentice. He was teaching me. He knew I understood the language and the poetry of those gems and metals as well as he did. I was going to work by his side. You ruined all that. You made it so we couldn't go on together, all of us, together.

"You owe me, Jordan. You owe me so many days and so many nights that I gave up for you. Thousands of unendurable nights while I lay on my pathetic bed staring at a ceiling that didn't even have cracks in it to relieve the monotony. Even when I slept, I thought of you. My body gave in to my dreams and my dick would wake me: thick, hot, and desperately wanting some relief. No glory in masturbating. No smells of skin, no hair brushing my face, no breasts pressed against my chest. No legs wrapped around my waist. No feminine moans or whimpers."

My daughter's face was drained of all color and her teeth were chattering. She was going into shock. Suddenly I knew what I had to do.

"Where are you going?" Mallory asked as I stood up.

"I want you to come with me into my bedroom so I can give you something to make up for everything you've been through." I had to get him away from Lilly long enough for her to get away.

He got up, started to follow me, then stopped and turned back. "Lilly, you come with us."

"No!" I shouted.

Mallory stuck the gun in my back. "Shhhh . . . the pretty little girl is going to come with us." He reached behind him and gently took Lilly's hand, leading her from the table as he followed me.

"Lilly is coming with us. I have wonderful plans for her. We just need to get all these secrets out in the open. And you have to start loving me again. And then it will all be fine. We can be a family."

My plan had backfired. Lilly had not been able to get away and now that we were all in the bedroom, Dan looked from the bed, then back to my face.

"Why are you doing that?" Mallory asked. He was looking down at my hands, and I realized I had been twisting the wedding bands furiously.

In the mirror I saw the reflection of the whole terrifying scene—at any moment Mallory might break and choose to use that gun. I couldn't waste any more time.

"Dan, there's a safe in my closet. What's in the safe is for you. Can I go and open it up?"

"That's not what I came in here for and you know it. What could be in your safe that I could want more than what you have in-between your legs or what Lilly has between hers? Don't you understand? I've been saving myself for you. I'm clean. I haven't touched a woman since I've been out because I was waiting for this."

"Dan, what's in the safe could change the rest of your life. You can take it and leave and start fresh anywhere you want. It's your dream, Dan. My father's raw stock—it's all in there. You can have it. Every emerald. Every sapphire. All the rubies and the amethysts and the rare stones he was saving."

As I spoke, a vein in Mallory's forehead twitched. "The raw stock from the store?" he asked.

"Yes, just let me go into the safe—"

"Wait a minute. I'm not that gullible. You might have a gun in there. How about if you let Lilly open the safe? I'll be right behind her, watching. So be careful, Jordan, no more teasing me. Not now."

"No, no teasing now, Dan. Just what's rightfully yours. Compensation for all the years you lost."

"Lilly." I looked at my daughter and tried to steady her with my eyes. "Please, open the safe."

"I don't know if I can," she whispered.

"You have to, sweetheart." I smiled at her.

She took a few tentative steps forward, moved the clothes aside, and revealed the steel door.

I gave my daughter instructions on how to spin the dial to the right and then the left and then back to the right, telling her what numbers to stop on.

"It's—it's open," Lilly said as she swung the metal door open and stepped to the side.

"Dan, it's all in there. It's all yours," I told him.

Mallory kept the gun against my spine. "Lilly," he said, "open those bags and show me what's in them."

Lilly reached inside the safe and pulled out the pouches, dropping some of them, spilling stones and jewelry onto the floor. Emeralds and sapphires and aquamarines and rubies and citrines shimmered in the light. Dozens stones spread out at Mallory's feet like Aladdin's treasure.

Without taking the gun out of my back, Mallory leaned down to scoop up a handful of the gemstones. He let them fall through his fingers like water.

Mallory's eyes reflected the glow of the stones as well as his astonishment.

"Take them and leave. The gems are far more valuable to you than we are. Dan, you can be a jeweler again. You can do what my father would have done with the stones. They're yours. The stones and all the jewelry that he made. Just take it and leave us alone."

He looked from me, to Lilly, and then to the bounty on the floor as if he were choosing.

"Lilly, will you pick them up for me?" he asked.

Quickly, as if they burned her fingers, she shoved the stones back into their pouches, handing each one to him as soon as she'd filled it. Taking each suede bag from her, he put them in his pockets one at a time.

"What's that?" He pointed to something Lilly still held on to in her hand. "Are you keeping something back?"

"It's mine. It's nothing. Please, let me keep it," Lilly whispered.

"What is it?" he asked. "Let me see it."

Gingerly, Lilly held up the mala that I had made for her. The little frog danced in the air so joyfully it was surreal.

"Those are emeralds." Mallory stared at the stones, recognizing them even after almost twenty years. "They are worth a fortune. Sloan took them out of an Indian necklace. A royal necklace."

"There are other emeralds in there, aren't there?" Lilly asked plaintively.

"Lilly, let him have them—" I said.

She ignored me and pleaded with Mallory. "Please, these were my birthday present from my mother. Let me keep them? Haven't you taken enough? Don't you already have more than you need?"

Mallory didn't answer her but instead walked to the door. Suddenly, he turned back to us. He looked at Lilly, wistfully as if he were leaving one of the best gemstones behind. Then his eyes moved to me and narrowed with anger. And something else I couldn't decipher.

"I'm leaving now," he said.

"Yes," I answered.

"You didn't turn out to be who I remembered," he said with a catch in his voice. "I wanted you to be the same. I had thought you would be the same."

"What happened to my father changed me," I said.

"It changed me to," he said.

"I suppose it did."

And then, finally, he left, but I didn't breathe until I heard the front door shut.

"Lilly, he's gone." I raced to the window and saw him walking down the stairs. "He's out on the street." I kept my eyes on him until he had turned the corner and I couldn't see him anymore.

At last, in the distance, I heard a police siren.

"Lilly, the police are on the way." I turned, expecting to find her beside me. But she was huddled on the floor of the closet, crouched low and hiding behind my clothes. My daughter did not make a sound, but she was shaking.

From between her fingers, the little jade frog poked his head out. Good was standing beside her, whimpering and licking the tears off her face, but she was deep in shock.

Pushing away skirts and pants and grabbing a thick sweater, I sat down on the floor beside my daughter and put the sweater around her shoulders. Slowly, carefully, I reached out and began to stroke her hair. "It's all right, sweetheart, he's gone. We're all right. You were so brave." I repeated the same phrases over and over trying to get through to her.

Finally she spoke: "You gave him everything you had. All you had left of your father's things," she said in a very small voice.

"It doesn't matter."

"But it's all gone," she repeated. "All those stones mattered to you so much."

"Lilly, look at me . . ."

My daughter picked up her head. She was still pale and she was breathing too hard, but she was responsive.

"All that matters is that you are all right and that your father is all right. The jewelry was part of the past. The stones were just things. I don't need them, sweetheart. Not anymore."

And then my beautiful dark-haired daughter, who had been so far away from me for so very long, laughed, and it was a wonderful sound.

"That is very enlightened, Mom," she said through tears.

"You don't think I could live in this house listening to you spouting Zen all the time and not pick some of it up, do you?"

I held Lilly and rocked her in my arms and let her cry. Good scampered up on my lap, and the three of us stayed in the cocoon we had created with our arms.

"You know what happens now?" I asked Lilly a few minutes later.

"What?" she hiccuped through a sob.

"You remember all those fairy tales I wouldn't tell you when you were a little girl?"

"Yes." She coughed.

I had tried so hard to protect my daughter from the power of those myths I had grown up on; the fairy tales that had given me such great and grand expectations of what life might be.

"What happens next, my darling Lilly, is we all live happily ever after."

It wasn't an exaggeration. I finally understood. If you accept that nothing is perfect and are willing to forgive, if you look at the people around you and recognize them for who they are and for the gifts they have to offer and not damn them for who they cannot be or what they cannot give, if you acknowledge that we are all are perfect and imperfect, then you really can live happily ever after.

TWENTY-EIGHT

Lilly and I walked into Robert's hospital room two hours later. He was sitting up in bed, talking to Simon. My husband's gray pallor was gone, and his eyes were alert as he smiled broadly at us.

Lilly was staring at him, afraid to move, to speak.

"Come here, Lilly. Come sit with me," he said, and patted a space beside him on the bed. "I can't tell you how happy I am to see you."

Lilly ran to his side and snuggled in beside him, and Robert put the arm that wasn't hooked up to the IV around her shoulders. "And to see you, Jordan," he said.

"I just filled him in on your morning," Simon said to me. "And Detective Tadlock just called. They caught up with Mallory at his mother's pawnshop. But he didn't have any of the jewels or jewelry with him."

"But he took them all—" Lilly sat up.

"Sweetheart, it's all right," I told her. "They'll find it. Or they won't. Let's not worry about that now."

She settled back down next to her father.

"I can't believe you figured out who Mallory was before I did," I told Robert. "I didn't know you could even hear me; I just knew that I had to tell you because you always could listen better than anyone I knew could. And you figured it out. You came out of that horrid sleep to warn me. Do you remember that?"

"At first I thought it was a dream—there was a man here and

he told you to go with him and I didn't want you to leave. I was trying so hard to yell out to you, to tell you not to go—that you had to be here so I could see you when I woke up. But he was so insistent, and I was angry with him because he was upsetting you. And then when I finally did open my eyes, you weren't here. No one was here."

I finally let the tears come then, and Robert somehow lifted his other arm—the one that was hooked up to the saline solution—and he offered me space next to him, and I joined him and our daughter on his narrow bed.

It didn't matter anymore if I cried. If I hurt. If there was pain. There would be other times when there was pleasure.

Simon left the three of us for a while, and when he came back an hour later, Lilly and I were both fussing over Robert, trying to make him eat.

"Robert," Simon said, "have you remembered anything about the accident yet?"

"No, not yet. The doc says that is fairly normal and that my memory should come back eventually."

"Well, from the fingerprints they found, the police have ruled out all of the suspects they had so far." Simon gave me a significant look. I was glad he hadn't yet mentioned Adrienne's name. Robert and I would deal with those questions later.

"You know what I'd like?" Robert looked at Lilly. "A burger and french fries from the coffee shop on Sixth Avenue. None of this hospital garbage, " he said. "Would you be a doll and go get dinner for me?"

"I think I'll go with you, Lilly," Simon said. "I'm kind of hungry myself."

Once they were gone, Robert's mood shifted and he became very serious. "Jordan, I know what happened in the darkroom, but I wanted to tell you without Lilly here."

I took a breath and tried to brace myself for the onslaught of words I was afraid would change everything again.

"It was Cooper."

"What?"

"After Lilly ran out, Cooper followed her, remember? When he couldn't find her, he came back and took out all his pent-up frustration on me. When I tried to talk to him, he snapped and accused me of suffocating Lilly. He told me I was too possessive of her and that my photographs of her were proof of how sick my relationship with her was. At first I tried to reason with him, but when it became obvious he wasn't listening, I got angry and told him to leave.

"He went into the darkroom to pack up—because that was where he'd stowed his stuff. He was in there for a while, then came out and left. A few minutes later I smelled something burning.

"Jordan, he set fire to all the negatives of Lilly. All that work. Ruined. Melting in front of my eyes. I tried to save them, even just one of them, but it was too late. The fire had already done its damage. I never stopped to think about the fire itself—the darkroom is fireproof—and I'd forgotten about the danger of heat with nitrate film. I was just furious so much hard work had been destroyed.

"And that's the last thing I remember. But obviously the fire was hot enough to combust the old film. I must have been inhaling the fumes the whole time I was trying to save the negatives of Lilly."

"Oh, no. Robert, I'm sorry."

We had both lost things that had mattered to us very much, but maybe we were finding other things that would matter more.

"How are we going to tell Lilly? I can't bear to think of how she'll deal with this blow. Even though Cooper didn't mean to hurt me, he did set fire to those negatives. She's going to be shattered, isn't she?" He sounded so sad; I put my hand on his.

"I know you want to protect her. But she'll be all right, Robert. I think she already knows that loving someone is worth whatever pain that comes with it."

In the end, we never had to tell Lilly.

Cooper had arrived at the hospital just as she and Simon had come back with the food.

"Apparently, Lilly had never really explained your accident to Cooper until she called him this afternoon," Simon told us. "Once Cooper understood what had happened, he realized it was his fault. So he borrowed his roommate's car and came straight here."

Just as Simon finished explaining, Lilly and Cooper walked in the door.

"I'm prepared to confess to the police and I expect you to press charges. I deserve to go to jail—" Cooper's face seemed about to dissolve into tears, but he controlled himself. "I don't know how to apologize, Mr. Falconer. When I think of what almost happened—I just can't—I just couldn't stand thinking that everyone was going to see those pictures of Lilly. On display, like that." He shrugged as if the weight of what had happened were resting on his shoulders and it was far too heavy a load. "But what I did was horribly wrong. I never meant to—" He was too upset to even finish the sentence.

Lilly's eyes were downcast. "I told him I can't see him anymore," she said.

She was so sad. I wanted to go to her and take her in my arms again, but she needed more from me than an embrace. I looked over at Cooper, and he met my gaze. He'd owned up to the crazy thing he'd done and wasn't hiding anymore. In his eyes I could see the remorse and the despair.

"People can change, Lilly," I said to her. "They can."

My daughter stared at me in surprise, and slowly a little of the old mischievous glint was back in her eye.

"Lilly, would you give me another chance?" Cooper asked.

Before answering him, she looked back at Robert and me, wanting our advice for the first time in months.

"It's up to you, Lilly," Robert said, and I nodded in agreement.

We had all changed.

Around six o'clock Lilly and I went home to take care of the dog and get some things Robert wanted us to bring from the studio. Simon was going to stay with him until we got back.

For the first time in three days, Lilly and I both took Good for a long walk. It was an odd feeling to pass people on the street and in the park and not look in the shadows, worried that Mallory might be lurking there.

"He's really gone now, isn't he?" Lilly asked. She couldn't say his name yet, but she didn't have to; I knew who she meant.

"Yes, he's gone and he may never leave prison again. He didn't just break his parole, he had a gun and he threatened our lives."

We talked about what had happened while we circled the park and then continued to discuss it on the way back home, but it would take much longer than one long walk for Lilly to work out her feelings about the encounter with Mallory and deal with Cooper's confession.

"Lilly, look—" I said, and pointed to the wisteria that climbed up the front of our brownstone. The thick vine was finally in full bloom, and the dripping violet blossoms scented the whole street.

Lilly looked at the wisteria and the sky and the sun and at the dog and at me, and she smiled. "Oh, Mom, I wish I'd brought my camera."

And then I knew she was going to be all right. She would heal. Like me, she would forever carry the memories of what had happened that day, but unlike me, she would not slip and slide on them. My daughter would process them and move on.

"Did you bring my things?" Robert asked later that night after Lilly left to go out to dinner with Simon and Perry and their kids.

I nodded, and as I handed him the tote bag, I noticed the basket of fruit on the bedside table.

Robert followed my glance. "What is it, Jordan?"

There was still one thing left to discuss.

"Do you know where that basket of fruit came from?" I asked him.

"No."

"Well, I'm not sure, but I think Adrienne Blessing sent it."

Robert put his hand on top of mine. "Jordan, Simon told me about Adrienne going to the police and that crazy story she told them. You never believed any of that, did you?"

I shrugged, suddenly embarrassed to admit that I had.

"I never went out with her. If only you'd told me she came to you as a patient, we could have avoided all this."

"It wouldn't have been appropriate. You know the rules. . . ." I said.

"The first time I met her was when she hired me to work on the Waves campaign. One night after a meeting we went out for drinks and she came on to me." He seemed to be remembering that night. "I explained that I wasn't interested, but she kept pursuing me. It made my job impossible, so finally I threatened to resign from the campaign. She seemed to be okay after that. I knew she was nuts, but I had no idea. What she did—going into therapy with you and accusing you—that was entirely my fault. To finally get her to stop bothering me I said I couldn't see her because of you—my wife—I said I was trying to work things out with you."

I started to think about Adrienne Blessing's neurosis. She was a narcissistic woman who had probably never been turned down before. Rather than accept that Robert wasn't interested in her, she blamed the wife whom he was trying to work things out with. And so she came to me to see what kind of competition I was.

I'd never know what she had thought she was achieving by becoming my patient or what caused her psychotic break. "We don't have to talk about her now," I said.

"No, Jordan, we never have to talk about her," Robert said.

EPILOGUE

There were many people milling around, sipping wine and talking about the photographs. The main room and the smaller gallery were equally crowded, and there were already red dots signifying sales under many of both Robert's and Lilly's photographs.

I walked slowly around the room, lingering, looking at the lovely photographs of my daughter, and then at the photographs she had taken.

The two shows were not only a success, but the protesters had never shown up; Robert had been right. Once the individual elements of his work had been assembled, merged, and seen as a whole, there was no question that these were not provocative images of a naked young girl, but the testimony of a father's pure love.

I marveled at how many of Robert's photographs had already been purchased: the prices were extremely high, since each was a one-of-a-kind print. That, too, somehow seemed right; every one was now more precious having earned the honor of being an original.

Chloe arrived and I went over to greet her.

"Where's John?" I asked after we'd exchanged kisses.

"He's meeting me here any minute."

Chloe glanced down at the floor and smiled. We were both wearing the same shoes—the mules we'd bought that afternoon not very long ago.

"Max went back to London," she said, answering the question before I had a chance to ask it. "Nothing really happened. One kiss. That's all." She added a wistful sigh, but she didn't seem unhappy.

"Are you okay with that?" I asked.

"Seeing Robert in the hospital shook me up. I kept thinking— what if something happened to John? I realized I didn't want to lose him; or do anything that would jeopardize what we have. I can be happy with—" Chloe stopped mid-sentence. Something had caught her attention.

"Do you recognize who Iago is talking to?" Chloe asked, point-ing to a tall portly man.

"No, who is he?"

"The curator of the photography department of the Museum of Modern Art."

Together we watched as the man nodded at one particular photograph and Iago reached over and placed a tiny red dot beneath it.

"Jordan, he just bought a photograph!" Chloe said, and grabbed my arm.

Robert's career had just reached a new zenith.

"Stay here. I have to go tell Robert. I'll be back in a minute."

Scanning the room, I searched for Robert and found him finally in the small gallery, where Lilly's photographs graced the walls. Lilly was talking to an elderly woman, and Robert, on her right, was smiling proudly.

Cooper stood to Lilly's left, smiling almost as broadly as Robert was. I was glad he was there. Lilly had told me Cooper had started to see a therapist about his jealousy, and so she'd agreed to resume seeing him.

Robert looked up and, reading my expression, excused himself. As he maneuvered around the crowd, several people stopped him to talk, and it took him a few minutes to reach me.

"Something wonderful just happened! Iago was with the cura-tor from the Museum of Modern Art. Robert, he bought one of your photographs."

For a moment Robert couldn't say anything, and then he sim-ply nodded. When he finally spoke, what he said surprised me.

"Come with me, Jordan. I have something more important to talk to you about."

What could be more important than the inclusion of one of his photographs into the museum?

Taking my hand, Robert led me outside.

The summer night was warm and breezy, and the SoHo street was almost empty. We stood outside the gallery and leaned against a car.

"You look lovely," he said, and reached out to touch my hair, which I'd worn down. My black sleeveless sheath was cut in a low V in both the front and the back, and my high heels made me almost level with Robert, who still had not taken his eyes off me.

"You cold?" he asked as I shivered.

"No, it's how you're looking at me."

"No, it's because you're not wearing enough."

"What do you mean? It's summer."

"You need something else to wear." Robert reached inside his jacket pocket and pulled out the jeweler's box he'd given me the weekend we'd spent in the Hamptons.

"I know how you felt about this when I tried to give it to you before; I thought you might feel differently now."

I stared down at his offering.

"Jordan, are you going to open this box or not?"

This time I did open the box and inside found a thin necklace of round rubies set in platinum. It was the most delicate piece of jewelry I'd ever seen.

Best of all, it wasn't something my father had made and had no memories attached to it.

I had always wondered if one day I would be able to forgive Robert, but now understanding him seemed all that was necessary. For a long time, I had lived with Robert's infidelity; perhaps it was time to start living with him again. Not the way we had been before, but the way we were now. A man who wasn't trying to compete with his wife's work. And a woman who could live beside a man, not for him.

"Do you remember what Lilly said about the thin red cord that connects people who belong together?" Robert asked.

I nodded and, looking down at the necklace, touched one of the red stones with my fingertip.

"We belong together, Jordan. We'll probably still cause each other pain. But we can give each other pleasures too," Robert said.

He hadn't asked a question, but he was waiting for an answer.

"I said I wouldn't put your gift on until I was ready to tell Lilly about us." I wasn't sure whether I was reminding him or myself.

"So are you going to put it on?" he asked.

"No—I'm not . . ."

Seeing the troubled look in Robert's eyes, I hurried to finish the thought. *"You* are going to put it on me, and then we'll go back inside and tell Lilly together."

Robert leaned forward, took the necklace out of my hand, and fastened it around my neck. Taking a deep breath, I felt the chilly metal on my skin, but I knew that it wouldn't stay cold. The change was already beginning. My body temperature was starting to heat the platinum. Soon it would be as warm as my skin. A transference between beating blood and inert metal.

In time, I would not even feel the chain around my neck but would have to reach up and touch it to know it was there.

Yes, Robert had changed.

And so had I.

Perhaps that was what his infidelity had taught us. That we both needed to change in order to come together again.

Perhaps his infidelity had, in a strange and roundabout way, saved our union.

"We'll tell her that we can't make promises about what is going to happen and that nothing is ever safe or certain . . ." I said.

Knowing what I was thinking, Robert finished my thought. "But that we are going to give each other—and being together—a chance."

There could be no better prayer than that, I thought as he took my hand and we turned around to go back inside the gallery and find our daughter.